EVERYMAN,

I WILL GO WITH THEE,

AND BE THY GUIDE,

IN THY MOST NEED

TO GO BY THY SIDE

✷

EVERYMAN'S POCKET CLASSICS

STORIES OF THE SEA

EDITED BY DIANA SECKER TESDELL

EVERYMAN'S POCKET CLASSICS
Alfred A. Knopf New York London Toronto

THIS IS A BORZOI BOOK
PUBLISHED BY ALFRED A. KNOPF

This selection by Diana Secker Tesdell first published in Everyman's Library, 2010

Second printing (US)

 Published in the United States by Alfred A. Knopf, a division of Random House, Inc., New York, and in Canada by Random House of Canada Limited, Toronto. Distributed by Random House, Inc., New York. Published in the United Kingdom by Everyman's Library, Northburgh House, 10 Northburgh Street, London EC1V 0AT, and distributed by Random House (UK) Ltd.

US website: www.randomhouse.com/everymans

ISBN: 978-0-307-59265-1 (US)
978-1-84159-605-1 (UK)

A CIP catalogue reference for this book is available from the British Library

Typography by Peter B. Willberg

Typeset in the UK by AccComputing, North Barrow, Somerset

Printed and bound in Germany by GGP Media GmbH, Pössneck

STORIES OF THE SEA

Contents

SURVIVAL AT SEA

THE CALL OF THE SEA

DANGERS OF THE DEEP

RAY BRADBURY

THE FOG HORN

OUT THERE IN the cold water, far from land, we waited every night for the coming of the fog, and it came, and we oiled the brass machinery and lit the fog light up in the stone tower. Feeling like two birds in the gray sky, McDunn and I sent the light touching out, red, then white, then red again, to eye the lonely ships. And if they did not see our light, then there was always our Voice, the great deep cry of our Fog Horn shuddering through the rags of mist to startle the gulls away like decks of scattered cards and make the waves turn high and foam.

'It's a lonely life, but you're used to it now, aren't you?' asked McDunn.

'Yes,' I said. 'You're a good talker, thank the Lord.'

'Well, it's your turn on land tomorrow,' he said, smiling, 'to dance the ladies and drink gin.'

'What do you think, McDunn, when I leave you out here alone?'

'On the mysteries of the sea.' McDunn lit his pipe. It was a quarter past seven of a cold November evening, the heat on, the light switching its tail in two hundred directions, the Fog Horn bumbling in the high throat of the tower. There wasn't a town for a hundred miles down the coast, just a road which came lonely through dead country to the sea, with few cars on it, a stretch of two miles of cold water out to our rock, and rare few ships.

'The mysteries of the sea,' said McDunn thoughtfully.

'You know, the ocean's the biggest damned snowflake ever? It rolls and swells a thousand shapes and colors, no two alike. Strange. One night, years ago, I was here alone, when all of the fish of the sea surfaced out there. Something made them swim in and lie in the bay, sort of trembling and staring up at the tower light going red, white, red, white, across them so I could see their funny eyes. I turned cold. They were like a big peacock's tail, moving out there until midnight. Then, without so much as a sound, they slipped away, the million of them was gone. I kind of think maybe, in some sort of way, they came all those miles to worship. Strange. But think how the tower must look to them, standing seventy feet above the water, the God-light flashing out from it, and the tower declaring itself with a monster voice. They never came back, those fish, but don't you think for a while they thought they were in the Presence?'

I shivered. I looked out at the long gray lawn of the sea stretching away into nothing and nowhere.

'Oh, the sea's full.' McDunn puffed his pipe nervously, blinking. He had been nervous all day and hadn't said why. 'For all our engines and so-called submarines, it'll be ten thousand centuries before we set foot on the real bottom of the sunken lands, in the fairy kingdoms there, and know *real* terror. Think of it, it's still the year 300,000 before Christ down under there. While we've paraded around with trumpets, lopping off each other's countries and heads, they have been living beneath the sea twelve miles deep and cold in a time as old as the beard of a comet.'

'Yes, it's an old world.'

'Come on. I got something special I been saving up to tell you.'

We ascended the eighty steps, talking and taking our time. At the top, McDunn switched off the room lights so there'd be no reflection in the plate glass. The great eye of the light was humming, turning easily in its oiled socket. The Fog Horn was blowing steadily, once every fifteen seconds.

'Sounds like an animal, don't it?' McDunn nodded to himself. 'A big lonely animal crying in the night. Sitting here on the edge of ten billion years calling out to the Deeps, I'm here, I'm here, I'm here. And the Deeps do answer, yes, they do. You been here now for three months, Johnny, so I better prepare you. About this time of year,' he said, studying the murk and fog, 'something comes to visit the lighthouse.'

'The swarms of fish like you said?'

'No, this is something else. I've put off telling you because you might think I'm daft. But tonight's the latest I can put it off, for if my calendar's marked right from last year, tonight's the night it comes. I won't go into detail, you'll have to see it yourself. Just sit down there. If you want, tomorrow you can pack your duffel and take the motorboat in to land and get your car parked there at the dinghy pier on the cape and drive on back to some little inland town and keep your lights burning nights, I won't question or blame you. It's happened three years now, and this is the only time anyone's been here with me to verify it. You wait and watch.'

Half an hour passed with only a few whispers between us. When we grew tired waiting, McDunn began describing some of his ideas to me. He had some theories about the Fog Horn itself.

'One day many years ago a man walked along and stood in the sound of the ocean on a cold sunless shore and said, "We need a voice to call across the water, to warn ships; I'll make one. I'll make a voice like all of time and all of the fog that ever was; I'll make a voice that is like an empty bed beside you all night long, and like an empty house when you open the door, and like trees in autumn with no leaves. A sound like the birds flying south, crying, and a sound like November wind and the sea on the hard, cold shore. I'll make a sound that's so alone that no one can miss it, that whoever hears it will weep in their souls, and hearths will seem warmer, and being inside will seem better to all who hear it in the distant towns. I'll make me a sound and an apparatus and they'll call it a Fog Horn and whoever hears it will know the sadness of eternity and the briefness of life." '

The Fog Horn blew.

'I made up that story,' said McDunn quietly, 'to try to explain why this thing keeps coming back to the lighthouse every year. The Fog Horn calls it, I think, and it comes. . . .'

'But—' I said.

'Sssst!' said McDunn. 'There!' He nodded out to the Deeps.

Something was swimming toward the lighthouse tower.

It was a cold night, as I have said; the high tower was cold, the light coming and going, and the Fog Horn calling and calling through the raveling mist. You couldn't see far and you couldn't see plain, but there was the deep sea moving on its way about the night earth, flat and quiet, the color of gray mud, and here were the two of us alone in the high tower, and there, far out at first, was a ripple, followed by a wave, a rising, a bubble, a bit of froth. And then, from the surface of the cold sea came a head, a large head, dark-colored, with immense eyes, and then a neck. And then – not a body – but more neck and more! The head rose a full forty feet above the water on a slender and beautiful dark neck. Only then did the body, like a little island of black coral and shells and crayfish, drip up from the subterranean. There was a flicker of tail. In all, from head to tip of tail, I estimated the monster at ninety or a hundred feet.

I don't know what I said. I said something.

'Steady, boy, steady,' whispered McDunn.

'It's impossible!' I said.

'No, Johnny, *we're* impossible. *It's* like it always was ten million years ago. *It* hasn't changed. It's *us* and the land that've changed, become impossible. *Us!*'

It swam slowly and with a great dark majesty out in the icy waters, far away. The fog came and went about it, momentarily erasing its shape. One of the monster eyes caught and held and flashed back our immense light, red, white, red, white, like a disk held high and sending a message in primeval code. It was as silent as the fog through which it swam.

'It's a dinosaur of some sort!' I crouched down, holding to the stair rail.

'Yes, one of the tribe.'

'But they died out!'

'No, only hid away in the Deeps. Deep, deep down in the deepest Deeps. Isn't *that* a word now, Johnny, a real word, it says so much: the Deeps. There's all the coldness and darkness and deepness in a word like that.'

'What'll we do?'

'Do? We got our job, we can't leave. Besides, we're safer here than in any boat trying to get to land. That thing's as big as a destroyer and almost as swift.'

'But here, why does it come *here*?'

The next moment I had my answer.

The Fog Horn blew.

And the monster answered.

A cry came across a million years of water and mist. A cry so anguished and alone that it shuddered in my head and my body. The monster cried out at the tower. The Fog Horn blew. The monster roared again. The Fog Horn blew. The monster opened its great toothed mouth and the sound that came from it was the sound of the Fog Horn itself. Lonely and vast and far away. The sound of isolation, a viewless sea, a cold night, apartness. That was the sound.

'Now,' whispered McDunn, 'do you know why it comes here?'

I nodded.

'All year long, Johnny, that poor monster there lying far out, a thousand miles at sea, and twenty miles deep maybe, biding its time, perhaps it's a million years old, this one creature. Think of it, waiting a million years; could *you* wait that long? Maybe it's the last of its kind. I sort of think that's true. Anyway, here come men on land and build this lighthouse, five years ago. And set up their Fog Horn and sound it and sound it out toward the place where you bury yourself in sleep and sea memories of a world where there were thousands like yourself, but now you're alone, all alone in a world not made for you, a world where you have to hide.

'But the sound of the Fog Horn comes and goes, comes and goes, and you stir from the muddy bottom of the Deeps, and your eyes open like the lenses of two-foot cameras and you move, slow, slow, for you have the ocean sea on your shoulders, heavy. But that Fog Horn comes through a thousand miles of water, faint and familiar, and the furnace in your belly stokes up, and you begin to rise, slow, slow. You feed yourself on great slakes of cod and minnow, on rivers of jellyfish, and you rise slow through the autumn months, through September when the fogs started, through October with more fog and the horn still calling you on, and then, late in November, after pressurizing yourself day by day, a few feet higher every hour, you are near the surface and still alive. You've got to go slow; if you surfaced all at once you'd explode. So it takes you all of three months to surface, and then a number of days to swim through the cold waters to the lighthouse. And there you are, out there, in the night, Johnny, the biggest damn monster in creation. And here's the lighthouse calling to you, with a long neck like your neck sticking way up out of the water, and a body like your body, and, most important of all, a voice like your voice. Do you understand now, Johnny, do you understand?'

The Fog Horn blew.

The monster answered.

I saw it all, I knew it all – the million years of waiting alone, for someone to come back who never came back. The million years of isolation at the bottom of the sea, the insanity of time there, while the skies cleared of reptile-birds, the swamps dried on the continental lands, the sloths and saber-tooths had their day and sank in tar pits, and men ran like white ants upon the hills.

The Fog Horn blew.

'Last year,' said McDunn, 'that creature swam round and round, round and round, all night. Not coming too near, puzzled, I'd say. Afraid, maybe. And a bit angry after coming all this way. But the next day, unexpectedly, the fog lifted, the sun came out fresh, the sky was as blue as a painting. And the monster swam off away from the heat and the silence and didn't come back. I suppose it's been brooding on it for a year now, thinking it over from every which way.'

The monster was only a hundred yards off now, it and the Fog Horn crying at each other. As the lights hit them, the monster's eyes were fire and ice, fire and ice.

'That's life for you,' said McDunn. 'Someone always waiting for someone who never comes home. Always someone loving some thing more than that thing loves them. And after a while you want to destroy whatever that thing is, so it can't hurt you no more.'

The monster was rushing at the lighthouse.

The Fog Horn blew.

'Let's see what happens,' said McDunn.

He switched the Fog Horn off.

The ensuing minute of silence was so intense that we could hear our hearts pounding in the glassed area of the tower, could hear the slow greased turn of the light.

The monster stopped and froze. Its great lantern eyes blinked. Its mouth gaped. It gave a sort of rumble, like a volcano. It twitched its head this way and that, as if to seek the sounds now dwindled off into the fog. It peered at the lighthouse. It rumbled again. Then its eyes caught fire. It reared up, threshed the water, and rushed at the tower, its eyes filled with angry torment.

'McDunn!' I cried. 'Switch on the horn!'

McDunn fumbled with the switch. But even as he flicked it on, the monster was rearing up. I had a glimpse of its gigantic paws, fishskin glittering in webs between the finger-like projections, clawing at the tower. The huge eye on the right side of its anguished head glittered before me like a caldron into which I might drop, screaming. The tower shook. The Fog Horn cried; the monster cried. It seized the tower and gnashed at the glass, which shattered in upon us.

McDunn seized my arm. 'Downstairs!'

The tower rocked, trembled, and started to give. The Fog Horn and the monster roared. We stumbled and half fell down the stairs. 'Quick!'

We reached the bottom as the tower buckled down toward us. We ducked under the stairs into the small stone cellar. There were a thousand concussions as the rocks rained down; the Fog Horn stopped abruptly. The monster crashed upon the tower. The tower fell. We knelt together, McDunn and I, holding tight, while our world exploded.

Then it was over, and there was nothing but darkness and the wash of the sea on the raw stones.

That and the other sound.

'Listen,' said McDunn quietly. 'Listen.'

We waited a moment. And then I began to hear it. First a great vacuumed sucking of air, and then the lament, the bewilderment, the loneliness of the great monster, folded over and upon us, above us, so that the sickening reek of its body filled the air, a stone's thickness away from our cellar. The monster gasped and cried. The tower was gone. The light was gone. The thing that had called to it across a million years was gone. And the monster was opening its mouth and sending out great sounds. The sounds of a Fog Horn, again and again. And ships far at sea, not finding the light, not seeing anything, but passing and hearing late that night, must've thought: There it is, the lonely sound, the Lonesome Bay horn. All's well. We've rounded the cape.

And so it went for the rest of that night.

The sun was hot and yellow the next afternoon when the rescuers came out to dig us from our stoned-under cellar.

'It fell apart, is all,' said Mr McDunn gravely. 'We had a few bad knocks from the waves and it just crumbled.' He pinched my arm.

There was nothing to see. The ocean was calm, the sky blue. The only thing was a great algaic stink from the green matter that covered the fallen tower stones and the shore rocks. Flies buzzed about. The ocean washed empty on the shore.

The next year they built a new lighthouse, but by that time I had a job in the little town and a wife and a good small warm house that glowed yellow on autumn nights, the doors locked, the chimney puffing smoke. As for

McDunn, he was master of the new lighthouse, built to his own specifications, out of steel-reinforced concrete. 'Just in case,' he said.

The new lighthouse was ready in November. I drove down alone one evening late and parked my car and looked across the gray waters and listened to the new horn sounding, once, twice, three, four times a minute far out there, by itself.

The monster?

It never came back.

'It's gone away,' said McDunn. 'It's gone back to the Deeps. It's learned you can't love anything too much in this world. It's gone into the deepest Deeps to wait another million years. Ah, the poor thing! Waiting out there, and waiting out there, while man comes and goes on this pitiful little planet. Waiting and waiting.'

I sat in my car, listening. I couldn't see the lighthouse or the light standing out in Lonesome Bay. I could only hear the Horn, the Horn, the Horn. It sounded like the monster calling.

I sat there wishing there was something I could say.

RUDYARD KIPLING

A MATTER OF FACT

And if ye doubt the tale I tell,
Steer through the South Pacific swell;
Go where the branching coral hives
Unending strife of endless lives,
Where, leagued about the 'wildered boat,
The rainbow jellies fill and float;
And, lilting where the laver lingers,
The starfish trips on all her fingers;
Where, 'neath his myriad spines ashock,
The sea-egg ripples down the rock;
An orange wonder dimly guessed,
From darkness where the cuttles rest,
Moored o'er the darker deeps that hide
The blind white Sea-snake and his bride
Who, drowsing, nose the long-lost ships
Let down through darkness to their lips.

The Palms.

ONCE A PRIEST, always a priest; once a mason, always a mason; but once a journalist, always and for ever a journalist.

There were three of us, all newspaper men, the only passengers on a little tramp steamer that ran where her owners told her to go. She had once been in the Bilbao iron ore business, had been lent to the Spanish Government for service at Manilla; and was ending her days in the Cape Town coolie-trade, with occasional trips to Madagascar and even as far as England. We found her going to Southampton in ballast, and shipped in her because the fares were nominal. There was Keller, of an American paper, on his way back to the States from palace executions in Madagascar; there was a burly half-Dutchman, called Zuyland, who owned and edited a paper up country near Johannesburg; and there was myself, who had solemnly put away all journalism, vowing to forget that I had ever known the difference between an imprint and a stereo advertisement.

Ten minutes after Keller spoke to me, as the *Rathmines* cleared Cape Town, I had forgotten the aloofness I desired to feign, and was in heated discussion on the immorality of expanding telegrams beyond a certain fixed point. Then Zuyland came out of his cabin, and we were all at home instantly, because we were men of the same profession needing no introduction. We annexed the boat formally, broke open the passengers' bathroom door – on the Manilla lines the Dons do not wash – cleaned out the orange-peel and cigar-ends at the bottom of the bath, hired a Lascar to shave us throughout the voyage, and then asked each other's names.

Three ordinary men would have quarrelled through sheer boredom before they reached Southampton. We, by virtue of our craft, were anything but ordinary men. A large percentage of the tales of the world, the thirty-nine that cannot be told to ladies and the one that can, are common property coming of a common stock. We told them all, as a matter of form, with all their local and specific variants which are surprising. Then came, in the intervals of steady card-play, more personal histories of adventure and things seen and suffered: panics among white folk, when the blind terror ran from man to man on the Brooklyn Bridge, and the people crushed each other to death they knew not why; fires, and faces that opened and shut their mouths horribly at red-hot window frames; wrecks in frost and snow, reported from the sleet-sheathed rescue-tug at the risk of frostbite; long rides after diamond thieves; skirmishes on the veldt and in municipal committees with the Boers; glimpses of lazy tangled Cape politics and the mule-rule in the Transvaal; card-tales, horse-tales, woman-tales, by the score and the half hundred; till the first mate, who had seen more than us all put together, but lacked words to clothe his tales with, sat open-mouthed far into the dawn.

When the tales were done we picked up cards till a curious hand or a chance remark made one or other of us say, 'That reminds me of a man who – or a business which –' and the anecdotes would continue while the *Rathmines* kicked her way northward through the warm water.

In the morning of one specially warm night we three were sitting immediately in front of the wheel-house, where an old Swedish boatswain whom we called 'Frithiof the Dane' was at the wheel, pretending that he could not hear our stories. Once or twice Frithiof spun the spokes curiously, and Keller lifted his head from a long chair to ask, 'What is it? Can't you get any steerage-way on her?'

'There is a feel in the water', said Frithiof, 'that I cannot understand. I think that we run downhills or somethings. She steers bad this morning.'

Nobody seems to know the laws that govern the pulse of the big waters. Sometimes even a landsman can tell that the solid ocean is atilt, and that the ship is working herself up a long unseen slope; and sometimes the captain says, when neither full steam nor fair wind justifies the length of a day's run, that the ship is sagging downhill; but how these ups and downs come about has not yet been settled authoritatively.

'No, it is a following sea,' said Frithiof; 'and with a following sea you shall not get good steerage-way.'

The sea was as smooth as a duck-pond, except for a regular oily swell. As I looked over the side to see where it might be following us from, the sun rose in a perfectly clear sky and struck the water with its light so sharply that it seemed as though the sea should clang like a burnished gong. The wake of the screw and the little white streak cut by the log-line hanging over the stern were the only marks on the water as far as eye could reach.

Keller rolled out of his chair and went aft to get a pineapple from the ripening stock that was hung inside the after awning.

'Frithiof, the log-line has got tired of swimming. It's coming home,' he drawled.

'What?' said Frithiof, his voice jumping several octaves.

'Coming home', Keller repeated, leaning over the stern. I ran to his side and saw the log-line, which till then had been drawn tense over the stern railing, slacken, loop, and come up off the port quarter. Frithiof called up the speaking-tube to the bridge, and the bridge answered, 'Yes, nine knots.' Then Frithiof spoke again, and the answer was, 'What do you want of the skipper?' and Frithiof bellowed, 'Call him up.'

By this time Zuyland, Keller, and myself had caught something of Frithiof's excitement, for any emotion on shipboard is most contagious. The captain ran out of his cabin, spoke to Frithiof, looked at the log-line, jumped on the bridge, and in a minute we felt the steamer swing round as Frithiof turned her.

' 'Going back to Cape Town?' said Keller.

Frithiof did not answer, but tore away at the wheel. Then he beckoned us three to help, and we held the wheel down till the *Rathmines* answered it, and we found ourselves looking into the white of our own wake, with the still oily sea tearing past our bows, though we were not going more than half steam ahead.

The captain stretched out his arm from the bridge and shouted. A minute later I would have given a great deal to have shouted too, for one-half of the sea seemed to shoulder itself above the other half, and came on in the shape of a hill. There was neither crest, comb, nor curl-over to it; nothing but black water with little waves chasing each other about the flanks. I saw it stream past and on a level with the *Rathmines'* bow-plates before the steamer hove up her bulk to rise, and I argued that this would be the last of all earthly voyages for me. Then we lifted for ever and ever and ever, till I heard Keller saying in my ear, 'The bowels of the deep, good Lord!' and the *Rathmines* stood poised, her screw racing and drumming on the slope of a hollow that stretched downwards for a good half-mile.

We went down that hollow, nose under for the most part, and the air smelt wet and muddy, like that of an emptied aquarium. There was a second hill to climb; I saw that much: but the water came aboard and carried me aft till it jammed me against the wheel-house door, and before I could catch breath or clear my eyes again we were rolling to and fro in torn water, with the scuppers pouring like eaves in a thunderstorm.

'There were three waves,' said Keller, 'and the stokehold's flooded.'

The firemen were on deck waiting, apparently, to be drowned. The engineer came and dragged them below, and the crew, gasping, began to work the clumsy Board of Trade pump. That showed nothing serious, and when I understood that the *Rathmines* was really on the water, and not beneath it, I asked what had happened.

'The captain says it was a blow-up under the sea – a volcano,' said Keller.

'It hasn't warmed anything,' I said. I was feeling bitterly cold, and cold was almost unknown in those waters. I went below to change my clothes, and when I came up everything was wiped out in clinging white fog.

'Are there going to be any more surprises?' said Keller to the captain.

'I don't know. Be thankful you're alive, gentlemen. That's a tidal wave thrown up by a volcano. Probably the bottom of the sea has been lifted a few feet somewhere or other. I can't quite understand this cold spell. Our sea-thermometer says the surface water is 44°, and it should be 68° at least.'

'It's abominable,' said Keller, shivering. 'But hadn't you better attend to the fog-horn? It seems to me that I heard something.'

'Heard! Good heavens!' said the captain from the bridge, 'I should think you did.' He pulled the string of our fog-horn, which was a weak one. It sputtered and choked, because the stokehold was full of water and the fires were half-drowned, and at last gave out a moan. It was answered from the fog by one of the most appalling steam-sirens I have ever heard. Keller turned as white as I did, for the fog, the cold fog, was upon us, and any man may be forgiven for fearing a death he cannot see.

'Give her steam there!' said the captain to the engine-room. 'Steam for the whistle, if we have to go dead slow.'

We bellowed again, and the damp dripped off the awnings on to the deck as we listened for the reply. It seemed to be astern this time, but much nearer than before.

'The *Pembroke Castle* on us!' said Keller; and then, viciously, 'Well, thank God, we shall sink her too.'

'It's a side-wheel steamer,' I whispered. 'Can't you hear the paddles?'

This time we whistled and roared till the steam gave out, and the answer nearly deafened us. There was a sound of frantic threshing in the water, apparently about fifty yards away, and something shot past in the whiteness that looked as though it were grey and red.

'The *Pembroke Castle* bottom up,' said Keller, who, being a journalist, always sought for explanations. 'That's the colours of a Castle liner. We're in for a big thing.'

'The sea is bewitched,' said Frithiof from the wheel-house. 'There are *two* steamers!'

Another siren sounded on our bow, and the little steamer rolled in the wash of something that had passed unseen.

'We're evidently in the middle of a fleet,' said Keller quietly. 'If one doesn't run us down, the other will. Phew! What in creation is that?'

I sniffed, for there was a poisonous rank smell in the cold air – a smell that I had smelt before.

'If I was on land I should say that it was an alligator. It smells like musk,' I answered.

'Not ten thousand alligators could make that smell,' said Zuyland; 'I have smelt them.'

'Bewitched! Bewitched!' said Frithiof. 'The sea she is turned upside down, and we are walking along the bottom.'

Again the *Rathmines* rolled in the wash of some unseen ship, and a silver-grey wave broke over the bow, leaving on the deck a sheet of sediment – the grey broth that has its place in the fathomless deeps of the sea. A sprinkling of the wave fell on my face, and it was so cold that it stung as boiling water stings. The dead and most untouched deep water of the sea had been heaved to the top by the submarine volcano – the chill still water that kills all life and smells of desolation and emptiness. We did not need either the blinding fog or that indescribable smell of musk to make us unhappy – we were shivering with cold and wretchedness where we stood.

'The hot air on the cold water makes this fog,' said the captain; 'it ought to clear in a little time.'

'Whistle, oh! whistle, and let's get out of it,' said Keller.

The captain whistled again, and far and far astern the invisible twin steam-sirens answered us. Their blasting shriek grew louder, till at last it seemed to tear out of the fog just above our quarter, and I cowered while the *Rathmines* plunged bows under on a double swell that crossed.

'No more,' said Frithiof, 'it is not good any more. Let us get away, in the name of God.'

'Now if a torpedo-boat with a *City of Paris* siren went mad and broke her moorings and hired a friend to help her, it's just conceivable that we might be carried as we are now. Otherwise this thing is—'

The last words died on Keller's lips, his eyes began to start from his head, and his jaw fell. Some six or seven feet above the port bulwarks, framed in fog, and as utterly unsupported as the full moon, hung a Face. It was not human, and it certainly was not animal, for it did not belong to this earth as known to man. The mouth was open, revealing a ridiculously tiny tongue – as absurd as the tongue of an elephant; there were tense wrinkles of white skin at the angles of the drawn lips, white feelers like those of a barbel sprung from the lower jaw, and there was no sign of teeth within the mouth. But the horror of the face lay in the eyes, for those were sightless – white, in sockets as white as scraped bone, and blind. Yet for all this the face, wrinkled as the mask of a lion is drawn in Assyrian sculpture, was alive with rage and terror. One long white feeler touched our bulwarks. Then the face disappeared with the swiftness of a blindworm popping into its burrow, and the next thing that I remember is my own voice in my own ears, saying gravely to the mainmast, 'But the air-bladder ought to have been forced out of its mouth, you know.'

Keller came up to me, ashy white. He put his hand into his pocket, took a cigar, bit it, dropped it, thrust his shaking thumb into his mouth and mumbled, 'The giant gooseberry and the raining frogs! Gimme a light – gimme a light! Say, gimme a light.' A little bead of blood dropped from his thumb-joint.

I respected the motive, though the manifestation was absurd. 'Stop, you'll bite your thumb off', I said, and Keller laughed brokenly as he picked up his cigar. Only Zuyland, leaning over the port bulwarks, seemed self-possessed. He declared later that he was very sick.

'We've seen it,' he said, turning round. 'That is it.'

'What?' said Keller, chewing the unlighted cigar.

As he spoke the fog was blown into shreds, and we saw the sea, grey with mud, rolling on every side of us and empty of all life. Then in one spot it bubbled and became like the pot of ointment that the Bible speaks of. From that wide-ringed trouble a Thing came up – a grey and red Thing with a neck – a Thing that bellowed and writhed in pain. Frithiof drew in his breath and held it till the red letters of the ship's name, woven across his jersey, straggled and opened out as though they had been type badly set. Then he said with a little cluck in his throat, 'Ah me! It is blind. *Hur illa!* That thing is blind,' and a murmur of pity went through us all, for we could see that the thing on the water was blind and in pain. Something had gashed and cut the great sides cruelly and the blood was spurting out. The grey ooze of the undermost sea lay in the monstrous wrinkles of the back, and poured away in sluices. The blind white head flung back and battered the wounds, and the body in its torment rose clear of the red and grey waves till we saw a pair of quivering shoulders streaked with weed and rough with shells, but as white in the clear spaces as the hairless, maneless, blind, toothless head. Afterwards, came a dot on the horizon and the sound of a shrill scream, and it was as though a shuttle shot all across the sea in one breath, and a second head and neck tore through the levels, driving a whispering wall of water to right and left. The two Things met – the one untouched and the other in its death-throe – male and female, we said, the female coming to the male. She circled round him bellowing, and laid her neck across the curve of his great turtle-back, and he disappeared under water for an instant, but flung up again, grunting in agony while the blood ran. Once the entire head and neck shot clear of the water and stiffened, and I heard Keller saying, as though he was watching a street accident, 'Give him air. For God's sake, give him air.' Then the death-struggle began, with crampings and twistings and jerkings of the white bulk to and fro, till our little steamer rolled again, and each grey wave coated her plates with the grey slime. The sun was clear, there was no wind, and we watched, the whole crew, stokers and all, in wonder and pity, but chiefly pity. The Thing was so helpless, and, save for his mate, so alone. No human eye should have beheld him; it was monstrous and indecent to exhibit him there in trade waters between atlas degrees of latitude. He had been spewed up, mangled and dying, from his rest on the sea-floor, where he might have lived till the Judgement Day, and we saw the tides of his life go from him as an angry tide goes out across rocks in the teeth of a landward gale. His mate lay rocking on the water a little distance off, bellowing continually, and the smell of musk came down upon the ship making us cough.

At last the battle for life ended in a batter of coloured seas.

We saw the writhing neck fall like a flail, the carcase turn sideways, showing the glint of a white belly and the inset of a gigantic hind leg or flipper. Then all sank, and sea boiled over it, while the mate swam round and round, darting her head in every direction. Though we might have feared that she would attack the steamer, no power on earth could have drawn any one of us from our places that hour. We watched, holding our breaths. The mate paused in her search; we could hear the wash beating along her sides; reared her neck as high as she could reach, blind and lonely in all that loneliness of the sea, and sent one desperate bellow booming across the swells as an oyster-shell skips across a pond. Then she made off to the westward, the sun shining on the white head and the wake behind it, till nothing was left to see but a little pin point of silver on the horizon. We stood on our course again; and the *Rathmines*, coated with the sea-sediment from bow to stern, looked like a ship made grey with terror.

'We must pool our notes,' was the first coherent remark from Keller. 'We're three trained journalists – we hold absolutely the biggest scoop on record. Start fair.'

I objected to this. Nothing is gained by collaboration in journalism when all deal with the same facts, so we went to work each according to his own lights. Keller triple-headed his account, talked about our 'gallant captain', and wound up with an allusion to American enterprise in that it was a citizen of Dayton, Ohio, that had seen the sea-serpent. This sort of thing would have discredited the Creation, much more a mere sea tale, but as a specimen of the picture-writing of a half-civilized people it was very interesting. Zuyland took a heavy column and a half, giving approximate lengths and breadths, and the whole list of the crew whom he had sworn on oath to testify to his facts. There was nothing fantastic or flamboyant in Zuyland. I wrote three-quarters of a leaded bourgeoïs column, roughly speaking, and refrained from putting any journalese into it for reasons that had begun to appear to me.

Keller was insolent with joy. He was going to cable from Southampton to the New York *World*, mail his account to America on the same day, paralyse London with his three columns of loosely knitted headlines, and generally efface the earth. 'You'll see how I work a big scoop when I get it', he said.

'Is this your first visit to England?' I asked.

'Yes', said he. 'You don't seem to appreciate the beauty of our scoop. It's pyramidal – the death of the sea-serpent! Good heavens alive, man, it's the biggest thing ever vouchsafed to a paper!'

'Curious to think that it will never appear in any paper, isn't it?' I said.

Zuyland was near me, and he nodded quickly.

'What do you mean?' said Keller. 'If you're enough of a Britisher to throw this thing away, I shan't. I thought you were a newspaperman.'

'I am. That's why I know. Don't be an ass, Keller. Remember, I'm seven hundred years your senior, and what your grandchildren may learn five hundred years hence, I learned from my grandfathers about five hundred years ago. You won't do it, because you can't.'

This conversation was held in open sea, where everything seems possible, some hundred miles from Southampton. We passed the Needles Light at dawn, and the lifting day showed the stucco villas on the green and the awful orderliness of England – line upon line, wall upon wall, solid stone dock and monolithic pier. We waited an hour in the Customs shed, and there was ample time for the effect to soak in.

'Now, Keller, you face the music. The *Havel* goes out today. Mail by her, and I'll take you to the telegraph-office,' I said.

I heard Keller gasp as the influence of the land closed about him, cowing him as they say Newmarket Heath cows a young horse unused to open courses.

'I want to retouch my stuff. Suppose we wait till we get to London?' he said.

Zuyland, by the way, had torn up his account and thrown it overboard that morning early. His reasons were my reasons.

In the train Keller began to revise his copy, and every time that he looked at the trim little fields, the red villas, and the embankments of the line, the blue pencil plunged remorselessly through the slips. He appeared to have dredged the dictionary for adjectives. I could think of none that he had not used. Yet he was a perfectly sound poker-player and never showed more cards than were sufficient to take the pool.

'Aren't you going to leave him a single bellow?' I asked sympathetically. 'Remember, everything goes in the States, from a trouser-button to a double-eagle.'

'That's just the curse of it', said Keller below his breath. 'We've played 'em for suckers so often that when it comes to the golden truth – I'd like to try this on a London paper. You have first call there, though.'

'Not in the least. I'm not touching the thing in our papers. I shall be happy to leave 'em all to you; but surely you'll cable it home?'

'No. Not if I can make the scoop here and see the Britishers sit up.'

'You won't do it with three columns of slushy headline, believe me. They don't sit up as quickly as some people.'

'I'm beginning to think that too. Does *nothing* make

any difference in this country?' he said, looking out of the window. 'How old is that farmhouse?'

'New. It can't be more than two hundred years at the most.'

'Um. Fields, too?'

'That hedge there must have been clipped for about eighty years.'

'Labour cheap – eh?'

'Pretty much. Well, I suppose you'd like to try the *Times*, wouldn't you?'

'No', said Keller, looking at Winchester Cathedral. ' 'Might as well try to electrify a haystack. And to think that the *World* would take three columns and ask for more – with illustrations too! It's sickening.'

'But the *Times* might,' I began.

Keller flung his paper across the carriage, and it opened in its austere majesty of solid type – opened with the crackle of an encyclopedia.

'Might! You *might* work your way through the bow-plates of a cruiser. Look at that first page!'

'It strikes you that way, does it?' I said. 'Then I'd recommend you to try a light and frivolous journal.'

'With a thing like this of mine – of ours? It's sacred history!'

I showed him a paper which I conceived would be after his own heart, in that it was modelled on American lines.

'That's homey,' he said, 'but it's not the real thing. Now, I should like one of these fat old *Times* columns. Probably there'd be a bishop in the office, though.'

When we reached London Keller disappeared in the direction of the Strand. What his experiences may have been I cannot tell, but it seems that he invaded the office of an evening paper at 11.45 a.m. (I told him English editors were most idle at that hour), and mentioned my name as that of a witness to the truth of his story.

'I was nearly fired out,' he said furiously at lunch. 'As soon as I mentioned you, the old man said that I was to tell you that they didn't want any more of your practical jokes, and that you knew the hours to call if you had anything to sell, and that they'd see you condemned before they helped to puff one of your infernal yarns in advance. Say, what record do you hold for truth in this country, anyway?'

'A beauty. You ran up against it, that's all. Why don't you leave the English papers alone and cable to New York? Everything goes over there.'

'Can't you see that's just why?' he repeated.

'I saw it a long time ago. You don't intend to cable, then?'

'Yes, I do,' he answered, in the over-emphatic voice of one who does not know his own mind.

That afternoon I walked him abroad and about, over the streets that run between the pavements like channels of grooved and tongued lava, over the bridges that are made of enduring stone, through subways floored and sided with yard-thick concrete, between houses that are never rebuilt, and by river-steps hewn, to the eye, from the living rock. A black fog chased us into Westminster Abbey, and, standing there in the darkness, I could hear the wings of the dead centuries circling round the head of Litchfield A. Keller, journalist, of Dayton, Ohio, USA, whose mission it was to make the Britishers sit up.

He stumbled gasping into the thick gloom, and the roar of the traffic came to his bewildered ears.

'Let's go to the telegraph-office and cable,' I said. 'Can't you hear the New York *World* crying for news of the great sea-serpent, blind, white, and smelling of musk, stricken to death by a submarine volcano, and assisted by his loving wife to die in mid-ocean, as visualized by an American citizen, the breezy, newsy, brainy newspaper man of Dayton, Ohio? 'Rah for the Buckeye State. Step lively! Both gates! Szz! Boom! Aah!' Keller was a Princeton man, and he seemed to need encouragement.

'You've got me on your own ground,' said he, tugging at his overcoat pocket. He pulled out his copy, with the cable forms – for he had written out his telegram – and put them all into my hand, groaning, 'I pass. If I hadn't come to your cursed country – If I'd sent it off at Southampton – If I ever get you west of the Alleghannies, if—'

'Never mind, Keller. It isn't your fault. It's the fault of your country. If you had been seven hundred years older you'd have done what I am going to do.'

'What are you going to do?'

'Tell it as a lie.'

'Fiction?' This with the full-blooded disgust of a journalist for the illegitimate branch of the profession.

'You can call it that if you like. I shall call it a lie.'

And a lie it has become; for Truth is a naked lady, and if by accident she is drawn up from the bottom of the sea, it behoves a gentleman either to give her a print petticoat or to turn his face to the wall and vow that he did not see.

EDGAR ALLAN POE

A DESCENT INTO THE MAELSTRÖM

The ways of God in Nature, as in Providence, are not as *our* ways; nor are the models that we frame in any way commensurate to the vastness, profundity, and unsearchableness of His works, *which have a depth in them greater than the well of Democritus.*

– *Joseph Glanville*

WE HAD NOW reached the summit of the loftiest crag. For some minutes the old man seemed too much exhausted to speak.

'Not long ago,' said he at length, 'and I could have guided you on this route as well as the youngest of my sons; but, about three years past, there happened to me an event such as never happened before to mortal man – or at least such as no man ever survived to tell of – and the six hours of deadly terror which I then endured have broken me up body and soul. You suppose me a *very* old man – but I am not. It took less than a single day to change these hairs from a jetty black to white, to weaken my limbs, and to unstring my nerves, so that I tremble at the least exertion, and am frightened at a shadow. Do you know I can scarcely look over this little cliff without getting giddy?'

The 'little cliff,' upon whose edge he had so carelessly thrown himself down to rest that the weightier portion of his body hung over it, while he was only kept from falling by the tenure of his elbow on its extreme and slippery edge

– this 'little cliff' arose, a sheer unobstructed precipice of black shining rock, some fifteen or sixteen hundred feet from the world of crags beneath us. Nothing would have tempted me to be within half a dozen yards of its brink. In truth so deeply was I excited by the perilous position of my companion, that I fell at full length upon the ground, clung to the shrubs around me, and dared not even glance upward at the sky – while I struggled in vain to divest myself of the idea that the very foundations of the mountain were in danger from the fury of the winds. It was long before I could reason myself into sufficient courage to sit up and look out into the distance.

'You must get over these fancies,' said the guide, 'for I have brought you here that you might have the best possible view of the scene of that event I mentioned – and to tell you the whole story with the spot just under your eye.

'We are now,' he continued, in that particularizing manner which distinguished him – 'we are now close upon the Norwegian coast – in the sixty-eighth degree of latitude – in the great province of Nordland – and in the dreary district of Lofoden. The mountain upon whose top we sit is Helseggen, the Cloudy. Now raise yourself up a little higher – hold on to the grass if you feel giddy – so – and look out, beyond the belt of vapor beneath us, into the sea.'

I looked dizzily, and beheld a wide expanse of ocean, whose waters wore so inky a hue as to bring at once to my mind the Nubian geographer's account of the *Mare Tenebrarum*. A panorama more deplorably desolate no human imagination can conceive. To the right and left, as far as the eye could reach, there lay outstretched, like ramparts of the world, lines of horridly black and beetling cliff, whose character of gloom was but the more forcibly illustrated by the surf which reared high up against it its white and ghastly crest, howling and shrieking for ever. Just opposite the promontory upon whose apex we were placed, and at a distance of some five or six miles out at sea, there was visible a small, bleak-looking island; or, more properly, its position was discernible through the wilderness of surge in which it was enveloped. About two miles nearer the land, arose another of smaller size, hideously craggy and barren, and encompassed at various intervals by a cluster of dark rocks.

The appearance of the ocean, in the space between the more distant island and the shore, had something very unusual about it. Although, at the time, so strong a gale was blowing landward that a brig in the remote offing lay to under a double-reefed trysail, and constantly plunged her whole hull out of sight, still there was here nothing like a regular swell, but only a short, quick, angry cross-dashing of water in every direction – as well in the teeth of the wind as otherwise. Of foam there was little except in the immediate vicinity of the rocks.

'The island in the distance,' resumed the old man, 'is called by the Norwegians Vurrgh. The one midway is Moskoe. That a mile to the northward is Ambaaren. Yonder are Islesen, Hotholm, Keildhelm, Suarven, and Buckholm. Further off – between Moskoe and Vurrgh – are Otterholm, Flimen, Sandflesen, and Stockholm. These are the true names of the places – but why it has been thought necessary to name them at all, is more than either you or I can understand. Do you hear any thing? Do you see any change in the water?'

We had now been about ten minutes upon the top of Helseggen, to which we had ascended from the interior of Lofoden, so that we had caught no glimpse of the sea until it had burst upon us from the summit. As the old man spoke, I became aware of a loud and gradually increasing sound, like the moaning of a vast herd of buffaloes upon an

American prairie; and at the same moment I perceived that what seamen term the *chopping* character of the ocean beneath us, was rapidly changing into a current which set to the eastward. Even while I gazed, this current acquired a monstrous velocity. Each moment added to its speed – to its headlong impetuosity. In five minutes the whole sea, as far as Vurrgh, was lashed into ungovernable fury; but it was between Moskoe and the coast that the main uproar held its sway. Here the vast bed of the waters, seamed and scarred into a thousand conflicting channels, burst suddenly into phrensied convulsion – heaving, boiling, hissing – gyrating in gigantic and innumerable vortices, and all whirling and plunging on to the eastward with a rapidity which water never elsewhere assumes, except in precipitous descents.

In a few minutes more, there came over the scene another radical alteration. The general surface grew somewhat more smooth, and the whirlpools, one by one, disappeared, while prodigious streaks of foam became apparent where none had been seen before. These streaks, at length, spreading out to a great distance, and entering into combination, took unto themselves the gyratory motion of the subsided vortices, and seemed to form the germ of another more vast. Suddenly – very suddenly – this assumed a distinct and definite existence, in a circle of more than a mile in diameter. The edge of the whirl was represented by a broad belt of gleaming spray; but no particle of this slipped into the mouth of the terrific funnel, whose interior, as far as the eye could fathom it, was a smooth, shining, and jet-black wall of water, inclined to the horizon at an angle of some forty-five degrees, speeding dizzily round and round with a swaying and sweltering motion, and sending forth to the winds an appalling voice, half shriek, half roar, such as not even the mighty cataract of Niagara ever lifts up in its agony to Heaven.

The mountain trembled to its very base, and the rock rocked. I threw myself upon my face, and clung to the scant herbage in an excess of nervous agitation.

'This,' said I at length, to the old man – 'this *can* be nothing else than the great whirlpool of the Maelström.'

'So it is sometimes termed,' said he. 'We Norwegians call it the Moskoe-ström, from the island of Moskoe in the midway.'

The ordinary account of this vortex had by no means prepared me for what I saw. That of Jonas Ramus, which is perhaps the most circumstantial of any, cannot impart the faintest conception either of the magnificence, or of the horror of the scene – or of the wild bewildering sense of *the novel* which confounds the beholder. I am not sure from what point of view the writer in question surveyed it, nor at what time; but it could neither have been from the summit of Helseggen, nor during a storm. There are some passages of his description, nevertheless, which may be quoted for their details, although their effect is exceedingly feeble in conveying an impression of the spectacle.

'Between Lofoden and Moskoe,' he says, 'the depth of the water is between thirty-six and forty fathoms; but on the other side, toward Ver (Vurrgh) this depth decreases so as not to afford a convenient passage for a vessel, without the risk of splitting on the rocks, which happens even in the calmest weather. When it is flood, the stream runs up the country between Lofoden and Moskoe with a boisterous rapidity; but the roar of its impetuous ebb to the sea is scarce equalled by the loudest and most dreadful cataracts; the noise being heard several leagues off, and the vortices or pits are of such an extent and depth, that if a ship comes within its attraction, it is inevitably absorbed and carried down to the bottom, and there beat to pieces against the rocks; and when the water relaxes, the fragments thereof are thrown up again. But these intervals of tranquillity are only at the turn of the ebb and flood, and in calm weather, and last but a quarter of an hour, its violence gradually returning. When the stream is most boisterous, and its fury heightened by a storm, it is dangerous to come within a Norway mile of it. Boats, yachts, and ships have been carried away by not guarding against it before they were carried within its reach. It likewise happens frequently, that whales come too near the stream, and are overpowered by its violence; and then it is impossible to describe their howlings and bellowings in their fruitless struggles to disengage themselves. A bear once, attempting to swim from Lofoden to Moskoe, was caught by the stream and borne down, while he roared terribly, so as to be heard on shore. Large stocks of firs and pine trees, after being absorbed by the current, rise again broken and torn to such a degree as if bristles grew upon them. This plainly shows the bottom to consist of craggy rocks, among which they are whirled to and fro. This stream is regulated by the flux and reflux of the sea – it being constantly high and low water every six hours. In the year 1645, early in the morning of Sexagesima Sunday, it raged with such noise and impetuosity that the very stones of the houses on the coast fell to the ground.'

In regard to the depth of the water, I could not see how this could have been ascertained at all in the immediate vicinity of the vortex. The 'forty fathoms' must have reference only to portions of the channel close upon the shore either of Moskoe or Lofoden. The depth in the centre of the Moskoe-ström must be unmeasurably greater; and no better proof of this fact is necessary than can be obtained from even the sidelong glance into the abyss of the whirl which may be had from the highest crag of Helseggen.

Looking down from this pinnacle upon the howling Phlegethon below, I could not help smiling at the simplicity with which the honest Jonas Ramus records, as a matter difficult of belief, the anecdotes of the whales and the bears, for it appeared to me, in fact, a self-evident thing, that the largest ships of the line in existence, coming within the influence of that deadly attraction, could resist it as little as a feather the hurricane, and must disappear bodily and at once.

The attempts to account for the phenomenon – some of which I remember, seemed to me sufficiently plausible in perusal – now wore a very different and unsatisfactory aspect. The idea generally received is that this, as well as three smaller vortices among the Ferroe Islands, 'have no other cause than the collision of waves rising and falling, at flux and reflux, against a ridge of rocks and shelves, which confines the water so that it precipitates itself like a cataract; and thus the higher the flood rises, the deeper must the fall be, and the natural result of all is a whirlpool or vortex, the prodigious suction of which is sufficiently known by lesser experiments.' – These are the words of the *Encyclopædia Britannica*. Kircher and others imagine that in the centre of the channel of the maelström is an abyss penetrating the globe, and issuing in some very remote part – the Gulf of Bothnia being somewhat decidedly named in one instance. This opinion, idle in itself, was the one to which, as I gazed, my imagination most readily assented; and, mentioning it to the guide, I was rather surprised to hear him say that, although it was the view almost universally entertained of the subject by the Norwegians, it nevertheless was not his own. As to the former notion he confessed his inability to comprehend it; and here I agreed with him – for, however conclusive on paper, it becomes altogether unintelligible, and even absurd, amid the thunder of the abyss.

'You have had a good look at the whirl now,' said the old man, 'and if you will creep round this crag, so as to get in its lee, and deaden the roar of the water, I will tell you a story that will convince you I ought to know something of the Moskoe-ström.'

I placed myself as desired, and he proceeded.

'Myself and my two brothers once owned a schooner-rigged smack of about seventy tons burthen, with which we were in the habit of fishing among the islands beyond Moskoe, nearly to Vurrgh. In all violent eddies at sea there is good fishing, at proper opportunities, if one has only the courage to attempt it, but among the whole of the Lofoden coastmen, we three were the only ones who made a regular business of going out to the islands, as I tell you. The usual grounds are a great way lower down to the southward. There fish can be got at all hours, without much risk, and therefore these places are preferred. The choice spots over here among the rocks, however, not only yield the finest variety, but in far greater abundance; so that we often got in a single day, what the more timid of the craft could not scrape together in a week. In fact, we made it a matter of desperate speculation – the risk of life standing instead of labor, and courage answering for capital.

'We kept the smack in a cove about five miles higher up the coast than this; and it was our practice, in fine weather, to take advantage of the fifteen minutes' slack to push across the main channel of the Moskoe-ström, far above the pool, and then drop down upon anchorage somewhere near Otterholm, or Sandflesen, where the eddies are not so violent as elsewhere. Here we used to remain until nearly time for slack-water again, when we weighed and made for home. We never set out upon this expedition without a steady side wind for going and coming – one that we felt sure would not fail us before our return – and we seldom made a miscalculation upon this point. Twice, during six years, we were forced to stay all night at anchor on account of a dead calm, which is a rare thing indeed just about here; and once we had to remain on the grounds nearly a week, starving to death, owing to a gale which blew up shortly after our arrival, and made the channel too boisterous to be thought of. Upon this occasion we should have been driven out to sea in spite of every thing (for the whirlpools threw us round and round so violently, that, at length, we fouled our anchor and dragged it), if it had not been that we drifted into one of the innumerable cross currents – here today and gone tomorrow – which drove us under the lee of Filmen, where, by good luck, we brought up.

'I could not tell you the twentieth part of the difficulties we encountered "on the ground" – it is a bad spot to be in, even in good weather – but we make shift always to run the gauntlet of the Moskoe-ström itself without accident; although at times my heart has been in my mouth when we happened to be a minute or so behind or before the slack. The wind sometimes was not as strong as we thought it at starting, and then we made rather less way than we could wish, while the current rendered the smack unmanageable. My eldest brother had a son eighteen years old, and I had two stout boys of my own. These would have been of great assistance at such times, in using the sweeps as well as afterward in fishing – but, somehow, although we ran the risk ourselves, we had not the heart to let the young ones get into the danger – for, after all said and done, it *was* a horrible danger, and that is the truth.

'It is now within a few days of three years since what I am going to tell you occurred. It was on the tenth of July, 18—, a day which the people of this part of the world will never forget – for it was one in which blew the most terrible hurricane that ever came out of the heavens. And yet all the morning, and indeed until late in the afternoon, there was a gentle and steady breeze from the southwest, while the sun shone brightly, so that the oldest seaman among us could not have foreseen what was to follow.

'The three of us – my two brothers and myself – had crossed over to the islands about two o'clock p.m; and soon nearly loaded the smack with fine fish, which, we all remarked, were more plenty that day than we had ever known them. It was just seven, *by my watch*, when we weighed and started for home, so as to make the worst of the Ström at slack water, which we knew would be at eight.

'We set out with a fresh wind on our starboard quarter, and for some time spanked along at a great rate, never dreaming of danger, for indeed we saw not the slightest reason to apprehend it. All at once we were taken aback by a breeze from over Helseggen. This was most unusual – something that had never happened to us before – and I began to feel a little uneasy, without exactly knowing why. We put the boat on the wind, but could make no headway at all for the eddies, and I was upon the point of proposing to return to the anchorage, when, looking astern, we saw the whole horizon covered with a singular copper-colored cloud that rose with the most amazing velocity.

'In the meantime the breeze that had headed us off fell away and we were dead becalmed, drifting about in every direction. This state of things, however, did not last long enough to give us time to think about it. In less than a minute the storm was upon us – in less than two the sky was entirely overcast – and what with this and the driving spray, it became suddenly so dark that we could not see each other in the smack.

'Such a hurricane as then blew it is folly to attempt describing. The oldest seaman in Norway never experienced any thing like it. We had let our sails go by the run before it cleverly took us; but, at the first puff, both our masts went by the board as if they had been sawed off – the mainmast taking with it my youngest brother, who had lashed himself to it for safety.

'Our boat was the lightest feather of a thing that ever sat upon water. It had a complete flush deck, with only a small hatch near the bow, and this hatch it had always been our custom to batten down when about to cross the Ström, by way of precaution against the chopping seas. But for this circumstance we should have foundered at once – for we lay entirely buried for some moments. How my elder brother escaped destruction I cannot say, for I never had an opportunity of ascertaining. For my part, as soon as I had let the foresail run, I threw myself flat on deck, with my feet against the narrow gunwale of the bow, and with my hands grasping a ring-bolt near the foot of the foremast. It was mere instinct that prompted me to do this – which was undoubtedly the very best thing I could have done – for I was too much flurried to think.

'For some moments we were completely deluged, as I say, and all this time I held my breath, and clung to the bolt. When I could stand it no longer I raised myself upon my knees, still keeping hold with my hands, and thus got my head clear. Presently our little boat gave herself a shake, just as a dog does in coming out of the water, and thus rid herself, in some measure, of the seas. I was now trying to get the better of the stupor that had come over me, and to collect my senses so as to see what was to be done, when I felt somebody grasp my arm. It was my elder brother, and my heart leaped for joy, for I had made sure that he was overboard – but the next moment all this joy was turned into horror – for he put his mouth close to my ear, and screamed out the word "*Moskoe-ström!*"

'No one ever will know what my feelings were at that moment. I shook from head to foot as if I had had the most violent fit of the ague. I knew what he meant by that one word well enough – I knew what he wished to make me understand. With the wind that now drove us on, we were bound for the whirl of the Ström, and nothing could save us!

'You perceive that in crossing the Ström *channel*, we always went a long way up above the whirl, even in the calmest weather, and then had to wait and watch carefully for the slack – but now we were driving right upon the pool itself, and in such a hurricane as this! "To be sure," I thought, "we shall get there just about the slack – there is some little hope in that" – but in the next moment I cursed myself for being so great a fool as to dream of hope at all. I knew very well that we were doomed, had we been ten times a ninety-gun ship.

'By this time the first fury of the tempest had spent itself, or perhaps we did not feel it so much, as we scudded before it, but at all events the seas, which at first had been kept down by the wind, and lay flat and frothing, now got up into absolute mountains. A singular change, too, had come over the heavens. Around in every direction it was still as black as pitch, but nearly overhead there burst out, all at once, a circular rift of clear sky – as clear as I ever saw – and of a deep bright blue – and through it there blazed forth the full moon with a lustre that I never before knew her to wear. She lit up every thing about us with the greatest distinctness – but, oh God, what a scene it was to light up!

'I now made one or two attempts to speak to my brother – but in some manner which I could not understand, the din had so increased that I could not make him hear a single word, although I screamed at the top of my voice in his ear. Presently he shook his head, looking as pale as death, and held up one of his fingers, as if to say "*listen!*"

'At first I could not make out what he meant – but soon a hideous thought flashed upon me. I dragged my watch from its fob. It was not going. I glanced at its face by the moonlight, and then burst into tears as I flung it far away into the ocean. *It had run down at seven o'clock! We were behind the time of the slack, and the whirl of the Ström was in full fury!*

'When a boat is well built, properly trimmed, and not deep laden, the waves in a strong gale, when she is going large, seem always to slip from beneath her – which appears strange to a landsman – and this is what is called *riding*, in sea phrase.

'Well, so far we had ridden the swells very cleverly; but presently a gigantic sea happened to take us right under the counter, and bore us with it as it rose – up – up – as if into the sky. I would not have believed that any wave could rise so high. And then down we came with a sweep, a slide, and a plunge that made me feel sick and dizzy, as if I was falling from some lofty mountain-top in a dream. But while we were up I had thrown a quick glance around and that one glance was all-sufficient. I saw our exact position in an instant. The Moskoe-ström whirlpool was about a quarter of a mile dead ahead – but no more like the every-day Moskoe-ström than the whirl, as you now see it, is like a mill-race. If I had not known where we were, and what we had to expect, I should not have recognized the place at all. As it was, I involuntarily closed my eyes in horror. The lids clenched themselves together as if in a spasm.

'It could not have been more than two minutes afterwards

until we suddenly felt the waves subside, and were enveloped in foam. The boat made a sharp half turn to larboard, and then shot off in its new direction like a thunderbolt. At the same moment the roaring noise of the water was completely drowned in a kind of shrill shriek – such a sound as you might imagine given out by the water-pipes of many thousand steam-vessels letting off their steam all together. We were now in the belt of surf that always surrounds the whirl; and I thought, of course, that another moment would plunge us into the abyss, down which we could only see indistinctly on account of the amazing velocity with which we were borne along. The boat did not seem to sink into the water at all, but to skim like an air-bubble upon the surface of the surge. Her starboard side was next the whirl, and on the larboard arose the world of ocean we had left. It stood like a huge writhing wall between us and the horizon.

'It may appear strange, but now, when we were in the very jaws of the gulf, I felt more composed than when we were only approaching it. Having made up my mind to hope no more, I got rid of a great deal of that terror which unmanned me at first. I supposed it was despair that strung my nerves.

'It may look like boasting – but what I tell you is truth – I began to reflect how magnificent a thing it was to die in such a manner, and how foolish it was in me to think of so paltry a consideration as my own individual life, in view of so wonderful a manifestation of God's power. I do believe that I blushed with shame when this idea crossed my mind. After a little while I became possessed with the keenest curiosity about the whirl itself. I positively felt a *wish* to explore its depths, even at the sacrifice I was going to make; and my principal grief was that I should never be able to tell my old companions on shore about the mysteries I should see.

These, no doubt, were singular fancies to occupy a man's mind in such extremity – and I have often thought since, that the revolutions of the boat around the pool might have rendered me a little light-headed.

'There was another circumstance which tended to restore my self-possession; and this was the cessation of the wind, which could not reach us in our present situation – for, as you saw for yourself, the belt of the surf is considerably lower than the general bed of the ocean, and this latter now towered above us, a high, black, mountainous ridge. If you have never been at sea in a heavy gale, you can form no idea of the confusion of mind occasioned by the wind and spray together. They blind, deafen, and strangle you, and take away all power of action or reflection. But we were now, in a great measure, rid of these annoyances – just as death-condemned felons in prison are allowed petty indulgences, forbidden them while their doom is yet uncertain.

'How often we made the circuit of the belt it is impossible to say. We careered round and round for perhaps an hour, flying rather than floating, getting gradually more and more into the middle of the surge, and then nearer and nearer to its horrible inner edge. All this time I had never let go of the ring-bolt. My brother was at the stern, holding on to a small empty water-cask which had been securely lashed under the coop of the counter, and was the only thing on deck that had not been swept overboard when the gale first took us. As we approached the brink of the pit he let go his hold upon this, and made for the ring, from which, in the agony of his terror, he endeavored to force my hands, as it was not large enough to afford us both a secure grasp. I never felt deeper grief than when I saw him attempt this act – although I knew he was a madman when he did it – a raving maniac through sheer fright. I did not care, however, to contest the point with him. I knew it could make no difference whether either of us held on at all; so I let him have the bolt, and went astern to the cask. This there was no great difficulty in doing; for the smack flew round steadily enough, and upon an even keel – only swaying to and fro with the immense sweeps and swelters of the whirl. Scarcely had I secured myself in my new position, when we gave a wild lurch to starboard, and rushed headlong into the abyss. I muttered a hurried prayer to God, and thought all was over.

'As I felt the sickening sweep of the descent, I had instinctively tightened my hold upon the barrel, and closed my eyes. For some seconds I dared not open them – while I expected instant destruction, and wondered that I was not already in my death-struggles with the water. But moment after moment elapsed. I still lived. The sense of falling had ceased; and the motion of the vessel seemed much as it had been before, while in the belt of foam, with the exception that she now lay more along. I took courage and looked once again upon the scene.

'Never shall I forget the sensation of awe, horror, and admiration with which I gazed about me. The boat appeared to be hanging, as if by magic, midway down, upon the interior surface of a funnel vast in circumference, prodigious in depth, and whose perfectly smooth sides might have been mistaken for ebony, but for the bewildering rapidity with which they spun around, and for the gleaming and ghastly radiance they shot forth, as the rays of the full moon, from that circular rift amid the clouds which I have already described, streamed in a flood of golden glory along the black walls, and far away down into the inmost recesses of the abyss.

'At first I was too much confused to observe any thing accurately. The general burst of terrific grandeur was all that I beheld. When I recovered myself a little, however, my gaze fell instinctively downward. In this direction I was able to obtain an unobstructed view, from the manner in which the smack hung on the inclined surface of the pool. She was quite upon an even keel – that is to say, her deck lay in a plane parallel with that of the water – but this latter sloped at an angle of more than forty-five degrees, so that we seemed to be lying upon our beam-ends. I could not help observing, nevertheless, that I had scarcely more difficulty in maintaining my hold and footing in this situation, than if we had been upon a dead level; and this, I suppose, was owing to the speed at which we revolved.

'The rays of the moon seemed to search the very bottom of the profound gulf; but still I could make out nothing distinctly on account of a thick mist in which every thing there was enveloped, and over which there hung a magnificent rainbow, like that narrow and tottering bridge which Mussulmen say is the only pathway between Time and Eternity. This mist, or spray, was no doubt occasioned by the clashing of the great walls of the funnel, as they all met together at the bottom – but the yell that went up to the Heavens from out of that mist I dare not attempt to describe.

'Our first slide into the abyss itself, from the belt of foam above, had carried us to a great distance down the slope; but our farther descent was by no means proportionate. Round and round we swept – not with any uniform movement – but in dizzying swings and jerks, that sent us sometimes only a few hundred yards – sometimes nearly the complete circuit of the whirl. Our progress downward, at each revolution, was slow, but very perceptible.

'Looking about me upon the wide waste of liquid ebony on which we were thus borne, I perceived that our boat was not the only object in the embrace of the whirl. Both above and below us were visible fragments of vessels, large masses of building-timber and trunks of trees, with many smaller articles, such as pieces of house furniture, broken boxes, barrels and staves. I have already described the unnatural curiosity which had taken the place of my original terrors. It appeared to grow upon me as I drew nearer and nearer to my dreadful doom. I now began to watch, with a strange interest, the numerous things that floated in our company. I *must* have been delirious, for I even sought *amusement* in speculating upon the relative velocities of their several descents toward the foam below. "This fir-tree," I found myself at one time saying, "will certainly be the next thing that takes the awful plunge and disappears," – and then I was disappointed to find that the wreck of a Dutch merchant ship overtook it and went down before. At length, after making several guesses of this nature, and being deceived in all – this fact – the fact of my invariable miscalculation, set me upon a train of reflection that made my limbs again tremble, and my heart beat heavily once more.

'It was not a new terror that thus affected me, but the dawn of a more exciting *hope*. This hope arose partly from memory, and partly from present observation. I called to mind the great variety of buoyant matter that strewed the coast of Lofoden, having been absorbed and then thrown forth by the Moskoe-ström. By far the greater number of the articles were shattered in the most extraordinary way – so chafed and roughened as to have the appearance of being stuck full of splinters – but then I distinctly recollected that there were *some* of them which were not disfigured at all. Now I could not account for this difference except by supposing that the roughened fragments were the only ones which had been *completely absorbed* – that the others had entered the whirl at so late a period of the tide, or, from some reason, had descended so slowly after entering, that they did not reach the bottom before the turn of the flood came, or of the ebb, as the case might be. I conceived it possible, in either instance, that they might thus be whirled up again to the level of the ocean, without undergoing the fate of those which had been drawn in more early or absorbed more rapidly. I made, also, three important observations. The first was, that as a general rule, the larger the bodies were, the more rapid their descent – the second, that, between two masses of equal extent, the one spherical, and the other *of any other shape*, the superiority in speed of descent was with the sphere – the third, that, between two masses of equal size, the one cylindrical, and the other of any other shape, the cylinder was absorbed the more slowly. Since my escape, I have had several conversations on this subject with an old school-master of the district; and it was from him that I learned the use of the words "cylinder" and "sphere." He explained to me – although I have forgotten the explanation – how what I observed was, in fact, the natural consequence of the forms of the floating fragments – and showed me how it happened that a cylinder, swimming in a vortex, offered more resistance to its suction, and was drawn in with greater difficulty than an equally bulky body, of any form whatever.*

'There was one startling circumstance which went a great way in enforcing these observations, and rendering me anxious to turn them to account, and this was that, at every revolution, we passed something like a barrel, or else the yard or the mast of a vessel, while many of these things, which had been on our level when I first opened my eyes upon the wonders of the whirlpool, were now high up above us, and seemed to have moved but little from their original station.

* See Archimedes, '*De Incidentibus in Fluido.*' – lib. 2.

'I no longer hesitated what to do. I resolved to lash myself securely to the water-cask upon which I now held, to cut it loose from the counter, and to throw myself with it into the water. I attracted my brother's attention by signs, pointed to the floating barrels that came near us, and did every thing in my power to make him understand what I was about to do. I thought at length that he comprehended my design – but, whether this was the case or not, he shook his head despairingly, and refused to move from his station by the ring-bolt. It was impossible to reach him; the emergency admitted of no delay; and so, with a bitter struggle, I resigned him to his fate, fastened myself to the cask by means of the lashings which secured it to the counter, and precipitated myself with it into the sea, without another moment's hesitation.

'The result was precisely what I had hoped it might be. As it is myself who now tell you this tale – as you see that I *did* escape – and as you are already in possession of the mode in which this escape was effected, and must therefore anticipate all that I have farther to say – I will bring my story quickly to conclusion. It might have been an hour, or thereabout, after my quitting the smack, when, having descended to a vast distance beneath me, it made three or four wild gyrations in rapid succession, and, bearing my loved brother with it, plunged headlong, at once and forever, into the chaos of foam below. The barrel to which I was attached sunk very little farther than half the distance between the bottom of the gulf and the spot at which I leaped overboard, before a great change took place in the character of the whirlpool. The slope of the sides of the vast funnel became momently less and less steep. The gyrations of the whirl grew, gradually, less and less violent. By degrees, the froth and the rainbow disappeared, and the bottom of the gulf seemed slowly to uprise. The sky was clear, the winds had gone down, and the full moon was setting radiantly in the west, when I found myself on the surface of the ocean, in full view of the shores of Lofoden, and above the spot where the pool of the Moskoe-ström *had been*. It was the hour of the slack – but the sea still heaved in mountainous waves from the effects of the hurricane. I was borne violently into the channel of the Ström, and in a few minutes, was hurried down the coast into the "grounds" of the fishermen. A boat picked me up – exhausted from fatigue – and (now that the danger was removed) speechless from the memory of its horror. Those who drew me on board were my old mates and daily companions – but they knew me no more than they would have known a traveller from the spirit-land. My hair, which had been raven black the day before, was as white as you see it now. They say too that the whole expression of my countenance had changed. I told them my story – they did not believe it. I now tell it to *you* – and I can scarcely expect you to put more faith in it than did the merry fishermen of Lofoden.'

ROBERT LOUIS STEVENSON

THE MERRY MEN

I

Eilean Aros

IT WAS A BEAUTIFUL morning in the late July when I set forth on foot for the last time for Aros. A boat had put me ashore the night before at Grisapol; I had such breakfast as the little inn afforded, and leaving all my baggage till I had an occasion to come round for it by sea, struck right across the promontory with a cheerful heart.

I was far from being a native of these parts, springing, as I did, from an unmixed lowland stock. But an uncle of mine, Gordon Darnaway, after a poor, rough youth, and some years at sea, had married a young wife in the islands; Mary Maclean she was called, the last of her family; and when she died in giving birth to a daughter, Aros, the sea-girt farm, had remained in his possession. It brought him in nothing but the means of life, as I was well aware; but he was a man whom ill-fortune had pursued; he feared, cumbered as he was with the young child, to make a fresh adventure upon life; and remained in Aros, biting his nails at destiny. Years passed over his head in that isolation, and brought neither help nor contentment. Meantime our family was dying out in the lowlands; there is little luck for any of that race; and perhaps my father was the luckiest of all, for not only was he one of the last to die, but he left a son to his name and a little money to support it. I was a student of Edinburgh University, living well enough at my own charges, but without kith or kin; when some news of me found its way to Uncle Gordon on the Ross of Grisapol; and he, as he was a man who held blood thicker than water, wrote to me the day he heard of my existence, and taught me to count Aros as my home. Thus it was that I came to spend my vacations in that part of the country, so far from all society and comfort, between the codfish and the moorcocks; and thus it was that now, when I had done with my classes, I was returning thither with so light a heart that July day.

The Ross, as we call it, is a promontory neither wide nor high, but as rough as God made it to this day; the deep sea on either hand of it, full of rugged isles and reefs most perilous to seamen – all overlooked from the eastward by some very high cliffs and the great peak of Ben Kyaw. *The Mountain of the Mist*, they say the words signify in the Gaelic tongue; and it is well named. For that hilltop, which is more than three thousand feet in height, catches all the clouds that come blowing from the seaward; and indeed, I used often to think that it must make them for itself; since when all heaven was clear to the sea level, there would ever be a streamer on Ben Kyaw. It brought water, too, and was mossy* to the top in consequence. I have seen us sitting in broad sunshine on the Ross, and the rain falling black like crape upon the mountain. But the wetness of it made it often appear more beautiful to my eyes; for when the sun struck upon the hillsides, there were many wet rocks and watercourses that shone like jewels even as far as Aros, fifteen miles away.

The road that I followed was a cattle track. It twisted so

* Boggy. [R.L.S.]

as nearly to double the length of my journey; it went over rough boulders so that a man had to leap from one to another, and through soft bottoms where the moss came nearly to the knee. There was no cultivation anywhere, and not one house in the ten miles from Grisapol to Aros. Houses of course there were – three at least; but they lay so far on the one side or the other that no stranger could have found them from the track. A large part of the Ross is covered with big granite rocks, some of them larger than a two-roomed house, one beside another, with fern and deep heather in between them where the vipers breed. Any way the wind was, it was always sea air, as salt as on a ship; the gulls were as free as moorfowl over all the Ross; and whenever the way rose a little, your eye would kindle with the brightness of the sea. From the very midst of the land, on a day of wind and a high spring, I have heard the Roost roaring like a battle where it runs by Aros, and the great and fearful voices of the breakers that we call the Merry Men.

Aros itself – Aros Jay, I have heard the natives call it, and they say it means *the House of God* – Aros itself was not properly a piece of the Ross, nor was it quite an islet. It formed the southwest corner of the land, fitted close to it, and was in one place only separated from the coast by a little gut of the sea, not forty feet across the narrowest. When the tide was full, this was clear and still, like a pool on a land river; only there was a difference in the weeds and fishes, and the water itself was green instead of brown; but when the tide went out, in the bottom of the ebb, there was a day or two in every month when you could pass dryshod from Aros to the mainland. There was some good pasture, where my uncle fed the sheep he lived on; perhaps the feed was better because the ground rose higher on the islet than the main level of the Ross, but this I am not skilled enough to settle. The house was a good one for that country, two storeys high. It looked westward over a bay, with a pier hard by for a boat, and from the door you could watch the vapours blowing on Ben Kyaw.

On all this part of the coast, and especially near Aros, these great granite rocks that I have spoken of go down together in troops into the sea, like cattle on a summer's day. There they stand, for all the world like their neighbours ashore; only the salt water sobbing between them instead of the quiet earth, and clots of sea pink blooming on their sides instead of heather; and the great sea conger to wreathe about the base of them instead of the poisonous viper of the land. On calm days you can go wandering between them in a boat for hours, echoes following you about the labyrinth; but when the sea is up, Heaven help the man that hears that cauldron boiling.

Off the southwest end of Aros these blocks are very many, and much greater in size. Indeed, they must grow monstrously bigger out to sea, for there must be ten sea miles of open water sown with them as thick as a country place with houses, some standing thirty feet above the tides, some covered, but all perilous to ships; so that on a clear, westerly blowing day, I have counted, from the top of Aros, the great rollers breaking white and heavy over as many as six-and-forty buried reefs. But it is nearer in shore that the danger is worst; for the tide, here running like a mill race, makes a long belt of broken water – a *Roost* we call it – at the tail of the land. I have often been out there in a dead calm at the slack of the tide; and a strange place it is, with the sea swirling and combing up and boiling like the cauldrons of a linn, and now and again a little dancing mutter of sound as though the Roost were talking to itself. But when the tide begins to run again, and above all in heavy weather, there is no man could take a boat within half a mile of it, nor a ship afloat that could either steer or live in such a place. You can hear the roaring of it six miles away. At the seaward end there comes the strongest of the bubble; and it's here that these big breakers dance together – the dance of death, it may be called – that have got the name, in these parts, of the Merry Men. I have heard it said that they run fifty feet high; but that must be the green water only, for the spray runs twice as high as that. Whether they got the name from their movements, which are swift and antic, or from the shouting they make about the turn of the tide, so that all Aros shakes with it, is more than I can tell.

The truth is, that in a southwesterly wind, that part of our archipelago is no better than a trap. If a ship got through the reefs, and weathered the Merry Men, it would be to come ashore on the south coast of Aros, in Sandag Bay, where so many dismal things befell our family, as I propose to tell. The thought of all these dangers, in the place I knew so long, makes me particularly welcome the works now going forward to set lights upon the headlands and buoys along the channels of our iron-bound, inhospitable islands.

The country people had many a story about Aros, as I used to hear from my uncle's man, Rorie, an old servant of the Macleans, who had transferred his services without afterthought on the occasion of the marriage. There was some tale of an unlucky creature, a sea-kelpie, that dwelt and did business in some fearful manner of his own among the boiling breakers of the Roost. A mermaid had once met a piper on Sandag beach, and there sang to him a long, bright midsummer's night so that in the morning he was found stricken crazy, and from thenceforward, till the day he died, said only one form of words; what they were in the original Gaelic I cannot tell, but they were thus translated:

'Ah, the sweet singing out of the sea.' Seals that haunted on that coast have been known to speak to man in his own tongue, presaging great disasters. It was here that a certain saint first landed on his voyage out of Ireland to convert the Hebrideans. And, indeed, I think he had some claim to be called saint; for, with the boats of that past age, to make so rough a passage, and land on such a ticklish coast, was surely not far short of the miraculous. It was to him, or to some of his monkish underlings who had a cell there, that the islet owes its holy and beautiful name, the House of God.

Among these old wives' stories there was one which I was inclined to hear with more credulity. As I was told, in that tempest which scattered the ships of the Invincible Armada over all the north and west of Scotland, one great vessel came ashore on Aros, and before the eyes of some solitary people on a hilltop, went down in a moment with all hands, her colours flying even as she sank. There was some likelihood in this tale; for another of that fleet lay sunk on the north side, twenty miles from Grisapol. It was told, I thought, with more detail and gravity than its companion stories, and there was one particularity which went far to convince me of its truth: the name, that is, of the ship was still remembered, and sounded, in my ears, Spanishly. The *Espirito Santo* they called it, a great ship of many decks of guns, laden with treasure and grandees of Spain, and fierce soldadoes, that now lay fathom deep to all eternity, done with her wars and voyages, in Sandag Bay, upon the west of Aros. No more salvos of ordnance for that tall ship, the 'Holy Spirit,' no more fair winds or happy ventures; only to rot there deep in the sea tangle and hear the shoutings of the Merry Men as the tide ran high about the island. It was a strange thought to me first and last, and only grew stranger as I learned the more of Spain, from which she had set sail with so proud a company, and King Philip, the wealthy king, that sent her on that voyage.

And now I must tell you, as I walked from Grisapol that day, the *Espirito Santo* was very much in my reflections. I had been favourably remarked by our then Principal in Edinburgh College, that famous writer, Dr Robertson, and by him had been set to work on some papers of an ancient date to rearrange and sift of what was worthless; and in one of these, to my great wonder, I found a note of this very ship, the *Espirito Santo*, with her captain's name, and how she carried a great part of the Spaniard's treasure, and had been lost upon the Ross of Grisapol; but in what particular spot, the wild tribes of that place and period would give no information to the king's inquiries. Putting one thing with another, and taking our island tradition together with this note of old King Jamie's perquisitions after wealth, it had come strongly on my mind that the spot for which he sought in vain could be no other than the small bay of Sandag on my uncle's land; and being a fellow of a mechanical turn, I had ever since been plotting how to weigh that good ship up again with all her ingots, ounces, and doubloons, and bring back our house of Darnaway to its long-forgotten dignity and wealth.

This was a design of which I soon had reason to repent. My mind was sharply turned on different reflections; and since I became the witness of a strange judgment of God's, the thought of dead men's treasures has been intolerable to my conscience. But even at that time I must acquit myself of sordid greed; for if I desired riches, it was not for their own sake, but for the sake of a person who was dear to my heart – my uncle's daughter, Mary Ellen. She had been educated well, and had been a time to school upon the mainland; which, poor girl, she would have been happier without. For

Aros was no place for her, with old Rorie the servant, and her father, who was one of the unhappiest men in Scotland, plainly bred up in a country place among Cameronians, long a skipper sailing out of the Clyde about the islands, and now, with infinite discontent, managing his sheep and a little 'long shore fishing for the necessary bread. If it was sometimes weariful to me, who was there but a month or two, you may fancy what it was to her who dwelt in that same desert all the year round, with the sheep and flying sea gulls, and the Merry Men singing and dancing in the Roost!

II

What the wreck had brought to Aros

It was half-flood when I got the length of Aros; and there was nothing for it but to stand on the far shore and whistle for Rorie with the boat. I had no need to repeat the signal. At the first sound, Mary was at the door flying a handkerchief by way of answer, and the old long-legged servingman was shambling down the gravel to the pier. For all his hurry, it took him a long while to pull across the bay; and I observed him several times to pause, go into the stern, and look over curiously into the wake. As he came nearer, he seemed to me aged and haggard, and I thought he avoided my eye. The coble had been repaired, with two new thwarts and several patches of some rare and beautiful foreign wood, the name of it unknown to me.

'Why, Rorie,' said I, as we began the return voyage, 'this is fine wood. How came you by that?'

'It will be hard to cheesel,' Rorie opined reluctantly; and just then, dropping the oars, he made another of those dives into the stern which I had remarked as he came across to fetch me, and, leaning his hand on my shoulder, stared with an awful look into the waters of the bay.

'What is wrong?' I asked, a good deal startled.

'It will be a great feesh,' said the old man, returning to his oars; and nothing more could I get out of him, but strange glances and an ominous nodding of the head. In spite of myself, I was infected with a measure of uneasiness; I turned also, and studied the wake. The water was still and transparent, but, out here in the middle of the bay, exceeding deep. For some time I could see naught; but at last it did seem to me as if something dark – a great fish, or perhaps only a shadow – followed studiously in the track of the moving coble. And then I remembered one of Rorie's superstitions: how in a ferry in Morven, in some great, exterminating feud among the clans, a fish, the like of it unknown in all our waters, followed for some years the passage of the ferryboat, until no man dared to make the crossing.

'He will be waiting for the right man,' said Rorie.

Mary met me on the beach, and led me up the brae and into the house of Aros. Outside and inside there were many changes. The garden was fenced with the same wood that I had noted in the boat; there were chairs in the kitchen covered with strange brocade; curtains of brocade hung from the window; a clock stood silent on the dresser; a lamp of brass was swinging from the roof; the table was set for dinner with the finest of linen and silver; and all these new riches were displayed in the plain old kitchen that I knew so well, with the high-backed settle, and the stools, and the closet bed for Rorie; with the wide chimney the sun shone into, and the clear-smouldering peats; with the pipes on the mantelshelf and the three-cornered spittoons, filled with sea-shells instead of sand, on the floor; with the bare stone walls and the bare wooden floor, and the three patchwork rugs that were of yore its sole adornment – poor man's patchwork, the like of it unknown in cities, woven with homespun, and Sunday black, and sea cloth polished on the bench of rowing. The room, like the house, had been a sort of wonder in that countryside, it was so neat and habitable; and to see it now, shamed by these incongruous additions, filled me with indignation and a kind of anger. In view of the errand I had come upon to Aros, the feeling was baseless and unjust; but it burned high, at the first moment, in my heart.

'Mary, girl,' said I, 'this is the place I had learned to call my home, and I do not know it.'

'It is my home by nature, not by the learning,' she replied; 'the place I was born and the place I'm like to die in; and I neither like these changes, nor the way they came, nor that which came with them. I would have liked better, under God's pleasure, they had gone down into the sea, and the Merry Men were dancing on them now.'

Mary was always serious; it was perhaps the only trait that she shared with her father; but the tone with which she uttered these words was even graver than of custom.

'Ay,' said I, 'I feared it came by wreck, and that's by death; yet when my father died, I took his goods without remorse.'

'Your father died a clean strae death, as the folk say,' said Mary.

'True,' I returned; 'and a wreck is like a judgment. What was she called?'

'They ca'd her the *Christ-Anna*,' said a voice behind me; and, turning round, I saw my uncle standing in the doorway.

He was a sour, small, bilious man, with a long face and very dark eyes; fifty-six years old, sound and active in body, and with an air somewhat between that of a shepherd and that of a man following the sea. He never laughed, that I heard; read long at the Bible; prayed much, like the

Cameronians he had been brought up among; and indeed, in many ways, used to remind me of one of the hill-preachers in the killing times before the Revolution. But he never got much comfort, nor even, as I used to think, much guidance, by his piety. He had his black fits when he was afraid of hell; but he had led a rough life, to which he would look back with envy, and was still a rough, cold, gloomy man.

As he came in at the door out of the sunlight, with his bonnet on his head and a pipe hanging in his buttonhole, he seemed, like Rorie, to have grown older and paler, the lines were deeplier ploughed upon his face, and the whites of his eyes were yellow, like old stained ivory, or the bones of the dead.

'Ay,' he repeated, dwelling upon the first part of the word, 'the *Christ-Anna*. It's an awfu' name.'

I made him my salutations, and complimented him upon his look of health; for I feared he had perhaps been ill.

'I'm in the body,' he replied, ungraciously enough; 'aye in the body and the sins of the body, like yoursel.' Denner,' he said abruptly to Mary, and then ran on to me: 'They're grand braws, thir that we hae gotten, are they no? Yon's a bonny knock,* but it'll no gang; and the napery's by ordnar. Bonny, bairnly braws; it's for the like o' them folk sells the peace of God that passeth understanding; it's for the like o' them, an' maybe no even sae muckle worth, folk daunton God to His face and burn in muckle hell; and it's for that reason the Scripture ca's them, as I read the passage, the accursed thing. Mary, ye girzie,' he interrupted himself to cry with some asperity, 'what for hae ye no put out the twa candlesticks?'

'Why should we need them at high noon?' she asked.

* Clock. [R.L.S.]

But my uncle was not to be turned from his idea. 'We'll bruik* them while we may,' he said; and so two massive candlesticks of wrought silver were added to the table equipage, already so unsuited to that rough seaside farm.

'She cam' ashore Februar' 10, about ten at nicht,' he went on to me. 'There was nae wind, and a sair run o' sea; and she was in the sook o' the Roost, as I jaloose. We had seen her a' day, Rorie and me, beating to the wind. She wasnae a handy craft, I'm thinking, that *Christ-Anna*; for she would neither steer nor stey wi' them. A sair day they had of it; their hands was never aff the sheets, and it perishin' cauld – ower cauld to snaw; and aye they would get a bit nip o' wind, and awa' again, to put the emp'y hope into them. Eh, man! but they had a sair day for the last o't! He would have had a prood, prood heart that won ashore upon the back o' that.'

'And were all lost?' I cried. 'God help them!'

'Wheesht!' he said sternly. 'Nane shall pray for the deid on my hearth-stane.'

I disclaimed a Popish sense for my ejaculation; and he seemed to accept my disclaimer with unusual facility, and ran on once more upon what had evidently become a favourite subject.

'We fand her in Sandag Bay, Rorie an' me, and a' thae braws in the inside of her. There's a kittle bit, ye see, about Sandag; whiles the sook rins strong for the Merry Men; an' whiles again, when the tide's makin' hard an' ye can hear the Roost blawin' at the far-end of Aros, there comes a backspang of current straucht into Sandag Bay. Weel, there's the thing that got the grip on the *Christ-Anna*. She but to have come in ram-stam an' stern forrit; for the bows of her are

* Enjoy. [R.L.S.]

aften under, and the back-side of her is clear at hie-water o' neaps. But, man! the dunt that she cam doon wi' when she struck! Lord save us a'! but it's an unco life to be a sailor – a cauld, wanchancy life. Mony's the gliff I got mysel' in the great deep; and why the Lord should hae made yon unco water is mair than ever I could win to understand. He made the vales and the pastures, the bonny green yaird, the halesome, canty land –

> And now they shout and sing to Thee,
> For Thou hast made them glad,

as the Psalms say in the metrical version. No that I would preen my faith to that clink neither; but it's bonny, and easier to mind. "Who go to sea in ships," they hae't again –

> And in
> Great waters trading be,
> Within the deep these men God's works
> And His great wonders see.

Weel, it's easy sayin' sae. Maybe Dauvit wasnae very weel acquant wi' the sea. But, troth, if it wasnae prentit in the Bible, I wad whiles be temp'it to think it wasnae the Lord, but the muckle, black deil that made the sea. There's naething good comes oot o't but the fish; an' the spentacle o' God riding on the tempest, to be shüre, whilk would be what Dauvit was likely ettling at. But, man, they were sair wonders that God showed to the *Christ-Anna* – wonders, do I ca' them? Judgments, rather: judgments in the mirk nicht among the draygons o' the deep. And their souls – to think o' that – their souls, man, maybe no prepared! The sea – a muckle yett to hell!'

I observed, as my uncle spoke, that his voice was unnaturally moved and his manner unwontedly demonstrative. He leaned forward at these last words, for example, and touched me on the knee with his spread fingers, looking up into my face with a certain pallor, and I could see that his eyes shone with a deep-seated fire, and that the lines about his mouth were drawn and tremulous.

Even the entrance of Rorie, and the beginning of our meal, did not detach him from his train of thought beyond a moment. He condescended, indeed, to ask me some questions as to my success at college, but I thought it was with half his mind; and even in his extempore grace, which was, as usual, long and wandering, I could find the trace of his preoccupation, praying, as he did, that God would 'remember in mercy fower puir, feckless, fiddling, sinful creatures here by their lee-lane beside the great and dowie waters.'

Soon there came an interchange of speeches between him and Rorie.

'Was it there?' asked my uncle.

'Ou, ay!' said Rorie.

I observed that they both spoke in a manner of aside, and with some show of embarrassment, and that Mary herself appeared to colour, and looked down on her plate. Partly to show my knowledge, and so relieve the party from an awkward strain, partly because I was curious, I pursued the subject.

'You mean the fish?' I asked.

'Whatten fish?' cried my uncle. 'Fish, quo' he! Fish! Your een are fu' o' fatness, man; your heid dozened wi' carnal leir. Fish! it's a bogle!'

He spoke with great vehemence, as though angry; and perhaps I was not very willing to be put down so shortly, for young men are disputatious. At least I remember I retorted hotly, crying out upon childish superstitions.

'And ye come frae the College!' sneered Uncle Gordon.

'Gude kens what they learn folk there; it's no muckle service onyway. Do ye think, man, that there's naething in a' yon saut wilderness o' a world oot wast there, wi' the sea grasses growin', an' the sea beasts fechtin', an' the sun glintin' down into it, day by day? Na; the sea's like the land, but fearsomer. If there's folk ashore, there's folk in the sea – deid they may be, but they're folk whatever; and as for deils, there's nane that's like the sea deils. There's no sae muckle harm in the land deils, when a's said and done. Lang syne, when I was a callant in the south country, I mind there was an auld, bald bogle in the Peewie Moss. I got a glisk o' him mysel', sittin' on his hunkers in a hag, as gray's a tombstane. An', troth, he was a fearsome-like taed. But he steered naebody. Nae doobt, if ane that was a reprobate, ane the Lord hated, had gane by there wi' his sin still upon his stamach, nae doobt the creature would hae lowped upo' the likes o' him. But there's deils in the deep sea would yoke on a communicant! Eh, sirs, if ye had gane doon wi' the puir lads in the *Christ-Anna*, ye would ken by now the mercy o' the seas. If ye had sailed it for as lang as me, ye would hate the thocht of it as I do. If ye had but used the een God gave ye, ye would hae learned the wickedness o' that fause, saut, cauld, bullering creature, and of a' that's in it by the Lord's permission: labsters an' partans, an' sic like, howking in the deid; muckle, gutsy, blawing whales; an' fish – the hale clan o' them – cauld-wamed, blind-eed uncanny ferlies. O, sirs,' he cried, 'the horror – the horror o' the sea!'

We were all somewhat staggered by this outburst; and the speaker himself, after that last hoarse apostrophe, appeared to sink gloomily into his own thoughts. But Rorie, who was greedy of superstitious lore, recalled him to the subject by a question.

'You will not ever have seen a teevil of the sea?' he asked.

'No clearly,' replied the other. 'I misdoobt if a mere man could see ane clearly and conteenue in the body. I hae sailed wi' a lad – they ca'd him Sandy Gabart; he saw ane, shüre eneuch, an' shüre eneuch it was the end of him. We were seeven days oot frae the Clyde – a sair wark we had had – gaun north wi' seeds an' braws an' things for the Macleod. We had got in ower near under the Cutchull'ns, an' had just gane about by Soa, an' were off on a lang tack, we thocht would maybe hauld as far's Copnahow. I mind the nicht weel; a mune smoored wi' mist; a fine gaun breeze upon the water, but no steedy; an' – what nane o' us likit to hear – anither wund gurlin' owerheid, amang thae fearsome, auld stane craigs o' the Cutchull'ns. Weel, Sandy was forrit wi' the jib sheet; we couldnae see him for the mains'l, that had just begude to draw, when a' at ance he gied a skirl. I luffed for my life, for I thocht we were ower near Soa; but na, it wasnae that, it was puir Sandy Gabart's deid skreigh, or near hand, for he was deid in half an hour. A't he could tell was that a sea deil, or sea bogle, or sea spenster, or sic-like, had clum up by the bowsprit, an' gi'en him ae cauld, uncanny look. An', or the life was oot o' Sandy's body, we kent weel what the thing betokened, and why the wund gurled in the taps o' the Cutchull'ns; for doon it cam' – a wund do I ca' it! it was the wund o' the Lord's anger – an' a' that nicht we foucht like men dementit, and the niest that we kenned we were ashore in Loch Uskevagh, an' the cocks were crawin' in Benbecula.'

'It will have been a merman,' Rorie said.

'A merman!' screamed my uncle with immeasurable scorn. 'Auld wives' clavers! There's nae sic things as mermen.'

'But what was the creature like?' I asked.

'What like was it? Gude forbid that we suld ken what like it was! It had a kind of a heid upon it – man could say nae mair.'

Then Rorie, smarting under the affront, told several tales of mermen, mermaids, and sea-horses that had come ashore upon the islands and attacked the crews of boats upon the sea; and my uncle, in spite of his incredulity, listened with uneasy interest.

'Aweel, aweel,' he said, 'it may be sae; I may be wrang; but I find nae word o' mermen in the Scriptures.'

'And you will find nae word of Aros Roost, maybe,' objected Rorie, and his argument appeared to carry weight.

When dinner was over, my uncle carried me forth with him to a bank behind the house. It was a very hot and quiet afternoon; scarce a ripple anywhere upon the sea, nor any voice but the familiar voice of sheep and gulls; and perhaps in consequence of this repose in nature, my kinsman showed himself more rational and tranquil than before. He spoke evenly and almost cheerfully of my career, with every now and then a reference to the lost ship or the treasures it had brought to Aros. For my part, I listened to him in a sort of trance, gazing with all my heart on that remembered scene, and drinking gladly the sea air and the smoke of peats that had been lit by Mary.

Perhaps an hour had passed when my uncle, who had all the while been covertly gazing on the surface of the little bay, rose to his feet and bade me follow his example. Now I should say that the great run of tide at the southwest end of Aros exercises a perturbing influence round all the coast. In Sandag Bay, to the south, a strong current runs at certain periods of the flood and ebb respectively; but in this northern bay – Aros Bay, as it is called – where the house stands and on which my uncle was now gazing, the only sign of disturbance is towards the end of the ebb, and even then it is too slight to be remarkable. When there is any swell, nothing can be seen at all; but when it is calm, as it often is, there appear certain strange, undecipherable marks – sea-runes, as we may name them – on the glassy surface of the bay. The like is common in a thousand places on the coast; and many a boy must have amused himself as I did, seeking to read in them some reference to himself or those he loved. It was to these marks that my uncle now directed my attention, struggling, as he did so, with an evident reluctance.

'Do ye see yon scart upo' the water?' he inquired; 'yon ane wast the gray stane? Ay? Weel, it'll no be like a letter, wull it?'

'Certainly it is,' I replied. 'I have often remarked it. It is like a C.'

He heaved a sigh as if heavily disappointed with my answer, and then added below his breath: 'Ay, for the *Christ-Anna*.'

'I used to suppose, sir, it was for myself,' said I; 'for my name is Charles.'

'And so ye saw't afore?' he ran on, not heeding my remark. 'Weel, weel, but that's unco strange. Maybe, it's been there waitin', as a man wad say, through a' the weary ages. Man, but that's awfu'.' And then, breaking off: 'Ye'll no see anither, will ye?' he asked.

'Yes,' said I. 'I see another very plainly, near the Ross side, where the road comes down – an M.'

'An M,' he repeated very low; and then, again after another pause: 'An' what wad ye make o' that?' he inquired.

'I had always thought it to mean Mary, sir,' I answered, growing somewhat red, convinced as I was in my own mind that I was on the threshold of a decisive explanation.

But we were each following his own train of thought to the exclusion of the other's. My uncle once more paid no attention to my words; only hung his head and held his peace; and I might have been led to fancy that he had not heard me, if his next speech had not contained a kind of echo from my own.

'I would say naething o' thae clavers to Mary,' he observed, and began to walk forward.

There is a belt of turf along the side of Aros Bay where walking is easy; and it was along this that I silently followed my silent kinsman. I was perhaps a little disappointed at having lost so good an opportunity to declare my love; but I was at the same time far more deeply exercised at the change that had befallen my uncle. He was never an ordinary, never, in the strict sense, an amiable, man; but there was nothing in even the worst that I had known of him before, to prepare me for so strange a transformation. It was impossible to close the eyes against one fact; that he had, as the saying goes, something on his mind; and as I mentally ran over the different words which might be represented by the letter M – misery, mercy, marriage, money, and the like – I was arrested with a sort of start by the word murder. I was still considering the ugly sound and fatal meaning of the word, when the direction of our walk brought us to a point from which a view was to be had to either side, back towards Aros Bay and homestead, and forward on the ocean, dotted to the north with isles, and lying to the southward blue and open to the sky. There my guide came to a halt, and stood staring for awhile on that expanse. Then he turned to me and laid a hand on my arm.

'Ye think there's naething there?' he said, pointing with his pipe; and then cried out aloud, with a kind of exultation: 'I'll tell ye, man! The deid are down there – thick like rattons!'

He turned at once, and, without another word, we retraced our steps to the house of Aros.

I was eager to be alone with Mary; yet it was not till after supper, and then but for a short while, that I could have a word with her. I lost no time beating about the bush, but spoke out plainly what was on my mind.

'Mary,' I said, 'I have not come to Aros without a hope. If that should prove well founded, we may all leave and go somewhere else, secure of daily bread and comfort; secure, perhaps, of something far beyond that, which it would seem extravagant in me to promise. But there's a hope that lies nearer to my heart than money.' And at that I paused. 'You can guess fine what that is, Mary,' I said. She looked away from me in silence, and that was small encouragement, but I was not to be put off. 'All my days I have thought the world of you,' I continued; 'the time goes on and I think always the more of you; I could not think to be happy or hearty in my life without you: you are the apple of my eye.' Still she looked away, and said never a word; but I thought I saw that her hands shook. 'Mary,' I cried in fear, 'do ye no like me?'

'O, Charlie man,' she said, 'is this a time to speak of it? Let me be, a while; let me be the way I am; it'll not be you that loses by the waiting!'

I made out by her voice that she was nearly weeping, and this put me out of any thought but to compose her. 'Mary Ellen,' I said, 'say no more; I did not come to trouble you: your way shall be mine, and your time too; and you have told me all I wanted. Only just this one thing more: what ails you?'

She owned it was her father, but would enter into no particulars, only shook her head, and said he was not well and not like himself, and it was a great pity. She knew nothing of the wreck. 'I havenae been near it,' said she. 'What for would I go near it, Charlie lad? The poor souls are gone to their account long syne; and I would just have wished they had ta'en their gear with them – poor souls!'

This was scarcely any great encouragement for me to tell her of the *Espirito Santo*; yet I did so, and at the very first word she cried out in surprise. 'There was a man at Grisapol,' she said, 'in the month of May – a little, yellow, black-avised body, they tell me, with gold rings upon his fingers, and a beard; and he was speiring high and low for that same ship.'

It was towards the end of April that I had been given these papers to sort out by Dr Robertson: and it came suddenly back upon my mind that they were thus prepared for a Spanish historian, or a man calling himself such, who had come with high recommendations to the Principal, on a mission of inquiry as to the dispersion of the great Armada. Putting one thing with another, I fancied that the visitor 'with the gold rings upon his fingers' might be the same with Dr Robertson's historian from Madrid. If that were so, he would be more likely after treasure for himself than information for a learned society. I made up my mind, I should lose no time over my undertaking; and if the ship lay sunk in Sandag Bay, as perhaps both he and I supposed, it should not be for the advantage of this ringed adventurer, but for Mary and myself, and for the good, old, honest, kindly family of the Darnaways.

III

Land and sea in Sandag Bay

I was early afoot next morning; and as soon as I had a bite to eat, set forth upon a tour of exploration. Something in my heart distinctly told me that I should find the ship of the Armada; and although I did not give way entirely to such hopeful thoughts, I was still very light in spirits and walked upon air. Aros is a very rough islet, its surface strewn with great rocks and shaggy with fern and heather; and my way lay almost north and south across the highest knoll; and though the whole distance was inside of two miles, it took more time and exertion than four upon a level road. Upon the summit, I paused. Although not very high – not three hundred feet, as I think – it yet out-tops all the neighbouring lowlands of the Ross, and commands a great view of sea and islands. The sun, which had been up some time, was already hot upon my neck; the air was listless and thundery, although purely clear; away over the northwest, where the isles lie thickliest congregated, some half-a-dozen small and ragged clouds hung together in a covey; and the head of Ben Kyaw wore, not merely a few streamers, but a solid hood of vapour. There was a threat in the weather. The sea, it is true, was smooth like glass: even the Roost was but a seam on that wide mirror, and the Merry Men no more than caps of foam; but to my eye and ear, so long familiar with these places, the sea also seemed to lie uneasily; a sound of it, like a long sigh, mounted to me where I stood; and, quiet as it was, the Roost itself appeared to be revolving mischief. For I ought to say that all we dwellers in these parts attributed, if not prescience, at least a quality of warning, to that strange and dangerous creature of the tides.

I hurried on, then, with the greater speed, and had soon descended the slope of Aros to the part that we call Sandag Bay. It is a pretty large piece of water compared with the size of the isle; well sheltered from all but the prevailing wind; sandy and shoal and bounded by low sandhills to the west, but to the eastward lying several fathoms deep along a ledge of rocks. It is upon that side that, at a certain time each flood, the current mentioned by my uncle sets so strong into the bay; a little later, when the Roost begins to work higher, an undertow runs still more strongly in the reverse direction; and it is the action of this last, as I suppose, that has scoured that part so deep. Nothing is to be seen out of Sandag Bay but one small segment of the horizon and, in heavy weather, the breakers flying high over a deep sea reef.

From halfway down the hill, I had perceived the wreck of February last, a brig of considerable tonnage, lying, with her back broken, high and dry on the east corner of the sands; and I was making directly towards it, and already almost on the margin of the turf, when my eyes were suddenly arrested by a spot, cleared of fern and heather, and marked by one of those long, low, and almost human-looking mounds that we see so commonly in graveyards. I stopped like a man shot. Nothing had been said to me of any dead man or interment on the island; Rorie, Mary, and my uncle had all equally held their peace; of her at least, I was certain that she must be ignorant; and yet here, before my eyes, was proof indubitable of the fact. Here was a grave; and I had to ask myself, with a chill, what manner of man lay there in his last sleep, awaiting the signal of the Lord in that solitary, sea-beat resting-place? My mind supplied no answer but what I feared to entertain. Shipwrecked, at least, he must have been; perhaps, like the old Armada mariners, from some far and rich land oversea; or perhaps one of my own race, perishing within eyesight of the smoke of home. I stood awhile uncovered by his side, and I could have desired that it had lain in our religion to put up some prayer for that unhappy stranger, or, in the old classic way, outwardly to honour his misfortune. I knew, although his bones lay there, a part of Aros, till the trumpet sounded, his imperishable soul was forth and far away, among the raptures of the everlasting Sabbath or the pangs of hell; and yet my mind misgave me even with a fear, that perhaps he was near me where I stood, guarding his sepulchre, and lingering on the scene of his unhappy fate.

Certainly it was with a spirit somewhat overshadowed that

I turned away from the grave to the hardly less melancholy spectacle of the wreck. Her stem was above the first arc of the flood; she was broken in two a little abaft the foremast – though indeed she had none, both masts having broken short in her disaster; and as the pitch of the beach was very sharp and sudden, and the bows lay many feet below the stern, the fracture gaped widely open, and you could see right through her poor hull upon the farther side. Her name was much defaced, and I could not make out clearly whether she was called *Christiania*, after the Norwegian city, or *Christiana*, after the good woman, Christian's wife, in that old book the *Pilgrim's Progress.* By her build she was a foreign ship, but I was not certain of her nationality. She had been painted green, but the colour was faded and weathered, and the paint peeling off in strips. The wreck of the mainmast lay alongside, half-buried in sand. She was a forlorn sight, indeed, and I could not look without emotion at the bits of rope that still hung about her, so often handled of yore by shouting seamen; or the little scuttle where they had passed up and down to their affairs; or that poor noseless angel of a figurehead that had dipped into so many running billows.

I do not know whether it came most from the ship or from the grave, but I fell into some melancholy scruples, as I stood there, leaning with one hand against the battered timbers. The homelessness of men and even of inanimate vessels, cast away upon strange shores, came strongly in upon my mind. To make a profit of such pitiful misadventures seemed an unmanly and a sordid act; and I began to think of my then quest as of something sacrilegious in its nature. But when I remembered Mary, I took heart again. My uncle would never consent to an imprudent marriage, nor would she, as I was persuaded, wed without his full approval. It behoved me, then, to be up and doing for my wife; and I thought with a laugh how long it was since that great sea-castle, the *Espirito Santo*, had left her bones in Sandag Bay, and how weak it would be to consider rights so long extinguished and misfortunes so long forgotten in the process of time.

I had my theory of where to seek for her remains. The set of the current and the soundings both pointed to the east side of the bay under the ledge of rocks. If she had been lost in Sandag Bay, and if, after these centuries, any portion of her held together, it was there that I should find it. The water deepens, as I have said, with great rapidity, and even close alongside the rocks several fathoms may be found. As I walked upon the edge I could see far and wide over the sandy bottom of the bay; the sun shone clear and green and steady in the deeps; the bay seemed rather like a great transparent crystal, as one sees them in a lapidary's shop; there was naught to show that it was water but an internal trembling, a hovering within of sun-glints and netted shadows, and now and then a faint lap and a dying bubble round the edge. The shadows of the rocks lay out for some distance at their feet, so that my own shadow, moving, pausing, and stooping on the top of that, reached sometimes half across the bay. It was above all in this belt of shadows that I hunted for the *Espirito Santo*; since it was there the undertow ran strongest, whether in or out. Cool as the whole water seemed this broiling day, it looked, in that part, yet cooler, and had a mysterious invitation for the eyes. Peer as I pleased, however, I could see nothing but a few fishes or a bush of sea tangle, and here and there a lump of rock that had fallen from above and now lay separate on the sandy floor. Twice did I pass from one end to the other of the rocks, and in the whole distance I could see nothing of the wreck, nor any place but one where it was possible for it to be. This was a large terrace in five fathoms of water; raised off the surface of the sand to a considerable height, and looking from above like a mere outgrowth of the rocks on which I walked. It was one mass of great sea tangles like a grove, which prevented me judging of its nature, but in shape and size it bore some likeness to a vessel's hull. At least it was my best chance. If the *Espirito Santo* lay not there under the tangles, it lay nowhere at all in Sandag Bay; and I prepared to put the question to the proof, once and for all, and either go back to Aros a rich man or cured for ever of my dreams of wealth.

I stripped to the skin, and stood on the extreme margin with my hands clasped, irresolute. The bay at that time was utterly quiet; there was no sound but from a school of porpoises somewhere out of sight behind the point; yet a certain fear withheld me on the threshold of my venture. Sad sea-feelings, scraps of my uncle's superstitions, thoughts of the dead, of the grave, of the old broken ships, drifted through my mind. But the strong sun upon my shoulders warmed me to the heart, and I stooped forward and plunged into the sea.

It was all that I could do to catch a trail of the sea-tangle that grew so thickly on the terrace; but once so far anchored I secured myself by grasping a whole armful of these thick and slimy stalks, and, planting my feet against the edge, I looked around me. On all sides the clear sand stretched forth unbroken; it came to the foot of the rocks, scoured into the likeness of an alley in a garden by the action of the tides; and before me, for as far as I could see, nothing was visible but the same many-folded sand upon the sun-bright bottom of the bay. Yet the terrace to which I was then holding was as thick with strong sea-growths as a tuft of heather, and the cliff from which it bulged hung draped below the waterline with brown lianas. In this complexity of forms, all swaying together in the current, things were hard to be distinguished; and I was still uncertain whether my feet were pressed upon the natural rock or upon the timbers of the Armada treasure ship, when the whole tuft of tangle came away in my hand, and in an instant I was on the surface, and the shores of the bay and the bright water swam before my eyes in a glory of crimson.

I clambered back upon the rocks, and threw the plant of tangle at my feet. Something at the same moment rang sharply, like a falling coin. I stooped, and there, sure enough, crusted with the red rust, there lay an iron shoe-buckle. The sight of this poor human relic thrilled me to the heart, but not with hope nor fear, only with a desolate melancholy. I held it in my hand, and the thought of its owner appeared before me like the presence of an actual man. His weather-beaten face, his sailor's hands, his sea-voice hoarse with singing at the capstan, the very foot that had once worn that buckle and trod so much along the swerving decks – the whole human fact of him, as a creature like myself, with hair and blood and seeing eyes, haunted me in that sunny, solitary place, not like a spectre, but like some friend whom I had basely injured. Was the great treasure ship indeed below there, with her guns and chain and treasure, as she had sailed from Spain; her decks a garden for the seaweed, her cabin a breeding place for fish, soundless but for the dredging water, motionless but for the waving of the tangle upon her battlements – that old, populous, sea-riding castle, now a reef in Sandag Bay? Or, as I thought it likelier, was this a waif from the disaster of the foreign brig – was this shoe-buckle bought but the other day and worn by a man of my own period in the world's history, hearing the same news from day to day, thinking the same thoughts, praying, perhaps, in the same temple with myself? However it was, I was assailed with dreary thoughts; my uncle's words, 'the dead are down there,' echoed in my ears; and though I determined to dive once more, it was with a strong repugnance that I stepped forward to the margins of the rocks.

A great change passed at that moment over the appearance of the bay. It was no more that clear, visible interior, like a house roofed with glass, where the green, submarine sunshine slept so stilly. A breeze, I suppose, had flawed the surface, and a sort of trouble and blackness filled its bosom, where flashes of light and clouds of shadow tossed confusedly together. Even the terrace below obscurely rocked and quivered. It seemed a graver thing to venture on this place of ambushes; and when I leaped into the sea the second time it was with a quaking in my soul.

I secured myself as at first, and groped among the waving tangle. All that met my touch was cold and soft and gluey. The thicket was alive with crabs and lobsters, trundling to and fro lopsidedly, and I had to harden my heart against the horror of their carrion neighbourhood. On all sides I could feel the grain and the clefts of hard, living stone; no planks, no iron, not a sign of any wreck; the *Espirito Santo* was not there. I remember I had almost a sense of relief in my disappointment, and I was about ready to leave go, when something happened that sent me to the surface with my heart in my mouth. I had already stayed somewhat late over my explorations; the current was freshening with the change of the tide, and Sandag Bay was no longer a safe place for a single swimmer. Well, just at the last moment there came a sudden flush of current, dredging through the tangles like a wave. I lost one hold, was flung sprawling on my side, and, instinctively grasping for a fresh support, my fingers closed on something hard and cold. I think I knew at that moment what it was. At least I instantly left hold of the tangle, leaped for the surface, and clambered out next moment on the friendly rocks with the bone of a man's leg in my grasp.

Mankind is a material creature, slow to think and dull to perceive connections. The grave, the wreck of the brig, and the rusty shoe-buckle were surely plain advertisements. A child might have read their dismal story, and yet it was not until I touched that actual piece of mankind that the full horror of the charnel ocean burst upon my spirit. I laid the bone beside the buckle, picked up my clothes, and ran as I was along the rocks towards the human shore. I could not be far enough from the spot; no fortune was vast enough to tempt me back again. The bones of the drowned dead should henceforth roll undisturbed by me, whether on tangle or minted gold. But as soon as I trod the good earth again, and had covered my nakedness against the sun, I knelt down over against the ruins of the brig, and out of the fulness of my heart prayed long and passionately for all poor souls upon the sea. A generous prayer is never presented in vain; the petition may be refused, but the petitioner is always, I believe, rewarded by some gracious visitation. The horror, at least, was lifted from my mind; I could look with calm of spirit on that great bright creature, God's ocean; and as I set off homeward up the rough sides of Aros, nothing remained of my concern beyond a deep determination to meddle no more with the spoils of wrecked vessels or the treasures of the dead.

I was already some way up the hill before I paused to breathe and look behind me. The sight that met my eyes was doubly strange.

For, first, the storm that I had foreseen was now advancing with almost tropical rapidity. The whole surface of the sea had been dulled from its conspicuous brightness to an ugly hue of corrugated lead; already in the distance the white waves, the 'skipper's daughters,' had begun to flee before a breeze that was still insensible on Aros; and already along the curve of Sandag Bay there was a splashing run of sea that I could hear from where I stood. The change upon the sky was even more remarkable. There had begun to arise out of the southwest a huge and solid continent of scowling cloud; here and there, through rents in its contexture, the sun still poured a sheaf of spreading rays; and here and there, from all its edges, vast inky streamers lay forth along the yet unclouded sky. The menace was express and imminent. Even as I gazed, the sun was blotted out. At any moment the tempest might fall upon Aros in its might.

The suddenness of this change of weather so fixed my eyes on heaven that it was some seconds before they alighted on the bay, mapped out below my feet, and robbed a moment later of the sun. The knoll which I had just surmounted overflanked a little amphitheatre of lower hillocks sloping towards the sea, and beyond that the yellow arc of beach and the whole extent of Sandag Bay. It was a scene on which I had often looked down, but where I had never before beheld a human figure. I had but just turned my back upon it and left it empty, and my wonder may be fancied when I saw a boat and several men in that deserted spot. The boat was lying by the rocks. A pair of fellows, bare-headed, with their sleeves rolled up, and one with a boathook, kept her with difficulty to her moorings, for the current was growing brisker every moment. A little way off upon the ledge two men in black clothes, whom I judged to be superior in rank, laid their heads together over some task which at first I did not understand, but a second after I had made it out – they were taking bearings with the compass; and just then I saw one of them unroll a sheet of paper and lay his finger down, as though identifying features in a map. Meanwhile a third was walking to and fro, poking among the rocks and peering over the edge into the water. While I was still watching them with the stupefaction of surprise, my mind hardly yet able to work on what my eyes reported, this third person suddenly stooped and summoned his companions with a cry so loud that it reached my ears upon the hill. The others ran to him, even dropping the compass in their hurry, and I could see the bone and the shoe-buckle going from hand to hand, causing the most unusual gesticulations of surprise and interest. Just then I could hear the seamen crying from the boat, and saw them point westward to that cloud continent which was ever the more rapidly unfurling its blackness over heaven. The others seemed to consult; but the danger was too pressing to be braved, and they bundled into the boat carrying my relics with them, and set forth out of the bay with all speed of oars.

I made no more ado about the matter, but turned and ran for the house. Whoever these men were, it was fit my uncle should be instantly informed. It was not then altogether too late in the day for a descent of the Jacobites; and maybe Prince Charlie, whom I knew my uncle to detest, was one of the three superiors whom I had seen upon the rock. Yet as I ran, leaping from rock to rock, and turned the matter loosely in my mind, this theory grew ever the longer the less welcome to my reason. The compass, the map, the interest awakened by the buckle, and the conduct of that one among the strangers who had looked so often below him in the water, all seemed to point to a different explanation of their presence on that outlying, obscure islet of the western sea. The Madrid historian, the search instituted by Dr Robertson, the bearded stranger with the rings, my own fruitless search that very morning in the deep water of Sandag Bay, ran together, piece by piece, in my memory, and I made sure that these strangers must be Spaniards in quest of ancient treasure and the lost ship of the Armada. But the people living in outlying islands, such as Aros, are answerable for their own security; there is none nearby to protect or even to help them; and the presence in such a spot of a crew of foreign adventurers – poor, greedy, and most likely lawless – filled me with apprehensions for my uncle's money, and even for the safety of his daughter. I was still wondering how we were to get rid of them when I came, all breathless, to the top of Aros. The whole world was shadowed over; only in the extreme east, on a hill of the mainland, one last gleam of sunshine lingered like a jewel; rain had begun to fall, not heavily, but in great drops; the sea was rising with each moment, and already a band of white encircled Aros and the nearer coasts of Grisapol. The boat was still pulling seaward, but I now became aware of what had been hidden from me lower down – a large, heavily sparred, handsome schooner, lying to at the south end of Aros. Since I had not seen her in the morning when I had looked around so closely at the signs of the weather, and upon these lone waters where a sail was rarely visible, it was clear she must have lain last night behind the uninhabited Eilean Gour, and this proved conclusively that she was manned by strangers to our coast, for that anchorage, though good enough to look at, is little better than a trap for ships. With such ignorant sailors upon so wild a coast, the coming gale was not unlikely to bring death upon its wings.

IV

The gale

I found my uncle at the gable end, watching the signs of the weather, with a pipe in his fingers.

'Uncle,' said I, 'there were men ashore at Sandag Bay—'

I had no time to go further; indeed, I not only forgot my words, but even my weariness, so strange was the effect on Uncle Gordon. He dropped his pipe and fell back against the end of the house with his jaw fallen, his eyes staring, and his long face as white as paper. We must have looked at one another silently for a quarter of a minute, before he made answer in this extraordinary fashion: 'Had he a hair kep on?'

I knew as well as if I had been there that the man who now lay buried at Sandag had worn a hairy cap, and that he had come ashore alive. For the first and only time I lost toleration for the man who was my benefactor and the father of the woman I hoped to call my wife.

'These were living men,' said I, 'perhaps Jacobites, perhaps the French, perhaps pirates, perhaps adventurers come here to seek the Spanish treasure ship; but, whatever they may be, dangerous at least to your daughter and my cousin. As for your own guilty terrors, man, the dead sleeps well where you have laid him. I stood this morning by his grave; he will not wake before the trump of doom.'

My kinsman looked upon me, blinking, while I spoke; then he fixed his eyes for a little on the ground, and pulled his fingers foolishly; but it was plain that he was past the power of speech.

'Come,' said I. 'You must think for others. You must come up the hill with me, and see this ship.'

He obeyed without a word or a look, following slowly after my impatient strides. The spring seemed to have gone out of his body, and he scrambled heavily up and down the rocks, instead of leaping, as he was wont, from one to another. Nor could I, for all my cries, induce him to make better haste. Only once he replied to me complainingly, and like one in bodily pain: 'Ay, ay, man, I'm coming.' Long before we had reached the top, I had no other thought for him but pity. If the crime had been monstrous, the punishment was in proportion.

At last we emerged above the skyline of the hill, and could see around us. All was black and stormy to the eye; the last gleam of sun had vanished; a wind had sprung up, not yet high, but gusty and unsteady to the point; the rain, on the other hand, had ceased. Short as was the interval, the sea already ran vastly higher than when I had stood there last; already it had begun to break over some of the outward reefs, and already it moaned aloud in the sea-caves of Aros. I looked, at first, in vain for the schooner.

'There she is,' I said at last. But her new position, and the course she was now lying, puzzled me. 'They cannot mean to beat to sea,' I cried.

'That's what they mean,' said my uncle, with something like joy; and just then the schooner went about and stood upon another tack, which put the question beyond the reach of doubt. These strangers, seeing a gale on hand, had thought first of sea room. With the wind that threatened, in these reef-sown waters and contending against so violent a stream of tide, their course was certain death.

'Good God!' said I, 'they are all lost.'

'Ay,' returned my uncle, 'a' – a' lost. They hadnae a chance but to rin for Kyle Dona. The gate they're gaun the noo, they couldnae win through an the muckle deil were there to pilot them. Eh, man,' he continued, touching me on the sleeve, 'it's a braw nicht for a shipwreck! Twa in ae twalmonth! Eh, but the Merry Men'll dance bonny!'

I looked at him, and it was then that I began to fancy him no longer in his right mind. He was peering up to me, as if for sympathy, a timid joy in his eyes. All that had passed between us was already forgotten in the prospect of this fresh disaster.

'If it were not too late,' I cried with indignation, 'I would take the coble and go out to warn them.'

'Na, na,' he protested, 'ye maunnae interfere; ye maunnae meddle wi' the like o' that. It's His' – doffing his bonnet – 'His wull. And, eh, man! but it's a braw nicht for't!'

Something like fear began to creep into my soul; and, reminding him that I had not yet dined, I proposed we should return to the house. But no; nothing would tear him from his place of outlook.

'I maun see the hail thing, man, Cherlie,' he explained; and then as the schooner went about a second time, 'Eh, but they han'le her bonny!' he cried. 'The *Christ-Anna* was naething to this.'

Already the men on board the schooner must have begun to realize some part, but not yet the twentieth, of the dangers that environed their doomed ship. At every lull of the capricious wind they must have seen how fast the current swept them back. Each tack was made shorter, as they saw how little it prevailed. Every moment the rising swell began to boom and foam upon another sunken reef; and ever and again a breaker would fall in sounding ruin under the very bows of her, and the brown reef and streaming tangle appear in the hollow of the wave. I tell you, they had to stand to their tackle: there was no idle man aboard that ship, God knows. It was upon the progress of a scene so horrible to any human-hearted man that my misguided uncle now pored and gloated like a connoisseur. As I turned to go down the hill, he was lying on his belly on the summit, with his hands stretched forth and clutching in the heather. He seemed rejuvenated, mind and body.

When I got back to the house already dismally affected,

I was still more sadly downcast at the sight of Mary. She had her sleeves rolled up over her strong arms, and was quietly making bread. I got a bannock from the dresser and sat down to eat it in silence.

'Are ye wearied, lad?' she asked after a while.

'I am not so much wearied, Mary,' I replied, getting on my feet, 'as I am weary of delay, and perhaps of Aros too. You know me well enough to judge me fairly, say what I like. Well, Mary, you may be sure of this: you had better be anywhere but here.'

'I'll be sure of one thing,' she returned: 'I'll be where my duty is.'

'You forget, you have a duty to yourself,' I said.

'Ay, man?' she replied, pounding at the dough; 'will you have found that in the Bible, now?'

'Mary,' I said solemnly, 'you must not laugh at me just now. God knows I am in no heart for laughing. If we could get your father with us, it would be best; but with him or without him, I want you far away from here, my girl; for your own sake, and for mine, ay, and for your father's too, I want you far – far away from here. I came with other thoughts; I came here as a man comes home; now it is all changed, and I have no desire nor hope but to flee – for that's the word – flee, like a bird out of the fowler's snare, from this accursed island.'

She had stopped her work by this time.

'And do you think, now,' said she, 'do you think, now, I have neither eyes nor ears? Do ye think I havenae broken my heart to have these braws (as he calls them, God forgive him!) thrown into the sea? Do ye think I have lived with him, day in, day out, and not seen what you saw in an hour or two? No,' she said, 'I know there's wrong in it; what wrong, I neither know nor want to know. There was never an ill thing made better by meddling, that I could hear of. But, my lad, you must never ask me to leave my father. While the breath is in his body, I'll be with him. And he's not long for here, either: that I can tell you, Charlie – he's not long for here. The mark is on his brow; and better so – maybe better so.'

I was a while silent, not knowing what to say; and when I roused my head at last to speak, she got before me.

'Charlie,' she said, 'what's right for me, neednae be right for you. There's sin upon this house and trouble; you are a stranger; take your things upon your back and go your ways to better places and to better folk, and if you were ever minded to come back, though it were twenty years syne, you would find me aye waiting.'

'Mary Ellen,' I said, 'I asked you to be my wife, and you said as good as yes. That's done for good. Wherever you are, I am; as I shall answer to my God.'

As I said the words, the wind suddenly burst out raving, and then seemed to stand still and shudder round the house of Aros. It was the first squall, or prologue, of the coming tempest, and as we started and looked about us, we found that a gloom, like the approach of evening, had settled round the house.

'God pity all poor folks at sea!' she said. 'We'll see no more of my father till the morrow's morning.'

And then she told me, as we sat by the fire and hearkened to the rising gusts, of how this change had fallen upon my uncle. All last winter he had been dark and fitful in his mind. Whenever the Roost ran high, or, as Mary said, whenever the Merry Men were dancing, he would lie out for hours together on the Head, if it were at night, or on the top of Aros by day, watching the tumult of the sea, and sweeping the horizon for a sail. After February the tenth, when the wealth-bringing wreck was cast ashore at Sandag, he had been at first unnaturally gay, and his excitement had never fallen in degree, but only changed in kind from dark to darker. He neglected his work, and kept Rorie idle. The two would speak together by the hour at the gable end, in guarded tones and with an air of secrecy and almost of guilt; and if she questioned either, as at first she sometimes did, her inquiries were put aside with confusion. Since Rorie had first remarked the fish that hung about the ferry, his master had never set foot but once upon the mainland of the Ross. That once – it was in the height of the springs – he had passed dryshod while the tide was out; but, having lingered overlong on the far side, found himself cut off from Aros by the returning waters. It was with a shriek of agony that he had leaped across the gut, and he had reached home thereafter in a fever-fit of fear. A fear of the sea, a constant haunting thought of the sea, appeared in his talk and devotions, and even in his looks when he was silent.

Rorie alone came in to supper; but a little later my uncle appeared, took a bottle under his arm, put some bread in his pocket, and set forth again to his outlook, followed this time by Rorie. I heard that the schooner was losing ground, but the crew were still fighting every inch with hopeless ingenuity and courage; and the news filled my mind with blackness.

A little after sundown the full fury of the gale broke forth, such a gale as I have never seen in summer, nor, seeing how swiftly it had come, even in winter. Mary and I sat in silence, the house quaking overhead, the tempest howling without, the fire between us sputtering with raindrops. Our thoughts were far away with the poor fellows on the schooner, or my not less unhappy uncle, houseless on the promontory; and yet ever and again we were startled back to ourselves, when the wind would rise and strike the gable like a solid body, or suddenly fall and draw away, so that the fire leaped into flame and our hearts bounded in our sides. Now the storm in its might would seize and shake the four corners of the roof, roaring like Leviathan in anger. Anon, in a lull, cold eddies of tempest moved shudderingly in the room, lifting the hair upon our heads and passing between us as we sat. And again the wind would break forth in a chorus of melancholy sounds, hooting low in the chimney, wailing with flutelike softness round the house.

It was perhaps eight o'clock when Rorie came in and pulled me mysteriously to the door. My uncle, it appeared, had frightened even his constant comrade; and Rorie, uneasy at his extravagance, prayed me to come out and share the watch. I hastened to do as I was asked; the more readily as, what with fear and horror, and the electrical tension of the night, I was myself restless and disposed for action. I told Mary to be under no alarm, for I should be a safeguard on her father; and wrapping myself warmly in a plaid, I followed Rorie into the open air.

The night, though we were so little past midsummer, was as dark as January. Intervals of a groping twilight alternated with spells of utter blackness; and it was impossible to trace the reason of these changes in the flying horror of the sky. The wind blew the breath out of a man's nostrils; all heaven seemed to thunder overhead like one huge sail; and when there fell a momentary lull on Aros, we could hear the gusts dismally sweeping in the distance. Over all the lowlands of the Ross, the wind must have blown as fierce as on the open sea; and God only knows the uproar that was raging around the head of Ben Kyaw. Sheets of mingled spray and rain were driven in our faces. All round the isle of Aros the surf, with an incessant, hammering thunder, beat upon the reefs and beaches. Now louder in one place, now lower in another, like the combinations of orchestral music, the constant mass of sound was hardly varied for a moment. And loud above all this hurly-burly I could hear the changeful voices of the Roost and the intermittent roaring of the Merry Men. At that hour, there flashed into my mind the reason of the name that they were called. For the noise of them seemed almost mirthful, as it out-topped the other noises of the night; or if not mirthful, yet instinct with a portentous joviality. Nay, and it seemed even human. As when savage men have drunk away their reason, and, discarding speech, bawl together in their madness by the hour; so, to my ears, these deadly breakers shouted by Aros in the night.

Arm in arm, and staggering against the wind, Rorie and I won every yard of ground with conscious effort. We slipped on the wet sod, we fell together sprawling on the rocks. Bruised, drenched, beaten, and breathless, it must have taken us near half an hour to get from the house down to the Head that overlooks the Roost. There, it seemed, was my uncle's favourite observatory. Right in the face of it, where the cliff is highest and most sheer, a hump of earth, like a parapet, makes a place of shelter from the common winds, where a man may sit in quiet and see the tide and the mad billows contending at his feet. As he might look down from the window of a house upon some street disturbance, so, from this post, he looks down upon the tumbling of the Merry Men. On such a night, of course, he peers upon a world of blackness, where the waters wheel and boil, where the waves joust together with the noise of an explosion, and the foam towers and vanishes in the twinkling of an eye. Never before had I seen the Merry Men thus violent. The fury, height, and transiency of their spoutings was a thing to be seen and not recounted. High over our heads on the cliff rose their white columns in the darkness; and the same instant, like phantoms, they were gone. Sometimes three at a time would thus aspire and vanish; sometimes a gust took them, and the spray would fall about us, heavy as a wave. And yet the spectacle was rather maddening in its levity than impressive by its force. Thought was beaten down by the confounding uproar; a gleeful vacancy possessed the brains of men, a state akin to madness; and I found myself at times following the dance of the Merry Men as it were a tune upon a jigging instrument.

I first caught sight of my uncle when we were still some yards away in one of the flying glimpses of twilight that chequered the pitch darkness of the night. He was standing up behind the parapet, his head thrown back and the bottle to his mouth. As he put it down, he saw and recognized us with a toss of one hand fleetingly above his head.

'Has he been drinking?' shouted I to Rorie.

'He will aye be drunk when the wind blaws,' returned Rorie in the same high key, and it was all that I could do to hear him.

'Then – was he so – in February?' I inquired.

Rorie's 'Ay' was a cause of joy to me. The murder, then, had not sprung in cold blood from calculation; it was an act of madness no more to be condemned than to be pardoned. My uncle was a dangerous madman, if you will, but he was not cruel and base as I had feared. Yet what a scene for a carouse, what an incredible vice, was this that the poor man had chosen! I have always thought drunkenness a wild and almost fearful pleasure, rather demoniacal than human; but drunkenness, out here in the roaring blackness, on the edge of a cliff above that hell of waters, the man's head spinning like the Roost, his foot tottering on the edge of death, his ear watching for the signs of shipwreck, surely that, if it were credible in anyone, was morally impossible in a man like my uncle, whose mind was set upon a damnatory creed and haunted by the darkest superstitions. Yet so it was; and, as we reached the bight of shelter and could breathe again, I saw the man's eyes shining in the night with an unholy glimmer.

'Eh, Charlie, man, it's grand!' he cried. 'See to them!' he continued, dragging me to the edge of the abyss from whence arose that deafening clamour and those clouds of spray; 'see to them dancin,' man! Is that no wicked?'

He pronounced the word with gusto, and I thought it suited with the scene.

'They're yowlin' for thon schooner,' he went on, his thin, insane voice clearly audible in the shelter of the bank, 'an' she's comin' aye nearer, aye nearer, aye nearer an' nearer an' nearer; an' they ken't, the folk kens it, they ken weel it's by wi' them. Charlie, lad, they're a' drunk in yon schooner, a' dozened wi' drink. They were a' drunk in the *Christ-Anna*, at the hinder end. There's nane could droon at sea wantin' the brandy. Hoot awa, what do you ken?' with a sudden blast of anger. 'I tell ye, it cannae be; they daurnae droon withoot it. Ha'e,' holding out the bottle, 'tak' a sowp.'

I was about to refuse, but Rorie touched me as if in warning; and indeed I had already thought better of the movement. I took the bottle, therefore, and not only drank freely myself, but contrived to spill even more as I was doing so. It was pure spirit, and almost strangled me to swallow. My kinsman did not observe the loss, but, once more throwing back his head, drained the remainder to the dregs. Then, with a loud laugh, he cast the bottle forth among the Merry Men, who seemed to leap up, shouting to receive it.

'Ha'e, bairns!' he cried, 'there's your han'sel. Ye'll get bonnier nor that, or morning.'

Suddenly, out in the black night before us, and not two hundred yards away, we heard, at a moment when the wind was silent, the clear note of a human voice. Instantly the wind swept howling down upon the Head, and the Roost bellowed, and churned, and danced with a new fury. But we had heard the sound, and we knew, with agony, that this was the doomed ship now close on ruin, and that what we had heard was the voice of her master issuing his last command. Crouching together on the edge, we waited, straining every sense, for the inevitable end. It was long, however, and to us it seemed like ages, ere the schooner suddenly appeared for one brief instant, relieved against a tower of glimmering foam. I still see her reefed mainsail flapping loose, as the boom fell heavily across the deck; I still see the black outline of the hull, and still think I can distinguish the figure of a man stretched upon the tiller. Yet the whole sight we had of her passed swifter than lightning; the very wave that disclosed her fell burying her for ever; the mingled cry of many voices at the point of death rose and was quenched in the roaring of the Merry Men. And with that the tragedy was at an end. The strong ship, with all her gear, and the lamp perhaps still burning in the cabin, the lives of so many men, precious surely to others, dear, at least, as heaven to themselves, had all, in that one moment, gone down into the surging waters. They were gone like a dream. And the wind still ran and shouted, and the senseless waters in the Roost still leaped and tumbled as before.

How long we lay there together, we three, speechless and motionless, is more than I can tell, but it must have been for long. At length, one by one, and almost mechanically, we crawled back into the shelter of the bank. As I lay against the parapet, wholly wretched and not entirely master of my mind, I could hear my kinsman maundering to himself in an altered and melancholy mood. Now he would repeat to himself with maudlin iteration, 'Sic a fecht as they had – sic a sair fecht as they had, puir lads, puir lads!' and anon he would bewail that 'a' the gear was as gude's tint,' because the ship had gone down among the Merry Men instead of stranding on the shore; and throughout, the name – the *Christ-Anna* – would come and go in his divagations, pronounced with shuddering awe. The storm all this time was rapidly abating. In half an hour the wind had fallen to a breeze, and the change was accompanied or caused by a heavy, cold, and plumping rain. I must then have fallen asleep, and when I came to myself, drenched, stiff, and unrefreshed, day had already broken, grey, wet, discomfortable day; the wind blew in faint and shifting capfuls, the tide was out, the Roost was at its lowest, and only the strong beating surf round all the coasts of Aros remained to witness of the furies of the night.

V

A man out of the sea

Rorie set out for the house in search of warmth and breakfast; but my uncle was bent upon examining the shores of Aros, and I felt it a part of duty to accompany him throughout. He was now docile and quiet, but tremulous and weak in mind and body; and it was with the eagerness of a child that he pursued his exploration. He climbed far down upon the rocks; on the beaches, he pursued the retreating breakers. The merest broken plank or rag of cordage was a treasure in his eyes to be secured at the peril of his life. To see him, with weak and stumbling footsteps, expose himself to the pursuit of the surf, or the snares and pitfalls of the weedy rock, kept me in a perpetual terror. My arm was ready to support him, my hand clutched him by the skirt, I helped him to draw his pitiful discoveries beyond the reach of the returning wave; a nurse accompanying a child of seven would have had no different experience.

Yet, weakened as he was by the reaction from his madness of the night before, the passions that smouldered in his nature were those of a strong man. His terror of the sea, although conquered for the moment, was still undiminished; had the sea been a lake of living flames, he could not have shrunk more panically from its touch; and once, when his foot slipped and he plunged to the midleg into a pool of water, the shriek that came up out of his soul was like the cry of death. He sat still for a while, panting like a dog, after that; but his desire for the spoils of shipwreck triumphed once more over his fears; once more he tottered among the curded foam; once more he crawled upon the rocks among the bursting bubbles; once more his whole heart seemed to be set on driftwood, fit, if it was fit for anything, to throw upon the fire. Pleased as he was with what he found, he still incessantly grumbled at his ill-fortune.

'Aros,' he said, 'is no a place for wrecks ava' – no ava'. A' the years I've dwalt here, this ane maks the second; and the best o' the gear clean tint!'

'Uncle,' said I, for we were now on a stretch of open sand, where there was nothing to divert his mind, 'I saw you last night, as I never thought to see you – you were drunk.'

'Na, na,' he said, 'no as bad as that. I had been drinking, though. And to tell ye the God's truth, it's a thing I cannae mend. There's nae soberer man than me in my ordnar; but when I hear the wind blaw in my lug, it's my belief that I gang gyte.'

'You are a religious man,' I replied, 'and this is sin.'

'Oh,' he returned, 'if it wasnae sin, I dinnae ken that I

would care for't. Ye see, man, it's defiance. There's a sair spang o' the auld sin o' the warld in yon sea; it's an unchristian business at the best o't; an' whiles when it gets up, an' the wind skreighs – the wind an' her are a kind of sib, I'm thinkin' – an' thae Merry Men, the daft callants, blawin' and lauchin,' and puir souls in the deid thraws warstlin' the leelang nicht wi' their bit ships – weel, it comes ower me like a glamour. I'm a deil, I ken't. But I think naething o' the puir sailor lads; I'm wi' the sea, I'm just like ane o' her ain Merry Men.'

I thought I should touch him in a joint of his harness. I turned me towards the sea; the surf was running gaily, wave after wave, with their manes blowing behind them, riding one after another up the beach, towering, curving, falling one upon another on the trampled sand. Without, the salt air, the scared gulls, the widespread army of the sea-chargers, neighing to each other, as they gathered together to the assault of Aros; and close before us, that line on the flat sands that, with all their number and their fury, they might never pass.

'Thus far shalt thou go,' said I, 'and no farther.' And then I quoted as solemnly as I was able a verse that I had often before fitted to the chorus of the breakers:

> But yet the Lord that is on high,
> Is more of might by far,
> Than noise of many waters is,
> As great sea billows are.

'Ay,' said my kinsman, 'at the hinder end, the Lord will triumph; I dinnae misdoobt that. But here on earth, even silly menfolk daur Him to His face. It is nae wise; I am nae sayin' that it's wise; but it's the pride of the eye, and it's the lust o' life, an' it's the wale o' pleesures.'

I said no more, for we had now begun to cross a neck of land that lay between us and Sandag; and I withheld my last appeal to the man's better reason till we should stand upon the spot associated with his crime. Nor did he pursue the subject; but he walked beside me with a firmer step. The call that I had made upon his mind acted like a stimulant, and I could see that he had forgotten his search for worthless jetsam, in a profound, gloomy, and yet stirring train of thought. In three or four minutes we had topped the brae and begun to go down upon Sandag. The wreck had been roughly handled by the sea; the stem had been spun round and dragged a little lower down; and perhaps the stern had been forced a little higher, for the two parts now lay entirely separate on the beach. When we came to the grave I stopped, uncovered my head in the thick rain, and, looking my kinsman in the face, addressed him.

'A man,' said I, 'was in God's providence suffered to escape from mortal dangers; he was poor, he was naked, he was wet, he was weary, he was a stranger; he had every claim upon the bowels of your compassion; it may be that he was the salt of the earth, holy, helpful, and kind; it may be he was a man laden with iniquities to whom death was the beginning of torment. I ask you in the sight of heaven: Gordon Darnaway, where is the man for whom Christ died?'

He started visibly at the last words; but there came no answer, and his face expressed no feeling but a vague alarm.

'You were my father's brother,' I continued; 'you have taught me to count your house as if it were my father's house; and we are both sinful men walking before the Lord among the sins and dangers of this life. It is by our evil that God leads us into good; we sin, I dare not say by His temptation, but I must say with His consent; and to any but the brutish man his sins are the beginning of wisdom.

God has warned you by this crime; He warns you still by the bloody grave between our feet; and if there shall follow no repentance, no improvement, no return to Him, what can we look for but the following of some memorable judgment?'

Even as I spoke the words, the eyes of my uncle wandered from my face. A change fell upon his looks that cannot be described; his features seemed to dwindle in size, the colour faded from his cheeks, one hand rose waveringly and pointed over my shoulder into the distance, and the oft-repeated name fell once more from his lips: 'The *Christ-Anna*!'

I turned; and if I was not appalled to the same degree, as I return thanks to Heaven that I had not the cause, I was still startled by the sight that met my eyes. The form of a man stood upright on the cabin-hutch of the wrecked ship; his back was towards us; he appeared to be scanning the offing with shaded eyes, and his figure was relieved to its full height, which was plainly very great, against the sea and sky. I have said a thousand times that I am not superstitious; but at that moment, with my mind running upon death and sin, the unexplained appearance of a stranger on that sea-girt, solitary island filled me with a surprise that bordered close on terror. It seemed scarce possible that any human soul should have come ashore alive in such a sea as had raged last night along the coasts of Aros; and the only vessel within miles had gone down before our eyes among the Merry Men. I was assailed with doubts that made suspense unbearable, and, to put the matter to the touch at once, stepped forward and hailed the figure like a ship.

He turned about, and I thought he started to behold us. At this my courage instantly revived, and I called and signed to him to draw near, and he, on his part, dropped immediately to the sands, and began slowly to approach, with many stops and hesitations. At each repeated mark of the man's uneasiness I grew the more confident myself; and I advanced another step, encouraging him as I did so with my head and hand. It was plain the castaway had heard indifferent accounts of our island hospitality; and indeed, about this time, the people farther north had a sorry reputation.

'Why,' I said, 'the man is black!'

And just at that moment, in a voice that I could scarce have recognized, my kinsman began swearing and praying in a mingled stream. I looked at him; he had fallen on his knees, his face was agonized; at each step of the castaway's the pitch of his voice rose, the volubility of his utterance and the fervour of his language redoubled. I call it prayer, for it was addressed to God; but surely no such ranting incongruities were ever before addressed to the Creator by a creature: surely if prayer can be a sin, this mad harangue was sinful. I ran to my kinsman, I seized him by the shoulders, I dragged him to his feet.

'Silence, man,' said I, 'respect your God in words, if not in action. Here, on the very scene of your transgressions, He sends you an occasion of atonement. Forward and embrace it; welcome like a father yon creature who comes trembling to your mercy.'

With that, I tried to force him towards the black; but he felled me to the ground, burst from my grasp, leaving the shoulder of his jacket, and fled up the hillside towards the top of Aros like a deer. I staggered to my feet again, bruised and somewhat stunned; the negro had paused in surprise, perhaps in terror, some halfway between me and the wreck; my uncle was already far away, bounding from rock to rock; and I thus found myself torn for a time between two duties. But I judged, and I pray Heaven that I judged rightly, in favour of the poor wretch upon the sands; his misfortune was at least not plainly of his own creation; it was one, besides, that I could certainly relieve; and I had begun by that time to regard my uncle as an incurable and dismal lunatic. I advanced accordingly towards the black, who now awaited my approach with folded arms, like one prepared for either destiny. As I came nearer, he reached forth his hand with a great gesture, such as I had seen from the pulpit, and spoke to me in something of a pulpit voice, but not a word was comprehensible. I tried him first in English, then in Gaelic, both in vain; so that it was clear we must rely upon the tongue of looks and gestures. Thereupon I signed to him to follow me, which he did readily and with a grave obeisance like a fallen king; all the while there had come no shade of alteration in his face, neither of anxiety while he was still waiting, nor of relief now that he was reassured; if he were a slave, as I supposed, I could not but judge he must have fallen from some high place in his own country, and fallen as he was, I could not but admire his bearing. As we passed the grave, I paused and raised my hands and eyes to heaven in token of respect and sorrow for the dead; and he, as if in answer, bowed low and spread his hands abroad; it was a strange motion, but done like a thing of common custom; and I supposed it was ceremonial in the land from which he came. At the same time he pointed to my uncle, whom we could just see perched upon a knoll, and touched his head to indicate that he was mad.

We took the long way round the shore, for I feared to excite my uncle if we struck across the island; and as we walked, I had time enough to mature the little dramatic exhibition by which I hoped to satisfy my doubts. Accordingly, pausing on a rock, I proceeded to imitate before the negro the action of the man whom I had seen the day before taking bearings with the compass at Sandag. He understood me at once, and, taking the imitation out of my hands, showed me where the boat was, pointed out seaward as if to indicate the position of the schooner, and then down along the edge of the rock with the words 'Espirito Santo,' strangely pronounced, but clear enough for recognition. I had thus been right in my conjecture; the pretended historical inquiry had been but a cloak for treasure hunting; the man who had played on Dr Robertson was the same as the foreigner who visited Grisapol in spring, and now, with many others, lay dead under the Roost of Aros: there had their greed brought them, there should their bones be tossed for evermore. In the meantime the black continued his imitation of the scene, now looking up skyward as though watching the approach of the storm; now, in the character of a seaman, waving the rest to come aboard; now as an officer, running along the rock and entering the boat; and anon bending over imaginary oars with the air of a hurried boatman; but all with the same solemnity of manner, so that I was never even moved to smile. Lastly, he indicated to me, by a pantomime not to be described in words, how he himself had gone up to examine the stranded wreck, and, to his grief and indignation, had been deserted by his comrades; and thereupon folded his arms once more, and stooped his head, like one accepting fate.

The mystery of his presence being thus solved for me, I explained to him by means of a sketch the fate of the vessel and of all aboard her. He showed no surprise nor sorrow, and, with a sudden lifting of his open hand, seemed to dismiss his former friends or masters (whichever they had been) into God's pleasure. Respect came upon me and grew stronger, the more I observed him; I saw he had a powerful mind and a sober and severe character, such as I loved to commune with; and before we reached the house of Aros

I had almost forgotten, and wholly forgiven him, his uncanny colour.

To Mary I told all that had passed without suppression, though I own my heart failed me; but I did wrong to doubt her sense of justice.

'You did the right,' she said. 'God's will be done.' And she set out meat for us at once.

As soon as I was satisfied, I bade Rorie keep an eye upon the castaway, who was still eating, and set forth again myself to find my uncle. I had not gone far before I saw him sitting in the same place, upon the very topmost knoll, and seemingly in the same attitude as when I had last observed him. From that point, as I have said, the most of Aros and the neighbouring Ross would be spread below him like a map; and it was plain that he kept a bright lookout in all directions, for my head had scarcely risen above the summit of the first ascent before he had leaped to his feet and turned as if to face me. I hailed him at once, as well as I was able, in the same tones and words as I had often used before, when I had come to summon him to dinner. He made not so much as a movement in reply. I passed on a little farther, and again tried parley, with the same result. But when I began a second time to advance, his insane fears blazed up again, and still in dead silence, but with incredible speed, he began to flee from before me along the rocky summit of the hill. An hour before, he had been dead weary, and I had been comparatively active. But now his strength was recruited by the fervour of insanity, and it would have been vain for me to dream of pursuit. Nay, the very attempt, I thought, might have inflamed his terrors, and thus increased the miseries of our position. And I had nothing left but to turn homeward and make my sad report to Mary.

She heard it, as she had heard the first, with a concerned

composure, and, bidding me lie down and take that rest of which I stood so much in need, set forth herself in quest of her misguided father. At that age it would have been a strange thing that put me from either meat or sleep; I slept long and deep; and it was already long past noon before I awoke and came downstairs into the kitchen. Mary, Rorie, and the black castaway were seated about the fire in silence; and I could see that Mary had been weeping. There was cause enough, as I soon learned, for tears. First she, and then Rorie, had been forth to seek my uncle; each in turn had found him perched upon the hilltop, and from each in turn he had silently and swiftly fled. Rorie had tried to chase him, but in vain; madness lent a new vigour to his bounds; he sprang from rock to rock over the widest gullies; he scoured like the wind along the hilltops; he doubled and twisted like a hare before the dogs; and Rorie at length gave in; and the last that he saw, my uncle was seated as before upon the crest of Aros. Even during the hottest excitement of the chase, even when the fleet-footed servant had come, for a moment, very near to capture him, the poor lunatic had uttered not a sound. He fled, and he was silent, like a beast; and this silence had terrified his pursuer.

There was something heartbreaking in the situation. How to capture the madman, how to feed him in the meanwhile, and what to do with him when he was captured, were the three difficulties that we had to solve.

'The black,' said I, 'is the cause of this attack. It may even be his presence in the house that keeps my uncle on the hill. We have done the fair thing; he has been fed and warmed under this roof; now I propose that Rorie put him across the bay in the coble, and take him through the Ross as far as Grisapol.'

In this proposal Mary heartily concurred; and bidding the

black follow us, we all three descended to the pier. Certainly, Heaven's will was declared against Gordon Darnaway; a thing had happened, never paralleled before in Aros; during the storm, the coble had broken loose, and, striking on the rough splinters of the pier, now lay in four feet of water with one side stove in. Three days of work at least would be required to make her float. But I was not to be beaten. I led the whole party round to where the gut was narrowest, swam to the other side, and called to the black to follow me. He signed, with the same clearness and quiet as before, that he knew not the art; and there was truth apparent in his signals, it would have occurred to none of us to doubt his truth; and that hope being over, we must all go back even as we came to the house of Aros, the negro walking in our midst without embarrassment.

All we could do that day was to make one more attempt to communicate with the unhappy madman. Again he was visible on his perch; again he fled in silence. But food and a great cloak were at least left for his comfort; the rain, besides, had cleared away, and the night promised to be even warm. We might compose ourselves, we thought, until the morrow; rest was the chief requisite, that we might be strengthened for unusual exertions; and as none cared to talk, we separated at an early hour.

I lay long awake, planning a campaign for the morrow. I was to place the black on the side of Sandag, whence he should head my uncle towards the house; Rorie in the west, I on the east, were to complete the cordon, as best we might. It seemed to me, the more I recalled the configuration of the island, that it should be possible, though hard, to force him down upon the low ground along Aros Bay; and once there, even with the strength of his madness, ultimate escape was hardly to be feared. It was on his terror of the black that

I relied; for I made sure, however he might run, it would not be in the direction of the man whom he supposed to have returned from the dead, and thus one point of the compass at least would be secure.

When at length I fell asleep, it was to be awakened shortly after by a dream of wrecks, black men, and submarine adventure; and I found myself so shaken and fevered that I arose, descended the stair, and stepped out before the house. Within, Rorie and the black were asleep together in the kitchen; outside was a wonderful clear night of stars, with here and there a cloud still hanging, last stragglers of the tempest. It was near the top of the flood, and the Merry Men were roaring in the windless quiet of the night. Never, not even in the height of the tempest, had I heard their song with greater awe. Now, when the winds were gathered home, when the deep was dandling itself back into its summer slumber, and when the stars rained their gentle light over land and sea, the voice of these tide-breakers was still raised for havoc. They seemed, indeed, to be a part of the world's evil and the tragic side of life. Nor were their meaningless vociferations the only sounds that broke the silence of the night. For I could hear, now shrill and thrilling and now almost drowned, the note of a human voice that accompanied the uproar of the Roost. I knew it for my kinsman's; and a great fear fell upon me of God's judgments, and the evil in the world. I went back again into the darkness of the house as into a place of shelter, and lay long upon my bed, pondering these mysteries.

It was late when I again woke, and I leaped into my clothes and hurried to the kitchen. No one was there; Rorie and the black had both stealthily departed long before; and my heart stood still at the discovery. I could rely on Rorie's heart, but I placed no trust in his discretion. If he had thus set out without a word, he was plainly bent upon some service to my uncle. But what service could he hope to render even alone, far less in the company of the man in whom my uncle found his fears incarnated? Even if I were not already too late to prevent some deadly mischief, it was plain I must delay no longer. With the thought I was out of the house; and often as I have run on the rough sides of Aros, I never ran as I did that fatal morning. I do not believe I put twelve minutes to the whole ascent.

My uncle was gone from his perch. The basket had indeed been torn open and the meat scattered on the turf; but, as we found afterwards, no mouthful had been tasted; and there was not another trace of human existence in that wide field of view. Day had already filled the clear heavens; the sun already lighted in a rosy bloom upon the crest of Ben Kyaw; but all below me the rude knolls of Aros and the shield of sea lay steeped in the clear darkling twilight of the dawn.

'Rorie!' I cried; and again 'Rorie!' My voice died in the silence, but there came no answer back. If there were indeed an enterprise afoot to catch my uncle, it was plainly not in fleetness of foot, but in dexterity of stalking, that the hunters placed their trust. I ran on farther, keeping the higher spurs, and looking right and left, nor did I pause again till I was on the mount above Sandag. I could see the wreck, the uncovered belt of sand, the waves idly beating, the long ledge of rocks, and on either hand the tumbled knolls, boulders, and gullies of the island. But still no human thing.

At a stride the sunshine fell on Aros, and the shadows and colours leaped into being. Not half a moment later, below me to the west, sheep began to scatter as in a panic. There came a cry. I saw my uncle running. I saw the black jump up in hot pursuit; and before I had time to understand, Rorie also had appeared, calling directions in Gaelic as to a dog herding sheep.

I took to my heels to interfere, and perhaps I had done better to have waited where I was, for I was the means of cutting off the madman's last escape. There was nothing before him from that moment but the grave, the wreck, and the sea in Sandag Bay. And yet Heaven knows that what I did was for the best.

My uncle Gordon saw in what direction, horrible to him, the chase was driving him. He doubled, darting to the right and left; but high as the fever ran in his veins, the black was still the swifter. Turn where he would, he was still forestalled, still driven toward the scene of his crime. Suddenly he began to shriek aloud, so that the coast re-echoed; and now both I and Rorie were calling on the black to stop. But all was vain, for it was written otherwise. The pursuer still ran, the chase still sped before him screaming; they avoided the grave, and skimmed close past the timbers of the wreck; in a breath they had cleared the sand; and still my kinsman did not pause, but dashed straight into the surf; and the black, now almost within reach, still followed swiftly behind him. Rorie and I both stopped, for the thing was now beyond the hands of men, and these were the decrees of God that came to pass before our eyes. There was never a sharper ending. On that steep beach they were beyond their depth at a bound; neither could swim; the black rose once for a moment with a throttling cry; but the current had them, racing seaward; and if ever they came up again, which God alone can tell, it would be ten minutes after, at the far end of Aros Roost, where the seabirds hover fishing.

ERNEST HEMINGWAY

AFTER THE STORM

IT WASN'T ABOUT anything, something about making punch, and then we started fighting and I slipped and he had me down kneeling on my chest and choking me with both hands like he was trying to kill me and all the time I was trying to get the knife out of my pocket to cut him loose. Everybody was too drunk to pull him off me. He was choking me and hammering my head on the floor and I got the knife out and opened it up; and I cut the muscle right across his arm and he let go of me. He couldn't have held on if he wanted to. Then he rolled and hung on to that arm and started to cry and I said:

'What the hell you want to choke me for?'

I'd have killed him. I couldn't swallow for a week. He hurt my throat bad.

Well, I went out of there and there were plenty of them with him and some came out after me and I made a turn and was down by the docks and I met a fellow and he said somebody killed a man up the street. I said, 'Who killed him?' and he said, 'I don't know who killed him but he's dead all right,' and it was dark and there was water standing in the street and no lights and windows broke and boats all up in the town and trees blown down and everything all blown and I got a skiff and went out and found my boat where I had her inside of Mango Key and she was all right only she was full of water. So I bailed her out and pumped her out and there was a moon but plenty of clouds and still plenty rough and I took it down along; and when it was daylight I was off Eastern Harbour.

Brother, that was some storm. I was the first boat out and you never saw water like that was. It was just as white as a lye barrel and coming from Eastern Harbour to Sou'west Key you couldn't recognize the shore. There was a big channel blown right out through the middle of the beach. Trees and all blown out and a channel cut through and all the water white as chalk and everything on it; branches and whole trees and dead birds, and all floating. Inside the keys were all the pelicans in the world and all kinds of birds flying. They must have gone inside there when they knew it was coming.

I lay at Sou'west Key a day and nobody came after me. I was the first boat out and I seen a spar floating and I knew there must be a wreck and I started out to look for her. I found her. She was a three-masted schooner and I could just see the stumps of her spars out of water. She was in too deep water and I didn't get anything off of her. So I went on looking for something else. I had the start on all of them and I knew I ought to get whatever there was. I went on down over the sand-bar from where I left that three-masted schooner and I didn't find anything and I went on a long way. I was way out toward the quicksands and I didn't find anything so I went on. Then when I was in sight of the Rebecca Light I saw all kinds of birds making over something and I headed over for them to see what it was and there was a cloud of birds all right.

I could see something looked like a spar up out of the water and when I got over close the birds all went up in the air and stayed all around me. The water was clear out there and there was a spar of some kind sticking out just above the water and when I come up close to it I saw it was all dark under water like a long shadow and I came right over it and there under water was a liner; just lying there all under water as big as the whole world. I drifted over her in the boat. She lay on her side and the stern was deep down. The portholes were all shut tight and I could see the glass shine in the water and the whole of her; the biggest boat I ever saw in my life lying there and I went along the whole length of her and then I went over and anchored and I had the skiff on the deck forward and I shoved it down into the water and sculled over with the birds all around me.

I had a water glass like we use sponging and my hand shook so I could hardly hold it. All the portholes were shut that you could see going along over her but way down below near the bottom something must have been open because there were pieces of things floating out all the time. You couldn't tell what they were. Just pieces. That's what the birds were after. You never saw so many birds. They were all around me; crazy yelling.

I could see everything sharp and clear. I could see her rounded over and she looked a mile long under the water. She was lying on a clear white bank of sand and the spar was a sort of foremast or some sort of tackle that slanted out of water the way she was lying on her side. Her bow wasn't very far under. I could stand on the letters of her name on her bow and my head was just out of water. But the nearest porthole was twelve feet down. I could just reach it with the grains pole and I tried to break it with that but I couldn't. The glass was too stout. So I sculled back to the boat and got a wrench and lashed it to the end of the grains pole and I couldn't break it. There I was looking down through the glass at that liner with everything in her and I was the first one to her and I couldn't get into her. She must have had five million dollars' worth in her.

It made me shaky to think how much she must have in her. Inside the porthole that was closed I could see something but I couldn't make it out through the water glass. I couldn't do any good with the grains pole and I took off my clothes and stood and took a couple of deep breaths and dove over off the stern with the wrench in my hand and swam down. I could hold on for a second to the edge of the porthole, and I could see in and there was a woman inside with her hair floating all out. I could see her floating plain and I hit the glass twice with the wrench hard and I heard the noise clink in my ears but it wouldn't break and I had to come up.

I hung on to the dinghy and got my breath and then I climbed in and took a couple of breaths and dove again. I swam down and took hold of the edge of the porthole with my fingers and held it and hit the glass as hard as I could with the wrench. I could see the woman floated in the water through the glass. Her hair was tied once close to her head and it floated all out in the water. I could see the rings on one of her hands. She was right up close to the porthole and I hit the glass twice and I didn't even crack it. When I came up I thought I wouldn't make it to the top before I'd have to breathe.

I went down once more and I cracked the glass, only cracked it, and when I came up my nose was bleeding and I stood on the bow of the liner with my bare feet on the letters of her name and my head just out and rested there and then I swam over to the skiff and pulled up into it and sat there waiting for my head to stop aching and looking down into the water glass, but I bled so I had to wash out the water glass. Then I lay back in the skiff and held my hand under my nose to stop it and I lay there with my head back looking up and there was a million birds above and all around.

When I quit bleeding I took another look through the

glass and then I sculled over to the boat to try and find something heavier than the wrench but I couldn't find a thing; not even a sponge hook. I went back and the water was clearer all the time and you could see everything that floated out over that white bank of sand. I looked for sharks but there weren't any. You could have seen a shark a long way away. The water was so clear and the sand white. There was a grapple for an anchor on the skiff and I cut it off and went overboard and down with it. It carried me right down and past the porthole and I grabbed and couldn't hold anything and went on down and down, sliding along the curved side of her. I had to let go of the grapple. I heard it bump once and it seemed like a year before I came up through to the top of the water. The skiff was floated away with the tide and I swam over to her with my nose bleeding in the water while I swam and I was plenty glad there weren't sharks; but I was tired.

My head felt cracked open and I lay in the skiff and rested and then I sculled back. It was getting along in the afternoon. I went down once more with the wrench and it didn't do any good. That wrench was too light. It wasn't any good diving unless you had a big hammer or something heavy enough to do good. Then I lashed the wrench to the grains pole again and I watched through the water glass and pounded on the glass and hammered until the wrench came off and I saw it in the glass, clear and sharp, go sliding down along her and then off and down to the quicksand and go in. Then I couldn't do a thing. The wrench was gone and I'd lost the grapple so I sculled back to the boat. I was too tired to get the skiff aboard and the sun was pretty low. The birds were all pulling out and leaving her and I headed for Sou'west Key towing the skiff and the birds going on ahead of me and behind me. I was plenty tired.

That night it came on to blow and it blew for a week.

You couldn't get out to her. They come out from town and told me the fellow I'd had to cut was all right except for his arm and I went back to town and they put me under five hundred dollar bond. It came out all right because some of them, friends of mine, swore he was after me with an axe, but by the time we got back out to her the Greeks had blown her open and cleaned her out. They got the safe out with dynamite. Nobody ever knows how much they got. She carried gold and they got it all. They stripped her clean. I found her and I never got a nickel out of her.

It was a hell of a thing all right. They say she was just outside of Havana harbour when the hurricane hit and she couldn't get in or the owners wouldn't let the captain chance coming in; they say he wanted to try; so she had to go with it and in the dark they were running with it trying to go through the gulf between Rebecca and Tortugas when she struck on the quicksands. Maybe her rudder was carried away. Maybe they weren't even steering. But anyway they couldn't have known they were quicksands and when she struck the captain must have ordered them to open up the ballast tanks so she'd lay solid. But it was quicksand she'd hit and when they opened the tank she went in stern first and then over on her beam ends. There were four hundred and fifty passengers and the crew on board of her and they must all have been aboard of her when I found her. They must have opened the tanks as soon as she struck and the minute she settled on it the quicksands took her down. Then her boilers must have burst and that must have been what made those pieces that came out. It was funny there weren't any sharks though. There wasn't a fish. I could have seen them on that clear white sand.

Plenty of fish now though; jewfish, the biggest kind. The biggest part of her's under the sand now but they live inside of her; the biggest kind of jewfish. Some weigh three to four hundred pounds. Sometime we'll go out and get some. You can see the Rebecca light from where she is. They've got a buoy on her now. She's right at the end of the quicksand right at the edge of the gulf. She only missed going through by about a hundred yards. In the dark in the storm they just missed it; raining the way it was they couldn't have seen the Rebecca. Then they're not used to that sort of thing. The captain of a liner isn't used to scudding that way. They have a course and they tell me they set some sort of a compass and it steers itself. They probably didn't know where they were when they ran with that blow but they come close to making it. Maybe they'd lost the rudder though. Anyway there wasn't another thing for them to hit till they'd get to Mexico once they were in that gul. Must have been something though when they struck in that rain and wind and he told them to open her tanks. Nobody could have been on deck in that blow and rain. Everybody must have been below. They couldn't have lived on deck. There must have been some scenes inside all right because you know she settled fast. I saw that wrench go into the sand. The captain couldn't have known it was quicksand when she struck unless he knew these waters. He just knew it wasn't rock. He must have seen it all up in the bridge. He must have known what it was about when she settled. I wonder how fast she made it. I wonder if the mate was there with him. Do you think they stayed inside the bridge or do you think they took it outside? They never found any bodies. Not a one. Nobody floating. They float a long way with lifebelts too. They must have took it inside. Well, the Greeks got it all. Everything. They must have come fast all right. They picked her clean. First there was the birds, then me, then the Greeks, and even the birds got more out of her than I did.

SAKI

THE TREASURE-SHIP

THE GREAT GALLEON lay in semi-retirement under the sand weed and water of the northern bay where the fortune of war and weather had long ago ensconced it. Three and a quarter centuries had passed since the day when it had taken the high seas as an important unit of a fighting squadron – precisely which squadron the learned were not agreed. The galleon had brought nothing into the world, but it had, according to tradition and report, taken much out of it. But how much? There again the learned were in disagreement. Some were as generous in their estimate as an income-tax assessor, others applied a species of higher criticism to the submerged treasure chests, and debased their contents to the currency of goblin gold. Of the former school was Lulu, Duchess of Dulverton.

The Duchess was not only a believer in the existence of a sunken treasure of alluring proportions; she also believed that she knew of a method by which the said treasure might be precisely located and cheaply disembedded. An aunt on her mother's side of the family had been Maid of Honour at the Court of Monaco, and had taken a respectful interest in the deep-sea researches in which the Throne of that country, impatient perhaps of its terrestrial restrictions, was wont to immerse itself. It was through the instrumentality of this relative that the Duchess learned of an invention, perfected and very nearly patented by a Monegaskan savant, by means of which the home-life of the Mediterranean sardine might be studied at a depth of many fathoms in a cold white light of more than ball-room brilliancy. Implicated in this invention (and, in the Duchess's eyes, the most attractive part of it) was an electric suction dredge, specially designed for dragging to the surface such objects of interest and value as might be found in the more accessible levels of the ocean-bed. The rights of the invention were to be acquired for a matter of eighteen hundred francs, and the apparatus for a few thousand more. The Duchess of Dulverton was rich, as the world counted wealth; she nursed the hope of being one day rich at her own computation. Companies had been formed and efforts had been made again and again during the course of three centuries to probe for the alleged treasures of the interesting galleon; with the aid of this invention she considered that she might go to work on the wreck privately and independently. After all, one of her ancestors on her mother's side was descended from Medina Sidonia, so she was of opinion that she had as much right to the treasure as any one. She acquired the invention and bought the apparatus.

Among other family ties and encumbrances, Lulu possessed a nephew, Vasco Honiton, a young gentleman who was blessed with a small income and a large circle of relatives, and lived impartially and precariously on both. The name Vasco had been given him possibly in the hope that he might live up to its adventurous tradition, but he limited himself strictly to the home industry of adventurer, preferring to exploit the assured rather than to explore the unknown. Lulu's intercourse with him had been restricted of recent years to the negative processes of being out of town when he called on her, and short of money when he wrote to her. Now, however, she bethought herself of his eminent suitability for the direction of a treasure-seeking experiment;

if any one could extract gold from an unpromising situation it would certainly be Vasco – of course, under the necessary safeguards in the way of supervision. Where money was in question Vasco's conscience was liable to fits of obstinate silence.

Somewhere on the west coast of Ireland the Dulverton property included a few acres of shingle, rock, and heather, too barren to support even an agrarian outrage, but embracing a small and fairly deep bay where the lobster yield was good in most seasons. There was a bleak little house on the property, and for those who liked lobsters and solitude, and were able to accept an Irish cook's ideas as to what might be perpetrated in the name of mayonnaise, Innisgluther was a tolerable exile during the summer months. Lulu seldom went there herself, but she lent the house lavishly to friends and relations. She put it now at Vasco's disposal.

'It will be the very place to practise and experiment with the salvage apparatus,' she said; 'the bay is quite deep in places, and you will be able to test everything thoroughly before starting on the treasure hunt.'

In less than three weeks Vasco turned up in town to report progress.

'The apparatus works beautifully,' he informed his aunt; 'the deeper one got the clearer everything grew. We found something in the way of a sunken wreck to operate on, too!'

'A wreck in Innisgluther Bay!' exclaimed Lulu.

'A submerged motor-boat, the *Sub-Rosa*,' said Vasco.

'No! really?' said Lulu; 'poor Billy Yuttley's boat. I remember it went down somewhere off that coast some three years ago. His body was washed ashore at the Point. People said at the time that the boat was capsized intentionally – a case of suicide, you know. People always say that sort of thing when anything tragic happens.'

'In this case they were right,' said Vasco.

'What do you mean?' asked the Duchess hurriedly. 'What makes you think so?'

'I know,' said Vasco simply.

'Know? How can you know? How can any one know? The thing happened three years ago.'

'In a locker of the *Sub-Rosa* I found a water-tight strong-box. It contained papers.' Vasco paused with dramatic effect and searched for a moment in the inner breast-pocket of his coat. He drew out a folded slip of paper. The Duchess snatched at it in almost indecent haste and moved appreciably nearer the fireplace.

'Was this in the *Sub-Rosa*'s strong-box?' she asked.

'Oh, no,' said Vasco carelessly, 'that is a list of the well-known people who would be involved in a very disagreeable scandal if the *Sub-Rosa*'s papers were made public. I've put you at the head of it, otherwise it follows alphabetical order.'

The Duchess gazed helplessly at the string of names, which seemed for the moment to include nearly every one she knew. As a matter of fact, her own name at the head of the list exercised an almost paralyzing effect on her thinking faculties.

'Of course you have destroyed the papers?' she asked, when she had somewhat recovered herself. She was conscious that she made the remark with an entire lack of conviction.

Vasco shook his head.

'But you should have,' said Lulu angrily; 'if, as you say, they are highly compromising –'

'Oh, they are, I assure you of that,' interposed the young man.

'Then you should put them out of harm's way at once. Supposing anything should leak out, think of all these poor, unfortunate people who would be involved in the disclosures,' and Lulu tapped the list with an agitated gesture.

'Unfortunate, perhaps, but not poor,' corrected Vasco; 'if you read the list carefully you'll notice that I haven't troubled to include any one whose financial standing isn't above question.'

Lulu glared at her nephew for some moments in silence. Then she asked hoarsely: 'What are you going to do?'

'Nothing – for the remainder of my life,' he answered meaningly. 'A little hunting, perhaps,' he continued, 'and I shall have a villa at Florence. The Villa Sub-Rosa would sound rather quaint and picturesque, don't you think, and quite a lot of people would be able to attach a meaning to the name. And I suppose I must have a hobby; I shall probably collect Raeburns.'

Lulu's relative, who lived at the Court of Monaco, got quite a snappish answer when she wrote recommending some further invention in the realm of marine research.

VOYAGES OF DISCOVERY

DORIS LESSING

THROUGH THE TUNNEL

GOING TO THE shore on the first morning of the vacation, the young English boy stopped at a turning of the path and looked down at a wild and rocky bay, and then over to the crowded beach he knew so well from other years. His mother walked on in front of him, carrying a bright striped bag in one hand. Her other arm, swinging loose, was very white in the sun. The boy watched that white naked arm, and turned his eyes, which had a frown behind them, towards the bay and back again to his mother. When she felt he was not with her, she swung around. 'Oh, there you are, Jerry!' she said. She looked impatient, then smiled. 'Why, darling, would you rather not come with me? Would you rather –' She frowned, conscientiously worrying over what amusements he might secretly be longing for, which she had been too busy or too careless to imagine. He was very familiar with that anxious, apologetic smile. Contrition sent him running after her. And yet, as he ran, he looked back over his shoulder at the wild bay; and all morning, as he played on the safe beach, he was thinking of it.

Next morning, when it was time for the routine of swimming and sunbathing, his mother said, 'Are you tired of the usual beach, Jerry? Would you like to go somewhere else?'

'Oh, no!' he said quickly, smiling at her out of that unfailing impulse of contrition – a sort of chivalry. Yet, walking down the path with her, he blurted out, 'I'd like to go and have a look at those rocks down there.'

She gave the idea her attention. It was a wild-looking place, and there was no one there; but she said, 'Of course, Jerry. When you've had enough, come to the big beach. Or just go straight back to the villa, if you like.' She walked away, that bare arm, now slightly reddened from yesterday's sun, swinging. And he almost ran after her again, feeling it unbearable that she should go by herself, but he did not.

She was thinking, Of course he's old enough to be safe without me. Have I been keeping him too close? He mustn't feel he ought to be with me. I must be careful.

He was an only child, eleven years old. She was a widow. She was determined to be neither possessive nor lacking in devotion. She went worrying off to her beach.

As for Jerry, once he saw that his mother had gained her beach, he began the steep descent to the bay. From where he was, high up among red-brown rocks, it was a scoop of moving blueish green fringed with white. As he went lower, he saw that it spread among small promontories and inlets of rough, sharp rock, and the crisping, lapping surface showed stains of purple and darker blue. Finally, as he ran sliding and scraping down the last few yards, he saw an edge of white surf and the shallow, luminous movement of water over white sand, and, beyond that, a solid, heavy blue.

He ran straight into the water and began swimming. He was a good swimmer. He went out fast over the gleaming sand, over a middle region where rocks lay like discoloured monsters under the surface, and then he was in the real sea – a warm sea where irregular cold currents from the deep water shocked his limbs.

When he was so far out that he could look back not only on the little bay but past the promontory that was between it and the big beach, he floated on the buoyant surface and looked for his mother. There she was, a speck of yellow under an umbrella that looked like a slice of orange peel. He swam back to shore, relieved at being sure she was there, but all at once very lonely.

On the edge of a small cape that marked the side of the bay away from the promontory was a loose scatter of rocks. Above them, some boys were stripping off their clothes. They came running, naked, down to the rocks. The English boy swam towards them, but kept his distance at a stone's throw. They were of that coast; all of them were burned smooth dark brown and speaking a language he did not understand. To be with them, of them, was a craving that filled his whole body. He swam a little closer; they turned and watched him with narrowed, alert dark eyes. Then one smiled and waved. It was enough. In a minute, he had swum in and was on the rocks beside them, smiling with a desperate, nervous supplication. They shouted cheerful greetings at him; and then, as he preserved his nervous, uncomprehending smile, they understood that he was a foreigner strayed from his own beach, and they proceeded to forget him. But he was happy. He was with them.

They began diving again and again from a high point into a well of blue sea between rough, pointed rocks. After they had dived and come up, they swam around, hauled themselves up, and waited their turn to dive again. They were big boys – men, to Jerry. He dived, and they watched him; and when he swam around to take his place, they made way for him. He felt he was accepted and he dived again, carefully, proud of himself.

Soon the biggest of the boys poised himself, shot down into the water, and did not come up. The others stood about, watching. Jerry, after waiting for the sleek brown head to appear, let out a yell of warning; they looked at him idly and turned their eyes back towards the water. After a long time, the boy came up on the other side of a big dark rock, letting the air out of his lungs in a sputtering gasp and a shout of triumph. Immediately the rest of them dived in. One moment, the morning seemed full of chattering boys; the next, the air and the surface of the water were empty. But through the heavy blue, dark shapes could be seen moving and groping.

Jerry dived, shot past the school of underwater swimmers, saw a black wall of rock looming at him, touched it, and bobbed up at once to the surface, where the wall was a low barrier he could see across. There was no one visible; under him, in the water, the dim shapes of the swimmers had disappeared. Then one, and then another of the boys came up on the far side of the barrier of rock, and he understood that they had swum through some gap or hole in it. He plunged down again. He could see nothing through the stinging salt water but the blank rock. When he came up the boys were all on the diving rock, preparing to attempt the feat again. And now, in a panic of failure, he yelled up, in English, 'Look at me! Look!' and he began splashing and kicking in the water like a foolish dog.

They looked down gravely, frowning. He knew the frown. At moments of failure, when he clowned to claim his mother's attention, it was with just this grave, embarrassed inspection that she rewarded him. Through his hot shame, feeling the pleading grin on his face like a scar that he could never remove, he looked up at the group of big brown boys on the rock and shouted '*Bonjour! Merci! Au revoir! Monsieur, monsieur!*' while he hooked his fingers round his ears and waggled them.

Water surged into his mouth; he choked, sank, came up. The rock, lately weighted with boys, seemed to rear up out of the water as their weight was removed. They were flying down past him now, into the water; the air was full of falling bodies. Then the rock was empty in the hot sunlight. He counted one, two, three . . .

At fifty, he was terrified. They must all be drowning beneath him, in the watery caves of the rock! At a hundred, he stared around him at the empty hillside, wondering if he should yell for help. He counted faster, faster, to hurry them up, to bring them to the surface quickly, to drown them quickly – anything rather than the terror of counting on and on into the blue emptiness of the morning. And then, at a hundred and sixty, the water beyond the rock was full of boys blowing like brown whales. They swam back to the shore without a look at him.

He climbed back to the diving rock and sat down, feeling the hot roughness of it under his thighs. The boys were gathering up their bits of clothing and running off along the shore to another promontory. They were leaving to get away from him. He cried openly, fists in his eyes. There was no one to see him, and he cried himself out.

It seemed to him that a long time had passed, and he swam out to where he could see his mother. Yes, she was still there, a yellow spot under an orange umbrella. He swam back to the big rock, climbed up, and dived into the blue pool among the fanged and angry boulders. Down he went, until he touched the wall of rock again. But the salt was so painful in his eyes that he could not see.

He came to the surface, swam to shore and went back to the villa to wait for his mother. Soon she walked slowly up the path, swinging her striped bag, the flushed, naked arm dangling beside her. 'I want some swimming goggles,' he panted, defiant and beseeching.

She gave him a patient, inquisitive look as she said casually, 'Well, of course, darling.'

But now, now, now! He must have them this minute, and no other time. He nagged and pestered until she went with him to a shop. As soon as she had bought the goggles, he grabbed them from her hand as if she were going to claim them for herself, and was off, running down the steep path to the bay.

Jerry swam out to the big barrier rock, adjusted the goggles, and dived. The impact of the water broke the rubber-enclosed vacuum, and the goggles came loose. He understood that he must swim down to the base of the rock from the surface of the water. He fixed the goggles tight and firm, filled his lungs, and floated, face down, on the water. Now he could see. It was as if he had eyes of a different kind – fish eyes that showed everything clear and delicate and wavering in the bright water.

Under him, six or seven feet down, was a floor of perfectly clean, shining white sand, rippled firm and hard by the tides. Two greyish shapes steered there, like long, rounded pieces of wood or slate. They were fish. He saw them nose towards each other, poise motionless, make a dart forward, swerve off, and come around again. It was like a water dance. A few inches above them the water sparkled as if sequins were dropping through it. Fish again – myriads of minute fish, the length of his fingernail – were drifting through the water, and in a moment he could feel the innumerable tiny touches of them against his limbs. It was like swimming in flaked silver. The great rock the big boys had swum through rose sheer out of the white sand – black, tufted lightly with greenish weed. He could see no gap in it. He swam down to its base.

Again and again he rose, took a big chestful of air, and went down. Again and again he groped over the surface of the rock, feeling it, almost hugging it in the desperate need to find the entrance. And then, once, while he was clinging to the black wall, his knees came up and he shot his feet out forward and they met no obstacle. He had found the hole.

He gained the surface, clambered about the stones that littered the barrier rock until he found a big one, and, with this in his arms, let himself down over the side of the rock. He dropped, with the weight, straight to the sandy floor. Clinging tight to the anchor of stone, he lay on his side and looked in under the dark shelf at the place where his feet had gone. He could see the hole. It was an irregular, dark gap; but he could not see deep into it. He let go of his anchor, clung with his hands to the edges of the hole, and tried to push himself in.

He got his head in, found his shoulders jammed, moved them in sidewise, and was inside as far as his waist. He could see nothing ahead. Something soft and clammy touched his mouth; he saw a dark frond moving against the greyish rock, and panic filled him. He thought of octopuses, of clinging weed. He pushed himself out backwards and caught a glimpse, as he retreated, of a harmless tentacle of seaweed drifting in the mouth of the tunnel. But it was enough. He reached the sunlight, swam to shore, and lay on the diving rock. He looked down into the blue well of water. He knew he must find his way through that cave, or hole, or tunnel, and out the other side.

First, he thought, he must learn to control his breathing. He let himself down into the water with another big stone in his arms, so that he could lie effortlessly on the bottom of the sea. He counted. One, two, three. He counted steadily. He could hear the movement of blood in his chest. Fifty-one, fifty-two ... His chest was hurting. He let go of the rock and went up into the air. He saw that the sun was low. He rushed to the villa and found his mother at her supper. She said only 'Did you enjoy yourself?' and he said 'Yes.'

All night the boy dreamed of the water-filled cave in the rock, and as soon as breakfast was over he went to the bay.

That night, his nose bled badly. For hours he had been underwater, learning to hold his breath, and now he felt weak and dizzy. His mother said, 'I shouldn't overdo things, darling, if I were you.'

That day and the next, Jerry exercised his lungs as if everything, the whole of his life, all that he would become, depended upon it. Again his nose bled at night, and his mother insisted on his coming with her the next day. It was a torment to him to waste a day of his careful self-training, but he stayed with her on that other beach, which now seemed a place for small children, a place where his mother might lie safe in the sun. It was not his beach.

He did not ask for permission, on the following day, to go to his beach. He went, before his mother could consider the complicated rights and wrongs of the matter. A day's rest, he discovered, had improved his count by ten. The big boys had made the passage while he counted a hundred and sixty. He had been counting fast, in his fright. Probably now, if he tried, he could get through that long tunnel, but he was not going to try yet. A curious, most unchildlike persistence, a controlled impatience, made him wait. In the meantime, he lay underwater on the white sand, littered now by stones he had brought down from the upper air, and studied the entrance to the tunnel. He knew every jut and corner of it, as far as it was possible to see. It was as if he already felt its sharpness about his shoulders.

He sat by the clock in the villa, when his mother was not near, and checked his time. He was incredulous and then proud to find he could hold his breath without strain for two minutes. The words 'two minutes,' authorized by the clock, brought close the adventure that was so necessary to him.

In another four days, his mother said casually one morning, they must go home. On the day before they left, he would do it. He would do it if it killed him, he said defiantly to himself. But two days before they were to leave – a day of triumph when he increased his count by fifteen – his nose bled so badly that he turned dizzy and had to lie limply over the big rock like a bit of seaweed, watching the thick red blood flow on to the rock and trickle slowly down to the sea. He was frightened. Supposing he turned dizzy in the tunnel? Supposing he died there, trapped? Supposing – his head went around, in the hot sun, and he almost gave up. He thought he would return to the house and lie down, and next summer, perhaps, when he had another year's growth in him – *then* he would go through the hole.

But even after he had made the decision, or thought he had, he found himself sitting up on the rock and looking down into the water; and he knew that now, this moment, when his nose had only just stopped bleeding, when his head was still sore and throbbing – this was the moment when he would try. If he did not do it now, he never would. He was trembling with fear that he would not go; and he was trembling with horror at the long, long tunnel under the rock, under the sea. Even in the open sunlight, the barrier rock seemed very wide and very heavy; tons of rock pressed down on where he would go. If he died there, he would lie until one day – perhaps not before next year – those big boys would swim into it and find it blocked.

He put on his goggles, fitted them tight, tested the vacuum. His hands were shaking. Then he chose the biggest stone he could carry and slipped over the edge of the rock until half of him was in the cool enclosing water and half in the hot sun. He looked up once at the empty sky, filled his lungs once, twice, and then sank fast to the bottom with the stone. He let it go and began to count. He took the edges of the hole in his hands and drew himself into it, wriggling his shoulders in sidewise as he remembered he must, kicking himself along with his feet.

Soon he was clear inside. He was in a small rock-bound hole filled with yellowish-grey water. The water was pushing him up against the roof. The roof was sharp and pained his back. He pulled himself along with his hands – fast, fast – and used his legs as levers. His head knocked against something; a sharp pain dizzied him. Fifty, fifty-one, fifty-two . . . He was without light, and the water seemed to press upon him with the weight of rock. Seventy-one, seventy-two . . . There was no strain on his lungs. He felt like an inflated balloon, his lungs were so light and easy, but his head was pulsing.

He was being continually pressed against the sharp roof, which felt slimy as well as sharp. Again he thought of octopuses, and wondered if the tunnel might be filled with weed that could tangle him. He gave himself a panicky, convulsive kick forward, ducked his head, and swam. His feet and hands moved freely, as if in open water. The hole must have widened out. He thought he must be swimming fast, and he was frightened of banging his head if the tunnel narrowed.

A hundred, a hundred and one . . . The water paled. Victory filled him. His lungs were beginning to hurt. A few more strokes and he would be out. He was counting wildly; he said a hundred and fifteen, and then, a long time later, a hundred and fifteen again. The water was a clear jewel-green all around him. Then he saw, above his head, a crack running up through the rock. Sunlight was falling through it, showing the clean, dark rock of the tunnel, a single mussel shell, and darkness ahead.

He was at the end of what he could do. He looked up at

the crack as if it were filled with air and not water, as if he could put his mouth to it to draw in air. A hundred and fifteen, he heard himself say inside his head – but he had said that long ago. He must go on into the blackness ahead, or he would drown. His head was swelling, his lungs cracking. A hundred and fifteen, a hundred and fifteen pounded through his head, and he feebly clutched at rocks in the dark, pulling himself forward leaving the brief space of sunlit water behind. He felt he was dying. He was no longer quite conscious. He struggled on in the darkness between lapses into unconsciousness. An immense, swelling pain filled his head, and then the darkness cracked with an explosion of green light. His hands, groping forward, met nothing; and his feet, kicking back, propelled him out into the open sea.

He drifted to the surface, his face turned up to the air. He was gasping like a fish. He felt he would sink now and drown; he could not swim the few feet back to the rock. Then he was clutching it and pulling himself up on to it. He lay face down, gasping. He could see nothing but a red-veined, clotted dark. His eyes must have burst, he thought; they were full of blood. He tore off his goggles and a gout of blood went into the sea. His nose was bleeding, and the blood had filled the goggles.

He scooped up handfuls of water from the cool, salty sea, to splash on his face, and did not know whether it was blood or salt water he tasted. After a time, his heart quieted, his eyes cleared, and he sat up. He could see the local boys diving and playing half a mile away. He did not want them. He wanted nothing but to get back home and lie down.

In a short while, Jerry swam to shore and climbed slowly up the path to the villa. He flung himself on his bed and slept, waking at the sound of feet on the path outside. His mother was coming back. He rushed to the bathroom, thinking she must not see his face with bloodstains, or tear-stains, on it. He came out of the bathroom and met her as she walked into the villa, smiling, her eyes lighting up.

'Have a nice morning?' she asked, laying her hand on his warm brown shoulder a moment.

'Oh, yes, thank you,' he said.

'You look a bit pale.' And then, sharp and anxious, 'How did you bang your head?'

'Oh, just banged it,' he told her.

She looked at him closely. He was strained; his eyes were glazed-looking. She was worried. And then she said to herself, Oh, don't fuss! Nothing can happen. He can swim like a fish.

They sat down to lunch together.

'Mummy,' he said, 'I can stay underwater for two minutes – three minutes, at least.' It came bursting out of him.

'Can you, darling?' she said. 'Well, I shouldn't overdo it. I don't think you ought to swim any more today.'

She was ready for a battle of wills, but he gave in at once. It was no longer of the least importance to go to the bay.

JOHN UPDIKE

CRUISE

ISLANDS KEPT APPEARING outside their windows. Crete, Ogygia, Capri, Ponza. Calypso, who had became Neuman's cruisemate, his wife at sea, liked to make love sitting astride him while gazing out the porthole, feeling between her legs the surging and the bucking of the boat. Her eyes, the color of a blue hydrangea, tipped toward the violet end of the spectrum in these moments. Her skin was as smooth as a new statue's. He called her Calypso because the entire cruise, consisting of sixty-five passengers and forty crewpersons, was marketed as a duplicate of the tortuous homeward voyage of Ulysses, though everyone including their lecturers kept forgetting which port of call represented what in *The Odyssey.* Were the cliffs of Bonifacio, a chic and slanty tourist trap on the southern tip of Corsica, *really* the cliffs from which the giant, indiscriminately carnivorous Laestrygones had pelted the fleet with rocks, sinking all but the wily captain's dark-prowed hull? Was Djerba, a sleepy hot island off of the Tunisian coast, distinguished by a functioning synagogue and a disused thirteenth-century Aragonese fort, *really* the land of the Lotus Eaters?

'Well, what is "really"?' their male lecturer asked them in turn, returning a question for a question in Socratic style. '*Tί έστιν ἀληθεια*? Or, as the French might put it, "*Le soi-disant 'Ding an sich,' c'existe ou non?*" '

Their on-board lecturers were two: a small man and a large woman. The man preached a wry verbal deconstructionism and the woman a ringing cosmic feminism. Clytemnestra was her idea of a Greek hero. Medea and Hecuba she admired also. She wore gold sickles around her neck and her hair was done up in snakes of braid. Our lovers – cruel and flippant vis-à-vis the rest of humanity in their ecstasy of love newly entered upon – called her Killer. The male lecturer they called Homer. Homer sat up late in the ship's lounge each night, smoking cigarettes and planning what he was going to say the next day. He looked wearied by all his knowledge, all his languages, and sallow from too much indoors. Even while trudging up and down the slippery, scree-ridden slopes of archaeological digs, he wore a button-down shirt and laced black shoes. The lovers felt superior to him, in the exalted state brought on by repeated orgasms in the little cabin's swaying, clicking, cunningly outfitted space. '*Aiiiieeee!*' they cried. '*Aiae, aiae!* We are as gods!'

There were rough seas between Malta and Djerba. Neuman threw up, to his own surprise and disgust. He had thought, on the basis of several Atlantic crossings in gigantic passenger liners, that he was seaworthy. Calypso, who in her terrestrial life had been raised on a Nebraska wheat farm and not seen the ocean until she was twenty-one and unhappily married, had no mal-de-mer problem; when he bolted from their table in the seesawing dining room she stayed put, finished her poached sea-trout, helped herself to his squid stew, ate all of the delicious little Maltese biscuits in the breadbasket, and ordered caramelized *pomme Charlotte* for dessert, with Turkish coffee. In the tranquillity of her stomach she was indeed as a goddess – Calypso, the daughter of Thetis by Oceanus. Fleeing the dining room, Neuman held acid vomit back against his teeth for the length of his run down the second-deck corridor; when he got into his own bathroom he erupted like a fountain, disgustingly, epically. Ah, what is man but a bit of slime in the cistern of the void?

'You poor baby,' she said, descending to him at last. Her kiss smelled of caramel and brought on a minor attack of gagging. 'I think I'll spend the night back in my own cabin,' she told him. 'After a spot of anisette.'

'Don't go up to the lounge,' he begged, feeble and green-faced yet sexually jealous. 'There's a hard-drinking crowd up there every night. Hardened cruisers. Good-time Charlies. Tonight they're having a singalong, followed by a showing of *Casablanca*. Whenever they show *Casablanca* on one of these boats, all hell breaks loose.'

'I'll be fine,' she told him, her complicated blue eyes drifting evasively to the porthole, which was black but for the dim glow of the starboard lights and a diagonal slap of spray at the nadir of an especially sickening flop into watery nothingness. 'Just because we have good sex,' she told him, firmly, 'you don't own me, buster. I paid for this cruise with my own money and I intend to have a good time.'

She was one of the new women and he, despite his name, one of the old men. Female equality struck him as a brutish idea. Just the idea of her having a good time – of trying to milk some selfish happiness out of this inchoate hyperactive muddle of a universe – doubled and redoubled his nausea. 'Go, go, you bitch,' he said. His stomach, like a filmy jelly-fish floating within him, was organizing itself for a new convulsion, and he was planning his dash to the toilet once she had removed the obstacle of her trim, compact body, in its chiton of starched blue linen, belted with a rope of gold. She had good sturdy legs, like a cheerleader's without the white socks. Hips squared off like small bales of cotton. Narrow feet in gilded sandals. 'Easy come,' he told her queasily, with false jauntiness, 'easy go.'

* * *

They had sized each other up at the start, in the ruins of Troy. She was standing in khaki safari slacks and a lime-green tennis visor on Level VIIa, thought to be Priam's Troy if anything on this site 'really' was, and he was down in Level II, not far from where Schliemann and his racy Greek wife, Sophia, had discovered and surreptitiously hidden a hoard of golden treasures from the middle of the third millennium before Christ. Now it was all a mess of mounds and pebbles and blowing grasses and bobbing poppies and liquid-eyed guides and elderly Americans and tightly made limestone walls most probably too small to have been the walls of fabled Troy. 'Can this be all there was?' Homer was murmuring to their group. *'Est-ce que c'est tout?* A little rubbly village by the marshes? Schliemann decided, "*Es ist genug.* This was Troy." ' The poppies bobbed amid the nodding grasses. The rubble underfoot had been trod by Cassandra and Aeneas, venerable Priam and ravishing Helen.

The destined lovers' glances met, and remet; they measured each other for size and age and signs of socio-economic compatibility, and he carefully climbed through the levels to edge into her group. Their group's guide, a local Turk, was telling about the Judgment of Paris as if it had happened just yesterday, in the next village: 'So poor Zeus, what to do? One woman his wife, another his daughter, straight from head – *boom!*' He hit his fist against his broad brown brow. 'Each lady say she the absolute best, *she* deserve golden apple. So Zeus, he looking around in bad way and see far off in Mount Ida, over there, you can almost see' – he gestured, and the tourists looked, raking with their eyes the vacant plains of Troy, vast if not as windy as in the epic – 'he see this poor shepherd boy, son of King Priam, minding own business, tending the sheeps. His name, Paris. Zeus tell him, "You choose." "Who, me?" "Yes, you." ' The American tourists, broiling in the sun, obligingly laughed; the guide smiled, showing a gold fang. ' "Oh boy," Paris think to self. "Problem." One lady offer him much riches, Hera. Another say, "No, have much glory in battle and wars, thanks to me." That was Athena, daughter straight from Zeus's head. Third say, Aphrodite say, "No, forget all that. I give you most beautiful woman in world to be your wife." And Paris say, "O.K., you win. Good deal." '

By now Neuman had drawn level with his tennis-visored prey. He murmured in her ear, 'The "O.K." that launched a thousand ships.' A gravelly American witticism, here in this remote archaic place. He liked her ear very much, the marble whiteness and the squarish folds of it. It was feminine yet no-nonsense, like her level gaze.

She had sensed his proximity. The soul has hairs, which prickle. In profile Calypso barely smiled at the pleasantry, then turned to appraise him, calculating his physical and mental compatibility and the length of the cruise ahead of them. Nauplia, Valletta, Bonifacio, Sperlonga. O.K. As if by destiny, without planning it, they arrived at the lounge for pre-dinner drinks at the same moment. With utmost diffidence they chose the same banquette and, their increasingly excited recountings of their separate pasts far from finished, asked to be seated at the same dining table, as the sleek white cruise ship slipped off the tight-fitting Dardanelles and slipped on the sequinned blue gown of the Aegean.

Malta, a fairy-tale island. Everything was sand-colored – a series of giant sand castles unfolded as they wormed into the harbor. Groggy from one of their seaborne nights of love, Neuman and Calypso, strolling slightly apart from the sixty-three other cruisers, wandered hand in hand through the bustling streets of Valletta, where every swivel-hipped pedestrian wore a dark scowl. The prehistoric Maltese blood had been suffused with centuries of Italian immigration. The palace of the grand masters of the famous persecuted Knights was gloomy with tapestries, and the ruins of the temples of Tarxien were so ancient and their purpose was so conjectural that one went dizzy, right there in the roofless maze of it all, under the blazing overhead sun.

In the harbor of Marsaxlokk, the little fishing boats had painted eyes on the prows; Neuman wondered, though, if they were sincerely magical or just painted on to keep tourists happy. So many things were like that now – the hex signs on Pennsylvania barns, the beefeater costumes at the Tower of London. The world had become a rather tatty theme park, its attractions trumped-up and suspect. A little rusty playground existed here in Marsaxlokk, and Calypso got on one of the swings, and Neuman gave her a push, both of them fighting the sadness welling from underneath – a black sludge leaking up through the grid of the 'x's in Maltese place-names, a dark liquid sliding beneath the progress of the tightly scheduled days, the certainty that the cruise would one day be over. They were both between divorces, which was worse than being between marriages. Their spouses had point-blank declined to come on this educational cruise, and these refusals hung in the air like the humming in the eardrums after a twenty-one-gun salute. In the heat of Malta, on the hike from the bus up to the standing stones of Hagar Qim, her pink hand in his felt as sticky as a child's.

Marvels – marvels! – began to beset them. Mrs Druthers, a grossly overweight widow from Caldwell, New Jersey, who maneuvered herself about on metal arm crutches (very gallantly, everybody agreed, especially when she, several days before, had leveraged herself all the way to the top of the hilltop fortress of Mycenae, through the celebrated Lion Gate and along the lip of the great shaft tomb) exhaustedly sat down on one of the stones of Hagar Qim in her sand-colored raincoat and simply vanished. Vanished! A concerted search led by the ship's captain and the Maltese secret service failed to uncover her whereabouts, though a rubber crutch-tip turned up in a crevice, and a local archaeologist said there seemed to be one more stone than usual, somehow.

Then, at sea, the captain's Bolivian fiancée, with her striped poncho and bowler hat, began to dress diaphanously and to drape herself at the U-shaped bar with the ship's purser for hours at a time, while the stern-visaged captain steadfastly steered the ship. The purser was a grave, mustached young man given to exceedingly slow calculations, as he turned dollars into drachmas and dinars; lachrymosely reading a French translation of John Grisham by the ship's bathtub-sized pool while his surprisingly muscular body acquired a glowering, narcissistic tan, he had been thought by the passengers to be a still-closeted gay. Now he was revealed as a Lothario, a Prometheus flying in the face of authority, and all the female passengers began to need to have their money changed and their accounts audited; they found on the office door a sign saying HOURS / HEURES / HORAS / STUNDEN but not giving an hour, the blank space left blank.

One night, long after midnight, the passengers turned and moaned in their dreams as the ship made an unscheduled stop in mid-Mediterranean; the captain was putting his rival ashore on a barren rock, crinkled like papier-mâché, east of Ustica. Then in a rage he reduced his fiancée to the form of a bright-green parrot and wore her on his epauletted shoulder when he descended, fiery-eyed, from the bridge.

He was an erect middle-aged Samothracian, very proud, his uniform very clean. The parrot kept twisting its glistening small head and affirming, with a croak and a lisp, '*Sí. Sí.*'

But most marvellous was what happened to old Mr Breadloaf. He was the oldest passenger, well into his eighties. His mouth lacked a number of its teeth but he smiled nevertheless, at a benign slant; his white countenance was rendered eerie by the redness of the sagging lids below his eyes, like two bright breves on an otherwise unaccented page. From Djerba, a group including the elderly gentleman passed over to the Tunisian mainland on a ferry noisome with Mercedes-Benz diesel trucks. A bus met the cruise passengers and carried them through miles of olive groves to the ruin of a Roman city in Gigthis. Here, close to the sea, pale stones – pavements, steps, shattered columns, inverted Corinthian capitals – still conveyed the sense of a grid; milling about in their running shoes and blue cruise badges, the Americans could feel the presence of an ancient hope, an order projected from afar. AVRELIO VERO CAESARI GIGTHENSIS PUBLICE, an upstanding reddish stone stated. Killer stood on a truncated pillar and, with a jaunty diction originally designed to capture the attention of inner-city students, translated it for them: 'I, the emperor Aurelius, be sending you this boss little Roman town, with its forum and shops and public baths and spiffy grid street-plan, as a sample of what the power of Rome can do for *you*. Yo, guys, get with the program!'

Dinnertime was nearing; the bus drivers, slim men with two-day beards, smoking over in the dunes, were letting their Arabic conversation become louder, as a sign of growing impatience. The blue sky above them was turning dull; parallel shadows were lengthening in the orderly ruins. But as the tourists began to gather and to straggle toward the bus through the collapsed arcades of limestone, Mr Breadloaf, standing alone in a paved space like a slightly tilting column, was transfigured. He grew taller. His cane dangled down like a candy cane, and his knobby old hand released it with a clatter. His irradiated white face spread out along a smiling diagonal bias. His wife of fifty-six years, hard of sight and hearing both, stared upward in habitual admiration. Her husband's radiance was by now quite diffuse, and his disturbing eyelids were smeared into two thin red cloudlets near the horizon, above the storied wine-dark sea. Mr Breadloaf had become a sunset – the haunting end to a day satisfyingly full of sights.

Ah, as the ancients knew, nothing lasts. The lovers' supernal bliss was disturbed on the eleventh night by Calypso's repeated sniffing. 'There's a funny smell in this cabin,' she said. 'Worse than funny. It's terrible.'

Neuman felt insulted. 'Do you think it's me?'

She bent down and sniffed his chest, his armpits. 'No. You're normal masculine. Nice.' She dismounted him gingerly and walked, nude, around his cabin, opening doors, bending down, sniffing. Glimmers from the starboard lights, bounced back by the waves, spotlit now her squarish buttocks, now the crescent of her shoulders and the swaying fall of her hair, unbound from its pins of spiralled gold wire. Her voice pounced: 'It's in here, down low.' She was at his closet, in the narrow corridor to his bathroom. 'Oh, it's *foul.*'

They turned on the light. There was nothing there but his shoes, including a pair of sandals he had bought in a row of shops near Houmt Souk. 'One dollar, one dollar,' the Tunisian outside had been chanting, but when Neuman went inside and was trapped in a rear room between walls of worked leather and horsehair fly whisks and souvenir mugs with a picture of the Aragonese fort on them, men kept tapping him and thrusting sandals in his face and saying, 'Thirty-five dollars, only thirty-five.' He had panicked, but as he crouched to barrel his way through the scrum and back into the open a voice had said, 'Ten,' and he – as keen as Odysseus to avoid unnecessary violence – had said, 'It's a deal.' The sandals were beige and cut rather flatteringly, he thought, across his instep. He had worn them once or twice to the ship's pool, which had been deserted since the Grisham-reading purser had been marooned for hubris.

Calypso held the sandals up close to her pretty white Doric nose, with its sunburned nostril wings. 'Ugh,' she said. 'Fish. Rotten fish. They used fish glue to hold the soles on. Throw them *out*, honey.'

Her tone reminded Neuman unpleasantly of his land wife, his legal wife, thousands of air-miles away. 'Listen,' he told her. 'I paid good money for those sandals. I risked my hide for them; suppose one of those guys in the back room had pulled a knife.'

'They were poor Tunisians,' she sniffed, 'trying to make a sale to a disgusting rich Westerner. You like to dramatize every little encounter. But you're wrong if you think I'm going to keep making love to a man whose cabin smells of dead fish.'

'I didn't even notice the smell,' he argued.

'You're not immensely sensitive, I can only conclude.'

'If you were really as carried away by me as you pretend, you wouldn't have noticed.'

'I *am* carried away, but I'm not rendered absolutely insensible. Drop those sandals overboard, Neuman, or do the rest of this cruise by yourself.'

'Let's compromise. I'll wrap them in a plastic shirt bag and tuck them under my dirty laundry.'

She accepted his compromise, but the relationship had

taken a wound. The islands seen through the porthole kept coming, faster and faster: Stromboli, Panarea, Lipari, Sicily. In the Strait of Messina, they held their breaths, between the Scylla of having loved and lost and the Charybdis of never having loved at all.

On Corfu, supposedly the land of the obliging Phaeacians, who turned Ulysses from a scruffy castaway into a well-fed, well-clad guest worthy of being returned to the island where he was king, Calypso took a dislike to the Achilleion Palace, built in 1890 to humor the Empress Elizabeth of Austria's extraordinary fondness for Achilles. 'It's so *pseu*do,' she said. 'It's so *Ger*man.'

Her dislike of his sandals' fishy smell still rankled with Neuman. 'To me,' he said, 'this grand villa in the neoclassical style has a lovely late-Victorian charm. Statues without broken noses and arms, for once, and infused with a scientific sensibility. Who says the nineteenth century couldn't sculpt? See how with what charming anatomical accuracy the boy and the dolphin, here in the fountain, are intertwined! And look, darling, in Ernst Herter's *Dying Achilles*, how the flesh of the tendon puckers around the arrow, as it were erotically! Scrap the "as it were." It *is* erotic. It's *us*.'

But she was harder to beguile, to amuse, each day. In anticipation of the injury that her susceptible, vain, and divine nature would soon suffer, she was trying to make their inevitable parting her own deed. No longer riding the boat's rise and fall, she huddled deep under the blankets beside him as the wistful scattered lights of coastal Greece and benighted Albania slid away to port. Just the sun-kissed pink tip of her Doric nose showed, and when he touched it, it, too, withdrew into the carapace of blankets.

At the Nekromanteion of Ephyra, once thought to be the mouth of Hades, they were led, in stark sunlight, through the maze that credulous pilgrims had long ago traced in the dark, in an ordeal that took days and many offerings. The modern pilgrims were shown the subterranean room where the priests shouted oracles up through the stone floor of the final chamber. The stones smelled of all those past lives, stumbling from birth to death by the flickering light of illusion.

In the little fan-shaped lecture hall, with its feeble slide projector and slippery green blackboard that resisted the imprint of chalk, Homer tried to prepare them for Ithaca. His sallow triangular face was especially melancholy, lit from beneath by the dim lectern bulb. The end of the journey meant for him the return to his university – its rosy-cheeked students invincible in their ignorance, its demonic faculty politics, its clamorous demands for ever-higher degrees of political correctness and cultural diversity. 'ΚΡΙΝΩ,' he wrote on the blackboard, pronouncing, '*krino* – to discern, to be able to distinguish the real from the unreal. To do this, we need *noos*, mind, consciousness.' He wrote, then, 'ΝΟΟΣ.' His face illumined from underneath was as eerie as that of a jack-in-the-box or a prompter hissing lines to stymied thespians. 'We need *no-os*,' he pronounced, scrabbling with his invisible chalk in a fury of insertion, 'to achieve our *nos-tos*, our homecoming.' He stood aside to reveal the completed word: ΝΟΣΤΟΣ. In afterthought he rapidly rubbed out two of the letters, created ΠΟΝΤΟΣ, and added with a small sly smile, 'After our crossing together of the sea, the *pontos*.'

And the marvellous thing about Ithaca was that it *did* feel like a homecoming, to the quintessential islands, green and brimming with memories and precipitous: *ithaki*, precipitous. The bus taking them up the hairpin road to the monastery of Kathara and to Ulysses' *soi-disant* citadel repeatedly had to back around, with much labored chuffing of the engine and tortured squealing of the brakes. Had the driver's foot slipped, Calypso and Neuman, sitting in the back holding hands, would have been among the first tourists killed, the bus sliding and tumbling down, down in Peckinpahish slow motion, over the creamy white crags of Korax down to the wooded plateau of Marathia, where loyal Eumaeus had watered his pigs and plotted with the returned monarch his slaughter of the suitors – the suitors whose only fault, really, had been to pick up on the languishing queen's mixed signals. The lovers' hands gripped, as tightly as their loins had gripped, at the thought of the long fall with death – *aiae!* – at the end.

But the driver, a tough local kid called Telemachus, drove this route all the time. In the monastery, bougainvillea was in bloom and a demented old blind monk waggled his hand for money and occasionally shrieked, sitting there on a stone bench intricately shaded by grapevines. 'At home, he'd be homeless,' Neuman shyly said.

'Somehow,' she said, unsmiling, 'it offends me, the suggestion that one must be insane to be religious.' A dirty white dog slept before a blue door, a blue of such an ineffable rightness that Calypso photographed it with bracketed exposure times. Below them, the cruise ship was as white as a sliver of soap resting on the bottom of a sapphire bathtub whose sides were mountainsides.

The bus went down a different way, and stopped at the sunny, terraced village of Stavros. Here in a small park a bust of Odysseus awaited them. Neuman posed for Calypso's camera beside it; though Neuman had no bronze beard, there was a resemblance, that of all men to one another. Wanderers, deserters, returners. Now in a mood of terminal holiday the

Harvard graduates posed for the Yale graduates, and vice versa, while those marginal cruise passengers from Columbia and the University of Chicago looked on scornfully.

Calypso and Neuman drifted away from the square with its monuments and taverna, and found a small store down a side street, where they bought souvenir scarves and aprons, baskets and vases for their spouses and children. He said, thinking of the grip of her loins, so feminine yet no-nonsense, 'I can't bear it.'

'Life is a voyage,' Calypso said. 'We take our pleasure at a price. The price is loss.'

'Don't lecture me,' he begged.

She shrugged, suggesting, 'Stay with me, then, and I'll make you divine. This was the last gasp of your youth. With me, you will be eternally youthful and never die.'

Neuman would never forget the electric, static quality she projected, there with her arms full of cloth and her hands full of drachmas, staring at him in the wake of this celestial challenge with irises as multiform as hydrangea blooms. Did her lower lip tremble? This was as vulnerable as the daughter of Oceanus could allow herself to appear. The disconcerted mortal defended himself as best he could, by distinguishing the real from the unreal: 'I am a mere man. Only gods and animals can withstand the monotony of eternity, however paradisiacal.'

She snapped her profile at him, with a wisecrack: 'So now who's lecturing?'

By mutual agreement they slept, on this last night at sea, in separate cabins. But at four in the morning, Aurora Mergenthaler, their melodious chief stewardess, announced to every cabin over the loudspeaking system that the ship was about to pass through the Corinth Canal. The project, cherished by Periander and Caligula, and actually begun by

Nero, had been taken up by a French company in 1882 and completed by the Greeks in 1893. The canal is four miles long, twenty-four yards wide, and two hundred sixty feet at the highest point. Dug entirely by hand, it transformed the Peloponnesus from a peninsula into an island.

In the dark of the hour, the walls of earth slid by ominously, growing higher and higher. There seemed to be many horizons, marked by receding bluish lights. The ship, formerly so free, plodded forward in the channel like a blinkered ox. The damp upper deck was surprisingly well populated by conscientious cruisers, some wearing ghostly pajamas, others sporting fanciful jogging outfits, and still others fully dressed for disembarkation on the mainland at Piraeus. Personalities that had grown distinct over the days now melted back into dim shapes: shades. Calypso was not among them. Or if she was – and Neuman searched, going from face to face with a thrashing heart – she had been transformed beyond recognition.

KURT VONNEGUT

THE CRUISE OF *THE JOLLY ROGER*

DURING THE Great Depression, Nathan Durant was homeless until he found a home in the United States Army. He spent seventeen years in the Army, thinking of the earth as terrain, of the hills and valleys as enfilade and defilade, of the horizon as something a man should never silhouette himself against, of the houses and woods and thickets as cover. It was a good life, and when he got tired of thinking about war, he got himself a girl and a bottle, and the next morning he was ready to think about war some more.

When he was thirty-six, an enemy projectile dropped into a command post under thick green cover in defilade in the terrain of Korea, and blew Major Durant, his maps, and his career through the wall of his tent.

He had always assumed that he was going to die young and gallantly. But he didn't die. Death was far, far away, and Durant faced unfamiliar and frightening battalions of peaceful years.

In the hospital, the man in the next bed talked constantly of the boat he was going to own when he was whole again. For want of exciting peacetime dreams of his own, for want of a home or family or civilian friends, Durant borrowed his neighbor's dream.

With a deep scar across his cheek, with the lobe of his right ear gone, with a stiff leg, he limped into a boatyard in New London, the port nearest the hospital, and bought a secondhand cabin cruiser. He learned to run it in the harbor there, christened the boat *The Jolly Roger* at the suggestion of some children who haunted the boatyard, and set out arbitrarily for Martha's Vineyard.

He stayed on the island but a day, depressed by the tranquility and permanence, by the feeling of deep, still lakes of time, by men and women so at one with the peace of the place as to have nothing to exchange with an old soldier but a few words about the weather.

Durant fled to Chatham, at the elbow of Cape Cod, and found himself beside a beautiful woman at the foot of a lighthouse there. Had he been in his old uniform, seeming as he'd liked to seem in the old days, about to leave on a dangerous mission, he and the woman might have strolled off together. Women had once treated him like a small boy with special permission to eat icing off cakes. But the woman looked away without interest. He was nobody and nothing. The spark was gone.

His former swashbuckling spirits returned for an hour or two during a brief blow off the dunes of Cape Cod's east coast, but there was no one aboard to notice. When he reached the sheltered harbor at Provincetown and went ashore, he was a hollow man again, who didn't have to be anywhere at any time, whose life was all behind him.

'Look up, please,' commanded a gaudily dressed young man with a camera in his hands and a girl on his arm.

Surprised, Durant did look up, and the camera shutter clicked. 'Thank you,' said the young man brightly.

'Are you a painter?' asked his girl.

'Painter?' said Durant. 'No – retired Army officer.'

The couple did a poor job of covering their disappointment.

'Sorry,' said Durant, and he felt dull and annoyed.

'Oh!' said the girl. 'There's some real painters over there.'

Durant glanced at the artists, three men and one woman, probably in their late twenties, who sat on the wharf, their backs to a silvered splintering pile, sketching. The woman, a tanned brunette, was looking right at Durant.

'Do you mind being sketched?' she said.

'No – no, I guess not,' said Durant bearishly. Freezing in his pose, he wondered what it was he'd been thinking about that had made him interesting enough to draw. He realized that he'd been thinking about lunch, about the tiny galley aboard *The Jolly Roger*, about the four wrinkled wieners, the half-pound of cheese, and the flat remains of a quart of beer that awaited him there.

'There,' said the woman, 'you see?' She held out the sketch.

What Durant saw was a big, scarred, hungry man, hunched over and desolate as a lost child. 'Do I really look that bad?' he said, managing to laugh.

'Do you really feel that awful?'

'I was thinking of lunch. Lunch can be pretty terrible.'

'Not where we eat it,' she said. 'Why not come with us?'

Major Durant went with them, with the three men, Ed, Teddy, and Lou, who danced through a life that seemed full of funny secrets, and with the girl, Marion. He found he was relieved to be with others again, even with these others, and his step down the walk was jaunty.

At lunch, the four spoke of painting, ballet, and drama. Durant grew tired of counterfeiting interest, but he kept at it.

'Isn't the food good here?' said Marion, in a casual and polite aside.

'Um,' said Durant. 'But the shrimp sauce is flat. Needs –' He gave up. The four were off again in their merry whirlwind of talk.

'Did you just drive here?' said Teddy, when he saw Durant staring at him disapprovingly.

'No,' said Durant. 'I came in my boat.'

'A boat!' they echoed, excited, and Durant found himself center stage.

'What kind?' said Marion.

'Cabin cruiser,' said Durant.

Their faces fell. 'Oh,' said Marion, 'one of those floating tourist cabins with a motor.'

'Well,' said Durant, tempted to tell them about the blow he'd weathered, 'it's certainly no picnic when –'

'What's its name?' said Lou.

'*The Jolly Roger*,' said Durant.

The four exchanged glances, and then burst into laughter, repeating the boat's name, to Durant's consternation and bafflement.

'If you had a dog,' said Marion, 'I'll bet you'd call it Spot.'

'Seems like a perfectly good name for a dog,' said Durant, reddening.

Marion reached across the table and patted his hand. 'Aaaaaah, you lamb, you musn't mind us.' She was an irresponsibly affectionate woman, and appeared to have no idea how profoundly her touch was moving the lonely Durant, in spite of his resentment. 'Here we've been talking away and not letting you say a word,' she said. 'What is it you do in the Army?'

Durant was startled. He hadn't mentioned the Army, and there were no insignia on his faded khakis. 'Well, I was in Korea for a little while,' he said, 'and I'm out of the Army now because of wounds.'

The four were impressed and respectful. 'Do you mind talking about it?' said Ed.

Durant sighed. He did mind talking about it to Ed,

Teddy, and Lou, but he wanted very much for Marion to hear about it – wanted to show her that while he couldn't speak her language, he could speak one of his own that had life to it. 'No,' he said, 'there are some things that would just as well stay unsaid, but for the most part, why not talk about it?' He sat back and lit a cigarette, and squinted into the past as though through a thin screen of shrubs in a forward observation post.

'Well,' he said, 'we were over on the east coast, and . . .' He had never tried to tell the tale before, and now, in his eagerness to be glib and urbane, he found himself including details, large and small, as they occurred to him, until his tale was no tale at all, but a formless, unwieldy description of war as it had really seemed: a senseless, complicated mess that in the telling was first-rate realism but miserable entertainment.

He had been talking for twenty minutes now, and his audience had finished coffee and dessert, and two cigarettes apiece, and the waitress was getting restive about the check. Durant, florid and irritated with himself, was trying to manage a cast of thousands spread over the forty thousand square miles of South Korea. His audience was listening with glazed eyes, brightening at any sign that the parts were about to be brought together into a whole and thence to an end. But the signs were always false, and at last, when Marion swallowed her third yawn, Durant blew himself in his story through the wall of his tent and fell silent.

'Well,' said Teddy, 'it's hard for us who haven't seen it to imagine.'

'Words can hardly convey it,' said Marion. She patted Durant's hand again. 'You've been through so much, and you're so modest about it.'

'Nothing, really,' said Durant.

After a moment of silence, Marion stood. 'It's certainly been pleasant and interesting, Major,' she said, 'and we all wish you bon voyage on *The Jolly Roger.*'

And there it ended.

Back aboard *The Jolly Roger*, Durant finished the stale quart of beer and told himself he was ready to give up – to sell the boat, return to the hospital, put on a bathrobe, and play cards and thumb through magazines until doomsday.

Moodily he studied his charts for a course back to New London. It was then he realized that he was only a few miles from the home village of a friend who had been killed in the Second World War. It struck him as wryly fitting that he should call on this ghost on his way back.

He arrived at the village through an early-morning mist, the day before Memorial Day, feeling ghostlike himself. He made a bad landing that shook the village dock, and tied up *The Jolly Roger* with a clumsy knot.

When he reached the main street, he found it quiet but lined with flags. Only two other people were abroad to glance at the dour stranger.

He stepped into the post office and spoke to the brisk old woman who was sorting mail in a rickety cage.

'Pardon me,' said Durant, 'I'm looking for the Pefko family.'

'Pefko? Pefko?' said the postmistress. 'That doesn't sound like any name around here. Pefko? They summer people?'

'No – I don't think so. I'm sure they're not. They may have moved away a while ago.'

'Well, if they lived here, you'd think I'd know. They'd come here for their mail. There's only four hundred of us year around, and I never heard of any Pefko.'

The secretary from the law office across the street came

in and knelt by Durant, and worked the combination lock of her mailbox.

'Annie,' said the postmistress, 'you know about anybody named Pefko around here?'

'No,' said Annie, 'unless they had one of the summer cottages out on the dunes. It's hard to keep track of who is in those. They're changing hands all the time.'

She stood, and Durant saw that she was attractive in a determinedly practical way, without wiles or ornamentation. But Durant was now so convinced of his own dullness that his manner toward her was perfunctory.

'Look,' he said, 'my name is Durant, Major Nathan Durant, and one of my best friends in the Army was from here. George Pefko – I know he was from here. He said so, and so did all his records. I'm sure of it.'

'Ohhhhhh,' said Annie. 'Now wait, wait, wait. That's right – certainly. Now I remember.'

'You knew him?' said Durant.

'I knew *of* him,' said Annie. 'I know now who you're talking about: the one that got killed in the war.'

'I was with him,' said Durant.

'Still can't say as I remember him,' said the postmistress.

'You don't remember him, probably, but you remember the family,' said Annie. 'And they *did* live out on the dunes, too. Goodness, that was a long time ago – ten or fifteen years. Remember that big family that talked Paul Eldredge into letting them live in one of his summer cottages all winter? About six kids or more. That was the Pefkos. A wonder they didn't freeze to death, with nothing but a fireplace for heat. The old man came out here to pick cranberries, and stayed on through the winter.'

'Wouldn't exactly call this their hometown,' said the postmistress.

'George did,' said Durant.

'Well,' said Annie, 'I suppose one hometown was as good as another for young George. Those Pefkos were wanderers.'

'George enlisted from here,' said Durant. 'I suppose that's how he settled on it.' By the same line of reasoning, Durant had chosen Pittsburgh as his hometown, though a dozen other places had as strong a claim.

'One of those people who found a home in the Army,' said the postmistress. 'Scrawny, tough boy. I remember now. His family never got any mail. That was it, and they weren't church people. That's why I forgot. Drifters. He must have been about your brother's age, Annie.'

'I know. But I tagged after my brother all the time in those days, and George Pefko never had anything to do with his gang. They kept to themselves, the Pefkos did.'

'There must be somebody who remembers him well,' said Durant. 'Somebody who –' He let the sentence die on a note of urgency. It was unbearable that every vestige of George had disappeared, unmissed.

'Now that I think about it,' said Annie, 'I'm almost sure there's a square named after him.'

'A square?' said Durant.

'Not really a square,' said Annie. 'They just call it a square. When a man from around here gets killed in a war, the town names some little plot of town property after him – a traffic circle or something like that. They put up a plaque with his name on it. That triangle down by the village dock – I'm almost sure that was named for your friend.'

'It's hard to keep track of them all, *these* days,' said the postmistress.

'Would you like to go down and see it?' said Annie. 'I'll be glad to show you.'

'A plaque?' said Durant. 'Never mind.' He dusted his

hands. 'Well, which way is the restaurant – the one with a bar?'

'After June fifteenth, any way you want to go,' said the postmistress. 'But right now everything is closed and shuttered. You can get a sandwich at the drugstore.'

'I might as well move on,' said Durant.

'As long as you've come, you ought to stay for the parade,' said Annie.

'After seventeen years in the Army, that would be a real treat,' said Durant. 'What parade?'

'Memorial Day,' said Annie.

'That's tomorrow, I thought,' said Durant.

'The children march today. School is closed tomorrow,' said Annie. She smiled. 'I'm afraid you're going to have to endure one more parade, Major, because here it comes.'

Durant followed her apathetically out onto the sidewalk. He could hear the sound of a band, but the marchers weren't yet in sight. There were no more than a dozen people waiting for the parade to pass.

'They go from square to square,' said Annie. 'We really ought to wait for them down by George's.'

'Whatever you say,' said Durant. 'I'll be closer to the boat.'

They walked down the slope toward the village dock and *The Jolly Roger.*

'They keep up the squares very nicely,' said Annie.

'They always do, they always do,' said Durant.

'Are you in a hurry to get somewhere else today?'

'Me?' said Durant bitterly. 'Me? Nothing's waiting for me anywhere.'

'I see,' said Annie, startled. 'Sorry.'

'It isn't your fault.'

'I don't understand.'

'I'm an Army bum like George. They should have handed me a plaque and shot me. I'm not worth a dime to anybody.'

'Here's the square,' said Annie gently.

'Where? Oh – that.' The square was a triangle of grass, ten feet on a side, an accident of intersecting lanes and a footpath. In its center was a low boulder on which was fixed a small metal plaque, easily overlooked.

'George Pefko Memorial Square,' said Durant. 'By golly, I wonder what George would make of that?'

'He'd like it, wouldn't he?' said Annie.

'He'd probably laugh.'

'I don't see that there's anything to laugh about.'

'Nothing, nothing at all – except that it doesn't have much to do with anything, does it? Who cares about George? Why should anyone care about George? It's just what people are expected to do, put up plaques.'

The bandsmen were in sight now, all eight of them, teenagers, out of step, rounding a corner with confident, proud, sour, and incoherent noise intended to be music.

Before them rode the town policeman, fat with leisure, authority, leather, bullets, pistol, handcuffs, club, and a badge. He was splendidly oblivious to the smoking, backfiring motorcycle beneath him as he swept slowly back and forth before the parade.

Behind the band came a cloud of purple, seeming to float a few feet above the street. It was lilacs carried by children. Along the curb, teachers looking as austere as New England churches called orders to the children.

'The lilacs came in time this year,' said Annie. 'Sometimes they don't. It's touch-and-go.'

'That so?' said Durant.

A teacher blew a whistle. The parade halted, and Durant

found a dozen children bearing down on him, their eyes large, their arms filled with flowers, their knees lifted high.

Durant stepped aside.

A bugler played taps badly.

The children laid their flowers before the plaque on George Pefko Memorial Square.

'Lovely?' whispered Annie.

'Yes,' said Durant. 'It would make a statue want to cry. But what does it mean?'

'Tom,' called Annie to a small boy who had just laid down his flowers, 'why did you do that?'

The boy looked around guiltily. 'Do what?'

'Put the flowers down there,' said Annie.

'Tell them you're paying homage to one of the fallen valiant who selflessly gave his life,' prompted a teacher.

Tom looked at her blankly, and then back at the flowers.

'Don't you know?' said Annie.

'Sure,' said Tom at last. 'He died fighting so we could be safe and free. And we're thanking him with flowers, because it was a nice thing to do.' He looked up at Annie, amazed that she should ask. 'Everybody knows that.'

The policeman raced his motorcycle engine. The teacher shepherded the children back into line. The parade moved on.

'Well,' said Annie, 'are you sorry you had to endure one more parade, Major?'

'It's true, isn't it,' murmured Durant. 'It's so damn simple, and so easy to forget.' Watching the innocent marchers under the flowers, he was aware of life, the beauty and importance of a village at peace. 'Maybe I never knew – never had any way of knowing. This *is* what war is about, isn't it. This.'

Durant laughed. 'George, you homeless, horny, wild old

rummy,' he said to George Pefko Memorial Square, 'damned if you didn't turn out to be a saint.'

The old spark was back. Major Durant, home from the wars, was somebody.

'I wonder,' he said to Annie, 'if you'd have lunch with me, and then, maybe, we could go for a ride in my boat.'

PATRICIA HIGHSMITH

ONE FOR THE ISLANDS

THE VOYAGE WASN'T to be much longer.

Most people were bound for the mainland, which was not far at all now. Others were bound for the islands to the west, some of which were very far indeed.

Dan was bound for a certain island that he believed probably farther than any of the others the ship would touch at. He supposed that he would be about the last passenger to disembark.

On the sixth day of the smooth, uneventful voyage, he was in excellent spirits. He enjoyed the company of his fellow-passengers, had joined them a few times in the games that were always in progress on the top deck forward, but mostly he strolled the deck with his pipe in his mouth and a book under his arm, the pipe unlighted and the book forgotten, gazing serenely at the horizon and thinking of the island to which he was going. It would be the finest island of them all, Dan imagined. For some months now, he had devoted much of his time to imagining its terrain. There was no doubt, he decided finally, that he knew more about his island than any man alive, a fact which made him smile whenever he thought of it. No, no one would ever know a hundredth of what he knew about his island, though he had never seen it. But then, perhaps no one else had ever seen it, either.

Dan was happiest when strolling the deck, alone, letting his eyes drift from soft cloud to horizon, from sun to sea, thinking always that his island might come into view before the mainland. He would know its outline at once, he was sure of that. Strangely, it would be like a place he had always known, but secretly, telling no one. And there he would finally be alone.

It startled him sometimes, unpleasantly, too, suddenly to encounter, face to face, a passenger coming round a corner. He found it disturbing to bump into a hurrying steward in one of the twisting, turning corridors of D-deck, which being third class was more like a catacomb than the rest, and which was the deck where Dan had his cabin. Then there had been the time, the second day of the voyage, when for an instant he saw very close to his eyes the ridged floor of the corridor, with a cigarette butt between two ridges, a chewing-gum wrapper, and a few discarded matches. That had been unpleasant, too.

'Are you for the mainland?' asked Mrs Gibson-Leyden, one of the first-class passengers, as they stood at the rail one evening.

Dan smiled a little and shook his head. 'No, the islands,' he said pleasantly, rather surprised that Mrs Gibson-Leyden didn't know by now. But on the other hand, there had been little talk among the passengers as to where each was going. 'You're for the mainland, I take it?' He spoke to be friendly knowing quite well that Mrs Gibson-Leyden was for the mainland.

'Oh, yes,' Mrs Gibson-Leyden said. 'My husband had some idea of going to an island, but I said, not for me!'

She laughed with an air of satisfaction, and Dan nodded. He liked Mrs Gibson-Leyden because she was cheerful. It was more than could be said for most of the first-class passengers. Now he leaned his forearms on the rail and looked out at the wake of moonlight on the sea that shimmered like the back of a gigantic sea dragon with silver scales. Dan couldn't imagine that anyone would go to the mainland when there were islands in abundance, but then he had never been able to understand such things, and with a person like Mrs Gibson-Leyden, there was no use in trying to discuss them and to understand. Dan drew gently on his empty pipe. He could smell a fragrance of lavender cologne from Mrs Gibson-Leyden's direction. It reminded him of a girl he had once known, and he was amused now that he could feel drawn to Mrs Gibson-Leyden, certainly old enough to have been his mother, because she wore a familiar scent.

'Well, I'm supposed to meet my husband back in the game room,' Mrs Gibson-Leyden said, moving away. 'He went down to get a sweater.'

Dan nodded, awkwardly now. Her departure made him feel abandoned, absurdly lonely, and immediately he reproached himself for not having made more of an effort at communication with her. He smiled, straightened, and peered into the darkness over his left shoulder, where the mainland would appear before dawn, then his island, later.

Two people, a man and a woman, walked slowly down the deck, side by side, their figures quite black in the darkness. Dan was conscious of their separateness from each other. Another isolated figure, short and fat, moved into the light of the windows in the superstructure: Dr Eubanks, Dan recognized. Forward, Dan saw a group of people standing on deck and at the rails, all isolated, too. He had a vision of stewards and stewardesses below, eating their solitary meals at tiny tables in the corridors, hurrying about with towels, trays, menus. They were all alone, too. There was nobody who touched anybody, he thought, no man who held his wife's hand, no lovers whose lips met – at least he hadn't seen any so far on this voyage.

Dan straightened still taller. An overwhelming sense of aloneness, of his own isolation, had taken possession of him, and because his impulse was to shrink within himself, he unconsciously stood as tall as he could. But he could not look at the ship any longer, and turned back to the sea.

It seemed to him that only the moon spread its arms, laid its web protectively, lovingly, over the sea's body. He stared at the veils of moonlight as hard as he could, for as long as he could – which was perhaps twenty-five seconds – then went below to his cabin and to sleep.

He was awakened by the sound of running feet on the deck, and a murmur of excited voices.

The mainland, he thought at once, and threw off his bedcovers. He did want a good look at the mainland. Then as his head cleared of sleep, he realized that the excitement on deck must be about something else. There was more running now, a woman's wondering 'Oh!' that was half a scream, half an exclamation of pleasure. Dan hurried into his clothes and ran out of his cabin.

His view from the A-deck companionway made him stop and draw in his breath. The ship was sailing *downward*, had been sailing downward on a long, broad path in the sea itself. Dan had never seen anything like it. No one else had either, apparently. No wonder everyone was so excited.

'When?' asked a man who was running after the hurrying captain. 'Did you see it? What happened?'

The captain had no time to answer him.

'It's all right. This is right,' said a petty officer, whose calm, serious face contrasted strangely with the wide-eyed alertness of everyone else.

'One doesn't notice it below,' Dan said quickly to Mr Steyne who was standing near him, and felt idiotic at once, because what did it matter whether one felt it below or not?

The ship was sailing downward, the sea sloped downward at about a twenty degree angle with the horizon, and such a thing had never been heard of before, even in the Bible.

Dan ran to join the passengers who were crowding the forward deck. 'When did it start? I mean, where?' Dan asked the person nearest him.

The person shrugged, though his face was as excited, as anxious as the rest.

Dan strained to see what the water looked like at the side of the swath, for the slope did not seem more than two miles broad. But whatever was happening, whether the swath ended in a sharp edge or sloped up to the main body of the sea, he could not make out, because a fine mist obscured the sea on either side. Now he noticed the golden light that lay on everything around them, the swath, the atmosphere, the horizon before them. The light was no stronger on one side than on the other, so it could not have been the sun. Dan couldn't find the sun, in fact. But the rest of the sky and the higher body of the sea behind them was bright as morning.

'Has anybody seen the mainland?' Dan asked, interrupting the babble around him.

'No,' said a man.

'There's no mainland,' said the same unruffled petty officer.

Dan had a sudden feeling of having been duped.

'This is right,' the petty officer added laconically. He was winding a thin line around and round his arm, bracing it on palm and elbow.

'Right?' asked Dan.

'This is it,' said the petty officer.

'That's right, this is it,' a man at the rail confirmed, speaking over his shoulder.

'No islands, either?' asked Dan, alarmed.

'No,' said the petty officer, not unkindly, but in an abrupt way that hurt Dan in his breast.

'Well – what's all this talk about the mainland?' Dan asked.

'Talk,' said the petty officer, with a twinkle now.

'Isn't it won-derful!' said a woman's voice behind him, and Dan turned to see Mrs Gibson-Leyden – Mrs Gibson-Leyden who had been so eager for the mainland – gazing rapturously at the empty white and gold mist.

'Do you know about this? How much farther does it go?' asked Dan, but the petty officer was gone. Dan wished he could be as calm as everyone else – generally he was calmer – but how could he be calm about his vanished island? How could the rest just stand there at the rails, for the most part taking it all quite calmly, he could tell by the voices now and their casual postures.

Dan saw the petty officer again and ran after him. 'What happens?' he asked. 'What happens next?' His questions struck him as foolish, but they were as good as any.

'This is *it*,' said the petty officer with a smile. 'Good God, boy!'

Dan bit his lips.

'This is *it*!' repeated the petty officer. 'What did you expect?'

Dan hesitated. 'Land,' he said in a voice that made it almost a question.

The petty officer laughed silently and shook his head. 'You can get off any time you like.'

Dan gave a startled look around him. It was true, people were getting off at the port rail, stepping over the side with their suitcases. 'Onto what?' Dan asked, aghast.

The petty officer laughed again, and disdaining to answer him, walked slowly away with his coiled line.

Dan caught his arm. 'Get off here? Why?'

'As good a place as any. Whatever spot strikes your fancy.' The petty officer chuckled. 'It's all alike.'

'All sea?'

'There's no sea,' said the petty officer. 'But there's certainly no land.'

And there went Mr and Mrs Gibson-Leyden now, off the starboard rail.

'Hey!' Dan called to them, but they didn't turn.

Dan watched them disappear quickly. He blinked his eyes. They had not been holding hands, but they had been near each other, they had been together.

Suddenly Dan realized that if he got off the boat as they had done, he could still be alone, if he wanted to be. It was strange, of course, to think of stepping out into space. But the instant he was able to conceive it, barely conceive it, it became right to do it. He could feel it filling him with a gradual but overpowering certainty, that he only reluctantly yielded to. This was right, as the petty officer had said. And this was as good a place as any.

Dan looked around him. The boat was really almost empty now. He might as well be last, he thought. He'd meant to be last. He'd go down and get his suitcase packed. What a nuisance! The mainland passengers, of course, had been packed since the afternoon before.

Dan turned impatiently on the companionway where he had once nearly fallen, and he climbed up again. He didn't want his suitcase after all. He didn't want anything with him.

He put a foot up on the starboard rail and stepped off. He walked several yards on an invisible ground that was softer than grass. It wasn't what he had thought it would be like, yet now that he was here, it wasn't strange, either. In fact there was even that sense of recognition that he had imagined he would feel when he set foot on his island. He turned for a last look at the ship that was still on its downward course. Then suddenly, he was impatient with himself. Why look at a ship, he asked himself, and abruptly turned and went on.

SURVIVAL AT SEA

STEPHEN CRANE

THE OPEN BOAT

A tale intended to be after the fact. Being the experience of four men from the sunk steamer Commodore

I

NONE OF THEM knew the color of the sky. Their eyes glanced level, and were fastened upon the waves that swept toward them. These waves were of the hue of slate, save for the tops, which were of foaming white, and all of the men knew the colors of the sea. The horizon narrowed and widened, and dipped and rose, and at all times its edge was jagged with waves that seemed thrust up in points like rocks.

Many a man ought to have a bath-tub larger than the boat which here rode upon the sea. These waves were most wrongfully and barbarously abrupt and tall, and each froth-top was a problem in small boat navigation.

The cook squatted in the bottom and looked with both eyes at the six inches of gunwale which separated him from the ocean. His sleeves were rolled over his fat forearms, and the two of his unbuttoned vest dangled as he bent to bail out the boat. Often he said: 'Gawd! That was a narrow clip.' As he remarked it he invariably gazed eastward over the broken sea.

The oiler, steering with one of the two oars in the boat, sometimes raised himself suddenly to keep clear of water that swirled in over the stern. It was a thin little oar and it seemed often ready to snap.

The correspondent, pulling at the other oar, watched the waves and wondered why he was there.

The injured captain, lying in the bow, was at this time buried in that profound dejection and indifference which comes, temporarily at least, to even the bravest and most enduring when, willy nilly, the firm fails, the army loses, the ship goes down. The mind of the master of a vessel is rooted deep in the timbers of her, though he command for a day or a decade, and this captain had on him the stern impression of a scene in the grays of dawn of seven turned faces, and later a stump of a top-mast with a white ball on it that slashed to and fro at the waves, went low and lower, and down. Thereafter there was something strange in his voice. Although steady, it was deep with mourning, and of a quality beyond oration or tears.

'Keep'er a little more south, Billie,' said he.

' "A little more south," sir,' said the oiler in the stern.

A seat in this boat was not unlike a seat upon a bucking bronco, and, by the same token, a bronco is not much smaller. The craft pranced and reared, and plunged like an animal. As each wave came, and she rose for it, she seemed like a horse making at a fence outrageously high. The manner of her scramble over these walls of water is a mystic thing, and, moreover, at the top of them were ordinarily these problems in white water, the foam racing down from the summit of each wave, requiring a new leap, and a leap from the air. Then, after scornfully bumping a crest, she would slide, and race, and splash down a long incline and arrive bobbing and nodding in front of the next menace.

A singular disadvantage of the sea lies in the fact that after successfully surmounting one wave you discover that there is another behind it just as important and just as nervously anxious to do something effective in the way of swamping boats. In a ten-foot dinghy one can get an idea of the resources of the sea in the line of waves that is not probable to the average experience, which is never at sea in a dinghy. As each slaty wall of water approached, it shut all else from the view of the men in the boat, and it was not difficult to imagine that this particular wave was the final outburst of the ocean, the last effort of the grim water. There was a terrible grace in the move of the waves, and they came in silence, save for the snarling of the crests.

In the wan light, the faces of the men must have been gray. Their eyes must have glinted in strange ways as they gazed steadily astern. Viewed from a balcony, the whole thing would doubtlessly have been weirdly picturesque. But the men in the boat had no time to see it, and if they had had leisure there were other things to occupy their minds. The sun swung steadily up the sky, and they knew it was broad day because the color of the sea changed from slate to emerald-green, streaked with amber lights, and the foam was like tumbling snow. The process of the breaking day was unknown to them. They were aware only of this effect upon the color of the waves that rolled toward them.

In disjointed sentences the cook and the correspondent argued as to the difference between a life-saving station and a house of refuge. The cook had said: 'There's a house of refuge just north of the Mosquito Inlet Light, and as soon as they see us, they'll come off in their boat and pick us up.'

'As soon as who see us?' said the correspondent.

'The crew,' said the cook.

'Houses of refuge don't have crews,' said the correspondent. 'As I understand them, they are only places where clothes and grub are stored for the benefit of shipwrecked people. They don't carry crews.'

'Oh, yes, they do,' said the cook.

'No, they don't,' said the correspondent.

'Well, we're not there yet, anyhow,' said the oiler, in the stern.

'Well,' said the cook, 'perhaps it's not a house of refuge that I'm thinking of as being near Mosquito Inlet Light. Perhaps it's a life-saving station.'

'We're not there yet,' said the oiler, in the stern.

II

As the boat bounced from the top of each wave, the wind tore through the hair of the hatless men, and as the craft plopped her stern down again the spray slashed past them. The crest of each of these waves was a hill, from the top of which the men surveyed, for a moment, a broad tumultuous expanse, shining and wind-riven. It was probably splendid. It was probably glorious, this play of the free sea, wild with lights of emerald and white and amber.

'Bully good thing it's an on-shore wind,' said the cook. 'If not, where would we be? Wouldn't have a show.'

'That's right,' said the correspondent.

The busy oiler nodded his assent.

Then the captain, in the bow, chuckled in a way that expressed humor, contempt, tragedy, all in one. 'Do you think we've got much of a show, now, boys?' said he.

Whereupon the three were silent, save for a trifle of hemming and hawing. To express any particular optimism at this time they felt to be childish and stupid, but they all doubtless possessed this sense of the situation in their mind. A young man thinks doggedly at such times. On the other hand, the ethics of their condition was decidedly against any open suggestion of hopelessness. So they were silent.

'Oh, well,' said the captain, soothing his children, 'we'll get ashore all right.'

But there was that in his tone which made them think, so the oiler quoth: 'Yes! If this wind holds!'

The cook was bailing. 'Yes! If we don't catch hell in the surf.'

Canton flannel gulls flew near and far. Sometimes they sat down on the sea, near patches of brown sea-weed that rolled over the waves with a movement like carpets on a line in a gale. The birds sat comfortably in groups, and they were envied by some in the dinghy, for the wrath of the sea was no more to them than it was to a covey of prairie chickens a thousand miles inland. Often they came very close and stared at the men with black bead-like eyes. At these times they were uncanny and sinister in their unblinking scrutiny, and the men hooted angrily at them, telling them to be gone. One came, and evidently decided to alight on the top of the captain's head. The bird flew parallel to the boat and did not circle, but made short sidelong jumps in the air in chicken-fashion. His black eyes were wistfully fixed upon the captain's head. 'Ugly brute,' said the oiler to the bird. 'You look as if you were made with a jack-knife.' The cook and the correspondent swore darkly at the creature. The captain naturally wished to knock it away with the end of the heavy painter, but he did not dare do it, because anything resembling an emphatic gesture would have capsized this freighted boat, and so with his open hand, the captain gently and carefully waved the gull away. After it had been discouraged from the pursuit the captain breathed easier on account of his hair, and others breathed easier because the bird struck their minds at this time as being somehow grewsome and ominous.

In the meantime the oiler and the correspondent rowed. And also they rowed.

They sat together in the same seat, and each rowed an oar. Then the oiler took both oars; then the correspondent took both oars; then the oiler; then the correspondent. They rowed and they rowed. The very ticklish part of the business was when the time came for the reclining one in the stern to take his turn at the oars. By the very last star of truth, it is easier to steal eggs from under a hen than it was to change seats in the dinghy. First the man in the stern slid his hand along the thwart and moved with care, as if he were of Sèvres. Then the man in the rowing seat slid his hand along the other thwart. It was all done with the most extraordinary care. As the two sidled past each other, the whole party kept watchful eyes on the coming wave, and the captain cried: 'Look out now! Steady there!'

The brown mats of sea-weed that appeared from time to time were like islands, bits of earth. They were travelling, apparently, neither one way nor the other. They were, to all intents, stationary. They informed the men in the boat that it was making progress slowly toward the land.

The captain, rearing cautiously in the bow, after the dinghy soared on a great swell, said that he had seen the lighthouse at Mosquito Inlet. Presently the cook remarked that he had seen it. The correspondent was at the oars, then, and for some reason he too wished to look at the lighthouse, but his back was toward the far shore and the waves were important, and for some time he could not seize an opportunity to turn his head. But at last there came a wave more gentle than the others, and when at the crest of it he swiftly scoured the western horizon.

'See it?' said the captain.

'No,' said the correspondent, slowly, 'I didn't see anything.'

'Look again,' said the captain. He pointed. 'It's exactly in that direction.'

At the top of another wave, the correspondent did as he

was bid, and this time his eyes chanced on a small still thing on the edge of the swaying horizon. It was precisely like the point of a pin. It took an anxious eye to find a lighthouse so tiny.

'Think we'll make it, Captain?'

'If this wind holds and the boat don't swamp, we can't do much else,' said the captain.

The little boat, lifted by each towering sea, and splashed viciously by the crests, made progress that in the absence of sea-weed was not apparent to those in her. She seemed just a wee thing wallowing, miraculously, top-up, at the mercy of five oceans. Occasionally, a great spread of water, like white flames, swarmed into her.

'Bail her, cook,' said the captain, serenely.

'All right, Captain,' said the cheerful cook.

III

It would be difficult to describe the subtle brotherhood of men that was here established on the seas. No one said that it was so. No one mentioned it. But it dwelt in the boat, and each man felt it warm him. They were a captain, an oiler, a cook, and a correspondent, and they were friends, friends in a more curiously iron-bound degree than may be common. The hurt captain, lying against the water-jar in the bow, spoke always in a low voice and calmly, but he could never command a more ready and swiftly obedient crew than the motley three of the dinghy. It was more than a mere recognition of what was best for the common safety. There was surely in it a quality that was personal and heart-felt. And after this devotion to the commander of the boat there was this comradeship that the correspondent, for instance, who had been taught to be cynical of men, knew even at the time was the best experience of his life. But no one said that it was so. No one mentioned it.

'I wish we had a sail,' remarked the captain. 'We might try my overcoat on the end of an oar and give you two boys a chance to rest.' So the cook and the correspondent held the mast and spread wide the overcoat. The oiler steered, and the little boat made good way with her new rig. Sometimes the oiler had to scull sharply to keep a sea from breaking into the boat, but otherwise sailing was a success.

Meanwhile the lighthouse had been growing slowly larger. It had now almost assumed color, and appeared like a little gray shadow on the sky. The man at the oars could not be prevented from turning his head rather often to try for a glimpse of this little gray shadow.

At last, from the top of each wave the men in the tossing boat could see land. Even as the lighthouse was an upright shadow on the sky, this land seemed but a long black shadow on the sea. It certainly was thinner than paper. 'We must be about opposite New Smyrna,' said the cook, who had coasted this shore often in schooners. 'Captain, by the way, I believe they abandoned that life-saving station there about a year ago.'

'Did they?' said the captain.

The wind slowly died away. The cook and the correspondent were not now obliged to slave in order to hold high the oar. But the waves continued their old impetuous swooping at the dinghy, and the little craft, no longer under way, struggled woundily over them. The oiler or the correspondent took the oars again.

Shipwrecks are *apropos* of nothing. If men could only train for them and have them occur when the men had reached pink condition, there would be less drowning at sea. Of the four in the dinghy none had slept any time worth mentioning for two days and two nights previous to embarking in the dinghy, and in the excitement of clambering about the deck of a foundering ship they had also forgotten to eat heartily.

For these reasons, and for others, neither the oiler nor the correspondent was fond of rowing at this time. The correspondent wondered ingenuously how in the name of all that was sane could there be people who thought it amusing to row a boat. It was not an amusement; it was a diabolical punishment, and even a genius of mental aberrations could never conclude that it was anything but a horror to the muscles and a crime against the back. He mentioned to the boat in general how the amusement of rowing struck him, and the weary-faced oiler smiled in full sympathy. Previously to the foundering, by the way, the oiler had worked double-watch in the engine-room of the ship.

'Take her easy, now, boys,' said the captain. 'Don't spend yourselves. If we have to run a surf you'll need all your strength, because we'll sure have to swim for it. Take your time.'

Slowly the land arose from the sea. From a black line it became a line of black and a line of white – trees and sand. Finally, the captain said that he could make out a house on the shore. 'That's the house of refuge, sure,' said the cook. 'They'll see us before long, and come out after us.'

The distant lighthouse reared high. 'The keeper ought to be able to make us out now, if he's looking through a glass,' said the captain. 'He'll notify the life-saving people.'

'None of those other boats could have got ashore to give word of the wreck,' said the oiler, in a low voice. 'Else the life-boat would be out hunting us.'

Slowly and beautifully the land loomed out of the sea. The wind came again. It had veered from the northeast to the southeast. Finally, a new sound struck the ears of the men in the boat. It was the low thunder of the surf on the shore. 'We'll never be able to make the lighthouse now,' said the captain. 'Swing her head a little more north, Billie.'

' "A little more north," sir,' said the oiler.

Whereupon the little boat turned her nose once more down the wind, and all but the oarsman watched the shore grow. Under the influence of this expansion doubt and direful apprehension was leaving the minds of the men. The management of the boat was still most absorbing, but it could not prevent a quiet cheerfulness. In an hour, perhaps, they would be ashore.

Their back-bones had become thoroughly used to balancing in the boat and they now rode this wild colt of a dinghy like circus men. The correspondent thought that he had been drenched to the skin, but happening to feel in the top pocket of his coat, he found therein eight cigars. Four of them were soaked with sea-water; four were perfectly scatheless. After a search, somebody produced three dry matches, and thereupon the four waifs rode impudently in their little boat, and with an assurance of an impending rescue shining in their eyes, puffed at the big cigars and judged well and ill of all men. Everybody took a drink of water.

IV

'Cook,' remarked the captain, 'there don't seem to be any signs of life about your house of refuge.'

'No,' replied the cook. 'Funny they don't see us!'

A broad stretch of lowly coast lay before the eyes of the men. It was of dunes topped with dark vegetation. The roar of the surf was plain, and sometimes they could see the white lip of a wave as it spun up the beach. A tiny house was blocked out black upon the sky. Southward, the slim lighthouse lifted its little gray length.

Tide, wind, and waves were swinging the dinghy northward. 'Funny they don't see us,' said the men.

The surf's roar was here dulled, but its tone was, nevertheless, thunderous and mighty. As the boat swam over the great rollers, the men sat listening to this roar. 'We'll swamp sure,' said everybody.

It is fair to say here that there was not a life-saving station within twenty miles in either direction, but the men did not know this fact and in consequence they made dark and opprobrious remarks concerning the eyesight of the nation's life-savers. Four scowling men sat in the dinghy and surpassed records in the invention of epithets.

'Funny they don't see us.'

The light-heartedness of a former time had completely faded. To their sharpened minds it was easy to conjure pictures of all kinds of incompetency and blindness and, indeed, cowardice. There was the shore of the populous land, and it was bitter and bitter to them that from it came no sign.

'Well,' said the captain, ultimately, 'I suppose we'll have to make a try for ourselves. If we stay out here too long, we'll none of us have strength left to swim after the boat swamps.'

And so the oiler, who was at the oars, turned the boat straight for the shore. There was a sudden tightening of muscles. There was some thinking.

'If we don't all get ashore –' said the captain. 'If we don't all get ashore, I suppose you fellows know where to send news of my finish?'

They then briefly exchanged some addresses and admonitions. As for the reflections of the men, there was a great deal of rage in them. Perchance they might be formulated thus: 'If I am going to be drowned – if I am going to be drowned – if I am going to be drowned, why, in the name of the seven mad gods who rule the sea, was I allowed to come thus far and contemplate sand and trees? Was I brought here merely to have my nose dragged away as I was about to nibble the sacred cheese of life? It is preposterous. If this old ninny-woman, Fate, cannot do better than this, she should be deprived of the management of men's fortunes. She is an old hen who knows not her intention. If she has decided to drown me, why did she not do it in the beginning and save me all this trouble. The whole affair is absurd. . . . But, no, she cannot mean to drown me. She dare not drown me. She cannot drown me. Not after all this work.' Afterward the man might have had an impulse to shake his fist at the clouds. 'Just you drown me, now, and then hear what I call you!'

The billows that came at this time were more formidable. They seemed always just about to break and roll over the little boat in a turmoil of foam. There was a preparatory and long growl in the speech of them. No mind unused to the sea would have concluded that the dinghy could ascend these sheer heights in time. The shore was still afar. The oiler was a wily surfman. 'Boys,' he said, swiftly, 'she won't live three minutes more and we're too far out to swim. Shall I take her to sea again, Captain?'

'Yes! Go ahead!' said the captain.

This oiler, by a series of quick miracles, and fast and steady oarsmanship, turned the boat in the middle of the surf and took her safely to sea again.

There was a considerable silence as the boat bumped over the furrowed sea to deeper water. Then somebody in gloom spoke. 'Well, anyhow, they must have seen us from the shore by now.'

The gulls went in slanting flight up the wind toward

the gray desolate cast. A squall, marked by dingy clouds, and clouds brick-red, like smoke from a burning building, appeared from the southeast.

'What do you think of those life-saving people? Ain't they peaches?'

'Funny they haven't seen us.'

'Maybe they think we're out here for sport! Maybe they think we're fishin'. Maybe they think we're damned fools.'

It was a long afternoon. A changed tide tried to force them southward, but wind and wave said northward. Far ahead, where coast-line, sea, and sky formed their mighty angle, there were little dots which seemed to indicate a city on the shore.

'St Augustine?'

The captain shook his head. 'Too near Mosquito Inlet.'

And the oiler rowed, and then the correspondent rowed. Then the oiler rowed. It was a weary business. The human back can become the seat of more aches and pains than are registered in books for the composite anatomy of a regiment. It is a limited area, but it can become the theatre of innumerable muscular conflicts, tangles, wrenches, knots, and other comforts.

'Did you ever like to row, Billie?' asked the correspondent.

'No,' said the oiler. 'Hang it.'

When one exchanged the rowing-seat for a place in the bottom of the boat, he suffered a bodily depression that caused him to be careless of everything save an obligation to wiggle one finger. There was cold sea-water swashing to and fro in the boat, and he lay in it. His head, pillowed on a thwart, was within an inch of the swirl of a wave crest, and sometimes a particularly obstreperous sea came in-board and drenched him once more. But these matters did not annoy him. It is almost certain that if the boat had capsized he would have tumbled comfortably out upon the ocean as if he felt sure that it was a great soft mattress.

'Look! There's a man on the shore!'

'Where?'

'There! See 'im? See 'im?'

'Yes, sure! He's walking along.'

'Now he's stopped. Look! He's facing us!'

'He's waving at us!'

'So he is! By thunder!'

'Ah, now, we're all right! Now we're all right! There'll be a boat out here for us in half an hour.'

'He's going on. He's running. He's going up to that house there.'

The remote beach seemed lower than the sea, and it required a searching glance to discern the little black figure. The captain saw a floating stick and they rowed to it. A bath-towel was by some weird chance in the boat, and, tying this on the stick, the captain waved it. The oarsman did not dare turn his head, so he was obliged to ask questions.

'What's he doing now?'

'He's standing still again. He's looking, I think. . . . There he goes again. Toward the house. . . . Now he's stopped again.'

'Is he waving at us?'

'No, not now! he was, though.'

'Look! There comes another man!'

'He's running.'

'Look at him go, would you.'

'Why, he's on a bicycle. Now he's met the other man. They're both waving at us. Look!'

'There comes something up the beach.'

'What the devil is that thing?'

'Why, it looks like a boat.'

'Why, certainly it's a boat.'

'No, it's on wheels.'

'Yes, so it is. Well, that must be the life-boat. They drag them along shore on a wagon.'

'That's the life-boat, sure.'

'No, by—, it's – it's an omnibus.'

'I tell you it's a life-boat.'

'It is not! It's an omnibus. I can see it plain. See? One of those big hotel omnibuses.'

'By thunder, you're right. It's an omnibus, sure as fate. What do you suppose they are doing with an omnibus? Maybe they are going around collecting the life-crew, hey?'

'That's it, likely. Look! There's a fellow waving a little black flag. He's standing on the steps of the omnibus. There come those other two fellows. Now they're all talking together. Look at the fellow with the flag. Maybe he ain't waving it!'

'That ain't a flag, is it? That's his coat. Why, certainly, that's his coat.'

'So it is. It's his coat. He's taken it off and is waving it around his head. But would you look at him swing it!'

'Oh, say, there isn't any life-saving station there. That's just a winter resort hotel omnibus that has brought over some of the boarders to see us drown.'

'What's that idiot with the coat mean? What's he signaling, anyhow?'

'It looks as if he were trying to tell us to go north. There must be a life-saving station up there.'

'No! He thinks we're fishing. Just giving us a merry hand. See? Ah, there, Willie.'

'Well, I wish I could make something out of those signals. What do you suppose he means?'

'He don't mean anything. He's just playing.'

'Well, if he'd just signal us to try the surf again, or to go to sea and wait, or go north, or go south, or go to hell – there would be some reason in it. But look at him. He just stands there and keeps his coat revolving like a wheel. The ass!'

'There come more people.'

'Now there's quite a mob. Look! Isn't that a boat?'

'Where? Oh, I see where you mean. No, that's no boat.'

'That fellow is still waving his coat.'

'He must think we like to see him do that. Why don't he quit it. It don't mean anything.'

'I don't know. I think he is trying to make us go north. It must be that there's a life-saving station there somewhere.'

'Say, he ain't tired yet. Look at 'im wave.'

'Wonder how long he can keep that up. He's been revolving his coat ever since he caught sight of us. He's an idiot. Why aren't they getting men to bring a boat out. A fishing boat – one of those big yawls – could come out here all right. Why don't he do something?'

'Oh, it's all right, now.'

'They'll have a boat out here for us in less than no time, now that they've seen us.'

A faint yellow tone came into the sky over the low land. The shadows on the sea slowly deepened. The wind bore coldness with it, and the men began to shiver.

'Holy smoke!' said one, allowing his voice to express his impious mood, 'if we keep on monkeying out here! If we've got to flounder out here all night!'

'Oh, we'll never have to stay here all night! Don't you worry. They've seen us now, and it won't be long before they'll come chasing out after us.'

The shore grew dusky. The man waving a coat blended gradually into this gloom, and it swallowed in the same manner the omnibus and the group of people. The spray, when it dashed uproariously over the side, made the voyagers shrink and swear like men who were being branded.

'I'd like to catch the chump who waved the coat. I feel like soaking him one, just for luck.'

'Why? What did he do?'

'Oh, nothing, but then he seemed so damned cheerful.'

In the meantime the oiler rowed, and then the correspondent rowed, and then the oiler rowed. Gray-faced and bowed forward, they mechanically, turn by turn, plied the leaden oars. The form of the lighthouse had vanished from the southern horizon, but finally a pale star appeared, just lifting from the sea. The streaked saffron in the west passed before the all-merging darkness, and the sea to the east was black. The land had vanished, and was expressed only by the low and drear thunder of the surf.

'If I am going to be drowned – if I am going to be drowned – if I am going to be drowned, why, in the name of the seven mad gods who rule the sea, was I allowed to come thus far and contemplate sand and trees? Was I brought here merely to have my nose dragged away as I was about to nibble the sacred cheese of life?'

The patient captain, drooped over the water-jar, was sometimes obliged to speak to the oarsman.

'Keep her head up! Keep her head up!'

' "Keep her head up," sir.' The voices were weary and low.

This was surely a quiet evening. All save the oarsman lay heavily and listlessly in the boat's bottom. As for him, his eyes were just capable of noting the tall black waves that swept forward in a most sinister silence, save for an occasional subdued growl of a crest.

The cook's head was on a thwart, and he looked without interest at the water under his nose. He was deep in other scenes. Finally he spoke. 'Billie,' he murmured, dreamfully, 'what kind of pie do you like best?'

V

'Pie,' said the oiler and the correspondent, agitatedly. 'Don't talk about those things, blast you!'

'Well,' said the cook, 'I was just thinking about ham sandwiches, and –'

A night on the sea in an open boat is a long night. As darkness settled finally, the shine of the light, lifting from the sea in the south, changed to full gold. On the northern horizon a new light appeared, a small bluish gleam on the edge of the waters. These two lights were the furniture of the world. Otherwise there was nothing but waves.

Two men huddled in the stern, and distances were so magnificent in the dinghy that the rower was enabled to keep his feet partly warmed by thrusting them under his companions. Their legs indeed extended far under the rowing-seat until they touched the feet of the captain forward. Sometimes, despite the efforts of the tired oarsman, a wave came piling into the boat, an icy wave of the night, and the chilling water soaked them anew. They would twist their bodies for a moment and groan, and sleep the dead sleep once more, while the water in the boat gurgled about them as the craft rocked.

The plan of the oiler and the correspondent was for one to row until he lost the ability, and then arouse the other from his sea-water couch in the bottom of the boat.

The oiler plied the oars until his head drooped forward, and the overpowering sleep blinded him. And he rowed yet afterward. Then he touched a man in the bottom of the boat, and called his name. 'Will you spell me for a little while?' he said, meekly.

'Sure, Billie,' said the correspondent, awakening and dragging himself to a sitting position. They exchanged places carefully, and the oiler, cuddling down in the sea-water at the cook's side, seemed to go to sleep instantly.

The particular violence of the sea had ceased. The waves came without snarling. The obligation of the man at the oars was to keep the boat headed so that the tilt of the rollers would not capsize her, and to preserve her from filling when the crests rushed past. The black waves were silent and hard to be seen in the darkness. Often one was almost upon the boat before the oarsman was aware.

In a low voice the correspondent addressed the captain. He was not sure that the captain was awake, although this iron man seemed to be always awake. 'Captain, shall I keep her making for that light north, sir?'

The same steady voice answered him. 'Yes. Keep it about two points off the port bow.'

The cook had tied a life-belt around himself in order to get even the warmth which this clumsy cork contrivance could donate, and he seemed almost stove-like when a rower, whose teeth invariably chattered wildly as soon as he ceased his labor, dropped down to sleep.

The correspondent, as he rowed, looked down at the two men sleeping under foot. The cook's arm was around the oiler's shoulders, and, with their fragmentary clothing and haggard faces, they were the babes of the sea, a grotesque rendering of the old babes in the wood.

Later he must have grown stupid at his work, for suddenly there was a growling of water, and a crest came with a roar and a swash into the boat, and it was a wonder that it did not set the cook afloat in his life-belt. The cook continued to sleep, but the oiler sat up, blinking his eyes and shaking with the new cold.

'Oh, I'm awful sorry, Billie,' said the correspondent, contritely.

'That's all right, old boy,' said the oiler, and lay down again and was asleep.

Presently it seemed that even the captain dozed, and the correspondent thought that he was the one man afloat on all the oceans. The wind had a voice as it came over the waves, and it was sadder than the end.

There was a long, loud swishing astern of the boat, and a gleaming trail of phosphorescence, like blue flame, was furrowed on the black waters. It might have been made by a monstrous knife.

Then there came a stillness, while the correspondent breathed with the open mouth and looked at the sea.

Suddenly there was another swish and another long flash of bluish light, and this time it was alongside the boat, and might almost have been reached with an oar. The correspondent saw an enormous fin speed like a shadow through the water, hurling the crystalline spray and leaving the long glowing trail.

The correspondent looked over his shoulder at the captain. His face was hidden, and he seemed to be asleep. He looked at the babes of the sea. They certainly were asleep. So, being bereft of sympathy, he leaned a little way to one side and swore softly into the sea.

But the thing did not then leave the vicinity of the boat. Ahead or astern, on one side or the other, at intervals long or short, fled the long sparkling streak, and there was to be heard the whiroo of the dark fin. The speed and power of the thing was greatly to be admired. It cut the water like a gigantic and keen projectile.

The presence of this biding thing did not affect the man with the same horror that it would if he had been a picnicker. He simply looked at the sea dully and swore in an undertone.

Nevertheless, it is true that he did not wish to be alone

with the thing. He wished one of his companions to awaken by chance and keep him company with it. But the captain hung motionless over the water-jar and the oiler and the cook in the bottom of the boat were plunged in slumber.

VI

'If I am going to be drowned – if I am going to be drowned – if I am going to be drowned, why, in the name of the seven mad gods who rule the sea, was I allowed to come thus far and contemplate sand and trees?'

During this dismal night, it may be remarked that a man would conclude that it was really the intention of the seven mad gods to drown him, despite the abominable injustice of it. For it was certainly an abominable injustice to drown a man who had worked so hard, so hard. The man felt it would be a crime most unnatural. Other people had drowned at sea since galleys swarmed with painted sails, but still –

When it occurs to a man that nature does not regard him as important, and that she feels she would not maim the universe by disposing of him, he at first wishes to throw bricks at the temple, and he hates deeply the fact that there are no bricks and no temples. Any visible expression of nature would surely be pelleted with his jeers.

Then, if there be no tangible thing to hoot he feels, perhaps, the desire to confront a personification and indulge in pleas, bowed to one knee, and with hands supplicant, saying: 'Yes, but I love myself.'

A high cold star on a winter's night is the word he feels that she says to him. Thereafter he knows the pathos of his situation.

The men in the dinghy had not discussed these matters, but each had, no doubt, reflected upon them in silence and according to his mind. There was seldom any expression upon their faces save the general one of complete weariness. Speech was devoted to the business of the boat.

To chime the notes of his emotion, a verse mysteriously entered the correspondent's head. He had even forgotten that he had forgotten this verse, but it suddenly was in his mind.

> A soldier of the Legion lay dying in Algiers,
> There was lack of woman's nursing, there was dearth
>   of woman's tears;
> But a comrade stood beside him, and he took that
>   comrade's hand,
> And he said: 'I never more shall see my own, my
>   native land.'

In his childhood, the correspondent had been made acquainted with the fact that a soldier of the Legion lay dying in Algiers, but he had never regarded it as important. Myriads of his school-fellows had informed him of the soldier's plight, but the dinning had naturally ended by making him perfectly indifferent. He had never considered it his affair that a soldier of the Legion lay dying in Algiers, nor had it appeared to him as a matter for sorrow. It was less to him than the breaking of a pencil's point.

Now, however, it quaintly came to him as a human, living thing. It was no longer merely a picture of a few throes in the breast of a poet, meanwhile drinking tea and warming his feet at the grate; it was an actuality – stern, mournful, and fine.

The correspondent plainly saw the soldier. He lay on the sand with his feet out straight and still. While his pale left hand was upon his chest in an attempt to thwart the going of his life, the blood came between his fingers. In the far

Algerian distance, a city of low square forms was set against a sky that was faint with the last sunset hues. The correspondent, plying the oars and dreaming of the slow and slower movements of the lips of the soldier, was moved by a profound and perfectly impersonal comprehension. He was sorry for the soldier of the Legion who lay dying in Algiers.

The thing which had followed the boat and waited had evidently grown bored at the delay. There was no longer to be heard the slash of the cut-water, and there was no longer the flame of the long trail. The light in the north still glimmered, but it was apparently no nearer to the boat. Sometimes the boom of the surf rang in the correspondent's ears, and he turned the craft seaward then and rowed harder. Southward, some one had evidently built a watch-fire on the beach. It was too low and too far to be seen, but it made a shimmering, roseate reflection upon the bluff back of it, and this could be discerned from the boat. The wind came stronger, and sometimes a wave suddenly raged out like a mountain-cat and there was to be seen the sheen and sparkle of a broken crest.

The captain, in the bow, moved on his water-jar and sat erect. 'Pretty long night,' he observed to the correspondent. He looked at the shore. 'Those life-saving people take their time.'

'Did you see that shark playing around?'

'Yes, I saw him. He was a big fellow, all right.'

'Wish I had known you were awake.'

Later the correspondent spoke into the bottom of the boat. 'Billie!' There was a slow and gradual disentanglement. 'Billie, will you spell me?'

'Sure,' said the oiler.

As soon as the correspondent touched the cold comfortable sea-water in the bottom of the boat, and had huddled close to the cook's life-belt he was deep in sleep, despite the fact that his teeth played all the popular airs. This sleep was so good to him that it was but a moment before he heard a voice call his name in a tone that demonstrated the last stages of exhaustion. 'Will you spell me?'

'Sure, Billie.'

The light in the north had mysteriously vanished, but the correspondent took his course from the wide-awake captain.

Later in the night they took the boat farther out to sea, and the captain directed the cook to take one oar at the stern and keep the boat facing the seas. He was to call out if he should hear the thunder of the surf. This plan enabled the oiler and the correspondent to get respite together. 'We'll give those boys a chance to get into shape again,' said the captain. They curled down and, after a few preliminary chatterings and trembles, slept once more the dead sleep. Neither knew they had bequeathed to the cook the company of another shark, or perhaps the same shark.

As the boat caroused on the waves, spray occasionally bumped over the side and gave them a fresh soaking, but this had no power to break their repose. The ominous slash of the wind and the water affected them as it would have affected mummies.

'Boys,' said the cook, with the notes of every reluctance in his voice, 'she's drifted in pretty close. I guess one of you had better take her to sea again.' The correspondent, aroused, heard the crash of the toppled crests.

As he was rowing, the captain gave him some whiskey and water, and this steadied the chills out of him. 'If I ever get ashore and anybody shows me even a photograph of an oar –'

At last there was a short conversation.

'Billie. . . . Billie, will you spell me?'

'Sure,' said the oiler.

VII

When the correspondent again opened his eyes, the sea and the sky were each of the gray hue of the dawning. Later, carmine and gold was painted upon the waters. The morning appeared finally, in its splendor, with a sky of pure blue, and the sunlight flamed on the tips of the waves.

On the distant dunes were set many little black cottages and a tall white wind-mill reared above them. No man, nor dog, nor bicycle appeared on the beach. The cottages might have formed a deserted village.

The voyagers scanned the shore. A conference was held in the boat. 'Well,' said the captain, 'if no help is coming, we might better try a run through the surf right away. If we stay out here much longer we will be too weak to do anything for ourselves at all.' The others silently acquiesced in this reasoning. The boat was headed for the beach. The correspondent wondered if none ever ascended the tall wind-tower, and if then they never looked seaward. This tower was a giant, standing with its back to the plight of the ants. It represented in a degree, to the correspondent, the serenity of nature amid the struggles of the individual – nature in the wind, and nature in the vision of men. She did not seem cruel to him then, nor beneficent, nor treacherous, nor wise. But she was indifferent, flatly indifferent. It is, perhaps, plausible that a man in this situation, impressed with the unconcern of the universe, should see the innumerable flaws of his life and have them taste wickedly in his mind and wish for another chance. A distinction between right and wrong seems absurdly clear to him, then, in this new ignorance of the grave-edge, and he understands that if he were given another opportunity he would mend his conduct and his words, and be better and brighter during an introduction, or at a tea.

'Now, boys,' said the captain, 'she is going to swamp sure. All we can do is to work her in as far as possible, and then when she swamps, pile out and scramble for the beach. Keep cool now, and don't jump until she swamps sure.'

The oiler took the oars. Over his shoulders he scanned the surf. 'Captain,' he said, 'I think I'd better bring her about, and keep her head-on to the seas and back her in.'

'All right, Billie,' said the captain. 'Back her in.' The oiler swung the boat then and, seated in the stern, the cook and the correspondent were obliged to look over their shoulders to contemplate the lonely and indifferent shore.

The monstrous inshore rollers heaved the boat high until the men were again enabled to see the white sheets of water scudding up the slanted beach. 'We won't get in very close,' said the captain. Each time a man could wrest his attention from the rollers, he turned his glance toward the shore, and in the expression of the eyes during this contemplation there was a singular quality. The correspondent, observing the others, knew that they were not afraid, but the full meaning of their glances was shrouded.

As for himself, he was too tired to grapple fundamentally with the fact. He tried to coerce his mind into thinking of it, but the mind was dominated at this time by the muscles, and the muscles said they did not care. It merely occurred to him that if he should drown it would be a shame.

There were no hurried words, no pallor, no plain agitation. The men simply looked at the shore. 'Now, remember to get well clear of the boat when you jump,' said the captain.

Seaward the crest of a roller suddenly fell with a thunderous crash, and the long white comber came roaring down upon the boat.

'Steady now,' said the captain. The men were silent. They

turned their eyes from the shore to the comber and waited. The boat slid up the incline, leaped at the furious top, bounced over it, and swung down the long back of the wave. Some water had been shipped and the cook bailed it out.

But the next crest crashed also. The tumbling boiling flood of white water caught the boat and whirled it almost perpendicular. Water swarmed in from all sides. The correspondent had his hands on the gunwale at this time, and when the water entered at that place he swiftly withdrew his fingers, as if he objected to wetting them.

The little boat, drunken with this weight of water, reeled and snuggled deeper into the sea.

'Bail her out, cook! Bail her out,' said the captain.

'All right, Captain,' said the cook.

'Now, boys, the next one will do for us, sure,' said the oiler. 'Mind to jump clear of the boat.'

The third wave moved forward, huge, furious, implacable. It fairly swallowed the dinghy, and almost simultaneously the men tumbled into the sea. A piece of life-belt had lain in the bottom of the boat, and as the correspondent went overboard he held this to his chest with his left hand.

The January water was icy, and he reflected immediately that it was colder than he had expected to find it off the coast of Florida. This appeared to his dazed mind as a fact important enough to be noted at the time. The coldness of the water was sad; it was tragic. This fact was somehow so mixed and confused with his opinion of his own situation that it seemed almost a proper reason for tears. The water was cold.

When he came to the surface he was conscious of little but the noisy water. Afterward he saw his companions in the sea. The oiler was ahead in the race. He was swimming strongly and rapidly. Off to the correspondent's left, the cook's great white and corked back bulged out of the water, and in the rear the captain was hanging with his one good hand to the keel of the overturned dinghy.

There is a certain immovable quality to a shore, and the correspondent wondered at it amid the confusion of the sea.

It seemed also very attractive, but the correspondent knew that it was a long journey, and he paddled leisurely. The piece of life-preserver lay under him, and sometimes he whirled down the incline of a wave as if he were on a hand-sled.

But finally he arrived at a place in the sea where travel was beset with difficulty. He did not pause swimming to inquire what manner of current had caught him, but there his progress ceased. The shore was set before him like a bit of scenery on a stage, and he looked at it and understood with his eyes each detail of it.

As the cook passed, much farther to the left, the captain was calling to him, 'Turn over on your back, cook! Turn over on your back and use the oar.'

'All right, sir.' The cook turned on his back, and, paddling with an oar, went ahead as if he were a canoe.

Presently the boat also passed to the left of the correspondent with the captain clinging with one hand to the keel. He would have appeared like a man raising himself to look over a board fence, if it were not for the extraordinary gymnastics of the boat. The correspondent marvelled that the captain could still hold to it.

They passed on, nearer to shore – the oiler, the cook, the captain – and following them went the water-jar, bouncing gayly over the seas.

The correspondent remained in the grip of this strange new enemy – a current. The shore, with its white slope of sand and its green bluff, topped with little silent cottages, was spread like a picture before him. It was very near to him then, but he was impressed as one who in a gallery looks at a scene from Brittany or Holland.

He thought: 'I am going to drown? Can it be possible? Can it be possible? Can it be possible?' Perhaps an individual must consider his own death to be the final phenomenon of nature.

But later a wave perhaps whirled him out of this small deadly current, for he found suddenly that he could again make progress toward the shore. Later still, he was aware that the captain, clinging with one hand to the keel of the dinghy, had his face turned away from the shore and toward him, and was calling his name. 'Come to the boat! Come to the boat!'

In his struggle to reach the captain and the boat, he reflected that when one gets properly wearied, drowning must really be a comfortable arrangement, a cessation of hostilities accompanied by a large degree of relief, and he was glad of it, for the main thing in his mind for some moments had been horror of the temporary agony. He did not wish to be hurt.

Presently he saw a man running along the shore. He was undressing with most remarkable speed. Coat, trousers, shirt, everything flew magically off him.

'Come to the boat,' called the captain.

'All right, Captain.' As the correspondent paddled, he saw the captain let himself down to bottom and leave the boat. Then the correspondent performed his one little marvel of the voyage. A large wave caught him and flung him with ease and supreme speed completely over the boat and far beyond it. It struck him even then as an event in gymnastics, and a true miracle of the sea. An overturned boat in the surf is not a plaything to a swimming man.

The correspondent arrived in water that reached only to

his waist, but his condition did not enable him to stand for more than a moment. Each wave knocked him into a heap, and the under-tow pulled at him.

Then he saw the man who had been running and undressing, and undressing and running, come bounding into the water. He dragged ashore the cook, and then waded toward the captain, but the captain waved him away, and sent him to the correspondent. He was naked, naked as a tree in winter, but a halo was about his head, and he shone like a saint. He gave a strong pull, and a long drag, and a bully heave at the correspondent's hand. The correspondent, schooled in the minor formulæ, said: 'Thanks, old man.' But suddenly the man cried: 'What's that?' He pointed a swift finger. The correspondent said: 'Go.'

In the shallows, face downward, lay the oiler. His forehead touched sand that was periodically, between each wave, clear of the sea.

The correspondent did not know all that transpired afterward. When he achieved safe ground he fell, striking the sand with each particular part of his body. It was as if he had dropped from a roof, but the thud was grateful to him.

It seems that instantly the beach was populated with men with blankets, clothes, and flasks, and women with coffee-pots and all the remedies sacred to their minds. The welcome of the land to the men from the sea was warm and generous, but a still and dripping shape was carried slowly up the beach, and the land's welcome for it could only be the different and sinister hospitality of the grave.

When it came night, the white waves paced to and fro in the moonlight, and the wind brought the sound of the great sea's voice to the men on shore, and they felt that they could then be interpreters.

JACK LONDON

THE HOUSE OF MAPUHI

DESPITE THE HEAVY clumsiness of her lines, the *Aorai* handled easily in the light breeze, and her captain ran her well in before he hove to just outside the suck of the surf. The atoll of Hikueru lay low on the water, a circle of pounded coral sand a hundred yards wide, twenty miles in circumference, and from three to five feet above high-water mark. On the bottom of the huge and glassy lagoon was much pearl shell, and from the deck of the schooner, across the slender ring of the atoll, the divers could be seen at work. But the lagoon had no entrance for even a trading schooner. With a favoring breeze cutters could win in through the tortuous and shallow channel, but the schooners lay off and on outside and sent in their small boats.

The *Aorai* swung out a boat smartly, into which sprang half a dozen brown-skinned sailors clad only in scarlet loin-cloths. They took the oars, while in the stem-sheets, at the steering sweep, stood a young man garbed in the tropic white that marks the European. But he was not all European. The golden strain of Polynesia betrayed itself in the sun-gilt of his fair skin and cast up golden sheens and lights through the glimmering blue of his eyes. Raoul he was, Alexandré Raoul, youngest son of Marie Raoul, the wealthy quarter-caste, who owned and managed half a dozen trading schooners similar to the *Aorai*. Across an eddy just outside the entrance, and in and through and over a boiling tide-rip, the boat fought its way to the mirrored calm of the lagoon.

Young Raoul leaped out upon the white sand and shook hands with a tall native. The man's chest and shoulders were magnificent, but the stump of a right arm, beyond the flesh of which the age-whitened bone projected several inches, attested the encounter with a shark that had put an end to his diving days and made him a fawner and an intriguer for small favors.

'Have you heard, Alec?' were his first words. 'Mapuhi has found a pearl – such a pearl. Never was there one like it ever fished up in Hikueru, nor in all the Paumotus, nor in all the world. Buy it from him. He has it now. And remember that I told you first. He is a fool and you can get it cheap. Have you any tobacco?'

Straight up the beach to a shack under a pandanus tree Raoul headed. He was his mother's supercargo, and his business was to comb all the Paumotus for the wealth of copra, shell, and pearls that they yielded up.

He was a young supercargo, it was his second voyage in such capacity, and he suffered much secret worry from his lack of experience in pricing pearls. But when Mapuhi exposed the pearl to his sight he managed to suppress the startle it gave him, and to maintain a careless, commercial expression on his face. For the pearl had struck him a blow. It was large as a pigeon egg, a perfect sphere, of a whiteness that reflected opalescent lights from all colors about it. It was alive. Never had he seen anything like it. When Mapuhi dropped it into his hand he was surprised by the weight of it. That showed that it was a good pearl. He examined it closely, through a pocket magnifying-glass. It was without flaw or blemish. The purity of it seemed almost to melt into the atmosphere out of his hand. In the shade it was softly luminous, gleaming like a tender moon. So translucently white was it, that when he dropped it into a glass of water he had difficulty in finding it. So straight and swiftly had it sunk to the bottom that he knew its weight was excellent.

'Well, what do you want for it?' he asked, with a fine assumption of nonchalance.

'I want –' Mapuhi began, and behind him, framing his own dark face, the dark faces of two women and a girl nodded concurrence in what he wanted. Their heads were bent forward, they were animated by a suppressed eagerness, their eyes flashed avariciously.

'I want a house,' Mapuhi went on. 'It must have a roof of galvanized iron and an octagon-drop-clock. It must be six fathoms long with a porch all around. A big room must be in the center, with a round table in the middle of it and the octagon-drop-clock on the wall. There must be four bedrooms, two on each side of the big room, and in each bedroom must be an iron bed, two chairs, and a washstand. And back of the house must be a kitchen, a good kitchen, with pots and pans and a stove. And you must build the house on my island, which is Fakarava.'

'Is that all?' Raoul asked incredulously.

'There must be a sewing-machine,' spoke up Tefara, Mapuhi's wife.

'Not forgetting the octagon-drop-clock,' added Nauri, Mapuhi's mother.

'Yes, that is all,' said Mapuhi.

Young Raoul laughed. He laughed long and heartily. But while he laughed he secretly performed problems in mental arithmetic. He had never built a house in his life, and his notions concerning house building were hazy. While he laughed, he calculated the cost of the voyage to Tahiti for materials, of the materials themselves, of the voyage back again to Fakarava, and the cost of landing the materials and of building the house. It would come to four thousand

French dollars, allowing a margin for safety – four thousand French dollars were equivalent to twenty thousand francs. It was impossible. How was he to know the value of such a pearl? Twenty thousand francs was a lot of money – and of his mother's money at that.

'Mapuhi,' he said, 'you are a big fool. Set a money price.'

But Mapuhi shook his head, and the three heads behind him shook with his.

'I want the house,' he said. 'It must be six fathoms long with a porch all around –'

'Yes, yes,' Raoul interrupted. 'I know all about your house, but it won't do. I'll give you a thousand Chili dollars.'

The four heads chorused a silent negative.

'And a hundred Chili dollars in trade.'

'I want the house,' Mapuhi began.

'What good will the house do you?' Raoul demanded. 'The first hurricane that comes along will wash it away. You ought to know. Captain Raffy says it looks like a hurricane right now.'

'Not on Fakarava,' said Mapuhi. 'The land is much higher there. On this island, yes. Any hurricane can sweep Hikueru. I will have the house on Fakarava. It must be six fathoms long with a porch all around –'

And Raoul listened again to the tale of the house. Several hours he spent in the endeavor to hammer the house-obsession out of Mapuhi's mind; but Mapuhi's mother and wife, and Ngakura, Mapuhi's daughter, bolstered him in his resolve for the house. Through the open doorway, while he listened for the twentieth time to the detailed description of the house that was wanted, Raoul saw his schooner's second boat draw up on the beach. The sailors rested on the oars, advertising haste to be gone. The first mate of the *Aorai* sprang ashore, exchanged a word with the one-armed native, then hurried toward Raoul. The day grew suddenly dark, as a squall obscured the face of the sun. Across the lagoon Raoul could see approaching the ominous line of the puff of wind.

'Captain Raffy says you've got to get to hell outa here,' was the mate's greeting. 'If there's any shell, we've got to run the risk of picking it up later on – so he says. The barometer's dropped to twenty-nine-seventy.'

The gust of wind struck the pandanus tree overhead and tore through the palms beyond, flinging half a dozen ripe cocoanuts with heavy thuds to the ground. Then came the rain out of the distance, advancing with the roar of a gale of wind and causing the water of the lagoon to smoke in driven windrows. The sharp rattle of the first drops was on the leaves when Raoul sprang to his feet.

'A thousand Chili dollars, cash down, Mapuhi,' he said. 'And two hundred Chili dollars in trade.'

'I want a house –' the other began.

'Mapuhi!' Raoul yelled, in order to make himself heard. 'You are a fool!'

He flung out of the house, and, side by side with the mate, fought his way down the beach toward the boat. They could not see the boat. The tropic rain sheeted about them so that they could see only the beach under their feet and the spiteful little waves from the lagoon that snapped and bit at the sand. A figure appeared through the deluge. It was Huru-Huru, the man with the one arm.

'Did you get the pearl?' he yelled in Raoul's ear.

'Mapuhi is a fool!' was the answering yell, and the next moment they were lost to each other in the descending water.

Half an hour later, Huru-Huru, watching from the seaward side of the atoll, saw the two boats hoisted in and the *Aorai* pointing her nose out to sea. And near her, just come in from the sea on the wings of the squall, he saw another schooner hove to and dropping a boat into the water. He knew her. It was the *Orohena*, owned by Toriki, the half-caste trader, who served as his own supercargo and who doubtlessly was even then in the stem-sheets of the boat. Huru-Huru chuckled. He knew that Mapuhi owed Toriki for trade-goods advanced the year before.

The squall had passed. The hot sun was blazing down, and the lagoon was once more a mirror. But the air was sticky like mucilage, and the weight of it seemed to burden the lungs and make breathing difficult.

'Have you heard the news, Toriki?' Huru-Huru asked. 'Mapuhi has found a pearl. Never was there a pearl like it ever fished up in Hikueru, nor anywhere in the Paumotus, nor anywhere in all the world. Mapuhi is a fool. Besides, he owes you money. Remember that I told you first. Have you any tobacco?'

And to the grass-shack of Mapuhi went Toriki. He was a masterful man, withal a fairly stupid one. Carelessly he glanced at the wonderful pearl – glanced for a moment only; and carelessly he dropped it into his pocket.

'You are lucky,' he said. 'It is a nice pearl. I will give you credit on the books.'

'I want a house,' Mapuhi began, in consternation. 'It must be six fathoms –'

'Six fathoms your grandmother!' was the trader's retort. 'You want to pay up your debts, that's what you want. You owed me twelve hundred dollars Chili. Very well; you owe them no longer. The amount is squared. Besides, I will give you credit for two hundred Chili. If, when I get to Tahiti, the pearl sells well, I will give you credit for another hundred – that will make three hundred. But mind, only if the pearl sells well. I may even lose money on it.'

Mapuhi folded his arms in sorrow and sat with bowed head. He had been robbed of his pearl. In place of the house, he had paid a debt. There was nothing to show for the pearl.

'You are a fool,' said Tefara.

'You are a fool,' said Nauri, his mother. 'Why did you let the pear into his hand?'

'What was I to do?' Mapuhi protested. 'I owed him the money. He knew I had the pearl. You heard him yourself ask to see it. I had not told him. He knew. Somebody else told him. And I owed him the money.'

'Mapuhi is a fool,' mimicked Ngakura.

She was twelve years old and did not know any better. Mapuhi relieved his feelings by sending her reeling from a box on the ear; while Tefara and Nauri burst into tears and continued to upbraid him after the manner of women.

Huru-Huru, watching on the beach, saw a third schooner that he knew heave to outside the entrance and drop a boat. It was the *Hira*, well named, for she was owned by Levy, the German Jew, the greatest pearl-buyer of them all, and, as was well known, Hira was the Tahitian god of fishermen and thieves.

'Have you heard the news?' Huru-Huru asked, as Levy, a fat man with massive asymmetrical features, stepped out upon the beach. 'Mapuhi has found a pearl. There was never a pearl like it in Hikueru, in all the Paumotus, in all the world. Mapuhi is a fool. He has sold it to Toriki for fourteen hundred Chili – I listened outside and heard. Toriki is likewise a fool. You can buy it from him cheap. Remember that I told you first. Have you any tobacco?'

'Where is Toriki?'

'In the house of Captain Lynch, drinking absinthe. He has been there an hour.'

And while Levy and Toriki drank absinthe and chaffered

over the pearl, Huru-Huru listened and heard the stupendous price of twenty-five thousand francs agreed upon.

It was at this time that both the *Orohena* and the *Hira*, running in close to the shore, began firing guns and signalling frantically. The three men stepped outside in time to see the two schooners go hastily about and head off shore, dropping mainsails and flying-jibs on the run in the teeth of the squall that heeled them far over on the whitened water. Then the rain blotted them out.

'They'll be back after it's over,' said Toriki. 'We'd better be getting out of here.'

'I reckon the glass has fallen some more,' said Captain Lynch.

He was a white-bearded sea-captain, too old for service, who had learned that the only way to live on comfortable terms with his asthma was on Hikueru. He went inside to look at the barometer.

'Great God!' they heard him exclaim, and rushed in to join him at staring at a dial, which marked twenty-nine-twenty.

Again they came out, this time anxiously to consult sea and sky. The squall had cleared away, but the sky remained overcast. The two schooners, under all sail and joined by a third, could be seen making back. A veer in the wind induced them to slack off sheets, and five minutes afterward a sudden veer from the opposite quarter caught all three schooners aback, and those on shore could see the boom-tackles being slacked away or cast off on the jump. The sound of the surf was loud, hollow, and menacing, and a heavy swell was setting in. A terrible sheet of lightning burst before their eyes, illuminating the dark day, and the thunder rolled wildly about them.

Toriki and Levy broke into a run for their boats, the latter ambling along like a panic-stricken hippopotamus. As their two boats swept out the entrance, they passed the boat of the *Aorai* coming in. In the stern-sheets, encouraging the rowers, was Raoul. Unable to shake the vision of the pearl from his mind, he was returning to accept Mapuhi's price of a house.

He landed on the beach in the midst of a driving thunder squall that was so dense that he collided with Huru-Huru before he saw him.

'Too late,' yelled Huru-Huru. 'Mapuhi sold it to Toriki for fourteen hundred Chili, and Toriki sold it to Levy for twenty-five thousand francs. And Levy will sell it in France for a hundred thousand francs. Have you any tobacco?'

Raoul felt relieved. His troubles about the pearl were over. He need not worry any more, even if he had not got the pearl. But he did not believe Huru-Huru. Mapuhi might well have sold it for fourteen hundred Chili, but that Levy, who knew pearls, should have paid twenty-five thousand francs was too wide a stretch. Raoul decided to interview Captain Lynch on the subject, but when he arrived at that ancient mariner's house, he found him looking wide-eyed at the barometer.

'What do you read it?' Captain Lynch asked anxiously, rubbing his spectacles and staring again at the instrument.

'Twenty-nine-ten,' said Raoul. 'I have never seen it so low before.'

'I should say not!' snorted the captain. 'Fifty years boy and man on all the seas, and I've never seen it go down to that. Listen!'

They stood for a moment, while the surf rumbled and shook the house. Then they went outside. The squall had passed. They could see the *Aorai* lying becalmed a mile away and pitching and tossing madly in the tremendous seas that rolled in stately procession down out of the northeast and flung themselves furiously upon the coral shore. One of the sailors from the boat pointed at the mouth of the passage and shook his head. Raoul looked and saw a white anarchy of foam and surge.

'I guess I'll stay with you tonight, Captain,' he said; then turned to the sailor and told him to haul the boat out and to find shelter for himself and fellows.

'Twenty-nine flat,' Captain Lynch reported, coming out from another look at the barometer, a chair in his hand.

He sat down and stared at the spectacle of the sea. The sun came out, increasing the sultriness of the day, while the dead calm still held. The seas continued to increase in magnitude.

'What makes that sea is what gets me,' Raoul muttered petulantly. 'There is no wind, yet look at it, look at that fellow there!'

Miles in length, carrying tens of thousands of tons in weight, its impact shook the frail atoll like an earthquake. Captain Lynch was startled.

'Gracious!' he exclaimed, half rising from his chair, then sinking back.

'But there is no wind,' Raoul persisted. 'I could understand it if there was wind along with it.'

'You'll get the wind soon enough without worryin' for it,' was the grim reply.

The two men sat on in silence. The sweat stood out on their skin in myriads of tiny drops that ran together, forming blotches of moisture, which, in turn, coalesced into rivulets that dripped to the ground. They panted for breath, the old man's efforts being especially painful. A sea swept up the beach, licking around the trunks of the cocoanuts and subsiding almost at their feet.

' 'Way past high-water mark,' Captain Lynch remarked,

'and I've been here eleven years.' He looked at his watch. 'It is three o'clock.'

A man and woman, at their heels a motley following of brats and curs, trailed disconsolately by. They came to a halt beyond the house, and, after much irresolution, sat down in the sand. A few minutes later another family trailed in from the opposite direction, the men and women carrying a heterogeneous assortment of possessions. And soon several hundred persons of all ages and sexes were congregated about the captain's dwelling. He called to one new arrival, a woman with a nursing babe in her arms, and in answer received the information that her house had just been swept into the lagoon.

This was the highest spot of land in miles, and already, in many places on either hand, the great seas were making a clean breach of the slender ring of the atoll and surging into the lagoon. Twenty miles around stretched the ring of the atoll, and in no place was it more than fifty fathoms wide. It was the height of the diving season, and from all the islands around, even as far as Tahiti, the natives had gathered.

'There are twelve hundred men, women, and children here,' said Captain Lynch. 'I wonder how many will be here tomorrow morning.'

'But why don't it blow? That's what I want to know,' Raoul demanded.

'Don't worry, young man, don't worry; you'll get your troubles fast enough.'

Even as Captain Lynch spoke, a great watery mass smote the atoll. The sea-water churned about them three inches deep under their chairs. A low wail of fear went up from the many women. The children, with clasped hands, stared at the immense rollers and cried piteously. Chickens and cats, wading perturbedly in the water, as by common consent, with flight and scramble took refuge on the roof of the captain's house. A Paumotan, with a litter of newborn puppies in a basket, climbed into a cocoanut tree and twenty feet above the ground made the basket fast. The mother floundered about in the water beneath, whining and yelping.

And still the sun shone brightly and the dead calm continued. They sat and watched the seas and the insane pitching of the *Aorai.* Captain Lynch gazed at the huge mountains of water sweeping in until he could gaze no more. He covered his face with his hands to shut out the sight; then went into the house.

'Twenty-eight-sixty,' he said quietly when he returned.

In his arm was a coil of small rope. He cut it into two-fathom lengths, giving one to Raoul and, retaining one for himself, distributed the remainder among the women with the advice to pick out a tree and climb.

A light air began to blow out of the northeast, and the fan of it on his cheek seemed to cheer Raoul up. He could see the *Aorai* trimming her sheets and heading off shore, and he regretted that he was not on her. She would get away at any rate, but as for the atoll – A sea breached across, almost sweeping him off his feet, and he selected a tree. Then he remembered the barometer and ran back to the house. He encountered Captain Lynch on the same errand and together they went in.

'Twenty-eight-twenty,' said the old mariner. 'It's going to be fair hell around here – what was that?'

The air seemed filled with the rush of something. The house quivered and vibrated, and they heard the thrumming of a mighty note of sound. The windows rattled. Two panes crashed. A draught of wind tore in, striking them and making them stagger. The door opposite banged shut, shattering the latch. The white doorknob crumbled in fragments to the floor. The room's walls bulged like a gas balloon in the process of sudden inflation. Then came a new sound like the rattle of musketry, as the spray from a sea struck the wall of the house. Captain Lynch looked at his watch. It was four o'clock. He put on a coat of pilot cloth, unhooked the barometer, and stowed it away in a capacious pocket. Again a sea struck the house, with a heavy thud, and the light building tilted, twisted quarter-around on its foundation, and sank down, its floor at an angle of ten degrees.

Raoul went out first. The wind caught him and whirled him away. He noted that it had hauled around to the east. With a great effort he threw himself on the sand, crouching and holding his own. Captain Lynch, driven like a wisp of straw, sprawled over him. Two of the *Aorai*'s sailors, leaving a cocoanut tree to which they had been clinging, came to their aid, leaning against the wind at impossible angles and fighting and clawing every inch of the way.

The old man's joints were stiff and he could not climb, so the sailors, by means of short ends of rope tied together, hoisted him up the trunk, a few feet at a time, till they could make him fast, at the top of the tree, fifty feet from the ground. Raoul passed his length of rope around the base of an adjacent tree and stood looking on. The wind was frightful. He had never dreamed it could blow so hard. A sea breached across the atoll, wetting him to the knees before it subsided into the lagoon. The sun had disappeared, and a lead-colored twilight settled down. A few drops of rain, driving horizontally, struck him. The impact was like that of leaden pellets. A splash of salt spray struck his face. It was like the slap of a man's hand. His cheeks stung, and involuntary tears of pain were in his smarting eyes. Several hundred natives had taken to the trees, and he could have laughed at the bunches of human fruit clustering in the tops. Then, being Tahitian-born, he doubled his body at the waist, clasped the trunk of his tree with his hands, pressed the soles of his feet against the near surface of the trunk, and began to walk up the tree. At the top he found two women, two children, and a man. One little girl clasped a housecat in her arms.

From his eyrie he waved his hand to Captain Lynch, and that doughty patriarch waved back. Raoul was appalled at the sky. It had approached much nearer – in fact, it seemed just over his head; and it had turned from lead to black. Many people were still on the ground grouped about the bases of the trees and holding on. Several such clusters were praying, and in one the Mormon missionary was exhorting. A weird sound, rhythmical, faint as the faintest chirp of a far cricket, enduring but for a moment, but in that moment suggesting to him vaguely the thought of heaven and celestial music, came to his ear. He glanced about him and saw, at the base of another tree, a large cluster of people holding on by ropes and by one another. He could see their faces working and their lips moving in unison. No sound came to him, but he knew that they were singing hymns.

Still the wind continued to blow harder. By no conscious process could he measure it, for it had long since passed beyond all his experience of wind; but he knew somehow, nevertheless, that it was blowing harder. Not far away a tree was uprooted, flinging its load of human beings to the ground. A sea washed across the strip of sand, and they were gone. Things were happening quickly. He saw a brown shoulder and a black head silhouetted against the churning white of the lagoon. The next instant that, too, had vanished. Other trees were going, falling and crisscrossing like matches. He was amazed at the power of the wind. His own tree was swaying perilously, one woman was wailing and clutching the little girl, who in turn still hung on to the cat.

The man, holding the other child, touched Raoul's arm and pointed. He looked and saw the Mormon church careering drunkenly a hundred feet away. It had been torn from its foundations, and wind and sea were heaving and shoving it toward the lagoon. A frightful wall of water caught it, tilted it, and flung it against half a dozen cocoanut trees. The bunches of human fruit fell like ripe cocoanuts. The subsiding wave showed them on the ground, some lying motionless, others squirming and writhing. They reminded him strangely of ants. He was not shocked. He had risen above horror. Quite as a matter of course he noted the succeeding wave sweep the sand clean of the human wreckage. A third wave, more colossal than any he had yet seen, hurled the church into the lagoon, where it floated off into the obscurity to leeward, half-submerged, reminding him for all the world of a Noah's ark.

He looked for Captain Lynch's house, and was surprised to find it gone. Things certainly were happening quickly. He noticed that many of the people in the trees that still held had descended to the ground. The wind had yet again increased. His own tree showed that. It no longer swayed or bent over and back. Instead, it remained practically stationary, curved in a rigid angle from the wind and merely vibrating. But the vibration was sickening. It was like that of a tuning-fork or the tongue of a jew's-harp. It was the rapidity of the vibration that made it so bad. Even though its roots held, it could not stand the strain for long. Something would have to break.

Ah, there was one that had gone. He had not seen it go, but there it stood, the remnant, broken off half-way up the trunk. One did not know what happened unless he saw it.

The mere crashing of trees and wails of human despair occupied no place in that mighty volume of sound. He chanced to be looking in Captain Lynch's direction when it happened. He saw the trunk of the tree, half-way up, splinter and part without noise. The head of the tree, with three sailors of the *Aorai* and the old captain, sailed off over the lagoon. It did not fall to the ground, but drove through the air like a piece of chaff. For a hundred yards he followed its flight, when it struck the water. He strained his eyes, and was sure that he saw Captain Lynch wave farewell.

Raoul did not wait for anything more. He touched the native and made signs to descend to the ground. The man was willing, but his women were paralyzed from terror, and he elected to remain with them. Raoul passed his rope around the tree and slid down. A rush of salt water went over his head. He held his breath and clung desperately to the rope. The water subsided, and in the shelter of the trunk he breathed once more. He fastened the rope more securely, and then was put under by another sea. One of the women slid down and joined him, the native remaining by the other woman, the two children, and the cat.

The supercargo had noticed how the groups clinging at the bases of the other trees continually diminished. Now he saw the process work out alongside him. It required all his strength to hold on, and the woman who had joined him was growing weaker. Each time he emerged from a sea he was surprised to find himself still there, and next, surprised to find the woman still there. At last he emerged to find himself alone. He looked up. The top of the tree had gone as well. At half its original height, a splintered end vibrated. He was safe. The roots still held, while the tree had been shorn of its windage. He began to climb up. He was so weak that he went slowly, and sea after sea caught him before he was above them. Then he tied himself to the trunk and stiffened his soul to face the night and he knew not what.

He felt very lonely in the darkness. At times it seemed to him that it was the end of the world and that he was the last one left alive. Still the wind increased. Hour after hour it increased. By what he calculated was eleven o'clock, the wind had become unbelievable. It was a horrible, monstrous thing, a screaming fury, a wall that smote and passed on but that continued to smite and pass on – a wall without end. It seemed to him that he had become light and ethereal; that it was he that was in motion; that he was being driven with inconceivable velocity through unending solidness. The wind was no longer air in motion. It had become substantial as water or quicksilver. He had a feeling that he could reach into it and tear it out in chunks as one might do with the meat in the carcass of a steer; that he could seize hold of the wind and hang on to it as a man might hang on to the face of a cliff.

The wind strangled him. He could not face it and breathe, for it rushed in through his mouth and nostrils, distending his lungs like bladders. At such moments it seemed to him that his body was being packed and swollen with solid earth. Only by pressing his lips to the trunk of the tree could he breathe. Also, the ceaseless impact of the wind exhausted him. Body and brain became wearied. He no longer observed, no longer thought, and was but semiconscious. One idea constituted his consciousness: So this was a hurricane. That one idea persisted irregularly. It was like a feeble flame that flickered occasionally. From a state of stupor he would return to it – So this was a hurricane. Then he would go off into another stupor.

The height of the hurricane endured from eleven at night till three in the morning, and it was at eleven that the tree in which clung Mapuhi and his women snapped off. Mapuhi rose to the surface of the lagoon, still clutching his daughter Ngakura. Only a South Sea islander could have lived in such a driving smother. The pandanus tree, to which he attached himself, turned over and over in the froth and churn; and it was only by holding on at times and waiting, and at other times shifting his grips rapidly, that he was able to get his head and Ngakura's to the surface at intervals sufficiently near together to keep the breath in them. But the air was mostly water, what with flying spray and sheeted rain that poured along at right angles to the perpendicular.

It was ten miles across the lagoon to the farther ring of sand. Here, tossing tree trunks, timbers, wrecks of cutters, and wreckage of houses, killed nine out of ten of the miserable beings who survived the passage of the lagoon. Half-drowned, exhausted, they were hurled into this mad mortar of the elements and battered into formless flesh. But Mapuhi was fortunate. His chance was the one in ten; it fell to him by the freakage of fate. He emerged upon the sand, bleeding from a score of wounds. Ngakura's left arm was broken; the fingers of her right hand were crushed; and cheek and forehead were laid open to the bone. He clutched a tree that yet stood, and clung on, holding the girl and sobbing for air, while the waters of the lagoon washed by knee-high and at times waist-high.

At three in the morning the backbone of the hurricane broke. By five no more than a stiff breeze was blowing. And by six it was dead calm and the sun was shining. The sea had gone down. On the yet restless edge of the lagoon, Mapuhi saw the broken bodies of those that had failed in the landing. Undoubtedly Tefara and Nauri were among them. He went along the beach examining them, and came upon his wife, lying half in and half out of the water. He sat down and wept, making harsh animal-noises after the manner of primitive grief. Then she stirred uneasily, and groaned. He looked more closely. Not only was she alive, but she was uninjured. She was merely sleeping. Hers also had been the one chance in ten.

Of the twelve hundred alive the night before but three hundred remained. The Mormon missionary and a gendarme made the census. The lagoon was cluttered with corpses. Not a house nor a hut was standing. In the whole atoll not two stones remained one upon another. One in fifty of the cocoanut palms still stood, and they were wrecks, while on not one of them remained a single nut. There was no fresh water. The shallow wells that caught the surface seepage of the rain were filled with salt. Out of the lagoon a few soaked bags of flour were recovered. The survivors cut the hearts out of the fallen cocoanut trees and ate them. Here and there they crawled into tiny hutches, made by hollowing out the sand and covering over with fragments of metal roofing. The missionary made a crude still, but he could not distill water for three hundred persons. By the end of the second day, Raoul, taking a bath in the lagoon, discovered that his thirst was somewhat relieved. He cried out the news, and thereupon three hundred men, women, and children could have been seen, standing up to their necks in the lagoon and trying to drink water in through their skins. Their dead floated about them, or were stepped upon where they still lay upon the bottom. On the third day the people buried their dead and sat down to wait for the rescue steamers.

In the meantime, Nauri, torn from her family by the hurricane, had been swept away on an adventure of her own. Clinging to a rough plank that wounded and bruised her and that filled her body with splinters, she was thrown clear over the atoll and carried away to sea. Here, under the amazing buffets of mountains of water, she lost her plank. She was an old woman nearly sixty; but she was Paumotan-born, and she had never been out of sight of the sea in her life. Swimming in the darkness, strangling, suffocating, fighting for air, she was struck a heavy blow on the shoulder by a cocoanut. On the instant her plan was formed, and she seized the nut. In the next hour she captured seven more. Tied together, they formed a lifebuoy that preserved her life – while at the same time it threatened to pound her to a jelly. She was a fat woman, and she bruised easily, but she had had experience of hurricanes, and, while she prayed to her shark god for protection from sharks, she waited for the wind to break. But at three o'clock she was in such a stupor that she did not know. Nor did she know at six o'clock when the dead calm settled down. She was shocked into consciousness when she was thrown upon the sand. She dug in with raw and bleeding hands and feet and clawed against the backwash until she was beyond the reach of the waves.

She knew where she was. This land could be no other than the tiny islet of Takokota. It had no lagoon. No one lived upon it. Hikueru was fifteen miles away. She could not see Hikueru, but she knew that it lay to the south. The days went by, and she lived on the cocoanuts that had kept her afloat. They supplied her with drinking water and with food. But she did not drink all she wanted, nor eat all she wanted. Rescue was problematical. She saw the smoke of the rescue steamers on the horizon, but what steamer could be expected to come to lonely, uninhabited Takokota?

From the first she was tormented by corpses. The sea persisted in flinging them upon her bit of sand, and she persisted, until her strength failed, in thrusting them back into the sea where the sharks tore at them and devoured them. When her strength failed, the bodies festooned her beach with ghastly horror, and she withdrew from them as far as she could, which was not far.

By the tenth day her last cocoanut was gone, and she was shrivelling from thirst. She dragged herself along the sand, looking for cocoanuts. It was strange that so many bodies floated up, and no nuts. Surely, there were more cocoanuts afloat than dead men! She gave up at last, and lay exhausted. The end had come. Nothing remained but to wait for death.

Coming out of a stupor, she became slowly aware that she was gazing at a patch of sandy-red hair on the head of a corpse. The sea flung the body toward her, then drew it back. It turned over, and she saw that it had no face. Yet there was something familiar about that patch of sandy-red hair. An hour passed. She did not exert herself to make the identification. She was waiting to die, and it mattered little to her what man that thing of horror once might have been.

But at the end of the hour she sat up slowly and stared at the corpse. An unusually large wave had thrown it beyond the reach of the lesser waves. Yes, she was right; that patch of red hair could belong to but one man in the Paumotus. It was Levy, the German Jew, the man who had bought the pearl and carried it away on the *Hira*. Well, one thing was evident: the *Hira* had been lost. The pearl-buyer's god of fishermen and thieves had gone back on him.

She crawled down to the dead man. His shirt had been torn away, and she could see the leather money-belt about his waist. She held her breath and tugged at the buckles. They gave easier than she had expected, and she crawled hurriedly away across the sand, dragging the belt after her. Pocket after pocket she unbuckled in the belt and found empty. Where could he have put it? In the last pocket of all she found it, the first and only pearl he had bought on the voyage. She crawled a few feet farther, to escape the pestilence of the belt, and examined the pearl. It was the one Mapuhi had found and been robbed of by Toriki. She weighed it in her hand and rolled it back and forth caressingly. But in it she saw no intrinsic beauty. What she did see was the house Mapuhi and Tefara and she had built so carefully in their minds. Each time she looked at the pearl she saw the house in all its details, including the octagon-drop-clock on the wall. That was something to live for.

She tore a strip from her *ahu* and tied the pearl securely about her neck. Then she went on along the beach, panting and groaning, but resolutely seeking for cocoanuts. Quickly she found one, and, as she glanced around, a second. She broke one, drinking its water, which was mildewy, and eating the last particle of the meat. A little later she found a shattered dugout. Its outrigger was gone, but she was hopeful, and, before the day was out, she found the outrigger. Every find was an augury. The pearl was a talisman. Late in the afternoon she saw a wooden box floating low in the water. When she dragged it out on the beach its contents rattled, and inside she found ten tins of salmon. She opened one by hammering it on the canoe. When a leak was started, she drained the tin. After that she spent several hours in extracting the salmon, hammering and squeezing it out a morsel at a time.

Eight days longer she waited for rescue. In the meantime she fastened the outrigger back on the canoe, using for lashings all the cocoanut-fibre she could find, and also what remained of her *ahu*. The canoe was badly cracked, and she could not make it water-tight, but a calabash made from a cocoanut she stored on board for a bailer. She was hard put for a paddle. With a piece of tin she sawed off all her hair close to the scalp. Out of the hair she braided a cord; and by means of the cord she lashed a three-foot piece of broom-handle to a board from the salmon case. She gnawed wedges with her teeth and with them wedged the lashing.

On the eighteenth day, at midnight, she launched the canoe through the surf and started back for Hikueru. She was an old woman. Hardship had stripped her fat from her till scarcely more than bones and skin and a few stringy muscles remained. The canoe was large and should have been paddled by three strong men. But she did it alone, with a make-shift paddle. Also, the canoe leaked badly, and one-third of her time was devoted to bailing. By clear daylight she looked vainly for Hikueru. Astern, Takokota had sunk beneath the sea-rim. The sun blazed down on her nakedness, compelling her body to surrender its moisture. Two tins of salmon were left, and in the course of the day she battered holes in them and drained the liquid. She had no time to waste in extracting the meat. A current was setting to the westward, she made westing whether she made southing or not.

In the early afternoon, standing upright in the canoe, she sighted Hikueru. Its wealth of cocoanut palms was gone. Only here and there, at wide intervals, could she see the ragged remnants of trees. The sight cheered her. She was nearer than she had thought. The current was setting her to the westward. She bore up against it and paddled on. The wedges in the paddle-lashing worked loose, and she lost much time, at frequent intervals, in driving them tight. Then there was the bailing. One hour in three she had to cease paddling in order to bail. And all the time she drifted to the westward.

By sunset Hikueru bore southeast from her, three miles away. There was a full moon, and by eight o'clock the land was due east and two miles away. She struggled on for another hour, but the land was as far away as ever. She was in the main grip of the current; the canoe was too large; the paddle was too inadequate; and too much of her time and strength was wasted in bailing. Besides, she was very weak and growing weaker. Despite her efforts, the canoe was drifting off to the westward.

She breathed a prayer to her shark god, slipped over the side, and began to swim. She was actually refreshed by the water, and quickly left the canoe astern. At the end of an hour the land was perceptibly nearer. Then came her fright. Right before her eyes, not twenty feet away, a large fin cut the water. She swam steadily toward it, and slowly it glided away, curving off toward the right and circling around her. She kept her eyes on the fin and swam on. When the fin disappeared, she lay face downward on the water and watched. When the fin reappeared she resumed her swimming. The monster was lazy – she could see that. Without doubt he had been well fed since the hurricane. Had he been very hungry, she knew he would not have hesitated from making a dash for her. He was fifteen feet long, and one bite, she knew, could cut her in half.

But she did not have any time to waste on him. Whether she swam or not, the current drew away from the land just the same. A half-hour went by, and the shark began to grow bolder. Seeing no harm in her he drew closer, in narrowing circles, cocking his eyes at her impudently as he slid past. Sooner or later, she knew well enough, he would get up sufficient courage to dash at her. She resolved to play first. It was a desperate act she meditated. She was an old woman, alone in the sea and weak from starvation and hardship; and yet she, in the face of this sea-tiger, must anticipate his dash by herself dashing at him. She swam on, waiting her chance. At last he passed languidly by, barely eight feet away. She rushed at him suddenly, feigning that she was attacking him. He gave a wild flirt of his tail as he fled away, and his sandpaper hide, striking her, took off her skin from elbow to shoulder. He swam rapidly, in a widening circle, and at last disappeared.

In the hole in the sand, covered over by fragments of metal roofing, Mapuhi and Tefara lay disputing.

'If you had done as I said,' charged Tefara, for the thousandth time, 'and hidden the pearl and told no one, you would have it now.'

'But Huru-Huru was with me when I opened the shell – have I not told you so times and times and times without end?'

'And now we shall have no house. Raoul told me today that if you had not sold the pearl to Toriki –'

'I did not sell it. Toriki robbed me.'

'– that if you had not sold the pearl, he would give you five thousand French dollars, which is ten thousand Chili.'

'He has been talking to his mother,' Mapuhi explained. 'She has an eye for a pearl.'

'And now the pearl is lost,' Tefara complained.

'It paid my debt with Toriki. That is twelve hundred I have made, anyway.'

'Toriki is dead,' she cried. 'They have heard no word of his schooner. She was lost along with the *Aorai* and the *Hira*. Will Toriki pay you the three hundred credit he promised? No, because Toriki is dead. And had you found no pearl, would you today owe Toriki the twelve hundred? No, because Toriki is dead, and you cannot pay dead men.'

'But Levy did not pay Toriki,' Mapuhi said. 'He gave him a piece of paper that was good for the money in Papeete; and now Levy is dead and cannot pay; and Toriki is dead and the paper lost with him, and the pearl is lost with Levy. You are right, Tefara. I have lost the pearl, and got nothing for it. Now let us sleep.'

He held up his hand suddenly and listened. From without came a noise, as of one who breathed heavily and with pain. A hand fumbled against the mat that served for a door.

'Who is there?' Mapuhi cried.

'Nauri,' came the answer. 'Can you tell me where is my son, Mapuhi?'

Tefara screamed and gripped her husband's arm.

'A ghost!' she chattered. 'A ghost!'

Mapuhi's face was a ghastly yellow. He clung weakly to his wife.

'Good woman,' he said in faltering tones, striving to disguise his voice, 'I know your son well. He is living on the east side of the lagoon.'

From without came the sound of a sigh. Mapuhi began to feel elated. He had fooled the ghost.

'But where do you come from, old woman?' he asked.

'From the sea,' was the dejected answer.

'I knew it! I knew it!' screamed Tefara, rocking to and fro.

'Since when has Tefara bedded in a strange house?' came Nauri's voice through the matting.

Mapuhi looked fear and reproach at his wife. It was her voice that had betrayed them.

'And since when has Mapuhi, my son, denied his old mother?' the voice went on.

'No, no, I have not – Mapuhi has not denied you,' he cried. 'I am not Mapuhi. He is on the east end of the lagoon, I tell you.'

Ngakura sat up in bed and began to cry. The matting started to shake.

'What are you doing?' Mapuhi demanded.

'I am coming in,' said the voice of Nauri.

One end of the matting lifted. Tefara tried to dive under the blankets, but Mapuhi held on to her. He had to hold on to something. Together, struggling with each other, with shivering bodies and chattering teeth, they gazed with protruding eyes at the lifting mat. They saw Nauri, dripping with sea-water, without her *ahu*, creep in. They rolled over backward from her and fought for Ngakura's blanket with which to cover their heads.

'You might give your old mother a drink of water,' the ghost said plaintively.

'Give her a drink of water,' Tefara commanded in a shaking voice.

'Give her a drink of water,' Mapuhi passed on the command to Ngakura.

And together they kicked out Ngakura from under the blanket. A minute later, peeping, Mapuhi saw the ghost drinking. When it reached out a shaking hand and laid it on his, he felt the weight of it and was convinced that it was no ghost. Then he emerged, dragging Tefara after him, and in a few minutes all were listening to Nauri's tale. And when she told of Levy, and dropped the pearl into Tefara's hand, even she was reconciled to the reality of her mother-in-law.

'In the morning,' said Tefara, 'you will sell the pearl to Raoul for five thousand French.'

'The house?' objected Nauri.

'He will build the house,' Tefara answered. 'He says it will cost four thousand French. Also will he give one thousand French in credit, which is two thousand Chili.'

'And it will be six fathoms long?' Nauri queried.

'Ay,' answered Mapuhi, 'six fathoms.'

'And in the middle room will be the octagon-drop-clock?'

'Ay, and the round table as well.'

'Then give me something to eat, for I am hungry,' said Nauri, complacently. 'And after that we will sleep, for I am weary. And tomorrow we will have more talk about the house before we sell the pearl. It will be better if we take the thousand French in cash. Money is ever better than credit in buying goods from the traders.'

JOSEPH CONRAD

YOUTH

THIS COULD HAVE occurred nowhere but in England, where men and sea interpenetrate, so to speak – the sea entering into the life of most men, and the men knowing something or everything about the sea, in the way of amusement, of travel, or of bread-winning.

We were sitting round a mahogany table that reflected the bottle, the claret-glasses, and our faces as we leaned on our elbows. There was a director of companies, an accountant, a lawyer, Marlow, and myself. The director had been a *Conway* boy, the accountant had served four years at sea, the lawyer – a fine crusted Tory, High Churchman, the best of old fellows, the soul of honor – had been chief officer in the P. & O. service in the good old days when mail-boats were square-rigged at least on two masts, and used to come down the China Sea before a fair monsoon with stun'-sails set alow and aloft. We all began life in the merchant service. Between the five of us there was the strong bond of the sea, and also the fellowship of the craft, which no amount of enthusiasm for yachting, cruising, and so on can give, since one is only the amusement of life and the other is life itself.

Marlow (at least I think that is how he spelt his name) told the story, or rather the chronicle, of a voyage:

'Yes, I have seen a little of the Eastern seas; but what I remember best is my first voyage there. You fellows know there are those voyages that seem ordered for the illustration of life, that might stand for a symbol of existence. You fight, work, sweat, nearly kill yourself, sometimes do kill yourself, trying to accomplish something – and you can't. Not from any fault of yours. You simply can do nothing, neither great nor little – not a thing in the world – not even marry an old maid, or get a wretched 600-ton cargo of coal to its port of destination.

'It was altogether a memorable affair. It was my first voyage to the East, and my first voyage as second mate; it was also my skipper's first command. You'll admit it was time. He was sixty if a day; a little man, with a broad, not very straight back, with bowed shoulders and one leg more bandy than the other, he had that queer twisted-about appearance you see so often in men who work in the fields. He had a nut-cracker face – chin and nose trying to come together over a sunken mouth – and it was framed in iron-gray fluffy hair, that looked like a chin strap of cotton-wool sprinkled with coal-dust. And he had blue eyes in that old face of his, which were amazingly like a boy's, with that candid expression some quite common men preserve to the end of their days by a rare internal gift of simplicity of heart and rectitude of soul. What induced him to accept me was a wonder. I had come out of a crack Australian clipper, where I had been third officer, and he seemed to have a prejudice against crack clippers as aristocratic and high-toned. He said to me, "You know, in this ship you will have to work." I said I had to work in every ship I had ever been in. "Ah, but this is different, and you gentlemen out of them big ships; . . . but there! I dare say you will do. Join tomorrow."

'I joined tomorrow. It was twenty-two years ago; and I was just twenty. How time passes! It was one of the happiest days of my life. Fancy! Second mate for the first time – a really responsible officer! I wouldn't have thrown up my new billet for a fortune. The mate looked me over carefully. He was also an old chap, but of another stamp. He had a Roman nose, a snow-white, long beard, and his name was Mahon, but he insisted that it should be pronounced Mann. He was well connected; yet there was something wrong with his luck, and he had never got on.

'As to the captain, he had been for years in coasters, then in the Mediterranean, and last in the West Indian trade. He had never been round the Capes. He could just write a kind of sketchy hand, and didn't care for writing at all. Both were thorough good seamen of course, and between those two old chaps I felt like a small boy between two grandfathers.

'The ship also was old. Her name was the *Judea*. Queer name, isn't it? She belonged to a man Wilmer, Wilcox – some name like that; but he has been bankrupt and dead these twenty years or more, and his name don't matter. She had been laid up in Shadwell basin for ever so long. You can imagine her state. She was all rust, dust, grime – soot aloft, dirt on deck. To me it was like coming out of a palace into a ruined cottage. She was about 400 tons, had a primitive windlass, wooden latches to the doors, not a bit of brass about her, and a big square stern. There was on it, below her name in big letters, a lot of scroll work, with the gilt off, and some sort of a coat of arms, with the motto "Do or Die" underneath. I remember it took my fancy immensely. There was a touch of romance in it, something that made me love the old thing – something that appealed to my youth!

'We left London in ballast – sand ballast – to load a cargo of coal in a northern port for Bankok. Bankok! I thrilled. I had been six years at sea, but had only seen Melbourne and Sydney, very good places, charming places in their way – but Bankok!

'We worked out of the Thames under canvas, with a North Sea pilot on board. His name was Jermyn, and he dodged all day long about the galley drying his handkerchief before the stove. Apparently he never slept. He was a dismal man, with a perpetual tear sparkling at the end of his nose, who either had been in trouble, or was in trouble, or expected to be in trouble – couldn't be happy unless something went wrong. He mistrusted my youth, my common-sense, and my seamanship, and made a point of showing it in a hundred little ways. I dare say he was right. It seems to me I knew very little then, and I know not much more now; but I cherish a hate for that Jermyn to this day.

'We were a week working up as far as Yarmouth Roads, and then we got into a gale – the famous October gale of twenty-two years ago. It was wind, lightning, sleet, snow, and a terrific sea. We were flying light, and you may imagine how bad it was when I tell you we had smashed bulwarks and a flooded deck. On the second night she shifted her ballast into the lee bow, and by that time we had been blown off somewhere on the Dogger Bank. There was nothing for it but go below with shovels and try to right her, and there we were in that vast hold, gloomy like a cavern, the tallow dips stuck and flickering on the beams, the gale howling above, the ship tossing about like mad on her side; there we all were, Jermyn, the captain, everyone, hardly able to keep our feet, engaged on that grave-digger's work, and trying to toss shovelfuls of wet sand up to the windward. At every tumble of the ship you could see vaguely in the dim light men falling down with a great flourish of shovels. One of the ship's boys (we had two), impressed by the weirdness of the scene, wept as if his heart would break. We could hear him blubbering somewhere in the shadows.

'On the third day the gale died out, and by-and-by a north-country tug picked us up. We took sixteen days in all to get from London to the Tyne! When we got into dock we had lost our turn for loading, and they hauled us off to a tier where we remained for a month. Mrs Beard (the captain's name was Beard) came from Colchester to see the old man. She lived on board. The crew of runners had left, and there remained only the officers, one boy, and the steward, a mulatto who answered to the name of Abraham. Mrs Beard was an old woman, with a face all wrinkled and ruddy like a winter apple, and the figure of a young girl. She caught sight of me once, sewing on a button, and insisted on having my shirts to repair. This was something different from the captains' wives I had known on board crack clippers. When I brought her the shirts, she said: "And the socks? They want mending, I am sure, and John's – Captain Beard's – things are all in order now. I would be glad of something to do." Bless the old woman. She overhauled my outfit for me, and meantime I read for the first time "Sartor Resartus" and Burnaby's "Ride to Khiva." I didn't understand much of the first then; but I remember I preferred the soldier to the philosopher at the time; a preference which life has only confirmed. One was a man, and the other was either more – or less. However, they are both dead, and Mrs Beard is dead, and youth, strength, genius, thoughts, achievements, simple hearts – all die. . . . No matter.

'They loaded us at last. We shipped a crew. Eight able seamen and two boys. We hauled off one evening to the buoys at the dock-gates, ready to go out, and with a fair prospect of beginning the voyage next day. Mrs Beard was to start for home by a late train. When the ship was fast we went to tea. We sat rather silent through the meal – Mahon, the old couple, and I. I finished first, and slipped away for a smoke, my cabin being in a deck-house just against the poop. It was high water, blowing fresh with a drizzle; the double dock-gates were opened, and the steam colliers were going in and out in the darkness with their lights burning bright, a great plashing of propellers, rattling of winches, and a lot of hailing on the pier-heads. I watched the procession of head-lights gliding high and of green lights gliding low in the night, when suddenly a red gleam flashed at me, vanished, came into view again, and remained. The fore-end of a steamer loomed up close. I shouted down the cabin, "Come up, quick!" and then heard a startled voice saying afar in the dark, "Stop her, sir." A bell jingled. Another voice cried warningly, "We are going right into that bark, sir." The answer to this was a gruff "All right," and the next thing was a heavy crash as the steamer struck a glancing blow with the bluff of her bow about our fore-rigging. There was a moment of confusion, yelling, and running about. Steam roared. Then somebody was heard saying, "All clear, sir." . . . "Are you all right?" asked the gruff voice. I had jumped forward to see the damage, and hailed back, "I think so." "Easy astern," said the gruff voice. A bell jingled. "What steamer is that?" screamed Mahon. By that time she was no more to us than a bulky shadow maneuvering a little way off. They shouted at us some name – a woman's name, Miranda or Melissa – or some such thing. "This means another month in this beastly hole," said Mahon to me, as we peered with lamps about the splintered bulwarks and broken braces. "But where's the captain?"

'We had not heard or seen anything of him all that time. We went aft to look. A doleful voice arose hailing somewhere in the middle of the dock, "*Judea* ahoy!" . . . How the devil did he get there? . . . "Hallo!" we shouted. "I am adrift in our boat without oars," he cried. A belated waterman offered his services, and Mahon struck a bargain with him for half-a-crown to tow our skipper alongside; but it was Mrs Beard that came up the ladder first. They had been floating about the dock in that mizzly cold rain for nearly an hour. I was never so surprised in my life.

'It appears that when he heard my shout "Come up," he understood at once what was the matter, caught up his wife, ran on deck, and across, and down into our boat, which was fast to the ladder. Not bad for a sixty-year-old. Just imagine that old fellow saving heroically in his arms that old woman – the woman of his life. He set her down on a thwart, and was ready to climb back on board when the painter came adrift somehow, and away they went together. Of course in the confusion we did not hear him shouting. He looked abashed. She said cheerfully, "I suppose it does not matter my losing the train now?" "No, Jenny – you go below and get warm," he growled. Then to us: "A sailor has no business with a wife – I say. There I was, out of the ship. Well, no harm done this time. Let's go and look at what that fool of a steamer smashed."

'It wasn't much, but it delayed us three weeks. At the end of that time, the captain being engaged with his agents, I carried Mrs Beard's bag to the railway-station and put her all comfy into a third-class carriage. She lowered the window to say, "You are a good young man. If you see John – Captain Beard – without his muffler at night, just remind him from me to keep his throat well wrapped up." "Certainly, Mrs Beard," I said. "You are a good young man; I noticed how attentive you are to John – to Captain—" The train pulled out suddenly; I took my cap off to the old woman: I never saw her again. . . . Pass the bottle.

'We went to sea next day. When we made that start for Bankok we had been already three months out of London. We had expected to be a fortnight or so – at the outside.

'It was January, and the weather was beautiful – the beautiful sunny winter weather that has more charm than in the summer-time, because it is unexpected, and crisp, and you know it won't, it can't, last long. It's like a windfall, like a god-send, like an unexpected piece of luck.

'It lasted all down the North Sea, all down Channel; and it lasted till we were three hundred miles or so to the westward of the Lizards: then the wind went round to the sou'-west and began to pipe up. In two days it blew a gale. The *Judea*, hove to, wallowed on the Atlantic like an old candle-box. It blew day after day; it blew with spite, without interval, without mercy, without rest. The world was nothing but an immensity of great foaming waves rushing at us, under a sky low enough to touch with the hand and dirty like a smoked ceiling. In the stormy space surrounding us there was as much flying spray as air. Day after day and night after night there was nothing round the ship but the howl of the wind, the tumult of the sea, the noise of water pouring over her deck. There was no rest for her and no rest for us. She tossed, she pitched, she stood on her head, she sat on her tail, she rolled, she groaned, and we had to hold on while on deck and cling to our bunks when below, in a constant effort of body, and worry of mind.

'One night Mahon spoke through the small window of my berth. It opened right into my very bed, and I was lying there sleepless, in my boots, feeling as though I had not slept for years, and could not if I tried. He said excitedly –

' "You got the sounding-rod in here, Marlow? I can't get the pumps to suck. By God! it's no child's play."

'I gave him the sounding-rod and lay down again, trying to think of various things – but I thought only of the pumps. When I came on deck they were still at it, and my watch relieved at the pumps. By the light of the lantern brought on deck to examine the sounding-rod I caught a glimpse of their weary, serious faces. We pumped all the four hours.

We pumped all night, all day, all week, – watch and watch. She was working herself loose, and leaked badly – not enough to drown us at once, but enough to kill us with the work at the pumps. And while we pumped the ship was going from us piecemeal: the bulwarks went, the stanchions were torn out, the ventilators smashed, the cabin-door burst in. There was not a dry spot in the ship. She was being gutted bit by bit. The long-boat changed, as if by magic, into matchwood where she stood in her gripes. I had lashed her myself, and was rather proud of my handiwork, which had withstood so long the malice of the sea. And we pumped. And there was no break in the weather. The sea was white like a sheet of foam, like a caldron of boiling milk; there was not a break in the clouds, no – not the size of a man's hand – no, not for so much as ten seconds. There was for us no sky, there were for us no stars, no sun, no universe – nothing but angry clouds and an infuriated sea. We pumped watch and watch, for dear life; and it seemed to last for months, for years, for all eternity, as though we had been dead and gone to a hell for sailors. We forgot the day of the week, the name of the month, what year it was, and whether we had ever been ashore. The sails blew away, she lay broadside on under a weather-cloth, the ocean poured over her, and we did not care. We turned those handles, and had the eyes of idiots. As soon as we had crawled on deck I used to take a round turn with a rope about the men, the pumps, and the mainmast, and we turned, we turned incessantly, with the water to our waists, to our necks, over our heads. It was all one. We had forgotten how it felt to be dry.

'And there was somewhere in me the thought: By Jove! this is the deuce of an adventure – something you read about; and it is my first voyage as second mate – and I am only twenty – and here I am lasting it out as well as any of these men, and keeping my chaps up to the mark. I was pleased. I would not have given up the experience for worlds. I had moments of exultation. Whenever the old dismantled craft pitched heavily with her counter high in the air, she seemed to me to throw up, like an appeal, like a defiance, like a cry to the clouds without mercy, the words written on her stern: "*Judea*, London. Do or Die."

'O youth! The strength of it, the faith of it, the imagination of it! To me she was not an old rattle-trap carting about the world a lot of coal for a freight – to me she was the endeavor, the test, the trial of life. I think of her with pleasure, with affection, with regret – as you would think of someone dead you have loved. I shall never forget her.... Pass the bottle.

'One night when tied to the mast, as I explained, we were pumping on, deafened with the wind, and without spirit enough in us to wish ourselves dead, a heavy sea crashed aboard and swept clean over us. As soon as I got my breath I shouted, as in duty bound, "Keep on, boys!" when suddenly I felt something hard floating on deck strike the calf of my leg. I made a grab at it and missed. It was so dark we could not see each other's faces within a foot – you understand.

'After that thump the ship kept quiet for a while, and the thing, whatever it was, struck my leg again. This time I caught it – and it was a sauce-pan. At first, being stupid with fatigue and thinking of nothing but the pumps, I did not understand what I had in my hand. Suddenly it dawned upon me, and I shouted, "Boys, the house on deck is gone. Leave this, and let's look for the cook."

'There was a deck-house forward, which contained the galley, the cook's berth, and the quarters of the crew. As we had expected for days to see it swept away, the hands had been ordered to sleep in the cabin – the only safe place in the ship. The steward, Abraham, however, persisted in clinging to his berth, stupidly, like a mule – from sheer fright I believe, like an animal that won't leave a stable falling in an earthquake. So we went to look for him. It was chancing death, since once out of our lashings we were as exposed as if on a raft. But we went. The house was shattered as if a shell had exploded inside. Most of it had gone overboard – stove, men's quarters, and their property, all was gone; but two posts, holding a portion of the bulkhead to which Abraham's bunk was attached, remained as if by a miracle. We groped in the ruins and came upon this, and there he was, sitting in his bunk, surrounded by foam and wreckage, jabbering cheerfully to himself. He was out of his mind; completely, and for ever mad, with this sudden shock coming upon the fag-end of his endurance. We snatched him up, lugged him aft, and pitched him head-first down the cabin companion. You understand there was no time to carry him down with infinite precautions and wait to see how he got on. Those below would pick him up at the bottom of the stairs all right. We were in a hurry to go back to the pumps. That business could not wait. A bad leak is an inhuman thing.

'One would think that the sole purpose of that fiendish gale had been to make a lunatic of that poor devil of a mulatto. It eased before morning, and next day the sky cleared, and as the sea went down the leak took up. When it came to bending a fresh set of sails the crew demanded to put back – and really there was nothing else to do. Boats gone, decks swept clean, cabin gutted, men without a stitch but what they stood in, stores spoiled, ship strained. We put her head for home, and – would you believe it? The wind came east right in our teeth. It blew fresh, it blew continuously. We had to beat up every inch of the way, but she did not leak so badly, the water keeping comparatively smooth. Two hours' pumping in every four is no joke – but it kept her afloat as far as Falmouth.

'The good people there live on casualties of the sea, and no doubt were glad to see us. A hungry crowd of shipwrights sharpened their chisels at the sight of that carcass of a ship. And, by Jove! they had pretty pickings off us before they were done. I fancy the owner was already in a tight place. There were delays. Then it was decided to take part of the cargo out and calk her topsides. This was done, the repairs finished, cargo reshipped; a new crew came on board, and we went out – for Bankok. At the end of a week we were back again. The crew said they weren't going to Bankok – a hundred and fifty days' passage – in a something hooker that wanted pumping eight hours out of the twenty-four; and the nautical papers inserted again the little paragraph: "*Judea*. Bark. Tyne to Bankok; coals; put back to Falmouth leaky and with crew refusing duty."

'There were more delays – more tinkering. The owner came down for a day, and said she was as right as a little fiddle. Poor old Captain Beard looked like the ghost of a Geordie skipper – through the worry and humiliation of it. Remember he was sixty, and it was his first command. Mahon said it was a foolish business, and would end badly. I loved the ship more than ever, and wanted awfully to get to Bankok. To Bankok! Magic name, blessed name. Mesopotamia wasn't a patch on it. Remember I was twenty, and it was my first second mate's billet, and the East was waiting for me.

'We went out and anchored in the outer roads with a fresh crew – the third. She leaked worse than ever. It was as if those confounded shipwrights had actually made a hole in her. This time we did not even go outside. The crew simply refused to man the windlass.

'They towed us back to the inner harbor, and we became a fixture, a feature, an institution of the place. People pointed us out to visitors as "That 'ere bark that's going to Bankok – has been here six months – put back three times." On holidays the small boys pulling about in boats would hail, "*Judea*, ahoy!" and if a head showed above the rail shouted, "Where you bound to? – Bankok?" and jeered. We were only three on board. The poor old skipper mooned in the cabin. Mahon undertook the cooking, and unexpectedly developed all a Frenchman's genius for preparing nice little messes. I looked languidly after the rigging. We became citizens of Falmouth. Every shopkeeper knew us. At the barbers or tobacconist's they asked familiarly, "Do you think you will ever get to Bankok?" Meantime the owner, the underwriters, and the charterers squabbled amongst themselves in London, and our pay went on. . . . Pass the bottle.

'It was horrid. Morally it was worse than pumping for life. It seemed as though we had been forgotten by the world, belonged to nobody, would get nowhere; it seemed that, as if bewitched, we would have to live for ever and ever in that inner harbor, a derision and a by-word to generations of long-shore loafers and dishonest boatmen. I obtained three months' pay and a five days' leave, and made a rush for London. It took me a day to get there and pretty well another to come back – but three months' pay went all the same. I don't know what I did with it. I went to a music-hall, I believe, lunched, dined, and supped in a swell place in Regent Street, and was back to time, with nothing but a complete set of Byron's works and a new railway rug to show for three months' work. The boatman who pulled me off to the ship said: "Hallo! I thought you had left the old thing. *She* will never get to Bankok." "That's all *you* know about it," I said scornfully – but I didn't like that prophecy at all.

'Suddenly a man, some kind of agent to somebody, appeared with full powers. He had grog blossoms all over his face, an indomitable energy, and was a jolly soul. We leaped into life again. A hulk came alongside, took our cargo, and then we went into dry dock to get our copper stripped. No wonder she leaked. The poor thing, strained beyond endurance by the gale, had, as if in disgust, spat out all the oakum of her lower seams. She was recalked, new coppered, and made as tight as a bottle. We went back to the hulk and reshipped our cargo.

'Then on a fine moonlight night, all the rats left the ship.

'We had been infested with them. They had destroyed our sails, consumed more stores than the crew, affably shared our beds and our dangers, and now, when the ship was made seaworthy, concluded to clear out. I called Mahon to enjoy the spectacle. Rat after rat appeared on our rail, took a last look over his shoulder, and leaped with a hollow thud into the empty hulk. We tried to count them, but soon lost the tale. Mahon said: "Well, well! don't talk to me about the intelligence of rats. They ought to have left before, when we had that narrow squeak from foundering. There you have the proof how silly is the superstition about them. They leave a good ship for an old rotten hulk, where there is nothing to eat, too, the fools! . . . I don't believe they know what is safe or what is good for them, any more than you or I."

'And after some more talk we agreed that the wisdom of rats had been grossly overrated, being in fact no greater than that of men.

'The story of the ship was known, by this, all up the Channel from Land's End to the Forelands, and we could get no crew on the south coast. They sent us one all complete from Liverpool, and we left once more – for Bankok.

'We had fair breezes, smooth water right into the tropics,

and the old *Judea* lumbered along in the sunshine. When she went eight knots everything cracked aloft, and we tied our caps to our heads; but mostly she strolled on at the rate of three miles an hour. What could you expect? She was tired – that old ship. Her youth was where mine is – where yours is – you fellows who listen to this yarn; and what friend would throw your years and your weariness in your face? We didn't grumble at her. To us aft, at least, it seemed as though we had been born in her, reared in her, had lived in her for ages, had never known any other ship. I would just as soon have abused the old village church at home for not being a cathedral.

'And for me there was also my youth to make me patient. There was all the East before me, and all life, and the thought that I had been tried in that ship and had come out pretty well. And I thought of men of old who, centuries ago, went that road in ships that sailed no better, to the land of palms, and spices, and yellow sands, and of brown nations ruled by kings more cruel than Nero the Roman and more splendid than Solomon the Jew. The old bark lumbered on, heavy with her age and the burden of her cargo, while I lived the life of youth in ignorance and hope. She lumbered on through an interminable procession of days; and the fresh gilding flashed back at the setting sun, seemed to cry out over the darkening sea the words painted on her stern, "*Judea*, London. Do or Die."

'Then we entered the Indian Ocean and steered northerly for Java Head. The winds were light. Weeks slipped by. She crawled on, do or die, and people at home began to think of posting us as overdue.

'One Saturday evening, I being off duty, the men asked me to give them an extra bucket of water or so – for washing clothes. As I did not wish to screw on the fresh-water pump so late, I went forward whistling, and with a key in my hand to unlock the forepeak scuttle, intending to serve the water out of a spare tank we kept there.

'The smell down below was as unexpected as it was frightful. One would have thought hundreds of paraffin-lamps had been flaring and smoking in that hole for days. I was glad to get out. The man with me coughed and said, "Funny smell, sir." I answered negligently, "It's good for the health, they say," and walked aft.

'The first thing I did was to put my head down the square of the midship ventilator. As I lifted the lid a visible breath, something like a thin fog, a puff of faint haze, rose from the opening. The ascending air was hot, and had a heavy, sooty, paraffiny smell. I gave one sniff, and put down the lid gently. It was no use choking myself. The cargo was on fire.

'Next day she began to smoke in earnest. You see it was to be expected, for though the coal was of a safe kind, that cargo had been so handled, so broken up with handling, that it looked more like smithy coal than anything else. Then it had been wetted – more than once. It rained all the time we were taking it back from the hulk, and now with this long passage it got heated, and there was another case of spontaneous combustion.

'The captain called us into the cabin. He had a chart spread on the table, and looked unhappy. He said, "The coast of West Australia is near, but I mean to proceed to our destination. It is the hurricane month too; but we will just keep her head for Bankok, and fight the fire. No more putting back anywhere, if we all get roasted. We will try to stifle this 'ere damned combustion by want of air."

'We tried. We battened down everything, and still she smoked. The smoke kept coming out through imperceptible crevices; it forced itself through bulkheads and covers; it oozed here and there and everywhere in slender threads, in an invisible film, in an incomprehensible manner. It made its way into the cabin, into the forecastle; it poisoned the sheltered places on the deck, it could be sniffed as high as the mainyard. It was clear that if the smoke came out the air came in. This was disheartening. This combustion refused to be stifled.

'We resolved to try water, and took the hatches off. Enormous volumes of smoke, whitish, yellowish, thick, greasy, misty, choking, ascended as high as the trucks. All hands cleared out aft. Then the poisonous cloud blew away, and we went back to work in a smoke that was no thicker now than that of an ordinary factory chimney.

'We rigged the force pump, got the hose along, and by-and-by it burst. Well, it was as old as the ship – a prehistoric hose, and past repair. Then we pumped with the feeble head-pump, drew water with buckets, and in this way managed in time to pour lots of Indian Ocean into the main hatch. The bright stream flashed in sunshine, fell into a layer of white crawling smoke, and vanished on the black surface of coal. Steam ascended mingling with the smoke. We poured salt water as into a barrel without a bottom. It was our fate to pump in that ship, to pump out of her, to pump into her; and after keeping water out of her to save ourselves from being drowned, we frantically poured water into her to save ourselves from being burnt.

'And she crawled on, do or die, in the serene weather. The sky was a miracle of purity, a miracle of azure. The sea was polished, was blue, was pellucid, was sparkling like a precious stone, extending on all sides, all round to the horizon – as if the whole terrestrial globe had been one jewel, one colossal sapphire, a single gem fashioned into a planet. And on the luster of the great calm waters the *Judea* glided imperceptibly, enveloped in languid and unclean vapors, in a lazy cloud that drifted to leeward, light and slow: a pestiferous cloud defiling the splendor of sea and sky.

'All this time of course we saw no fire. The cargo smoldered at the bottom somewhere. Once Mahon, as we were working side by side, said to me with a queer smile: "Now, if she only would spring a tidy leak – like that time when we first left the Channel – it would put a stopper on this fire. Wouldn't it?" I remarked irrelevantly, "Do you remember the rats?"

'We fought the fire and sailed the ship too as carefully as though nothing had been the matter. The steward cooked and attended on us. Of the other twelve men, eight worked while four rested. Everyone took his turn, captain included. There was equality, and if not exactly fraternity, then a deal of good feeling. Sometimes a man, as he dashed a bucketful of water down the hatchway, would yell out, "Hurrah for Bankok!" and the rest laughed. But generally we were taciturn and serious – and thirsty. Oh! how thirsty! And we had to be careful with the water. Strict allowance. The ship smoked, the sun blazed. . . . Pass the bottle.

'We tried everything. We even made an attempt to dig down to the fire. No good, of course. No man could remain more than a minute below. Mahon, who went first, fainted there, and the man who went to fetch him out did likewise. We lugged them out on deck. Then I leaped down to show how easily it could be done. They had learned wisdom by that time, and contented themselves by fishing for me with a chain-hook tied to a broom-handle, I believe. I did not offer to go and fetch up my shovel, which was left down below.

'Things began to look bad. We put the long-boat into the water. The second boat was ready to swing out. We had also another, a fourteen-foot thing, on davits aft, where it was quite safe.

'Then behold, the smoke suddenly decreased. We redoubled our efforts to flood the bottom of the ship. In two days there was no smoke at all. Everybody was on the broad grin. This was on a Friday. On Saturday no work, but sailing the ship of course was done. The men washed their clothes and their faces for the first time in a fortnight, and had a special dinner given them. They spoke of spontaneous combustion with contempt, and implied *they* were the boys to put out combustions. Somehow we all felt as though we each had inherited a large fortune. But a beastly smell of burning hung about the ship. Captain Beard had hollow eyes and sunken cheeks. I had never noticed so much before how twisted and bowed he was. He and Mahon prowled soberly about hatches and ventilators, sniffing. It struck me suddenly poor Mahon was a very, very old chap. As to me, I was as pleased and proud as though I had helped to win a great naval battle. O! Youth!

'The night was fine. In the morning a homeward-bound ship passed us hull down, – the first we had seen for months; but we were nearing the land at last, Java Head being about 190 miles off, and nearly due north.

'Next day it was my watch on deck from eight to twelve. At breakfast the captain observed, "It's wonderful how that smell hangs about the cabin." About ten, the mate being on the poop, I stepped down on the maindeck for a moment. The carpenter's bench stood abaft the mainmast: I leaned against it sucking at my pipe, and the carpenter, a young chap, came to talk to me. He remarked, "I think we have done very well, haven't we?" and then I perceived with annoyance the fool was trying to tilt the bench. I said curtly, "Don't, Chips," and immediately became aware of a queer sensation, of an absurd delusion, – I seemed somehow to be in the air. I heard all round me like a pent-up breath released

– as if a thousand giants simultaneously had said Phoo! – and felt a dull concussion which made my ribs ache suddenly. No doubt about it – I was in the air, and my body was describing a short parabola. But short as it was, I had the time to think several thoughts in, as far as I can remember, the following order: "This can't be the carpenter – What is it? – Some accident – Submarine volcano? – Coals, gas! – By Jove! we are being blown up – Everybody's dead – I am falling into the afterhatch – I see fire in it."

'The coal-dust suspended in the air of the hold had glowed dull-red at the moment of the explosion. In the twinkling of an eye, in an infinitesimal fraction of a second since the first tilt of the bench, I was sprawling full length on the cargo. I picked myself up and scrambled out. It was quick like a rebound. The deck was a wilderness of smashed timber, lying crosswise like trees in a wood after a hurricane; an immense curtain of soiled rags waved gently before me – it was the mainsail blown to strips. I thought, The masts will be toppling over directly; and to get out of the way bolted on all-fours towards the poop-ladder. The first person I saw was Mahon, with eyes like saucers, his mouth open, and the long white hair standing straight on end round his head like a silver halo. He was just about to go down when the sight of the maindeck stirring, heaving up, and changing into splinters before his eyes, petrified him on the top step. I stared at him in unbelief, and he stared at me with a queer kind of shocked curiosity. I did not know that I had no hair, no eyebrows, no eyelashes, that my young mustache was burnt off, that my face was black, one cheek laid open, my nose cut, and my chin bleeding. I had lost my cap, one of my slippers, and my shirt was torn to rags. Of all this I was not aware. I was amazed to see the ship still afloat, the poop-deck whole – and, most of all, to see anybody alive. Also the peace of the sky and the serenity of the sea were distinctly surprising. I suppose I expected to see them convulsed with horror. . . . Pass the bottle.

'There was a voice hailing the ship from somewhere – in the air, in the sky – I couldn't tell. Presently I saw the captain – and he was mad. He asked me eagerly, "Where's the cabin-table?" and to hear such a question was a frightful shock. I had just been blown up, you understand, and vibrated with that experience, – I wasn't quite sure whether I was alive. Mahon began to stamp with both feet and yelled at him, "Good God! don't you see the deck's blown out of her?" I found my voice, and stammered out as if conscious of some gross neglect of duty, "I don't know where the cabin-table is." It was like an absurd dream.

'Do you know what he wanted next? Well, he wanted to trim the yards. Very placidly, and as if lost in thought, he insisted on having the foreyard squared. "I don't know if there's anybody alive," said Mahon, almost tearfully. "Surely," he said, gently, "there will be enough left to square the foreyard."

'The old chap, it seems, was in his own berth, winding up the chronometers, when the shock sent him spinning. Immediately it occurred to him – as he said afterwards – that the ship had struck something, and he ran out into the cabin. There, he saw, the cabin-table had vanished somewhere. The deck being blown up, it had fallen down into the lazarette of course. Where we had our breakfast that morning he saw only a great hole in the floor. This appeared to him so awfully mysterious, and impressed him so immensely, that what he saw and heard after he got on deck were mere trifles in comparison. And, mark, he noticed directly the wheel deserted and his bark off her course – and his only thought was to get that miserable, stripped, undecked, smoldering shell of a ship back again with her head pointing at her port of destination. Bankok! That's what he was after. I tell you this quiet, bowed, bandy-legged, almost deformed little man was immense in the singleness of his idea and in his placid ignorance of our agitation. He motioned us forward with a commanding gesture, and went to take the wheel himself.

'Yes; that was the first thing we did – trim the yards of that wreck! No one was killed, or even disabled, but everyone was more or less hurt. You should have seen them! Some were in rags, with black faces, like coal-heavers, like sweeps, and had bullet heads that seemed closely cropped, but were in fact singed to the skin. Others, of the watch below, awakened by being shot out from their collapsing bunks, shivered incessantly, and kept on groaning even as we went about our work. But they all worked. That crew of Liverpool hard cases had in them the right stuff. It's my experience they always have. It is the sea that gives it – the vastness, the loneliness surrounding their dark stolid souls. Ah! Well! we stumbled, we crept, we fell, we barked our shins on the wreckage, we hauled. The masts stood, but we did not know how much they might be charred down below, it was nearly calm, but a long swell ran from the west and made her roll. They might go at any moment. We looked at them with apprehension. One could not foresee which way they would fall.

'Then we retreated aft and looked about us. The deck was a tangle of planks on edge, of planks on end, of splinters, of ruined woodwork. The masts rose from that chaos like big trees above a matted undergrowth. The interstices of that mass of wreckage were full of something whitish, sluggish, stirring – of something that was like a greasy fog. The smoke of the invisible fire was coming up again, was trailing, like a poisonous thick mist in some valley, choked with dead wood. Already lazy wisps were beginning to curl upwards amongst the mass of splinters. Here and there a piece of timber, stuck upright, resembled a post. Half of a fife-rail had been shot through the foresail, and the sky made a patch of glorious blue in the ignobly soiled canvas. A portion of several boards holding together had fallen across the rail, and one end protruded overboard, like a gangway leading upon nothing, like a gangway leading over the deep sea, leading to death – as if inviting us to walk the plank at once and be done with our ridiculous troubles. And still the air, the sky – a ghost, something invisible was hailing the ship.

'Someone had the sense to look over, and there was the helmsman, who had impulsively jumped overboard, anxious to come back. He yelled and swam lustily like a merman, keeping up with the ship. We threw him a rope, and presently he stood amongst us streaming with water and very crest-fallen. The captain had surrendered the wheel, and apart, elbow on rail and chin in hand, gazed at the sea wistfully. We asked ourselves, What next? I thought, Now, this is something like. This is great. I wonder what will happen. O youth!

'Suddenly Mahon sighted a steamer far astern. Captain Beard said, "We may do something with her yet." We hoisted two flags, which said in the international language of the sea, "On fire. Want immediate assistance." The steamer grew bigger rapidly, and by-and-by spoke with two flags on her foremast, "I am coming to your assistance."

'In half an hour she was abreast, to windward, within hail, and rolling slightly, with her engines stopped. We lost our composure, and yelled all together with excitement, "We've been blown up." A man in a white helmet, on the bridge, cried, "Yes! All right! all right!" and he nodded his head, and smiled, and made soothing motions with his hand as though at a lot of frightened children. One of the boats dropped in the water, and walked towards us upon the sea with her long oars. Four Calashes pulled a swinging stroke. This was my first sight of Malay seamen. I've known them since, but what struck me then was their unconcern: they came alongside, and even the bowman standing up and holding to our main-chains with the boat-hook did not deign to lift his head for a glance. I thought people who had been blown up deserved more attention.

'A little man, dry like a chip and agile like a monkey, clambered up. It was the mate of the steamer. He gave one look, and cried, "O boys – you had better quit."

'We were silent. He talked apart with the captain for a time, – seemed to argue with him. Then they went away together to the steamer.

'When our skipper came back we learned that the steamer was the *Sommerville*, Captain Nash, from West Australia to Singapore via Batavia with mails, and that the agreement was she should tow us to Anjer or Batavia, if possible, where we could extinguish the fire by scuttling, and then proceed on our voyage – to Bankok! The old man seemed excited. "We will do it yet," he said to Mahon, fiercely. He shook his fist at the sky. Nobody else said a word.

'At noon the steamer began to tow. She went ahead slim and high, and what was left of the *Judea* followed at the end of seventy fathom of tow-rope, – followed her swiftly like a cloud of smoke with mastheads protruding above. We went aloft to furl the sails. We coughed on the yards, and were careful about the bunts. Do you see the lot of us there, putting a neat furl on the sails of that ship doomed to arrive nowhere? There was not a man who didn't think that at any moment the masts would topple over. From aloft we could not see the ship for smoke, and they worked carefully, passing the gaskets with even turns. "Harbor furl – aloft there!" cried Mahon from below.

'You understand this? I don't think one of those chaps expected to get down in the usual way. When we did I heard them saying to each other, "Well, I thought we would come down overboard, in a lump – sticks and all – blame me if I didn't." "That's what I was thinking to myself," would answer wearily another battered and bandaged scarecrow. And, mind, these were men without the drilled-in habit of obedience. To an onlooker they would be a lot of profane scallywags without a redeeming point. What made them do it – what made them obey me when I, thinking consciously how fine it was, made them drop the bunt of the foresail twice to try and do it better? What? They had no professional reputation – no examples, no praise. It wasn't a sense of duty; they all knew well enough how to shirk, and laze, and dodge – when they had a mind to it – and mostly they had. Was it the two pounds ten a month that sent them there? They didn't think their pay half good enough. No; it was something in them, something inborn and subtle and everlasting. I don't say positively that the crew of a French or German merchant-man wouldn't have done it, but I doubt whether it would have been done in the same way. There was a completeness in it, something solid like a principle, and masterful like an instinct – a disclosure of something secret – of that hidden something, that gift, of good or evil that makes racial difference, that shapes the fate of nations.

'It was that night at ten that, for the first time since we had been fighting it, we saw the fire. The speed of the towing had fanned the smoldering destruction. A blue gleam appeared forward, shining below the wreck of the deck. It wavered in patches, it seemed to stir and creep like the light of a glowworm. I saw it first, and told Mahon. "Then the game's up," he said. "We had better stop this towing, or she will burst out suddenly fore and aft before we can clear out." We set up a yell; rang bells to attract their attention; they towed on. At last Mahon and I had to crawl forward and cut the rope with an ax. There was no time to cast off the lashings. Red tongues could be seen licking the wilderness of splinters under our feet as we made our way back to the poop.

'Of course they very soon found out in the steamer that the rope was gone. She gave a loud blast of her whistle, her lights were seen sweeping in a wide circle, she came up ranging close alongside, and stopped. We were all in a tight group on the poop looking at her. Every man had saved a little bundle or a bag. Suddenly a conical flame with a twisted top shot up forward and threw upon the black sea a circle of light, with the two vessels side by side and heaving gently in its center. Captain Beard had been sitting on the gratings still and mute for hours, but now he rose slowly and advanced in front of us, to the mizzen-shrouds. Captain Nash hailed: "Come along! Look sharp. I have mail-bags on board. I will take you and your boats to Singapore."

' "Thank you! No!" said our skipper. "We must see the last of the ship."

' "I can't stand by any longer," shouted the other. "Mails – you know."

' "Ay! ay' We are all right."

' "Very well! I'll report you in Singapore. . . . Good-by!"

'He waved his hand. Our men dropped their bundles quietly. The steamer moved ahead, and passing out of the circle of light, vanished at once from our sight, dazzled by the fire which burned fiercely. And then I knew that I would see the East first as commander of a small boat. I thought it fine; and the fidelity to the old ship was fine. We should see the last of her. Oh the glamour of youth! Oh the fire of it, more dazzling than the flames of the burning ship, throwing a magic light on the wide earth, leaping audaciously to the sky, presently to be quenched by time, more cruel, more pitiless, more bitter than the sea – and like the flames of the burning ship surrounded by an impenetrable night.

'The old man warned us in his gentle and inflexible way that it was part of our duty to save for the underwriters as much as we could of the ship's gear. According we went to work aft, while she blazed forward to give us plenty of light. We lugged out a lot of rubbish. What didn't we save? An old barometer fixed with an absurd quantity of screws nearly cost me my life: a sudden rush of smoke came upon me, and I just got away in time. There were various stores, bolts of canvas, coils of rope; the poop looked like a marine bazaar, and the boats were lumbered to the gunwales. One would have thought the old man wanted to take as much as he could of his first command with him. He was very, very quiet, but off his balance evidently. Would you believe it? He wanted to take a length of old stream-cable and a kedge-anchor with him in the long-boat. We said, "Ay, ay, sir," deferentially, and on the quiet let the thing slip overboard. The heavy medicine-chest went that way, two bags of green coffee, tins of paint – fancy, paint! – a whole lot of things. Then I was ordered with two hands into the boats to make a stowage and get them ready against the time it would be proper for us to leave the ship.

'We put everything straight, stepped the long-boat's mast for our skipper, who was in charge of her, and I was not sorry to sit down for a moment. My face felt raw, every limb ached as if broken, I was aware of all my ribs, and would have sworn to a twist in the backbone. The boats, fast astern, lay in a deep shadow, and all around I could see the circle of the sea lighted by the fire. A gigantic flame arose forward straight and clear. It flared fierce, with noises like the whir of wings, with rumbles as of thunder. There were cracks, detonations, and from the cone of flame the sparks flew upwards, as man is born to trouble, to leaky ships, and to ships that burn.

'What bothered me was that the ship, lying broadside to the swell and to such wind as there was – a mere breath – the boats would not keep astern where they were safe, but persisted, in a pig-headed way boats have, in getting under the counter and then swinging alongside. They were knocking about dangerously and coming near the flame, while the ship rolled on them, and, of course, there was always the danger of the masts going over the side at any moment. I and my two boat-keepers kept them off as best we could with oars and boat-hooks; but to be constantly at it became exasperating, since there was no reason why we should not leave at once. We could not see those on board, nor could we imagine what caused the delay. The boat-keepers were swearing feebly, and I had not only my share of the work, but also had to keep at it two men who showed a constant inclination to lay themselves down and let things slide.

'At last I hailed "On deck there," and someone looked over. "We're ready here," I said. The head disappeared, and very soon popped up again. "The captain says, All right, sir, and to keep the boats well clear of the ship."

'Half an hour passed. Suddenly there was a frightful racket, rattle, clanking of chain, hiss of water, and millions of sparks flew up into the shivering column of smoke that stood leaning slightly above the ship. The catheads had burned away, and the two red-hot anchors had gone to the bottom, tearing out after them two hundred fathom of red-hot chain. The ship trembled, the mass of flame swayed as if ready to collapse, and the fore top-gallant-mast fell. It darted down like an arrow of fire, shot under, and instantly leaping up within an oar's-length of the boats, floated quietly, very black on the luminous sea. I hailed the deck again. After some time a man in an unexpectedly cheerful but also muffled tone, as though he had been trying to speak with his mouth shut, informed me, "Coming directly, sir," and vanished. For a long time I heard nothing but the whir and roar of the fire. There were also whistling sounds. The boats jumped, tugged at the painters, ran at each other playfully, knocked their sides together, or, do what we would, swung in a bunch against the ship's side. I couldn't stand it any longer, and swarming up a rope, clambered aboard over the stern.

'It was as bright as day. Coming up like this, the sheet of fire facing me, was a terrifying sight, and the heat seemed hardly bearable at first. On a settee cushion dragged out of the cabin, Captain Beard, with his legs drawn up and one arm under his head, slept with the light playing on him. Do you know what the rest were busy about? They were sitting on deck right aft, around an open case, eating bread and cheese and drinking bottled stout.

'On the background of flames twisting in fierce tongues above their heads they seemed at home like salamanders, and looked like a band of desperate pirates. The fire sparkled in the whites of their eyes, gleamed on patches of white skin seen through the torn shirts. Each had the marks as of a battle about him – bandaged heads, tied-up arms, a strip of dirty rag round a knee – and each man had a bottle between his legs and a chunk of cheese in his hand. Mahon got up. With his handsome and disreputable head, his hooked profile, his long white beard, and with an uncorked bottle in his hand, he resembled one of those reckless sea-robbers of old making merry amidst violence and disaster. "The last meal on board," he explained solemnly. "We had nothing to eat all day, and it was no use leaving all this." He flourished the bottle and indicated the sleeping skipper. "He said he couldn't swallow anything, so I got him to lie down," he went on; and as I stared, "I don't know whether you are aware, young fellow, the man had no sleep to speak of for days – and there will be dam' little sleep in the boats." "There will be no boats by-and-by if you fool about much longer," I said, indignantly. I walked up to the skipper and shook him by the shoulder. At last he opened his eyes, but did not move. "Time to leave her, sir," I said, quietly.

'He got up painfully, looked at the flames, at the sea sparkling round the ship, and black, black as ink farther away; he looked at the stars shining dim through a thin veil of smoke in a sky black, black as Erebus.

' "Youngest first," he said.

'And the ordinary seaman, wiping his mouth with the back of his hand, got up, clambered over the taff-rail, and vanished. Others followed. One, on the point of going over, stopped short to drain his bottle, and with a great swing of his arm flung it at the fire. "Take this!" he cried.

'The skipper lingered disconsolately, and we left him to commune alone for awhile with his first command. Then I went up again and brought him away at last. It was time. The ironwork on the poop was hot to the touch.

'Then the painter of the long-boat was cut, and the three boats, tied together, drifted clear of the ship. It was just sixteen hours after the explosion when we abandoned her. Mahon had charge of the second boat, and I had the smallest – the 14-foot thing. The long-boat would have taken the lot of us; but the skipper said we must save as much property as we could – for the underwriters – and so I got my first command. I had two men with me, a bag of biscuits, a few tins of meat, and a breaker of water. I was ordered to keep close to the long-boat, that in case of bad weather we might be taken into her.

'And do you know what I thought? I thought I would part company as soon as I could. I wanted to have my first command all to myself. I wasn't going to sail in a squadron if there were a chance for independent cruising. I would make land by myself. I would beat the other boats. Youth! All youth! The silly, charming, beautiful youth.

'But we did not make a start at once. We must see the last of the ship. And so the boats drifted about that night, heaving and setting on the swell. The men dozed, waked, sighed, groaned. I looked at the burning ship.

'Between the darkness of earth and heaven she was burning fiercely, upon a disc of purple sea shot by the blood-red play of gleams; upon a disc of water glittering and sinister. A high, clear flame, an immense and lonely flame, ascended from the ocean, and from its summit the black smoke poured continuously at the sky. She burned furiously, mournful and imposing like a funeral pile kindled in the night, surrounded by the sea, watched over by the stars. A magnificent death had come like a grace, like a gift, like a reward to that old ship at the end of her laborious days. The surrender of her weary ghost to the keeping of stars and sea was stirring like the sight of a glorious triumph. The masts fell just before daybreak, and for a moment there was a burst and turmoil of sparks that seemed to fill with flying fire the night patient and watchful, the vast night lying silent upon the sea. At daylight she was only a charred shell, floating still under a cloud of smoke and bearing a glowing mass of coal within.

'Then the oars were got out, and the boats forming in a line moved round her remains as if in procession – the long-boat leading. As we pulled across her stern a slim dart of fire shot out viciously at us, and suddenly she went down, head first, in a great hiss of steam. The unconsumed stern was the last to sink; but the paint had gone, had cracked, had peeled off, and there were no letters, there was no word, no stubborn device that was like her soul, to flash at the rising sun her creed and her name.

'We made our way north. A breeze sprang up, and about noon all the boats came together for the last time. I had no mast or sail in mine, but I made a mast out of a spare oar and hoisted a boat-awning for a sail, with a boat-hook for a yard. She was certainly over-masted, but I had the satisfaction of knowing that with the wind aft I could beat the other two. I had to wait for them. Then we all had a look at the captain's chart, and, after a sociable meal of hard bread and water, got our last instructions. These were simple: steer north, and keep together as much as possible. "Be careful with that jury rig, Marlow," said the captain; and Mahon, as I sailed proudly past his boat, wrinkled his curved nose and hailed, "You will sail that ship of yours under water, if you don't look out, young fellow." He was a malicious old man – and may the deep sea where he sleeps now rock him gently, rock him tenderly to the end of time!

'Before sunset a thick rain-squall passed over the two boats, which were far astern, and that was the last I saw of them for a time. Next day I sat steering my cockle-shell – my first command – with nothing but water and sky around me. I did sight in the afternoon the upper sails of a ship far away, but said nothing, and my men did not notice her. You see I was afraid she might be homeward bound, and I had no mind to turn back from the portals of the East. I was steering for Java – another blessed name – like Bankok, you know. I steered many days.

'I need not tell you what it is to be knocking about in an

open boat. I remember nights and days of calm when we pulled, we pulled, and the boat seemed to stand still, as if bewitched within the circle of the sea horizon. I remember the heat, the deluge of rain-squalls that kept us baling for dear life (but filled our water-cask), and I remember sixteen hours on end with a mouth dry as a cinder and a steering-oar over the stern to keep my first command head on to a breaking sea. I did not know how good a man I was till then. I remember the drawn faces, the dejected figures of my two men, and I remember my youth and the feeling that will never come back any more – the feeling that I could last for ever, outlast the sea, the earth, and all men; the deceitful feeling that lures us on to joys, to perils, to love, to vain effort – to death; the triumphant conviction of strength, the heat of life in the handful of dust, the glow in the heart that with every year grows dim, grows cold, grows small, and expires – and expires, too soon – before life itself.

'And this is how I see the East. I have seen its secret places and have looked into its very soul; but now I see it always from a small boat, a high outline of mountains, blue and afar in the morning; like faint mist at noon; a jagged wall of purple at sunset. I have the feel of the oar in my hand, the vision of a scorching blue sea in my eyes. And I see a bay, a wide bay, smooth as glass and polished like ice, shimmering in the dark. A red light burns far off upon the gloom of the land, and the night is soft and warm. We drag at the oars with aching arms, and suddenly a puff of wind, a puff faint and tepid and laden with strange odors of blossoms, of aromatic wood, comes out of the still night – the first sigh of the East on my face. That I can never forget. It was impalpable and enslaving, like a charm, like a whispered promise of mysterious delight.

'We had been pulling this finishing spell for eleven hours.

Two pulled, and he whose turn it was to rest sat at the tiller. We had made out the red light in that bay and steered for it, guessing it must mark some small coasting port. We passed two vessels, outlandish and high-sterned, sleeping at anchor, and, approaching the light, now very dim, ran the boat's nose against the end of a jutting wharf. We were blind with fatigue. My men dropped the oars and fell off the thwarts as if dead. I made fast to a pile. A current rippled softly. The scented obscurity of the shore was grouped into vast masses, a density of colossal clumps of vegetation, probably – mute and fantastic shapes. And at their foot the semicircle of a beach gleamed faintly, like an illusion. There was not a light, not a stir, not a sound. The mysterious East faced me, perfumed like a flower, silent like death, dark like a grave.

'And I sat weary beyond expression, exulting like a conqueror, sleepless and entranced as if before a profound, a fateful enigma.

'A splashing of oars, a measured dip reverberating on the level of water, intensified by the silence of the shore into loud claps, made me jump up. A boat, a European boat, was coming in. I invoked the name of the dead; I hailed: *Judea* ahoy! A thin shout answered.

'It was the captain. I had beaten the flagship by three hours, and I was glad to hear the old man's voice, tremulous and tired. "Is it you, Marlow?" "Mind the end of that jetty, sir," I cried.

'He approached cautiously, and brought up with the deep-sea lead-line which we had saved – for the underwriters. I eased my painter and fell alongside. He sat, a broken figure at the stern, wet with dew, his hands clasped in his lap. His men were asleep already. "I had a terrible time of it," he murmured. "Mahon is behind – not very far." We conversed in whispers, in low whispers, as if afraid to wake up the land. Guns, thunder, earthquakes would not have awakened the men just then.

'Looking around as we talked, I saw away at sea a bright light traveling in the night. "There's a steamer passing the bay," I said. She was not passing, she was entering, and she even came close and anchored. "I wish," said the old man, "you would find out whether she is English. Perhaps they could give us a passage somewhere." He seemed nervously anxious. So by dint of punching and kicking I started one of my men into a state of somnambulism, and giving him an oar, took another and pulled towards the lights of the steamer.

'There was a murmur of voices in her, metallic hollow clangs of the engine-room, footsteps on the deck. Her ports shone, round like dilated eyes. Shapes moved about, and there was a shadowy man high up on the bridge. He heard my oars.

'And then, before I could open my lips, the East spoke to me, but it was in a Western voice. A torrent of words was poured into the enigmatical, the fateful silence; outlandish, angry words, mixed with words and even whole sentences of good English, less strange but even more surprising. The voice swore and cursed violently; it riddled the solemn peace of the bay by a volley of abuse. It began by calling me Pig, and from that went crescendo into unmentionable adjectives – in English. The man up there raged aloud in two languages, and with a sincerity in his fury that almost convinced me I had, in some way, sinned against the harmony of the universe. I could hardly see him, but began to think he would work himself into a fit.

'Suddenly he ceased, and I could hear him snorting and blowing like a porpoise. I said –

' "What steamer is this, pray?"

' "Eh? What's this? And who are you?"

‘“Castaway crew of an English bark burnt at sea. We came here tonight. I am the second mate. The captain is in the long-boat, and wishes to know if you would give us a passage somewhere.”

‘“Oh, my goodness! I say. . . . This is the *Celestial* from Singapore on her return trip. I’ll arrange with your captain in the morning, . . . and, . . . I say, . . . did you hear me just now?”

‘“I should think the whole bay heard you.”

‘“I thought you were a shore-boat. Now, look here – this infernal lazy scoundrel of a caretaker has gone to sleep again – curse him. The light is out, and I nearly ran foul of the end of this damned jetty. This is the third time he plays me this trick. Now, I ask you, can anybody stand this kind of thing? It’s enough to drive a man out of his mind. I’ll report him. . . . I’ll get the Assistant Resident to give him the sack, by . . . See – there’s no light. It’s out, isn’t it? I take you to witness the light’s out. There should be a light, you know. A red light on the –”

‘“There was a light,” I said, mildly.

‘“But it’s out, man! What’s the use of talking like this? You can see for yourself it’s out – don’t you? If you had to take a valuable steamer along this God-forsaken coast you would want a light too. I’ll kick him from end to end of his miserable wharf. You’ll see if I don’t. I will –”

‘“So I may tell my captain you’ll take us?” I broke in.

‘“Yes, I’ll take you. Good night,” he said, brusquely.

‘I pulled back, made fast again to the jetty, and then went to sleep at last. I had faced the silence of the East. I had heard some of its languages. But when I opened my eyes again the silence was as complete as though it had never been broken. I was lying in a flood of light, and the sky had never looked so far, so high, before. I opened my eyes and lay without moving.

'And then I saw the men of the East – they were looking at me. The whole length of the jetty was full of people. I saw brown, bronze, yellow faces, the black eyes, the glitter, the color of an Eastern crowd. And all these beings stared without a murmur, without a sigh, without a movement. They stared down at the boats, at the sleeping men who at night had come to them from the sea. Nothing moved. The fronds of palms stood still against the sky. Not a branch stirred along the shore, and the brown roofs of hidden houses peeped through the green foliage, through the big leaves that hung shining and still like leaves forged of heavy metal. This was the East of the ancient navigators, so old, so mysterious, resplendent and somber, living and unchanged, full of danger and promise. And these were the men. I sat up suddenly. A wave of movement passed through the crowd from end to end, passed along the heads, swayed the bodies, ran along the jetty like a ripple on the water, like a breath of wind on a field – and all was still again. I see it now – the wide sweep of the bay, the glittering sands, the wealth of green infinite and varied, the sea blue like the sea of a dream, the crowd of attentive faces, the blaze of vivid color – the water reflecting it all, the curve of the shore, the jetty, the high-sterned outlandish craft floating still, and the three boats with tired men from the West sleeping unconscious of the land and the people and of the violence of sunshine. They slept thrown across the thwarts, curled on bottom-boards, in the careless attitudes of death. The head of the old skipper, leaning back in the stern of the long-boat, had fallen on his breast, and he looked as though he would never wake. Farther out old Mahon's face was upturned to the sky, with the long white beard spread out on his breast, as though he been shot where he sat at the tiller; and a man, all in a heap in the bows of the boat, slept with both arms embracing the stem-head and with his cheek laid on the gunwale. The East looked at them without a sound.

'I have known its fascinations since: I have seen the mysterious shores, the still water, the lands of brown nations, where a stealthy Nemesis lies in wait, pursues, overtakes so many of the conquering race, who are proud of their wisdom, of their knowledge, of their strength. But for me all the East is contained in that vision of my youth. It is all in that moment when I opened my young eyes on it. I came upon it from a tussle with the sea – and I was young – and I saw it looking at me. And this is all that is left of it! Only a moment; a moment of strength, of romance, of glamour – of youth! . . . A flick of sunshine upon a strange shore, the time to remember, the time for a sigh, and – good-by! – Night – Good-by . . . !'

He drank.

'Ah! The good old time – the good old time. Youth and the sea. Glamour and the sea! The good, strong sea, the salt, bitter sea, that could whisper to you and roar at you and knock your breath out of you.'

He drank again.

'By all that's wonderful, it is the sea, I believe, the sea itself – or is it youth alone? Who can tell? But you here – you all had something out of life: money, love – whatever one gets on shore – and, tell me, wasn't that the best time, that time when we were young at sea; young and had nothing, on the sea that gives nothing, except hard knocks – and sometimes a chance to feel your strength – that only – what you all regret?'

And we all nodded at him: the man of finance, the man of accounts, the man of law, we all nodded at him over the polished table that like a still sheet of brown water reflected our faces, lined, wrinkled; our faces marked by toil, by deceptions, by success, by love; our weary eyes looking still, looking always, looking anxiously for something out of life, that while it is expected is already gone – has passed unseen, in a sigh, in a flash – together with the youth, with the strength, with the romance of illusions.

ROBERT OLEN BUTLER

TITANIC VICTIM SPEAKS THROUGH WATERBED

THIS IS A BIT of a puzzle, really. A certain thrashing about overhead. Swimmers with nowhere to go, I fear, though I don't recognize this body of water. I've grown quite used to this existence I now have. I'm fully conscious that I'm dead. And yet not so, somehow. I drift and drift, and I am that in which I drift, though what that is now, precisely, is unclear to me. There was darkness at first, and I failed to understand. But then I rose as some faint current from the depths of the North Atlantic and there were others around me, the corporeal creatures of the sea whom I had hitherto known strictly on fine china and dressed lightly in butter and lemon. I found that I was the very medium for the movement of their piscine limbs, and they seemed oblivious to my consciousness. Given their ignorance, I could not even haunt them. But I understood, by then, of what my fundamental state consisted, something that had eluded the wisdom of Canterbury. Something for which I was unprepared.

And after many years – I don't know how many, but it is clear to me that it is not an inconsiderable sum – there are still surprises awaiting me. This impulse now to shape words, for instance. And the thrashing above me, the agitation it brings upon me. I returned to the first-class smoking lounge soon after I realized what had happened to the ship. I sat in an overstuffed leather chair and then looked about for a dry match to light my cigar. But I was well aware of what was going on out in the darkness beyond the window.

Perhaps that accounts for the slight betrayal of fear, something only I could notice, since on the surface I seemed to be in control: I sat down and reached for a match. But I sat down already fearing that the matches would be wet. I should have searched for the match and then sat down. But I sat. And then I looked about. And, of course, the room was quite dry. On the table, just at arm's length, was a silver-plated ashtray with a silver matchbox engraved with the flag of the White Star Line rising on a pedestal from its center. The box was full of matches. I took one and struck it and it flared into life and I held it to my cigar and I thought, What a shame that this quite charming ashtray will be soon lost. My hand was steady. To anyone watching, it would seem I had never doubted that the matches in this room were dry. Of course they were. At that hour the ship was beginning to settle into the water, but only like a stout fellow standing in this very room after a long night of cards and feeling heavy in his lower limbs. It was, of course, impossible for water to be in this room as yet. That would come only very near the end. But still I feared that the matches would already be spoilt.

All through that night, the fear was never physical. I didn't mind so much, in point of fact, giving up a life in my body. The body was never a terribly interesting thing to me. Except perhaps to draw in the heavy curl of the smoke of my cigar, like a Hindu's rope in the market rising as if it were a thing alive. One needs a body to smoke a good cigar. I took the first draw there in that room just below the fourth funnel of the largest ship in the world as it sat dead still, filling with the North Atlantic ocean in the middle of the night, and the smoke was a splendid thing.

And as I did, I felt an issue of perspiration on my forehead. This was not unpleasant, however. I sat with many a fine cigar on the verandah of my bungalow in Madras, and though one of the boys was always there to fan the punkah, I would perspire on my forehead and it was just part of smoking a good cigar out in India. With a whisky and soda beside me. I thought, sitting on the sinking ship, about pouring myself a drink. But I didn't. I wanted a clear head. I had gone to my cabin when things seemed serious and I'd changed into evening dress. It was a public event, it seemed to me. It was a solemn occasion. With, I assumed, a King to meet somewhat higher even than our good King George. I didn't feel comfortable in tweeds.

What *is* that thrashing about above me now? The creatures of the sea are absent here, though I'm not risen into the air as I have done for some years, over and over, lifted and dispersed into cloud. I'm coalesced in a place that has no living creatures but is large enough for me to be unable quite to sense its boundaries. Perhaps not too large, since I am not moving except for a faint eddying from the activity above. But at least I am in a place larger than a teacup. I once dwelt in a cup of tea, and on that occasion, I sensed the constraints of the space.

I yearn to be clothed now in the evening dress I wore on that Sunday night in April in the year of 1912. I must say that a body is useful for formal occasions, as well. All this floating about seems much too casual to me. I expected something more rigorous in the afterlife. A propitiatory formality. A sensible accounting. Order. But there has been no sign, as yet, of that King of Kings. Just this long and elemental passage to a place I cannot recognize. And an odd sense of alertness now. And these words I feel compelled to speak.

There. I think I heard the sound of a human voice above me in this strange place. Very briefly. I cannot make out the words, if words this voice indeed uttered. It's been a rare thing for me, in all this time, to sense that a living human being might be close by. On that dark night in the North Atlantic, at the very moment we struck our fate out somewhere beneath the water line on our bow, I was in the midst of voices that did not resolve themselves into clear words, and none of us heard anything of that fateful event. I was sitting and smoking, and there was a voluble conversation over a card game near to me. It was late. Nearly midnight. I was reluctant to leave the company of these men, though I had not said more than two dozen words to any of them on this night, beyond 'good evening.' I am an indifferent card player. I sat and smoked all evening and I missed having the latest newspaper. I don't remember what I might have thought about, with all that smoke. India perhaps. Perhaps my sister and her husband in Toronto, towards whom we had just ceased to steam.

What did become clear to me quite quickly was that we had stopped. I looked at the others and they were continuing to play their game unaware of anything unusual. So I rose and stepped out under the wrought-iron and glass dome of the aft staircase. I had no apprehensions. The staircase was very elegant with polished oak wall paneling and gilt on the balustrades and it was lit bright with electric lights. My feeling was that in the absence of the threat of native rebellion, things such as this could not possibly be in peril.

That seems a bit naive now, of course, but at the time, I was straight from the leather chair of the first-class smoking lounge. And I was tutored in my views by the Civil Service in India. And I was a keen reader of the newspapers and all that they had to say about this new age of technology, an age for which this unsinkable ship stood as eloquent testament. And I was an old bachelor whose only sister lived in the safest dominion of the empire.

Owing to the lateness of the hour, there was no one about

on the staircase except for a steward who rushed past me and down the steps. 'What's the trouble?' I asked him.

He waved a hot water bottle he was carrying and said, 'Cold feet, I presume,' and he disappeared on the lower landing.

I almost stepped back into the smoking lounge. But there was no doubt that we had come to a full stop, and that was unquestionably out of the ordinary. Two or three of the card players were now standing in the doorway just behind me, murmuring about this very thing.

'I'll see what's the matter,' I said without looking at them, and I descended the steps and went out onto the open promenade.

The night was very still. There were people moving about, somewhat distractedly, but I paid them no attention. I stepped to the railing and the sea was vast and smooth in the moonlight. There were shapes out there, like water buffalo sleeping in the fields in the dark nights outside Madras. I would drive back to my bungalow in a trap, my head still cluttered with the talk and the music from the little dance band and the whirling around of the dancers, and I would think how the social rites of my own class sometimes felt as foreign to me as those of the people we were governing here. These pretenses the men and women made in order to touch, often someone else's spouse. I am not unobservant. But I would go to these events, nevertheless. Even if I kept to myself.

I looked out at these sleeping shapes in the water. A woman's voice was suddenly nearby.

'We're doomed now,' she said in the flat inflection of an American.

It took a moment to realize that she was addressing me. She said no more. But I think I heard her breathing. I turned and she was less than an arm's length from me along the railing. In the brightness of the moon I could see her face quite clearly. She seemed rather young, though less than two hours later I would revise that somewhat. The first impression, however, was that she was young, and that was all. Perhaps rather pretty, too, but I don't think I noticed that at the time. There were certain things that I suppose were beyond my powers of observation. When I realized to whom she was speaking, her words finally registered on me.

'Not at all.' I spoke from whatever ignorance I had learned all my life. 'Nothing that can't be handled. This is a fine ship.'

'I'm not in a panic,' she said. 'You can hear that in my voice, can't you?'

'Of course.'

'I just know this terrible thing to be true.'

I leaned on the rail and looked at these sleeping cattle. I knew what they were. I understood what this woman had concluded. 'It's the ice you fear,' I said.

'The deed is done, don't you think?' she said.

Her breath puffed out, white in the moonlight, and I felt suddenly responsible for her. There was nothing personal in it. But this was a lady in some peril, I realized. At least in peril from her own fears. I felt a familiar stiffening in me, and I was glad of it. Dissipated now were the effects of the cigar smoke and the comfort of a chair in a place where men gathered in their complacent ease. But I still felt I only needed to dispel some groundless fears of a woman too much given to her intuition.

'What deed might that be?' I asked her, trying to gentle my voice.

'We've struck an iceberg.'

I was surprised to find that this seemed entirely plausible. 'And suppose we have,' I said. 'This ship is the very most modern afloat. The watertight compartments make it quite unsinkable. We would, perhaps, at worst, be delayed.'

She turned her face to me, though she did not respond.

'Are you traveling alone?' I asked.

'Yes.'

'Perhaps that accounts for your anxiety.'

'No. It was the deep and distant sound of the collision. And the vibration I felt in my feet. And the speed with which we were hurtling among these things.' She nodded to the shapes in the dark. I looked and felt a chill from the night air. 'And the dead stop we instantly made,' she said. 'And it's a thing in the air. I can smell it. A thing that I smelled once before, when I was a little girl. A coal mine collapsed in my hometown. Many men were trapped and would die within a few hours. I smell that again . . . These are the things that account for my anxiety.'

'You shouldn't be traveling alone,' I said. 'If I might say so.'

'No, you might not say so,' she said, and she turned her face sharply to the sea.

'I'm sorry,' I said. Though I felt I was right. A woman alone could be subject to torments of the sensibility such as this and have no one to comfort her. I wanted to comfort this woman beside me.

Is this an eddy through what once was my mind? A stirring of the water in which I'm held? I ripple and suddenly I see this clearly: my wish to comfort her came from an impulse stronger than duty would strictly require. I see this now, dissolved as I have been for countless years in the thing that frightened her that night. But standing with her at the rail, I simply wished for a companion to comfort her on a troubling night, a father or a brother perhaps.

'You no doubt mean well,' she said.

'Yes. Of course.'

'I believe a woman should vote too,' she said.

'Quite,' I said. This was a notion I'd heard before and normally it seemed, in the voice of a woman, a hard and angry thing. But now this woman's voice was very small. She was arguing her right to travel alone and vote when, in fact, she feared she would soon die in the North Atlantic Ocean. I understood this much and her words did not seem provocative to me. Only sad.

'I'm certain you'll have a chance to express that view for many decades to come,' I said.

'The change is nearer than you think,' she said with some vigor now in her voice, even irritation. I was glad to hear it.

'I didn't mean to take up the political point,' I said. 'I simply meant you will survive this night and live a long time.'

She lowered her face.

'That's your immediate concern, isn't it?' I asked, trying to speak very gently.

Before she could answer, a man I knew from the smoking lounge approached along the promenade, coming from the direction of the bow of the ship. He had gone out of the lounge some time earlier.

'Look here,' he said, and he showed me his drink. It was full of chipped ice. 'It's from the forward well deck,' he said. 'It's all over the place.'

I felt the woman ease around my shoulder and look into the glass. The man was clearly drunk and shouldn't have been running about causing alarm.

'From the iceberg,' he said.

I heard her exhale sharply.

'I never take ice in my scotch and soda,' I said.

The man drew himself up. 'I do,' he said. And he moved away unsteadily, confirming my criticism of him.

She stood very still for a long moment.

All I could think to say was something along the lines of 'Here, here. There's nothing to worry about.' But she was not the type of woman to take comfort from that. I knew that much about her already. I felt no resentment at the fact. Indeed, I felt sorry for her. If she wanted to be the sort to travel alone and vote and not be consoled by the platitudes of a stiff old bachelor from the Civil Service in India, then it was sad for her to have these intense and daunting intuitions of disaster and death, as well.

So I kept quiet, and she eventually turned her face to me. The moon fell upon her. At the time, I did not clearly see her beauty. I can see it now, however. I have always been able to see in this incorporeal state. Quite vividly. Though not at the moment. There's only darkness. The activity above me has no shape. But in the sea, as I drifted inexorably to the surface, I began to see the fish and eventually the ceiling of light above me. And then there was the first time I rose – quite remarkable – lifting from the vastness of an ocean delicately wrinkled and athrash with the sunlight. I went up into a sky I knew I was a part of, spinning myself into the gossamer of a rain cloud, hiding from the sea, traced as a tiny wisp into a great gray mountain of vapor. And I wondered if there were others like me there. I listened for them. I tried to call to them, though I had no voice. Not even words. Not like these that now shape in me. If I'd had these words then, perhaps I could have called out to the others who had gone down with the *Titanic*, and they would have heard me. If, in fact, they were there. But as far as I knew – as far as I know now – I am a solitary traveler.

And then I was rain, and the cycle began. And I moved in the clouds and in the tides and eventually I became rivers and streams and lakes and dew and a cup of tea. Darjeeling.

In a place not unlike the one where I spent so many years. I had recently come out of the sea, but I don't think the place was Madras or near it, for the sea must have been the Arabian, not the Bay of Bengal. I was in a reservoir and then in a well and then in a boiling kettle and eventually in a porcelain cup, very thin: I could see the shadow of a woman's hand pick me up. I sensed it was Darjeeling tea, but I don't know how. Perhaps I can smell, too, in this state, but without the usual body, perhaps there is only the knowledge of the scent. I'm not sure. But I slipped inside a woman and then later I was – how shall I say this? – free again. I must emphasize that I kept my spirit's eyes tightly shut.

That was many years ago. I subsequently crossed the subcontinent and then Indochina and then I spent a very long time in another vast sea, the Pacific Ocean, I'm sure. And then, in recent times, I rolled in a storm front across a rough coast and rained hard in a new land. I think, in fact, I have arrived in the very country for which I'd set sail in that fateful spring of 1912.

Her country. I'm digressing now. I see that. I look at her face in this memory that drifts with me – I presume forever – and I am ready to understand that she was beautiful, from the first, and I look away, just as I did then. I talk of everything but her face. She turned to me and the moon fell upon her and I could not bring myself to be the pompous ass I am capable of being. I said nothing to reassure her. And that was an act of respect. I see that now. I wonder if she saw it. But neither did I say anything else. I looked away. I looked out to the sea that was even then trying to claim us both, and I finally realized she was gone.

She had said nothing more, either. Not good-bye. Nothing. Not that I blame her. I'd let her down somehow. And she knew that we were all in mortal peril. When I turned back around and found her gone, I had a feeling about her absence. A feeling that I quickly set aside. It had something to do with my body. I felt a chill. But, of course, we were in the North Atlantic with ice floating all about us. I wished I were in my bungalow near the Bay of Bengal, wrapped in mosquito netting and drifting into unconsciousness. I wished for that, at the time. I did not wish for her to return. I wanted only to be lying in a bed alone in a place I knew very well, a place where I could spend my days being as stiff as I needed to be to keep going. I wanted to lie wrapped tight, with the taste of cigars and whisky still faint in my mouth, and sleep.

And now I feel something quite strong, really. Though I have no body, whatever I am feels suddenly quite profoundly empty. Ah empty. Ah quite quite empty.

I have cried out. Just now. And the thrashing above me stops and turns into a low murmur of voices. The water moves, a sharp undulation, and then suddenly there's a faint light above me. I had rushed through dark tunnels into this place and had no idea what it was, and now I can see it is structured and tight. The light is a square ceiling above me. I see it through the water, but there is something else, as well, blurring the light. Mosquito netting. A shroud. Something. It is quite odd, really.

I want to think on this place I'm in, but I cannot. There's only the empty space on the promenade where she'd stood. I turned and she was gone and I looked both ways and there were people moving about, but I did not see her. It was then that I knew for certain that she was right. I knew the ship would go down, and I would die.

So I went to my cabin and closed the door and laid out my evening clothes on the bed. There were footsteps in the hallway, racing. Others knew. I imagined her moving about the ship like some Hindu spirit taken human form, visiting this truth upon whomever would listen. I once again stood still for a moment with a feeling. I wanted her to have spoken only to me. That we should keep that understanding strictly between the two of us. I straightened now and put the thought from my head. That thought, not the sinking of the ship, made me quake slightly inside. I straightened and stiffened with as much reserve and dignity as possible for a man in late middle age standing in his underwear, and I carefully dressed for this terrible event.

When I came out again on the promenade deck, I hesitated. But only briefly. Something very old and very strong in me brought me to the door of the smoking lounge. This was the only place that seemed familiar to me, that was filled with people whose salient qualities I could recognize easily. I stepped in and the card game was still on. Several faces turned to me.

'It's all up for us,' I said, matter-of-factly.

'Yes,' one of them said.

'You can bet rather more freely,' I said to him.

'Don't encourage him,' said another at the table.

'Right,' I said. Then I stood there for a moment. I knew that I'd come to join them. My chair sat empty near the card table. And I began to worry about finding a dry match. Force of habit – no, not habit; the indomitable instinct of my life – moved me into the room and to the chair and I sat and I worried about the matches and then I found that they were dry and I lit my cigar and I took a puff and I thought about getting a drink and I thought about meeting a King more powerful than King George and then I suddenly turned away from all that. I laid my cigar in the silver-plate ashtray and I rose and went out of the lounge.

It took me the better part of an hour to find her. At first, things were civilized. They were beginning to put women and children into the boats and people were keeping their heads about them. These were first-class passengers and I moved through them and we all of us exchanged careful apologies for being in each other's way or asking each other to move. With each exchanged request for pardon, I grew more concerned. From this very sharing of the grace of daily human affairs, I responded more and more to the contrast of the situation. I could tell there weren't enough lifeboats for this enterprise. Any fool could tell that. I searched these faces to whom I gently offered my apologies and who gently returned them, but I was not gentle inside. I wanted to find her. I prayed that if I did not, it was because she was already in a sound boat out on the sea, well away from what would soon happen.

Then I came up on the boat deck below the wheelhouse and I could see forward. The lights were still quite bright all over the ship and the orchestra was playing a waltz nearby and before me, at the bow, the forecastle deck already was awash. It was disappearing before my eyes. And now the people from steerage in rough blankets and flannel night-shirts and kersey caps were crowding up, and I felt bad for them. They'd been let down, too, trying to find a new life somewhere, and the gentlemen of the White Star Line were not prepared to save all these people.

A woman smelling of garlic pressed past me with a child swaddled against her chest and I looked forward again. The anchor crane was all that I could see of the forecastle. The blackness of the sea had smoothed away the bow of our ship, and I wanted to cry out the name of the woman I sought, and I realized that I did not even know it. We had never been introduced, of course. This woman and I had spoken together of life and death, and we had not even exchanged our names. That realization should have released me from my search, but in fact I grew quite intense now to find her.

There was a gunshot nearby and a voice cried out, 'Women and children only. Be orderly.' There was jostling behind me and voices rising, falling together in foreign words, full of panic now. I had already searched the first-class crowd in the midst of all that, and I slipped through a passage near the bridge and out onto the port side of the boat deck.

And there she was. There was order here, for the moment, women being helped into a boat by their husbands and by the ship's officers, though the movements were not refined now, there was a quick fumbling to them. But she was apart from all that. She was at the railing and looking forward. I came to her.

'Hello,' I said.

She turned her face to me and at last I could see her beauty. She was caught full in the bridge lights now. I wished it were the moon again, but in the glare of the incandescent bulbs I could see the delicate thinness of her face, the great darkness of her eyes, made more beautiful, it seemed to me, by the faint traces of her age around them. She was younger than I, but she was no young girl; she was a woman with a life lived in ways that perhaps would have been very interesting to share, in some other place. Though I know now that in some other place I never would have had occasion or even the impulse – even the impulse, I say – to speak to her of anything, much less the events of her life or the events of my own life, pitiful as it was, though I think she would have liked India. As I float here in this strange place beneath this muffled light I think she would have liked to go out to India and turn that remarkable intuition of hers, the subtle responsiveness of her ear and her sight and even the bottoms of her feet, which told her the truth of our doom, she would have liked to turn all that sensitivity to the days and nights of India, the animal cries in the dark and the smell of the Bay of Bengal and the comfort of a bed shrouded in mosquito netting and the drifting to sleep.

Can this possibly be me speaking? What is this feeling? This speaking of a bed in the same breath with this woman? The shroud above me is moving in this place where I float. It strips away and there are the shadows of two figures there. But it's the figure beside me on the night I died that compels me. She stood there and she turned her face to me and I know now that she must have understood what it is to live in a body. She looked at me and I said, 'You must go into a boat now.'

'I was about to go below and wait,' she said.

'Nonsense. You've known all along what's happening. You must go into the lifeboat.'

'I don't know why.'

'Because I ask you to.' How inadequate that answer should have been, I realize now. But she looked into my face and those dark eyes searched me.

'You've dressed up,' she said.

'To see you off,' I said.

She smiled faintly and lifted her hand. I braced for her touch, breathless, but her hand stopped at my tie, adjusted it, and then fell once more.

'Please hurry.' I tried to be firm but no more than whispered.

Nevertheless, she turned and I fell in beside her and we took a step together and another and another and we were before the lifeboat and a great flash of light lit us from above, a crackling fall of orange light, a distress flare, and she was beside me and she looked again into my eyes. My hands and arms were already dead, it seemed, they had already sunk deep beneath the sea, for they did not move. I turned and there was a man in uniform and I said, 'Officer, please board this lady now.'

He offered his hand to her and she took it and she moved into the end of the queue of women, and in a few moments she stepped into the boat. I shrank back into the darkness, terribly cold, feeling some terrible thing. One might expect it to be a fear of what was about to befall me, but one would be wrong. It was some other terrible thing that I did not try to think out. The winch began to turn and I stepped forward for one last look at her face, but the boat was gone. And my hands came up. They flailed before me, and I didn't understand. I could not understand this at all.

So I went back to the smoking lounge, and the place was empty. I was very glad for that. I sat in the leather chair and I struck a match and I held it before my cigar and then I put it down. I could not smoke, and I didn't understand that either.

But above me there are two faces, pressed close, trying to see into this place where I float. I move. I shape these words. I know that they heard me when I cried out. When I felt the emptiness, even of this spiritual body. They were the ones who thrashed above me. Not swimming in the sea. Not drowning with me in the night the *Titanic* sank. I stood before her and my arms were dead, my hands could not move, but I know now what it is that brought me to a quiet grief all my corporeal life long. And I know now what it is that I've interrupted with my cry. These two above me were floating on the face of this sea and they were touching. They had known to raise their hands and touch each other.

At the end of the night I met her, I put my cigar down, and I waited, and soon the floor rose up and I fell against the wall and the chair was on top of me, and I don't remember the moment of the water, but it made no difference whatsoever. I was already dead. I'd long been dead.

THE CALL OF THE SEA

ISAK DINESEN

THE YOUNG MAN WITH THE CARNATION

THREE-QUARTERS of a century ago there lay in Antwerp, near the harbour, a small hotel named the Queen's Hotel. It was a neat, respectable place, where sea captains stayed with their wives.

To this house there came, on a March evening, a young man, sunk in gloom. As he walked up from the harbour, to which he had come on a ship from England, he was, he felt, the loneliest being in the world. And there was no one to whom he could speak of his misery, for to the eyes of the world he must seem safe and fortunate, a young man to be envied by everyone.

He was an author who had had a great success with his first book. The public had loved it; the critics had been at one in praising it; and he had made money on it, after having been poor all his life. The book, from his own experience, treated the hard lot of poor children, and it had brought him into contact with social reformers. He had been enthusiastically received within a circle of highly cultivated, noble men and women. He had even married into their community, the daughter of a famous scientist, a beautiful young woman, who idolized him.

He was now going to Italy with his wife, there to finish his next book, and was, at the moment, carrying the manuscript in his portmanteau. His wife had preceded him by a few days, for she wanted to visit her old school in Brussels on the way. 'It will do me good,' she had said, smiling, 'to think and talk of other things than you.' She was now waiting for him at the Queen's Hotel, and would wish to think and talk of nothing else.

All these things looked pleasant. But things were not what they looked. They hardly ever were, he reflected, but in his case they were even exactly the opposite. The world had been turned upside down upon him; it was no wonder that he should feel sick, even to death, within it. He had been trapped, and had found out too late.

For he felt in his heart that he would never again write a great book. He had no more to tell, and the manuscript in his bag was nothing but a pile of paper that weighed down his arm. In his mind he quoted the Bible, because he had been to a Sunday School when he was a boy, and thought: 'I am good for nothing but to be cast out and be trodden under foot by men.'

How was he to face the people who loved him, and had faith in him: his public, his friends and his wife? He had never doubted but that they must love him better than themselves, and must consider his interests before their own, on account of his genius, and because he was a great artist. But when his genius had gone, there were only two possible future courses left. Either the world would despise and desert him, or else it might go on loving him, irrespective of his worthiness as an artist. From this last alternative, although in his thoughts he rarely shied at anything, he turned in a kind of *horror vaccui*; it seemed in itself to reduce the world to a void and a caricature, a Bedlam. He might bear anything better than that.

The idea of his fame augmented and intensified his despair. If in the past he had been unhappy, and had at times contemplated throwing himself in the river, it had at least been his own affair. Now he had had the glaring searchlight of renown set on him; a hundred eyes were watching him; and his failure, or suicide, would be the failure and the suicide of a world-famous author.

And even these considerations were but minor factors in his misfortune. If worse came to worst, he could do without his fellow-creatures. He had no great opinion of them, and might see them go, public, friends and wife, with infinitely less regret than they would ever have suspected, as long as he himself could remain face to face, and on friendly terms, with God.

The love of God and the certainty that in return God loved him beyond other human beings had upheld him in times of poverty and adversity. He had a talent for gratitude as well; his recent good luck had confirmed and sealed the understanding between God and him. But now he felt that God had turned away from him. And if he were not a great artist, who was he that God should love him? Without his visionary powers, without his retinue of fancies, jests and tragedies, how could he even approach the Lord and implore Him to redress him? The truth was that he was then no better than other people. He might deceive the world, but he had never in his life deceived himself. He had become estranged from God, and how was he now to live?

His mind wandered, and on its own brought home fresh material for suffering. He remembered his father-in-law's verdict on modern literature. 'Superficiality,' the old man had thundered, 'is the mark of it. The age lacks weight; its greatness is hollow. Now your own noble work, my dear boy . . .' Generally the views of his father-in-law were to him of no consequence whatever, but at the present moment he was so low in spirits that they made him writhe a little. Superficiality, he thought, was the word which the public and the critics would use about him, when they came to know the truth – lightness, hollowness. They called his work noble because he had moved their hearts when he described the sufferings of the poor. But he might as well have written of the sufferings of kings. And he had described them, because he happened to know them. Now that he had made his fortune, he found that he had got no more to say of the poor, and that he would prefer to hear no more of them. The word 'superficiality' made an accompaniment to his steps in the long street.

While he had meditated upon these matters he had walked on. The night was cold, a thin, sharp wind ran straight against him. He looked up, and reflected that it was going to rain.

The young man's name was Charlie Despard. He was a small, slight person, a tiny figure in the lonely street. He was not yet thirty, and looked extraordinarily young for his age; he might have been a boy of seventeen. He had brown hair and skin, but blue eyes, a narrow face and a nose with a faint bend to one side. He was extremely light of movement, and kept himself very straight, even in his present state of depression, and with the heavy portmanteau in his hand. He was well dressed, in a havelock, all his clothes had a new look on him, and were indeed new.

He turned his mind towards the hotel, wondering whether it would be any better to be in a house than out in the street. He decided that he would have a glass of brandy when he came there. Lately he had turned to brandy for consolation; sometimes he found it there and at other times not. He also thought of his wife, who was waiting for him. She might be asleep by now. If only she would not have locked the door, so that he should have to wake her up and talk, her nearness might be a comfort to him. He thought of her beauty and her kindness to him. She was a tall young woman with yellow hair and blue eyes, and a skin as white as marble. Her face would have been classic if the upper part of it had not been a little short and narrow in proportion to the jaw and chin. The same peculiarity was repeated in her body; the upper part of it was a little too short and slight for the hips and legs. Her name was Laura. She had a clear, grave, gentle gaze, and her blue eyes easily filled with tears of emotion, her admiration for him in itself would make them run full when she looked at him. What was the good of it all to him? She was not really his wife; she had married a phantom of her own imagination, and he was left out in the cold.

He came to the hotel, and found that he did not even want the brandy. He only stood in the hall, which to him looked like a grave, and asked the porter if his wife had arrived. The old man told him that Madame had arrived safely, and had informed him that Monsieur would come later. He offered to take the traveller's portmanteau upstairs for him, but Charlie reflected that he had better bear his own burdens. So he got the number of the room from him, and walked up the stairs and along the corridor alone. To his surprise he found the double door of the room unlocked, and went straight in. This seemed to him the first slight favour that fate had shown him for a long time.

The room, when he entered it, was almost dark; only a faint gas-jet burned by the dressing-table. There was a scent of violets in the air. His wife would have brought them and would have meant to give them to him with a line from a poem. But she lay deep down in the pillows. He was so easily swayed by little things at the present time that his heart warmed at his good luck. While he took off his shoes he looked round and thought: 'This room, with its sky-blue wallpaper and crimson curtains, has been kind to me; I will not forget it.'

But when he got into bed he could not sleep. He heard a

clock in the neighbourhood strike the quarter-stroke once, and twice, and three times. He felt that he had forgotten the art of sleeping and would have to lie awake for ever. 'That is,' he thought, 'because I am really dead. There is no longer any difference to me between life and death.'

Suddenly, without warning, for he had heard no steps approaching, he heard somebody gently turning the handle of the door. He had locked the door when he came in. When the person in the corridor discovered that, he waited a little, then tried it once more. He seemed to give it up, and after a moment softly drummed a little tune upon the door, and repeated it. Again there was a silence; then the stranger lowly whistled a bit of a tune. Charlie became deadly afraid that in the end all this would wake up his wife. He got out of bed, put on his green dressing-gown and went and opened the door with as little noise as possible.

The corridor was more clearly lighted than the room, and there was a lamp on the wall above the door. Outside, beneath it, stood a young man. He was tall and fair, and so elegantly dressed that Charlie was surprised to meet him in the Queen's Hotel. He had on evening clothes, with a cloak flung over them, and he wore in a buttonhole a pink carnation that looked fresh and romantic against the black and white. But what struck Charlie the moment he looked at him was the expression in the young man's face. It was so radiant with happiness, it shone with such gentle, humble, wild, laughing rapture that Charlie had never seen the like of it. An angelic messenger straight from Heaven could not have displayed a more exuberant, glorious ecstasy. It made the poet stare at him for a minute. Then he spoke, in French – since he took it that the distinguished young man of Antwerp must be French, and he himself spoke French well, for he had in his time been apprenticed to a French hairdresser. 'What is it you want?' he asked. 'My wife is asleep and I very much want to sleep myself.'

The young man with the carnation had appeared as deeply surprised at the sight of Charlie as Charlie at the sight of him. Still, his strange beatitude was so deeply rooted within him that it took him some time to change his expression into that of a gentleman who meets another gentleman. The light of it remained on his face, mingled with bewilderment, even when he spoke and said: 'I beg your pardon. I infinitely regret to have disturbed you. I have made a mistake.' Then Charlie closed the door and turned. With the corner of his eye he saw that his wife was sitting up in her bed. He said, shortly, for she might still be only half awake: 'It was a gentleman. I believe he was drunk.' At his words she lay down again, and he went back to bed himself.

The moment he was in his bed he was seized by a tremendous agitation; he felt that something irreparable had happened to him. For a while he did not know what it was, nor whether it was good or bad. It was as if a gigantic, blazing light had gone up on him, passed, and left him blinded. Then the impression slowly formed and consolidated, and made itself known in a pain so overwhelming that it contracted him as in a spasm.

For here, he knew, was the glory, the meaning and the key of life. The young man with the carnation had it. That infinite happiness which beamed on the face of the young man with the carnation was to be found somewhere in the world. The young man was aware of the way to it, but he, he had lost it. Once upon a time, it seemed to him, he too had known it, and had let go his hold, and here he was, forever doomed. O God, God in Heaven, at what moment had his own road taken off from the road of the young man with the carnation?

He saw clearly now that the gloom of his last weeks had been but the foreboding of this total perdition. In his agony, for he was really in the grip of death, he caught at any means of salvation, fumbled in the dark and struck at some of the most enthusiastic reviews of his book. His mind at the next moment shrank from them as if they had burnt him. Here, indeed, lay his ruin and damnation: with the reviewers, the publishers, the reading public, and with his wife. They were the people who wanted books, and to obtain their end would turn a human being into printed matter. He had let himself be seduced by the least seductive people in the world; they had made him sell his soul at a price which was in itself a penalty. 'I will put enmity,' he thought, 'between the author and the readers, and between thy seed and their seed; thou shalt bruise their heel, but they shall bruise thine head.' It was no wonder that God had ceased to love him, for he had, from his own free will, exchanged the things of the Lord – the moon, the sea, friendship, fights – for the words that describe them. He might now sit in a room and write down these words, to be praised by the critics, while outside, in the corridor, ran the road of the young man with the carnation into that light which made his face shine.

He did not know how long he had lain like this; he thought that he had wept, but his eyes were dry. In the end he suddenly fell asleep and slept for a minute. When he woke up he was perfectly calm and resolved. He would go away. He would save himself, and he would go in search of that happiness which existed somewhere. If he were to go to the end of the world for it, it did not signify; indeed it might be the best plan to go straight to the end of the world. He would now go down to the harbour and find a ship to take him away. At the idea of a ship he became calm.

He lay in bed for an hour more; then he got up and

dressed. The while he wondered what the young man with the carnation had thought of him. He will have thought, he said to himself: 'Ah, le pauvre petit bonhomme à la robe de chambre verte.' Very silently he packed his portmanteau; his manuscript he first planned to leave behind, then took it with him in order to throw it into the sea, and witness its destruction. As he was about to leave the room he bethought himself of his wife. It was not fair to leave a sleeping woman, forever, without some word of farewell. Theseus, he remembered, had done that. But it was hard to find the word of farewell. In the end, standing by the dressing-table he wrote on a sheet from his manuscript, 'I have gone away. Forgive me if you can.' Then he went down. In the loge the porter was nodding over a paper. Charlie thought: 'I shall never see him again. I shall never again open this door.'

When he came out the wind had lowered, it rained, and the rain was whispering and murmuring on all sides of him. He took off his hat; in a moment his hair was dripping wet, and the rain ran down his face. In this fresh, unexpected touch there was a purport. He went down the street by which he had come, since it was the only street he knew in Antwerp. As he walked, it seemed as if the world was no longer entirely indifferent to him, nor was he any longer absolutely lonely in it. The dispersed, dissipated phenomena of the universe were consolidating, very likely into the devil himself, and the devil had him by the hand or the hair.

Before he expected it, he was down by the harbour and stood upon the wharf, his portmanteau in his hand, gazing down into the water. It was deep and dark, the lights from the lamps on the quay played within it like young snakes. His first strong sensation about it was that it was salt. The rainwater came down on him from above; the salt water met him below. That was as it should be. He stood here for a long time, looking at the ships. He would go away on one of them.

The hulls loomed giant-like in the wet night. They carried things in their bellies, and were pregnant with possibilities; they were porters of destinies, his superiors in every way, with the water on all sides of them. They swam; the salt sea bore them wherever they wanted to go. As he looked, it seemed to him that a kind of sympathy was going forth from the big hulks to him; they had a message for him, but at first he did not know what it was. Then he found the word; it was superficiality. The ships were superficial, and kept to the surface. Therein lay their power; to ships the danger is to get to the bottom of things, to run aground. They were even hollow, and hollowness was the secret of their being; the great depths slaved for them as long as they remained hollow. A wave of happiness heaved Charlie's heart; after a while he laughed in the dark.

'My sisters,' he thought, 'I should have come to you long ago. You beautiful, superficial wanderers, gallant, swimming conquerors of the deep! You heavy, hollow angels, I shall thank you all my life. God keep you afloat, big sisters, you and me. God preserve our superficiality.' He was very wet by now; his hair and his havelock were shining softly, like the sides of the ships in the rain. 'And now,' he thought, 'I shall hold my mouth. My life has had altogether too many words; I cannot remember now why I have talked so much. Only when I came down here and was silent in the rain was I shown the truth of things. From now on I shall speak no more, but I shall listen to what the sailors will tell me, the people who are familiar with the floating ships, and keep off the bottom of things. I shall go to the end of the world, and hold my mouth.'

He had hardly made this resolution before a man on the

wharf came up and spoke to him. 'Are you looking for a ship?' he asked. He looked like a sailor, Charlie thought, and like a friendly monkey as well. He was a short man with a weather-bitten face and a neck-beard. 'Yes, I am,' said Charlie. 'For which ship?' asked the sailor. Charlie was about to answer: 'For the ark of Noah, from the flood.' But in time he realized that it would sound foolish. 'You see,' he said, 'I want to get aboard a ship, and go for a journey.' The sailor spat, and laughed. 'A journey?' he said. 'All right. You were staring down into the water, so that in the end I believed that you were going to jump in.' 'Ah, yes, to jump in!' said Charlie. 'And so you would have saved me? But there it is, you are too late to save me. You should have come last night, that would have been the right moment. The only reason why I did not drown myself last night,' he went on, 'was that I was short of water. If the water had come to me then! Here lies the water – good; here stands the man – good. If the water comes to him he drowns himself. It all goes to prove that the greatest of poets make mistakes, and that one should never become a poet.' The sailor by this time had made up his mind that the young stranger was drunk. 'All right, my boy,' he said, 'if you have thought better about drowning yourself, you may go your own way, and good night to you.' This was a great disappointment to Charlie, who thought that the conversation was going extraordinarily well. 'Nay, but can I not come with you?' he asked the sailor. 'I am going into the inn of La Croix du Midi,' the sailor answered, 'to have a glass of rum.' 'That,' Charlie exclaimed, 'is an excellent idea, and I am in luck to meet a man who has such ideas.'

They went together into the inn of La Croix du Midi close by, and there met two more sailors, whom the first sailor knew, and introduced them to Charlie as a mate and a supercargo. He himself was captain of a small ship riding at anchor outside the harbour. Charlie put his hand in his pocket and found it full of the money which he had taken with him for his journey. 'Let me have a bottle of your best rum for these gentlemen,' he said to the waiter, 'and a pot of coffee for myself.' He did not want any spirits in his present mood. He was actually scared of his companions, but he found it difficult to explain his case to them. 'I drink coffee,' he said, 'because I have taken' – he was going to say: a vow, but thought better of it – 'a bet. There was an old man on a ship – he is, by the way, an uncle of mine – and he bet me that I could not keep from drink for a year, but if I won, the ship would be mine.' 'And have you kept from it?' the captain asked. 'Yes, as God lives,' said Charlie. 'I declined a glass of brandy not twelve hours ago, and what, from my talk, you may take to be drunkenness, is nothing but the effect of the smell of the sea.' The mate asked: 'Was the man who bet you a small man with a big belly and only one eye?' 'Yes, that is Uncle!' cried Charlie. 'Then I have met him myself, on my way to Rio,' said the mate, 'and he offered me the same terms, but I would not take them.'

Here the drinks were brought and Charlie filled the glasses. He rolled himself a cigarette, and joyously inhaled the aroma of the rum and of the warm room. In the light of a dim hanging-lamp the three faces of his new acquaintances glowed fresh and genial. He felt honoured and happy in their company and thought: 'How much more they know than I do.' He himself was very pale, as always when he was agitated. 'May your coffee do you good,' said the captain. 'You look as if you had got the fever.' 'Nay, but I have had a great sorrow,' said Charlie. The others put on condolent faces, and asked him what sorrow it was. 'I will tell you,' said Charlie. 'It is better to speak of it, although a little while ago I thought the opposite. I had a tame monkey I was very fond of; his name was Charlie. I had bought him from an old woman who kept a house in Hongkong, and she and I had to smuggle him out in the dead of midday, otherwise the girls would never have let him go, for he was like a brother to them. He was like a brother to me, too. He knew all my thoughts, and was always on my side. He had been taught many tricks already when I got him, and he learned more while he was with me. But when I came home the English food did not agree with him, nor did the English Sunday. So he grew sick, and he grew worse, and one Sabbath evening he died on me.' 'That was a pity,' said the captain compassionately. 'Yes,' said Charlie. 'When there is only one person in the world whom you care for, and that is a monkey, and he is dead, then that is a pity.'

The supercargo, before the others came in, had been telling the mate a story. Now for the benefit of the others he told it all over. It was a cruel tale of how he had sailed from Buenos Aires with wool. When five days out in the doldrums the ship had caught fire, and the crew, after fighting the fire all night, had got into the boats in the morning and left her. The supercargo himself had had his hands burnt; all the same he had rowed for three days and nights, so that when they were picked up by a steamer from Rotterdam his hand had grown round his oar, and he could never again stretch out the two fingers. 'Then,' he said, 'I looked at my hand, and I swore an oath that if I ever came back on dry land, the Devil take me and the Devil hold me if ever I went to sea again.' The other two nodded their heads gravely at his tale, and asked him where he was off to now. 'Me?' said the supercargo. 'I have shipped for Sydney.'

The mate described a storm in the Bay, and the captain gave them a story of a blizzard in the North Sea, which he had experienced when he was but a sailor-boy. He had been set to the pumps, he narrated, and had been forgotten there, and as he dared not leave, he had pumped for eleven hours. 'At that time,' he said, 'I, too, swore to stay on land, and never to set foot on the sea again.'

Charlie listened, and thought: 'These are wise men. They know what they are talking about. For the people who travel for their pleasure when the sea is smooth, and smiles at them, and who declare that they love her, they do not know what love means. It is the sailors, who have been beaten and battered by the sea, and who have cursed and damned her, who are her true lovers. Very likely the same law applies to husbands and wives. I shall learn more from the seamen. I am a child and a fool, compared to them.'

The three sailors were conscious, from his silent, attentive attitude, of the young man's reverence and wonder. They took him for a student, and were content to divulge their experiences to him. They also thought him a good host, for he steadily filled their glasses, and ordered a fresh bottle when the first was empty. Charlie, in return for their stories, gave them a couple of songs. He had a sweet voice and tonight was pleased with it himself; it was a long time since he had sung a song. They all became friendly. The captain slapped him on the back and told him that he was a bright boy and might still be turned into a sailor.

But as, a little later, the captain began to talk tenderly of his wife and family, whom he had just left, and the supercargo, with pride and emotion, informed the party that within the last three months two barmaids of Antwerp had had twins, girls with red hair like their father's, Charlie remembered his own wife and became ill at ease. These sailors, he thought, seemed to know how to deal with their women. Probably there was not one of them so afraid of his wife as to run away from her in the middle of night. If they knew that he had done so, he reflected, they would think less well of him.

The sailors had believed him to be much younger than he was; so in their company he had come to feel himself like a very young man, and his wife now looked to him more like a mother than a mate. His real mother, although she had been a respectable tradeswoman, had had a drop of gypsy blood in her, and none of his quick resolutions had ever taken her by surprise. Indeed, he reflected, she kept upon the surface through everything, and swam there, majestically, like a proud, dark, ponderous goose. If tonight he had gone to her and told her of his decision to go to sea, the idea might very well have excited and pleased her. The pride and gratitude which he had always felt towards the old woman, now, as he drank his last cup of coffee, were transferred to the young. Laura would understand him, and side with him.

He sat for some time, weighing the matter. For experience had taught him to be careful here. He had, before now, been trapped as by a strange optical delusion. When he was away from her, his wife took on all the appearance of a guardian angel, unfailing in sympathy and support. But when again he met her face to face, she was a stranger, and he found his road paved with difficulties.

Still tonight all this seemed to belong to the past. For he was in power now; he had the sea and the ships with him, and before him the young man with the carnation. Great images surrounded him. Here, in the inn of La Croix du Midi he had already lived through much. He had seen a ship burn down, a snowstorm in the North Sea, and the sailor's homecoming to his wife and children. So potent did he feel that the figure of his wife looked pathetic. He remembered her as he had last seen her, asleep, passive and peaceful, and her whiteness, and her ignorance of the world, went to his heart. He suddenly blushed deeply at the thought of the letter he had written to her. He might go away, he now felt, with a lighter heart, if he had first explained everything to her. 'Home,' he thought, 'where is thy sting? Married life, where is thy victory?'

He sat and looked down at the table, where a little coffee had been spilled. The while the sailors' talk ebbed out, because they saw that he was no longer listening; in the end it stopped. The consciousness of silence round him woke up Charlie. He smiled at them. 'I shall tell you a story before we go home. A blue story,' he said.

'There was once,' he began, 'an immensely rich old Englishman who had been a courtier and a councillor to the Queen and who now, in his old age, cared for nothing but collecting ancient blue china. To that end he travelled to Persia, Japan and China, and he was everywhere accompanied by his daughter, the Lady Helena. It happened, as they sailed in the Chinese Sea, that the ship caught fire on a still night, and everybody went into the lifeboats and left her. In the dark and the confusion the old peer was separated from his daughter. Lady Helena got up on deck late, and found the ship quite deserted. In the last moment a young English sailor carried her down into a lifeboat that had been forgotten. To the two fugitives it seemed as if fire was following them from all sides, for the phosphorescence played in the dark sea, and, as they looked up, a falling star ran across the sky, as if it was going to drop into the boat. They sailed for nine days, till they were picked up by a Dutch merchantman, and came home to England.

'The old lord had believed his daughter to be dead. He now wept with joy, and at once took her off to a fashionable watering-place so that she might recover from the hardships she had gone through. And as he thought it must be unpleasant to her that a young sailor, who made his bread in the merchant service, should tell the world that he had sailed for nine days alone with a peer's daughter, he paid the boy a fine sum, and made him promise to go shipping in the other hemisphere and never come back. "For what," said the old nobleman, "would be the good of that?"

'When Lady Helena recovered, and they gave her the news of the Court and of her family, and in the end also told her how the young sailor had been sent away never to come back, they found that her mind had suffered from her trials, and that she cared for nothing in all the world. She would not go back to her father's castle in its park, nor go to Court, nor travel to any gay town of the continent. The only thing which she now wanted to do was to go, like her father before her, to collect rare blue china. So she began to sail, from one country to the other, and her father went with her.

'In her search she told the people, with whom she dealt, that she was looking for a particular blue colour, and would pay any price for it. But although she bought many hundred blue jars and bowls, she would always after a time put them aside and say: "Alas, alas, it is not the right blue." Her father, when they had sailed for many years, suggested to her that perhaps the colour which she sought did not exist. "O God, Papa," said she, "how can you speak so wickedly? Surely there must be some of it left from the time when all the world was blue."

'Her two old aunts in England implored her to come back, still to make a great match. But she answered them: "Nay, I have got to sail. For you must know, dear aunts, that it is all nonsense when learned people tell you that the seas have got a bottom to them. On the contrary, the water, which is the noblest of the elements, does, of course, go all through the earth, so that our planet really floats in the ether, like a soap-bubble. And there, on the other hemisphere, a ship sails, with which I have got to keep pace. We two are like the reflection of one another, in the deep sea, and the ship of which I speak is always exactly beneath my own ship, upon the opposite side of the globe. You have never seen a big fish swimming underneath a boat, following it like a dark-blue shade in the water. But in that way this ship goes, like the shadow of my ship, and I draw it to and fro wherever I go, as the moon draws the tides, all through the bulk of the earth. If I stopped sailing, what would those poor sailors who make their bread in the merchant service do? But I shall tell you a secret," she said. "In the end my ship will go down, to the centre of the globe, and at the very same hour the other ship will sink as well – for people call it sinking, although I can assure you that there is no up and down in the sea – and there, in the midst of the world, we two shall meet."

'Many years passed, the old lord died and Lady Helena became old and deaf, but she still sailed. Then it happened, after the plunder of the summer palace of the Emperor of China, that a merchant brought her a very old blue jar. The moment she set eyes on it she gave a terrible shriek. "There it is!" she cried. "I have found it at last. This is the true blue. Oh, how light it makes one. Oh, it is as fresh as a breeze, as deep as a deep secret, as full as I say not what." With trembling hands she held the jar to her bosom, and sat for six hours sunk in contemplation of it. Then she said to her doctor and her lady-companion: "Now I can die. And when I am dead you will cut out my heart and lay it in the blue jar. For then everything will be as it was then. All shall be blue round me, and in the midst of the blue world my heart will be innocent and free, and will beat gently, like a wake that sings, like the drops that fall from an oar blade." A little later she asked them: "Is it not a sweet thing to think that, if only you have patience, all that has ever been, will come back to you?" Shortly afterwards the old lady died.'

The party now broke up, the sailors gave Charlie their hands and thanked him for the rum and the story. Charlie wished them all good luck. 'You forgot your bag,' said the captain, and picked up Charlie's portmanteau with the manuscript in it. 'No,' said Charlie, 'I mean to leave that with you, till we are to sail together.' The captain looked at the initials on the bag. 'It is a heavy bag,' he said. 'Have you got anything of value in it?' 'Yes, it is heavy, God help me,' said Charlie, 'but that shall not happen again. Next time it will be empty.' He got the name of the captain's ship, and said good-bye to him.

As he came out he was surprised to find that it was nearly morning. The long spare row of street lamps held up their melancholy heads in the grey air.

A thin young girl with big black eyes, who had been walking up and down in front of the inn, came up and spoke to him, and, when he did not answer, repeated her invitation in English. Charlie looked at her. 'She too,' he thought, 'belongs to the ships, like the mussels and seaweeds that grow on their bottoms. Within her many good seamen, who escaped the deep, have been drowned. But all the same she will not run aground, and if I go with her I shall still be safe.' He put his hand in his pocket, but found only one shilling left there. 'Will you let me have a shilling's worth?' he asked the girl. She stared at him. Her face did not change as he took her hand, pulled down her old glove and pressed the palm, rough and clammy as fish-skin, to his lips and tongue. He gave her back her hand, placed a shilling in it, and walked away.

For the third time he walked along the street between the harbour and the Queen's Hotel. The town was now waking up, and he met a few people and carts. The windows of the hotel were lighted. When he came into the hall there was no one there, and he was about to walk up to his room, when, through a glass door, he saw his wife sitting in a small, lighted dining room next to the hall. So he went in there.

When his wife caught sight of him her face cleared up. 'Oh, you have come!' she cried. He bent his head. He was about to take her hand and kiss it when she asked him: 'Why are you so late?' 'Am I late?' he exclaimed, highly surprised by her question, and because the idea of time had altogether gone from him. He looked at a clock upon the mantelpiece, and said: 'It is only ten past seven.' 'Yes, but I thought you would be here earlier!' said she. 'I got up to be ready when you came.' Charlie sat down by the table. He did not answer her, for he had no idea what to say. 'Is it possible,' he thought, 'that she has the strength of soul to take me back in this way?'

'Will you have some coffee?' said his wife. 'No, thank you,' said he, 'I have had coffee.' He glanced round the room. Although it was nearly light and the blinds were up, the gas lamps were still burning, and from his childhood this had always seemed to him a great luxury. The fire on the fireplace played on a somewhat worn Brussels carpet and on the red plush chairs. His wife was eating an egg. As a little boy he had had an egg on Sunday mornings. The whole room, that smelled of coffee and fresh bread, with the white tablecloth and the shining coffee-pot, took on a sabbath-morning look. He gazed at his wife. She had on her grey travelling cloak, her bonnet was lying beside her, and her yellow hair, gathered in a net, shone in the lamplight. She was bright in her own way, a pure light came from her, and she seemed enduringly fixed on the sofa, the one firm object in a turbulent world.

An idea came to him: 'She is like a lighthouse,' he thought, 'the firm, majestic lighthouse that sends out its kindly light. To all ships it says: "Keep off." For where the lighthouse stands, there is shoal water, or rocks. To all floating objects the approach means death.' At this moment she looked up, and found his eyes on her. 'What are you thinking of?' she asked him. He thought: 'I will tell her. It is better to be honest with her, from now, and to tell her all.' So he said, slowly: 'I am thinking that you are to me, in life, like a lighthouse. A steady light, instructing me how to steer my course.' She looked at him, then away, and her eyes filled with tears. He became afraid that she was going to cry, even though till now she had been so brave. 'Let us go up to our own room,' he said, for it would be easier to explain things to her when they were alone.

They went up together, and the stairs, which, last night, had been so long to climb, now were so easy, that his wife said: 'No, you are going up too high. We are there.' She walked ahead of him down the corridor, and opened the door to their room.

The first thing that he noticed was that there was no longer any smell of violets in the air. Had she thrown them away in anger? Or had they all faded when he went away? She came up to him and laid her hand on his shoulder and her face on it. Over her fair hair, in the net, he looked round, and stood quite still. For the dressing-table, on which, last night, he had put his letter for her, was in a new place, and so, he found, was the bed he had lain in. In the corner there was now a cheval-glass which had not been there before. This was not his room. He quickly took in more details. There was no longer a canopy to the bed, but above it a steel-engraving of the Belgian Royal family that till now he had never seen. 'Did you sleep here last night?' he asked.

'Yes,' said his wife. 'But not well. I was worried when you did not come; I feared that you were having a bad crossing.' 'Did nobody disturb you?' he asked again. 'No,' she said. 'My door was locked. And this is a quiet hotel, I believe.'

As Charlie now looked back on the happenings of the night, with the experienced eye of an author of fiction, they moved him as mightily as if they had been out of one of his own books. He drew in his breath deeply. 'Almighty God,' he said from the bottom of his heart, 'as the heavens are higher than the earth, so are thy short stories higher than our short stories.'

He went through all the details slowly and surely, as a mathematician sets up and solves an equation. First he felt, like honey on his tongue, the longing and the triumph of the young man with the carnation. Then, like the grip of a hand round his throat, but with hardly less artistic enjoyment, the terror of the lady in the bed. As if he himself had possessed a pair of firm young breasts he was conscious of his heart stopping beneath them. He stood perfectly still, in his own thoughts, but his face took on such an expression of rapture, laughter and delight that his wife, who had lifted her head from his shoulder, asked him in surprise: 'What are you thinking of now?'

Charlie took her hand, his face still radiant. 'I am thinking,' he said very slowly, 'of the Garden of Eden, and the cherubim with the flaming sword. Nay,' he went on in the same way, 'I am thinking of Hero and Leander. Of Romeo and Juliet. Of Theseus and Ariadne, and the Minotaur as well. Have you ever tried, my dear, to guess how, upon the occasion, the Minotaur was feeling?'

'So you are going to write a love story, Troubadour?' she asked, smiling back upon him. He did not answer at once, but he let go her hand, and after a while asked: 'What did you say?' 'I asked you if you were going to write a love story?' she repeated timidly. He went away from her, up to the table, and put his hand upon it.

The light that had fallen upon him last night was coming back, and from all sides now – from his own lighthouse as well, he thought confusedly. Only then it had shone onward, upon the infinite world, while at this moment it was turned inwards, and was lightening up the room of the Queen's Hotel. It was very bright; it seemed that he was to see himself, within it, as God saw him, and under this test he had to steady himself by the table.

While he stood there the situation developed into a dialogue between Charlie and the Lord.

The Lord said: 'Your wife asked you twice if you are going to write a love story. Do you believe that this is indeed what you are going to do?' 'Yes, that is very likely,' said Charlie. 'Is it,' the Lord asked, 'to be a great and sweet tale, which will live in the hearts of young lovers?' 'Yes, I should say so,' said Charlie. 'And are you content with that?' asked the Lord.

'O Lord, what are you asking me?' cried Charlie. 'How can I answer yes? Am I not a human being, and can I write a love story without longing for that love which clings and embraces, and for the softness and warmth of a young woman's body in my arms?' 'I gave you all that last night,' said the Lord. 'It was you who jumped out of bed, to go to the end of the world from it.' 'Yes, I did that,' said Charlie. 'Did you behold it and think it very good? Are you going to repeat it on me? Am I to be, forever, he who lay in bed with the mistress of the young man with the carnation, and, by the way, what has become of her, and how is she to explain things to him? And who went off, and wrote to her: "I have gone away. Forgive me, if you can." ' 'Yes,' said the Lord.

'Nay, tell me, now that we are at it,' cried Charlie, 'am I, while I write of the beauty of young women, to get, from the live women of the earth, a shilling's worth, and no more?' 'Yes,' said the Lord. 'And you are to be content with that.' Charlie was drawing a pattern with his finger on the table; he said nothing. It seemed that the discourse was ended here, when again the Lord spoke.

'Who made the ships, Charlie?' he asked. 'Nay, I know not,' said Charlie, 'did you make them?' 'Yes,' said the Lord, 'I made the ships on their keels, and all floating things. The moon that sails in the sky, the orbs that swing in the universe, the tides, the generations, the fashions. You make me laugh, for I have given you all the world to sail and float in, and you have run aground here, in a room of the Queen's Hotel to seek a quarrel.'

'Come,' said the Lord again, 'I will make a covenant between me and you. I, I will not measure you out any more distress than you need to write your books.' 'Oh, indeed!' said Charlie. 'What did you say?' asked the Lord. 'Do you want any less than that?' 'I said nothing,' said Charlie. 'But you are to write the books,' said the Lord. 'For it is I who want them written. Not the public, not by any means the critics, but ME!' 'Can I be certain of that?' Charlie asked. 'Not always,' said the Lord. 'You will not be certain of it at all times. But I tell you now that it is so. You will have to hold on to that.' 'O good God,' said Charlie. 'Are you going,' said the Lord, 'to thank me for what I have done for you tonight?' 'I think,' said Charlie, 'that we will leave it at what it is, and say no more about it.'

His wife now went and opened the window. The cold, raw morning air streamed in, with the din of carriages from the street below, human voices and a great chorus of sparrows, and with the smell of smoke and horse manure.

When Charlie had finished his talk with God, and while

it was still so vivid to him that he might have written it down, he went to the window and looked out. The morning colours of the grey town were fresh and delicate, and there was a faint promise of sunshine in the sky. People were about; a young woman in a blue shawl and slippers was walking away quickly; and the omnibus of the hotel, with a white horse to it, was halting below, while the porter helped out the travellers and took down their luggage. Charlie gazed down into the street, a long way under him.

'I shall thank the Lord for one thing all the same,' he thought. 'That I did not lay my hand on anything that belonged to my brother, the young man with the carnation. It was within my reach, but I did not touch it.' He stood for a while in the window and saw the omnibus drive away. Where, he wondered, amongst the houses in the pale morning, was now the young man of last night?

'O the young man,' he thought. 'Ah, le pauvre jeune homme à l'œillet.'

HERMAN MELVILLE

JOHN MARR

JOHN MARR, TOWARD the close of the last century born in America of a mother unknown, and from boyhood up to maturity a sailor under divers flags, disabled at last from further maritime life by a crippling wound received at close quarters with pirates of the Keys, eventually betakes himself for a livelihood to less active employment ashore. There, too, he transfers his rambling disposition acquired as a seafarer.

After a variety of removals, at first as a sail-maker from sea-port to sea-port, then adventurously inland as a rough bench-carpenter, he, finally, in the last-named capacity, settles down about the year 1838 upon what was then a frontier-prairie, sparsely sprinkled with small oak-groves and yet fewer log-houses of a little colony but recently from one of our elder inland States. Here, putting a period to his rovings, he marries.

Ere long a fever, the bane of new settlements on teeming loam, and whose sallow livery was certain to show itself, after an interval, in the complexions of too many of these people, carries off his young wife and infant child. In one coffin, put together by his own hands, they are committed with meager rites to the earth – another mound, though a small one, in the wide prairie, not far from where the mound-builders of a race only conjecturable had left their pottery and bones, one common clay, under a strange terrace serpentine in form.

With an honest stillness in his general mien – swarthy and black-browed, with eyes that could soften or flash, but never harden, yet disclosing at times a melancholy depth – this kinless man had affections which, once placed, not readily could be dislodged or resigned to a substituted object. Being now arrived at middle-life, he resolves never to quit the soil that holds the only beings ever connected with him by love in the family tie. His log-house he lets to a new-comer, one glad enough to get it, and dwells with the household.

While the acuter sense of his bereavement becomes mollified by time, the void at heart abides. Fain, if possible, would he fill that void by cultivating social relations yet nearer than before with a people whose lot he purposes sharing to the end – relations superadded to that mere work-a-day bond arising from participation in the same outward hardships, making reciprocal helpfulness a matter of course. But here, and nobody to blame, he is obstructed.

More familiarly to consort, men of a practical turn must sympathetically converse, and upon topics of real life. But, whether as to persons or events, one cannot always be talking about the present, much less speculating about the future; one must needs recur to the past, which, with the mass of men, where the past is in any personal way a common inheritance, supplies to most practical natures the basis of sympathetic communion.

But the past of John Marr was not the past of these pioneers. Their hands had rested on the plow-tail, his upon the ship's helm. They knew but their own kind and their own usages; to him had been revealed something of the checkered globe. So limited unavoidably was the mental reach, and by consequence the range of sympathy, in this particular band of domestic emigrants, hereditary tillers of the soil, that the ocean, but a hearsay to their fathers, had now through yet deeper inland removal become to themselves little more than a rumor traditional and vague.

They were a staid people; staid through habituation to monotonous hardship; ascetics by necessity not less than through moral bias; nearly all of them sincerely, however narrowly, religious. They were kindly at need, after their fashion; but to a man wonted – as John Marr in his previous homeless sojournings could not but have been – to the free-and-easy tavern-clubs affording cheap recreation of an evening in certain old and comfortable sea-port towns of that time, and yet more familiar with the companionship afloat of the sailors of the same period, something was lacking. That something was geniality, the flower of life springing from some sense of joy in it, more or less. This their lot could not give to these hard-working endurers of the dispiriting malaria, – men to whom a holiday never came, – and they had too much of uprightness and no art at all or desire to affect what they did not really feel. At a corn-husking, their least grave of gatherings, did the lone-hearted mariner seek to divert his own thoughts from sadness, and in some degree interest theirs, by adverting to aught removed from the crosses and trials of their personal surroundings, naturally enough he would slide into some marine story or picture, but would soon recoil upon himself and be silent, finding no encouragement to proceed. Upon one such occasion an elderly man – a blacksmith, and at Sunday gatherings an earnest exhorter – honestly said to him, 'Friend, we know nothing of that here.'

Such unresponsiveness in one's fellow-creatures set apart from factitious life, and by their vocation – in those days little helped by machinery – standing, as it were, next of kin to Nature; this, to John Marr, seemed of a piece with the apathy of Nature herself as envisaged to him here on a prairie where none but the perished mound-builders had as yet left a durable mark.

The remnant of Indians thereabout – all but exterminated in their recent and final war with regular white troops, a war waged by the Red Men for their native soil and natural rights – had been coerced into the occupancy of wilds not very far beyond the Mississippi – wilds *then*, but now the seats of municipalities and States. Prior to that, the bisons, once streaming countless in processional herds, or browsing as in an endless battle-line over these vast aboriginal pastures, had retreated, dwindled in number, before the hunters, in main a race distinct from the agricultural pioneers, though generally their advance-guard. Such a double exodus of man and beast left the plain a desert, green or blossoming indeed, but almost as forsaken as the Siberian Obi. Save the prairie-hen, sometimes startled from its lurking-place in the rank grass; and, in their migratory season, pigeons, high overhead on the wing, in dense multitudes eclipsing the day like a passing stormcloud; save these – there being no wide woods with their underwood – birds were strangely few.

Blank stillness would for hours reign unbroken on this prairie. 'It is the bed of a dried-up sea,' said the companionless sailor – no geologist – to himself, musing at twilight upon the fixed undulations of that immense alluvial expanse bounded only by the horizon, and missing there the stir that, to alert eyes and ears, animates at all times the apparent solitudes of the deep.

But a scene quite at variance with one's antecedents may yet prove suggestive of them. Hooped round by a level rim, the prairie was to John Marr a reminder of ocean.

With some of his former shipmates, *chums* on certain cruises, he had contrived, prior to this last and more remote removal, to keep up a little correspondence at odd intervals. But from tidings of anybody or any sort he, in common with the other settlers, was now cut off; quite cut off, except from such news as might be conveyed over the grassy billows by the last-arrived prairie-schooner – the vernacular term, in those parts and times, for the emigrant-wagon arched high over with sail-cloth, and voyaging across the vast champaign. There was no reachable post-office as yet; not even the rude little receptive box with lid and leather hinges, set up at convenient intervals on a stout stake along some solitary green way, affording a perch for birds, and which, later in the unintermitting advance of the frontier, would perhaps decay into a mossy monument, attesting yet another successive overleaped limit of civilized life; a life which in America can today hardly be said to have any western bound but the ocean that washes Asia. Throughout these plains, now in places over-populous with towns over-opulent; sweeping plains, elsewhere fenced off in every direction into flourishing farms – pale townsmen and hale farmers alike, in part, the descendants of the first sallow settlers; a region that half a century ago produced little for the sustenance of man, but today launching its superabundant wheat-harvest on the world; – of this prairie, now everywhere intersected with wire and rail, hardly can it be said that at the period here written of there was so much as a traceable road. To the long-distance traveller the oak-groves, wide apart, and varying in compass and form; these, with recent settlements, yet more widely separate, offered some landmarks; but otherwise he steered by the sun. In early midsummer, even going but from one log-encampment to the next, a journey it might be of hours or good part of a day, travel was much like navigation. In some more enriched depressions between the long, green, graduated swells, smooth as those of ocean becalmed receiving and subduing to its own tranquillity the voluminous surge raised by some far-off hurricane of days previous, here one would catch the first indication of advancing strangers either in the distance, as a far sail at sea, by the glistening white canvas of the wagon, the wagon itself wading through the rank vegetation and hidden by it, or, failing that, when near to, in the ears of the team, peeking, if not above the tall tiger-lilies, yet above the yet taller grass.

Luxuriant, this wilderness; but, to its denizen, a friend left behind anywhere in the world seemed not alone absent to sight, but an absentee from existence.

Though John Marr's shipmates could not all have departed life, yet as subjects of meditation they were like phantoms of the dead. As the growing sense of his environment threw him more and more upon retrospective musings, these phantoms, next to those of his wife and child, became spiritual companions, losing something of their first indistinctness and putting on at last a dim semblance of mute life; and they were lit by that aureola circling over any object of the affections in the past for reunion with which an imaginative heart passionately yearns.

He invokes there visionary ones, – striving, as it were, to get into verbal communion with them, or, under yet stronger illusion, reproaching them for their silence: –

Since as in night's deck-watch ye show,
Why, lads, so silent here to me,
Your watchmate of times long ago?
Once, for all the darkling sea,
You your voices raised how clearly,
Striking in when tempest sung,
Hoisting up the storm-sail cheerly,
Life is storm – let storm! you rung.
Taking things as fated merely,

Child-like though the world ye spanned;
Nor holding unto life too dearly,
Ye who hold your lives in hand –
Skimmers, who on oceans four
Petrels were, and larks ashore.

O, not from memory lightly flung,
Forgot, like strains no more availing,
The heart to music haughtier strung;
Nay, frequent near me, never staleing,
Whose good feeling kept ye young.
Like tides that enter creek or stream,
Ye come, ye visit me, or seem
Swimming out from seas of faces,
Alien myriads memory traces,
To enfold me in a dream!

I yearn as ye. But rafts that strain,
Parted, shall they lock again?
Twined we were, entwined, then riven,
Ever to new embracements driven,
Shifting gulf-weed of the main!
And how if one here shift no more,
Lodged by the flinging surge ashore?
Nor less, as now, in eve's decline,
Your shadowy fellowship is mine.
Ye float around me, form and feature: –
Tattooings, ear-rings, love-locks curled;
Barbarians of man's simpler nature,
Unworldly servers of the world.
Yea, present all, and dear to me,
Though shades, or scouring China's sea.

Whither, whither, merchant-sailors,
Whitherward now in roaring gales?
Competing still, ye huntsman-whalers,
In leviathan's wake what boat prevails?
And man-of-war's men, whereaway?
If now no dinned drum beat to quarters
On the wilds of midnight waters –
Foemen looming through the spray;
Do yet your gangway lanterns, streaming,
Vainly strive to pierce below,
When, tilted from the slant plank gleaming,
A brother you see to darkness go?

But, gunmates lashed in shotted canvas,
If where long watch-below ye keep,
Never the shrill *'All hands up hammocks!'*
Breaks the spell that charms your sleep,
And summoning trumps might vainly call,
And booming guns implore –
A beat, a heart-beat musters all,
One heart-beat at heart-core.
It musters. But to clasp, retain;
To see you at the halyards main –
To hear your chorus once again!

J. G. BALLARD

NOW WAKES THE SEA

AGAIN AT NIGHT Mason heard the sounds of the approaching sea, the muffled thunder of breakers rolling up the near-by streets. Roused from his sleep, he ran out into the moonlight, where the white-framed houses stood like sepulchres among the washed concrete courts. Two hundred yards away the waves plunged and boiled, sluicing in and out across the pavement. Foam seethed through the picket fences, and the broken spray filled the air with the wine-sharp tang of brine.

Off-shore the deeper swells of the open sea rode across the roofs of the submerged houses, the white-caps cleft by isolated chimneys. Leaping back as the cold foam stung his feet, Mason glanced at the house where his wife lay sleeping. Each night the sea moved a few yards nearer, a hissing guillotine across the empty lawns.

For half an hour Mason watched the waves vault among the rooftops. The luminous surf cast a pale nimbus on the clouds racing overhead on the dark wind, and covered his hands with a waxy sheen.

At last the waves began to recede, and the deep bowl of illuminated water withdrew down the emptying streets, disgorging the lines of houses in the moonlight. Mason ran forwards across the expiring bubbles, but the sea shrank away from him, disappearing around the corners of the houses, sliding below the garage doors. He sprinted to the end of the road as a last glow was carried across the sky beyond the spire of the church. Exhausted, Mason returned to his bed, the sound of the dying waves filling his head as he slept.

'I saw the sea again last night,' he told his wife at breakfast.

Quietly, Miriam said: 'Richard, the nearest sea is a thousand miles away.' She watched her husband for a moment, her pale fingers straying to the coil of black hair lying against her neck. 'Go out into the drive and look. There's no sea.'

'Darling, I *saw* it.'

'Richard—!'

Mason stood up, and with slow deliberation raised his palms. 'Miriam, I felt the spray on my hands. The waves were breaking around my feet. I wasn't dreaming.'

'You must have been.' Miriam leaned against the door, as if trying to exclude the strange nightworld of her husband. With her long raven hair framing her oval face, and the scarlet dressing-gown open to reveal her slender neck and white breast, she reminded Mason of a Pre-Raphaelite heroine in an Arthurian pose. 'Richard, you must see Dr Clifton. It's beginning to frighten me.'

Mason smiled, his eyes searching the distant rooftops above the trees. 'I shouldn't worry. What's happening is really very simple. At night I hear the sounds of the sea, I go out and watch the waves in the moonlight, and then come back to bed.' He paused, a flush of fatigue on his face. Tall and slimly built, Mason was still convalescing from the illness which had kept him at home for the previous six months. 'It's curious, though,' he resumed, 'the water is remarkably luminous. I should guess its salinity is well above normal—'

'But Richard . . .' Miriam looked around helplessly, her husband's calmness exhausting her. 'The sea isn't *there*; it's only in your mind. No one else can see it.'

Mason nodded, hands lost in his pockets. 'Perhaps no one else has heard it yet.'

Leaving the breakfast-room, he went into his study. The couch on which he had slept during his illness still stood against the corner, his bookcase beside it. Mason sat down, taking a large fossil mollusc from a shelf. During the winter, when he had been confined to bed, the smooth trumpet-shaped conch, with its endless associations of ancient seas and drowned strands, had provided him with unlimited pleasure, a bottomless cornucopia of image and reverie. Cradling it reassuringly in his hands, as exquisite and ambiguous as a fragment of Greek sculpture found in a dry riverbed, he reflected that it seemed like a capsule of time, the condensation of another universe. He could almost believe that the midnight sea which haunted his sleep had been released from the shell when he had inadvertently scratched one of its helixes.

Miriam followed him into the room and briskly drew the curtains, as if aware that Mason was returning to the twilight world of his sick-bed. She took his shoulders in her hands.

'Richard, listen. Tonight, when you hear the waves, wake me and we'll go out together.'

Gently, Mason disengaged himself. 'Whether you see it or not is irrelevant, Miriam. The fact is that I see it.'

Later, walking down the street, Mason reached the point where he had stood the previous night, watching the waves break and roll towards him. The sounds of placid domestic activity came from the houses he had seen submerged. The grass on the lawns was bleached by the July heat, and sprays rotated in the bright sunlight, casting rainbows in the vivid air. Undisturbed since the rainstorms in the early spring, the long summer's dust lay between the wooden fences and water hydrants.

The street, one of a dozen suburban boulevards on the

perimeter of the town, ran north-west for some three hundred yards and then joined the open square of the neighbourhood shopping centre. Mason shielded his eyes and looked out at the clock tower of the library and the church spire, identifying the protuberances which had risen from the steep swells of the open sea. All were in exactly the positions he remembered.

The road shelved slightly as it approached the shopping centre, and by a curious coincidence marked the margins of the beach which would have existed if the area had been flooded. A mile or so from the town, this shallow ridge, which formed part of the rim of a large natural basin enclosing the alluvial plain below, culminated in a small chalk outcropping. Although it was partly hidden by the intervening houses, Mason now recognized it clearly as the promontory which had reared like a citadel above the sea. The deep swells had rolled against its flanks, sending up immense plumes of spray, that fell back with almost hypnotic slowness upon the receding water. At night the promontory seemed larger and more gaunt, an uneroded bastion against the sea. One evening, Mason promised himself, he would go out to the promontory and let the waves wake him as he slept on the peak.

A car moved past, the driver watching Mason curiously as he stood in the middle of the road, head raised to the air. Not wishing to appear any more eccentric than he was already considered – the solitary, abstracted husband of the beautiful but childless Mrs Mason – Mason turned into the avenue which ran along the ridge. As he approached the distant outcropping he glanced over the hedges for any signs of water-logged gardens or stranded cars. The houses had been inundated by the floodwater.

The first visions of the sea had come to Mason only three weeks earlier, but he was already convinced of their absolute validity. He recognized that after its nightly withdrawal the water failed to leave any mark on the hundreds of houses it submerged, and he felt no alarm for the drowned people who were, presumably, as he watched the luminous waves break across the rooftops, sleeping undisturbed in the sea's immense liquid locker. Despite this paradox, it was his complete conviction of the sea's reality that had made him admit to Miriam that he had woken one night to the sound of waves outside the window and gone out to find the sea rolling across the neighbourhood streets and houses. At first she had merely smiled at him, accepting this illustration of his strange private world. Then, three nights later, she had woken to the sound of him latching the door on his return, bewildered by his pumping chest and perspiring face.

From then on she spent all day looking over her shoulder through the window for any signs of the sea. What worried her as much as the vision itself was Mason's complete calm in the face of this terrifying unconscious apocalypse.

Tired by his walk, Mason sat down on a low ornamental wall, screened from the surrounding houses by the rhododendron bushes. For a few minutes he played with the dust at his feet, stirring the white grains with a branch. Although formless and passive, the dust shared something of the same evocative qualities of the fossil mollusc, radiating a curious compacted light.

In front of him, the road curved and dipped, the incline carrying it away on to the fields below. The chalk shoulder, covered by a mantle of green turf, rose into the clear sky. A metal shack had been erected on the slope, and a small group of figures moved about the entrance of a mine-shaft, adjusting a wooden hoist. Wishing that he had brought his wife's car, Mason watched the diminutive figures disappear one by one into the shaft.

The image of this elusive pantomime remained with him all day in the library, overlaying his memories of the dark waves rolling across the midnight streets. What sustained Mason was his conviction that others would soon also become aware of the sea.

When he went to bed that night he found Miriam sitting fully dressed in the armchair by the window, her face composed into an expression of calm determination.

'What are you doing?' he asked.

'Waiting.'

'For what?'

'The sea. Don't worry, simply ignore me and go to sleep. I don't mind sitting here with the light out.'

'Miriam . . .' Wearily, Mason took one of her slender hands and tried to draw her from the chair. 'Darling, what on earth will this achieve?'

'Isn't it obvious?'

Mason sat down on the foot of the bed. For some reason, not wholly concerned with the wish to protect her, he wanted to keep his wife from the sea. 'Miriam, don't you understand? I might not actually *see* it, in the literal sense. It might be . . .' he extemporized . . . 'an hallucination, or a dream.'

Miriam shook her head, hands clasped on the arms of the chair. 'I don't think it is. Anyway, I want to find out.'

Mason lay back on the bed. 'I wonder whether you're approaching this the right way—'

Miriam sat forward. 'Richard, you're taking it all so calmly; you accept this vision as if it were a strange headache. That's what frightens me. If you were really terrified by this sea I wouldn't worry, but . . .'

Half an hour later he fell asleep in the darkened room, Miriam's slim face watching him from the shadows.

* * *

Waves murmured, outside the windows the distant swish of racing foam drew him from sleep, the muffled thunder of rollers and the sounds of deep water drummed at his ears. Mason climbed out of bed, and dressed quickly as the hiss of receding water sounded up the street. In the corner, under the light reflected from the distant foam, Miriam lay asleep in the armchair, a bar of moonlight across her throat.

His bare feet soundless on the pavement, Mason ran towards the waves. He stumbled across the glistening tideline as one of the breakers struck with a guttural roar. On his knees, Mason felt the cold brilliant water, seething with animalcula, spurt across his chest and shoulders, slacken and then withdraw, sucked like a gleaming floor into the mouth of the next breaker. His wet suit clinging to him like a drowned animal, Mason stared out across the sea. In the moonlight the white houses advanced into the water like the palazzos of a spectral Venice, mausoleums on the causeways of some island necropolis. Only the church spire was still visible. The water rode in to its high tide, a further twenty yards down the street, the spray carried almost to the Masons' house.

Mason waited for an interval between two waves and then waded through the shallows to the avenue which wound towards the distant headland. By now the water had crossed the roadway, swilling over the dark lawns and slapping at the doorsteps.

Half a mile from the headland he heard the great surge and sigh of the deeper water. Out of breath, he leaned against a fence as the cold foam cut across his legs, pulling him with its undertow. Illuminated by the racing clouds, he saw the pale figure of a woman standing above the sea on a stone parapet at the cliff's edge, her black robe lifting behind her in the wind, her long hair white in the moonlight. Far below her feet, the luminous waves leapt and vaulted like acrobats.

Mason ran along the pavement, losing sight of her as the road curved and the houses intervened. The water slackened and he caught a last glimpse of the woman's icy-white profile through the spray. Turning, the tide began to ebb and fade, and the sea shrank away between the houses, draining the night of its light and motion.

As the last bubbles dissolved on the damp pavement, Mason searched the headland, but the luminous figure had gone. His damp clothes dried themselves as he walked back through the empty streets. A last tang of brine was carried away off the hedges on the midnight air.

The next morning he told Miriam: 'It *was* a dream, after all. I think the sea has gone now. Anyway, I saw nothing last night.'

'Thank heavens, Richard. Are you sure?'

'I'm certain.' Mason smiled encouragingly. 'Thanks for keeping watch over me.'

'I'll sit up tonight as well.' She held up her hand. 'I insist. I feel all right after last night, and I want to drive this thing away, once and for all.' She frowned over the coffee cups. 'It's strange, but once or twice I think I heard the sea too. It sounded very old and blind, like something waking again after millions of years.'

On his way to the library, Mason made a detour towards the chalk outcropping, and parked the car where he had seen the moonlit figure of the white-haired woman watching the sea. The sunlight fell on the pale turf, illuminating the mouth of the mine-shaft, around which the same desultory activity was taking place.

For the next fifteen minutes Mason drove in and out of the tree-lined avenues, peering over the hedges at the kitchen windows. Almost certainly she would live in one of the nearby houses, still wearing her black robe beneath a housecoat.

Later, at the library, he recognized a car he had seen on the headland. The driver, an elderly tweed-suited man, was examining the display cases of local geological finds.

'Who was that?' he asked Fellowes, the keeper of antiquities, as the car drove off. 'I've seen him on the cliffs.'

'Professor Goodhart, one of the party of paleontologists. Apparently they've uncovered an interesting bone-bed.' Fellowes gestured at the collection of femurs and jaw-bone fragments. 'With luck we may get a few pieces from them.'

Mason stared at the bones, aware of a sudden closing of the parallax within his mind.

Each night, as the sea emerged from the dark streets and the waves rolled farther towards the Masons' home, he would wake beside his sleeping wife and go out into the surging air, wading through the deep water towards the headland. There he would see the white-haired woman on the cliff's edge, her face raised above the roaring spray. Always he failed to reach her before the tide turned, and would kneel exhausted on the wet pavements as the drowned streets rose around him.

Once a police patrol car found him in its headlights, slumped against a gate-post in an open drive. On another night he forgot to close the front door when he returned. All through breakfast Miriam watched him with her old wariness, noticing the shadows which encircled his eyes like manacles.

'Richard, I think you should stop going to the library. You look worn out. It isn't that sea dream again?'

Mason shook his head, forcing a tired smile. 'No, that's finished with. Perhaps I've been overworking.'

Miriam held his hands. 'Did you fall over yesterday?' She examined Mason's palms. 'Darling, they're still *raw*! You must have grazed them only a few hours ago. Can't you remember?'

Abstracted, Mason invented some tale to satisfy her, then carried his coffee into the study and stared at the morning haze which lay across the rooftops, a soft lake of opacity that followed the same contours as the midnight sea. The mist dissolved in the sunlight, and for a moment the diminishing reality of the normal world reasserted itself, filling him with a poignant nostalgia.

Without thinking, he reached out to the fossil conch on the bookshelf, but involuntarily his hand withdrew before touching it.

Miriam stood beside him. 'Hateful thing,' she commented. 'Tell me, Richard, what do you think caused your dream?'

Mason shrugged. 'Perhaps it was a sort of memory . . .' He wondered whether to tell Miriam of the waves which he still heard in his sleep, and of the white-haired woman on the cliff's edge who seemed to beckon to him. But like all women Miriam believed that there was room for only one enigma in her husband's life. By an inversion of logic he felt that his dependence on his wife's private income, and the loss of self-respect, gave him the right to withhold something of himself from her.

'Richard, what's the matter?'

In his mind the spray opened like a diaphanous fan and the enchantress of the waves turned towards him.

Waist-high, the sea pounded across the lawn in a whirlpool. Mason pulled off his jacket and flung it into the water, and then waded out into the street. Higher than ever before, the waves had at last reached his house, breaking over the doorstep, but Mason had forgotten his wife. His attention was fixed upon the headland, which was lashed by a continuous storm of spray, almost obscuring the figure standing on its crest.

As Mason pressed on, sometimes sinking to his shoulders, shoals of luminous algae swarmed in the water around him. His eyes smarted in the saline air. He reached the lower slopes of the headland almost exhausted, and fell to his knees.

High above, he could hear the spray singing as it cut through the coigns of the cliff's edge, the deep base of the breakers overlaid by the treble of the keening air. Carried by the music, Mason climbed the flank of the headland, a thousand reflections of the moon in the breaking sea. As he reached the crest, the black robe hid the woman's face, but he could see her tall erect carriage and slender hips. Suddenly, without any apparent motion of her limbs, she moved away along the parapet.

'Wait!'

His shout was lost on the air. Mason ran forwards, and the figure turned and stared back at him. Her white hair swirled around her face like a spume of silver steam and then parted to reveal a face with empty eyes and notched mouth. A hand like a bundle of white sticks clawed towards him, and the figure rose through the whirling darkness like a gigantic bird.

Unaware whether the scream came from his own mouth or from this spectre, Mason stumbled back. Before he could catch himself he tripped over the wooden railing, and in a cackle of chains and pulleys fell backwards into the shaft, the sounds of the sea booming in its hurtling darkness.

* * *

After listening to the policeman's description, Professor Goodhart shook his head.

'I'm afraid not, sergeant. We've been working on the bed all week. No one's fallen down the shaft.' One of the flimsy wooden rails was swinging loosely in the crisp air. 'But thank you for warning me. I suppose we must build a heavier railing, if this fellow is wandering around in his sleep.'

'I don't think he'll bother to come up here,' the sergeant said. 'It's quite a climb.' As an afterthought he added: 'Down at the library where he works they said you'd found a couple of skeletons in the shaft yesterday. I know it's only two days since he disappeared, but one of them couldn't possibly be his?' The sergeant shrugged. 'If there was some natural acid, say . . .'

Professor Goodhart drove his heel into the chalky turf. 'Pure calcium carbonate, about a mile thick, laid down during the Triassic Period 200 million years ago when there was a large inland sea here. The skeletons we found yesterday, a man's and a woman's, belong to two Cro-Magnon fisher people who lived on the shore just before it dried up. I wish I could oblige you – it's quite a problem to understand how these Cro-Magnon relics found their way into the bone-bed. This shaft wasn't sunk until about thirty years ago. Still, that's my problem, not yours.'

Returning to the police car, the sergeant shook his head. As they drove off he looked out at the endless stretch of placid suburban homes.

'Apparently there was an ancient sea here once. A million years ago.' He picked a crumpled flannel jacket off the back seat. 'That reminds me, I know what Mason's coat smells of – brine.'

MARK HELPRIN

SAIL SHINING IN WHITE

AT FIVE IN the morning, the wind over Palm Island, off Cape Haze, took on a quality that could not fail to wake from his bed a man who twice had raced around the world, alone, in a sailboat. As always upon rising, he felt his loneliness more sharply than during the day, when both sunlight and the things that had to be done covered sorrow like the tide. He pulled on his tennis shorts, buttoned them, and went to the louvers to look out at the sea. The light over the waves early on a late August morning was a tangle of black and gunmetal blue, the whitecaps and foam a dirty gray that seemed to pulse as it appeared and disappeared in greater and lesser illumination, as if it were alive, beckoning, or sending a signal.

As he would do at sea, he carefully smelled the air. This was not tame air trapped in the Gulf of Mexico and backed up against the west coast of Florida, the hardly moving air that, like the retirees, like him, was going nowhere and would never go anywhere again, having finally come to the last stop and hit the stunning wall where nothing lies ahead.

This air said in less than a whisper that a storm was coming, the kind of storm that exists between the deserted coasts of Antarctica and Cape Horn, or thunders through the Bering Strait, or erupts off the sea-lanes in the empty Pacific and then spreads to overpower islands, the kind of storm that alters the scales by which such things are measured.

He knew before the satellites, the meteorologists, and the

television announcers who for the next week would broadcast without knowing what was coming. As if by some magic, he knew of the storm at the instant of its birth in the Atlantic off the coast of Africa, when satellites could not yet see it. He knew because the air over the Gulf, the light, and the waves themselves, knew. Several times, in sailing around the world, once at his own pace and once while racing scores of other boats, he had sensed the coming of a great storm.

The waves flatten, tighten, and darken. They reflect the changing light differently. Sharks have a similar intuition, sensing a kill hundreds of miles away. Perhaps it is electrical, or comes via a microscopic variation in the underlying sounds that travel from sea to sea with almost infinitely greater power than sounds in air. Whether by a process unknown or a hardly apprehensible variation in that which is understood, the message was clear as the waves drove in and the clouds unfurled at dawn.

After making the bed and shaving, he did old-man exercises for half an hour on the cool tile floor, following them with ten minutes of exercises that put his heart at risk. Then, when his heart had not failed and he was flushed with the color of life, he had the kind of unsatisfying breakfast a devoted athlete might eat – a discipline from which, at eighty-two, he had long before earned the right to be excused.

He was eighty-two, but his legs were not pipe cleaners and neither were his arms as frail as potato sticks. He still had muscle and grace of movement. He did not wear pastel Bermuda shorts without a belt, or a flat cap, or a shirt with seahorses on it (as many men his age did for a reason known perhaps to their wives, who wore straw hats with berries on the brims). He dressed habitually in a navy-blue polo shirt, white tennis shorts, and boating shoes.

He was without question an old man, but he did not carry

his money in a clip, he had never had to give up golf (never having played it), and he neither watched nor owned a television. This, in conjunction with other things, meant that he had no friends. But he didn't want friends, because it was over, or just about to be over, and in preparing for the greatest moment alone he did not want shuffleboard, crafts, dinner theater, book discussions, or college courses. He wanted, rather, to probe with a piercing eye to see in nature some clue to the mystery to come and the mysteries he would be leaving behind. He wanted a long and strenuous exercise of memory to summon in burning detail what he had loved. He wanted to bless, purify, and honor it, for if at the end he did not, he would by default have dishonored it.

No matter that nothing would come of this. No matter that all he thought and remembered would be unheard and unshared. The beauty of it as it burned within him was enough in itself, something like music, something that would set its seal even if all it did was vanish on the wind. But, then again, perhaps something would come of it. For very often, far away on the sea, a white sail will appear, running stiffly with the wind and shining in the sun, even if the sea is gray under dark and heavy cloud. These distant sails, proceeding with seeming purpose amid thin bands of sunlit green and blue, these persistent, silent flecks of white, are irresistible. You want to go to them, to be with them, and you wonder if they are a dream. They are so strong in purpose, so straight in direction, so steady, bright, and glowing, that it seems not unreasonable to follow them, to trust, to give oneself over to the light-filled other world of which they are the fleeting and resplendent edge.

Quite certain that the storm was coming, he would be the first one at the barge that morning, even before the carpenters and other early risers, and so his was the first footfall on the sandy road to mar the pattern of alligator tracks left overnight with remarkable delicacy in forms that suggested the passage of tanks or tractors. Alligators and lizards seemed unable to cross the road perpendicularly. They preferred a slash: whereas the snakes, whose imprint was like that of a garden hose, liked the perpendicular even if at a slither.

The rusty barge that slid across the water, though it floated, made no pretense of being a boat, as did many craft that operated close to shore, and even some on the open sea. These made him recoil, these boats that were top-heavy five times more than was safe, too wide by a factor of two, and either insufficiently rakish (as if born in a bathtub factory) or too much so, with needle bows to please the sensibilities of men who wore black shirts open to the navel. These boats, hubris in fiberglass, asked to be sunk in the wrath of waves, because they carried out upon the waters things that made a mockery of the fine line there between life and death. Instead of holding only what was essential, beautiful, or quick, they were sea-going repositories of every kind of vinyl, plastic, and sin. They carried waterbeds into parcels of sea where beneath them for seven miles lay unimaginable volumes of brine. And when they had metastasized into ships, they floated casinos, as if to be upon the ocean were not enough of a gamble in itself. They were places for nightclub reviews and various forms of prostitution, the carriers, upon the ineffable ocean, of pinball machines, lobster tanks, and bowling alleys.

The last time he had been in a ship at sea that was not propelled by the wind had been in a destroyer that not long before had shelled Iwo Jima. The rest had been sail, on purpose, from conviction, out of respect for the sea itself and for the wind that sang in sheets and stays. He wished he did not have to see the obese cabin cruisers with deep stern drafts and amusement-park wakes, and their speechless and beefy occupants in fluorescent bikinis and sun brims, rushing at thirty knots from nowhere to nowhere, with a deep rumble and the smell of perfume, gin, and suntan lotion.

The channel was clear except for a trawler moving downcast from a night having failed to break even, unlike the pelicans, whose every swoop put them in the black. 'Storm,' he said to the captain of the tug as they glided silently to the ferry slip, engines off. He casually pointed straight up.

The ferry captain turned his head in every direction, considering the air and clouds most carefully even as he was gliding toward the slip. 'What makes you think so?' he asked, puzzled.

'You can't tell?'

'No.'

'Really?'

'I've been listening to the Coast Guard. What storm?'

'It's coming.'

'Well,' said the ferry captain, dipping down to spin the wheel, 'if you wait long enough, a storm always comes.'

'In a week or less, this one will come, and no storm like it has hit this coast in my memory, which goes back to nineteen fifteen.'

'How do you know this?'

'How can you not know? Everything here,' he said, looking around at the houses and docks, 'will be destroyed. Everything on the island will be gone. Half the island itself, the sand and the trees, will be washed away. My house is on pilings, but the waves will be high enough to shatter it in one blow. The level of the sea will rise above the tops of those mangroves. Even things that float will be hard pressed to stay afloat, for the sea will shuffle, break, and overturn them.'

'If what you say is true,' the ferry captain said, 'there'll be a general evacuation. Everyone on the coast will have to get out.'

'Not everyone,' was the answer, which the ferry captain thought strange.

His car actually started, which was a miracle after so many years in the hot sun and salt air and use only every two weeks or so. The empty road was washed out in the morning sun that by now had climbed to beat down upon a coast of resilient green. Every time he saw the fragmented maroon debris that signified a crab killed on the road the night before, he thought of numbers, probability, and fate, and was reminded that most of his generation had already fallen, and would soon be fallen completely. Others would follow him where he was going, with both the certainty of the result and the absolute unpredictability of the means. The crabs in the road, scuttling by moonlight or in the tropical dark, were surprised by the sudden appearance of cars and trucks planing through the night air at eighty miles an hour. These and other kinds of small animals that littered the sides of the roads were returned in a week to the cycle of soil, sun, water, and wind. He noticed that their presence at the roadside diminished only when he came to the town, where stores on the tree-lined streets were just beginning to open. Watering cans and hose spray maintained the plants and cleansed the sidewalks. In the morning, when they are watered, plants seem to give off their most communicative scents. And store owners, waiting for the day to begin and hopeful of good sales, are often cheerful and engaging.

'What will you give me for this?' he asked of a jeweler who, even for a jeweler, was exceptionally calm.

'What is it?'

'The Scarborough Trophy, which you get, if you are lucky, for going out of the harbor at Scarborough and, with great excitement and hardly any sleep, passing the east coast of England in daylight and darkness, and then skating through the Channel to the open sea to drop down the entire length of the world, until the seasons change and summer becomes winter, though by the time you get there winter is over. And then across the Indian Ocean under stars that few people see and are brighter than you might think, through the Strait of Malacca, north of Australia, into the South Seas, and against the wind across the southern Pacific, where time is buried in the blue ocean. Around the Horn in storms with waves that seem like mountains, and then up the coast of South America, across the equator, with a glimpse of the lights of Tenerife, and anxious days in the Bay of Biscay. Into the Channel like a chip in a whirlpool, and to Scarborough once again, where the winter of your departure is long over.'

'In what?' the jeweler asked.

'In a sailboat that cannot be more than forty feet in length, cannot have an engine, and cannot carry anyone but you.'

'You won the race?'

'I did. I wasn't even young. When I was young I was working. It's gold,' he said of the trophy. 'It was the only prize, and it weighs at least ten pounds. I weighed it once.'

'We'll see,' the jeweler said, placing it on a balance and then expertly exchanging cylindrical brass weights until all came right. 'Five kilograms exactly – *eleven* pounds.'

'How much would that bring?' asked the 'round-the-world racer, who had to wait while the jeweler ran tests and weighed the mass of gold yet again before turning on his calculator.

'I can give you sixty thousand dollars.'

'You can, and you can also give me more and still make a large amount of money.'

'Sixty-two thousand, five hundred.'

'A little more.'

'Sixty-three thousand.'

'I mean more than that.'

'I stop there.'

'I go up the coast to Sarasota.'

'Sixty-five, that's it.' In the jeweler's mind, he had just lost several thousand dollars that he had hoped for, but he softened when he realized how much so few minutes of work would bring him still.

'Okay.'

'It's too bad that you have to give up the trophy.'

'No. Even though I've provided for her, and she can provide for herself, my daughter might need the money someday – one always lives and hopes just beyond one's capacities – and every time she might think of selling this her heart would break a little, not to mention when she actually did. I don't want to break the little girl's heart. I'll wire the money to the trust. She won't even know, but it will be there.'

'How old is she?' the jeweler asked.

'Thirty-nine.'

'That's not a little girl anymore.'

'She's a physicist,' he said proudly. 'She's at the Jet Propulsion Laboratory in Pasadena. And she's got a boy – my grandson – in high school, a brilliant jerk, just as I was when I was fifteen. Only I wasn't brilliant, and I apologize for that, but I never wore my clothes backwards, and I was able to speak in English.'

'Yeah, they wear their clothes backwards.'

'My daughter. . . . I was born to see her in her little corduroy jacket and at my very last I'll be thinking of what she looked like, buoyant and overjoyed, as she rode on my leg, standing with both feet on my foot, holding on below the knee. That's why I said "little girl." I know she's a woman, and so does she, but every time we embrace, we go back. And I know she knows exactly how I feel, now that her own son has long since been unable to ride in the crook of her arm.'

The last time his daughter had been at what she referred to as his 'house,' she had asked, 'How can you possibly think of disconnecting the telephone?'

'How can I possibly not think of it?' he answered, knowing that this made no sense.

'How are we supposed to speak to you when we're at home?' She was skirting the main subject, which both he and she knew was coming.

'You can use your cellular phone,' he said with a twinkle, mocking all the telephones in the world as he took yet another step on the plank of pretended senility that somehow pleases both parent and child – as inexplicably as the baby tooth, hanging by a thread, that his daughter would worry when she was six. 'Remember the baby tooth that you used to flap back and forth like a pet door?' he asked.

Stunned, she said, 'No.'

'Well, it's like that.'

'What's like that?'

'It's because I love you. You did it because you loved me, but we're different people.'

'I did what?' she asked.

'I know, Anna, and I know that two telephones are required to complete a discrete circuit, just as you knew not to worry your tooth.'

She tried another tack. 'How can you, a man who directed a great corporation. . . .'

'It was a shitty corporation. I hated it.'

'You hated it?'

'Yes.'

'You were rather cheerful, considering.'

'I did the best I could, but, believe me, I never liked that company.'

'Why?'

'Because it wasn't human and it wasn't alive, and all the thousands of people whose lives were molded around it were like sequins on a corpse. It had no desire or regret, it didn't know the difference between right and wrong, it couldn't breathe or kiss or sweat. I wasted my precious time on it, *my* life, and *it* will never die.'

'But that's how you made a living. It's how you provided for us.'

'That's why I did it,' he said, staring not so much into space as into the past. 'You know how you could spin your top for hour after hour, and see God-knows-what in the whirling city inside, where trains and boats moved ingeniously over painted fields and rivers?'

'Yes.'

'You weren't the only one. I could, too. I wasn't bored when I took care of you. I had to leave in the morning because I had to: I didn't want to.'

'Even when you were my age?'

'Yes.'

'Even as a man, back then?'

He smiled. 'Yes.'

'You have a baby's mind.'

'I do.'

'How did you survive the war? How did you command a destroyer?'

'Anna, a child knows what's important, what's essential,

what's eternal. It's no small thing to keep a child's mind. And to answer your question, war is a clash of essentials. People who in civilian life are taken in by the castle of clouds we build as we grow old don't understand the nature of the forces that in battle are both terrible and sublime. But that's just a comment. I got too old for war a long time ago.'

'Da Da,' she said. She had called him Da Da when she was a child. 'What if you fall, and can't get up?'

'Then I wouldn't be able to get to a telephone anyway.'

'We'll never hear from you again.'

'I'll use the phone at the dock. I'll call you.'

'What if you get sick?'

'That's okay, Anna. If I get sick and I can't get to the telephone, I'll die. That's the way it's supposed to be. I don't want to be a hospital case. Really. There's something to dying on the ground, or in a room where the air comes in the windows. You know how I hate fluorescent lights and windows that don't open, and how I love what I have here – the sound of birds, the deep green, the ocean, even the abject heat that makes the shadows so blessed.'

'What about your friends? How will you keep in touch with your friends?'

'In the past ten years or so, most of them have gone beyond the reach of the telephone.'

She nodded quickly, her eyes closed.

He knew what was coming. 'The world,' he said, 'the whole world, and all of time – sometime in my lifetime, and I don't know exactly when, it must have been a wide and diffuse line – crossed the line nonetheless between the two great ages. First was the age of patience, into which my mother and father brought me. And now we are in the age of impatience, which I have never loved. Impatience in everything. In loving, in understanding, in action, even in seeing. I'm not suited to it.'

Anna, his daughter, went to his arms, just as she had done as a baby, a child, and a young woman, and cried. And then, as always, she was better, very quickly becoming sunny, because, as he had many times, he took her cry into his heart.

In 1961, when his wife was not quite forty, someone in a passing yacht had photographed her in the bow of a sailboat they had chartered in Hawaii. Though neither party had hailed the other, an eight-by-ten Ektachrome print had been sent from Charlotte Amalie to '*Inverness II*, Honolulu,' eventually reaching New York in February.

A note with it said, 'I took this photograph off Lahaina, Maui, in December. We then made the passage back to Los Angeles, down the coast of Mexico, through the canal, and to Charlotte Amalie, where we're holding over. Normally, I would be surprised by a photograph, among hundreds, of someone I don't know. But I was not surprised. The image, and her smile, had never left me. I had thought that perhaps I was investing too much in memory, but when the pictures came back I realized that I had not invested enough.'

The stranger had photographed Anna's mother, Sabrina. Her grace and beauty had rolled across the water to him like the flower-scented air that cascades over a beach in the morning. The bow of the *Inverness II* was dipping into a smooth blue sea. Behind its white chevron were the green hills of Lahaina, topped by white clouds with shadowy blue bases. And above these clouds were pieces that had been torn from them by winds aloft and were engaged in battle with patches of Bristol, delft, and sapphire.

She was perched on the raked chrome rail, over the anchor that projected from the tip of the bow, so that, facing sternward, she appeared to be floating without care not merely above the rolling swell but above the deck. A scrim of foam had been knocked aside by the passage of the glistening hull. With her head turned to the passing boat, her hair fell across her shoulders and was lifted lightly by the wind into a soft fullness, semi-golden, chestnut brown.

As relaxed and unself-conscious as a young woman might be, she was a study in perfectly flowing limbs and flying, floating, weightless, airy majesty. During the war she had been a Wave, and her confidence had never shaken in even the war's most anxious moments. What had always impressed him about her most had been a natural, indelible grace that made even the loveliest things around her lovelier still; a tranquillity alert nonetheless to the excitement deep in all things; a self-possession that said she understood the shortness and beauty of the breath we take of the world. Without that impenetrable grace, every other quality could be shattered like glass – brilliance, beauty, force, spark, all would melt away in the face of loss and terror.

Anna's copy of the photograph was newer and brighter. His, slightly faded, though still the most vital color in his life, was on the huge pine table at which he ate, corresponded, and read. The lamp on that blond table, and the photograph of his wife, had become the center of a life that found itself migrating more and more toward the sea. She was gone, but he loved her so much in memory it was as if she were an angel perpetually rising from the waves,

When he had warned of the storm for a week before its coming they had mistaken his certainty of vision for fear. Now that they themselves knew, and were overtaken with panic, they forgot that he had told them, and could not understand how he could be unafraid. Every morning he had arisen before dawn and observed the insistence and darkness of the sea. The waves that rolled in now, even in the bright of day, were long and woolly. They seemed as tired as refugees, and moved not as if toward something but as if away from it.

A policeman visited. In his view, here was an old man who probably couldn't write checks or carry a bag of groceries, and who would have to be persuaded and cajoled for the purpose of saving his – to be truthful – worthless life. So the policeman had an air of exasperation even before he began to speak. 'The storm,' he said, 'will destroy everything.'

And the old man said to him, 'I know.'

'That seems to make you happy,' said the policeman, who had a mustache and a bullet-proof vest.

'What seems to make me happy?'

'That the storm will destroy everything.' The policeman was thinking of his own house on the mainland, close to shore, and his boat, his pool, his garden.

'No.'

'Then why are you happy?'

'If I appear to be happy, it's not because the storm will destroy everything, but because I know that it will.'

'There's a difference?'

'Of course. Knowing is more than half the battle. The rest is just stuff, you know.'

'Well I don't get that,' the policeman said.

'To get it, to really get it, you'd have to talk to my wife.'

'How is that?'

'She went through the war in the Pacific without flinching or bowing her head, or perhaps even shedding a tear. Her brother was killed. I was reported lost. The atmosphere was like what it is now, before the storm, but she glowed, always. As they say, she didn't miss a beat.'

'I understand, but you've got to get out. One trip in the car with as much as you can take. The roads will be jammed.'

'June, nineteen forty.'

'What?'

'Nothing.'

'We'll be coming through on a sweep starting at three tomorrow afternoon. If you're still here, we'll have to arrest you for your own safety.'

'You mean propel me, don't you? You don't want me to be arrested, you want me to be propelled.'

'I have no idea, but you have to do what the law says.'

'I agree,' said the 'round-the-world racer, with strange enthusiasm. 'If the law says that it knows the nature of the storm, it knows the strength of my house, and it knows what is in my soul, and that therefore I am to do what it dictates, who am I, what is the storm, what is my house, what is my soul, to contradict the law? Tomorrow, I won't be here. The house will be shut – windows boarded, power off, loose things battened – waiting to be destroyed.'

On the sea the only law was God's law, the physics of wind and blue water and the rolling of the waves that with continual urgency push boats across oceans that ring the world. War of any type is different on the sea, in that it is almost all maneuver. When ships are firing at other ships or planes, or planes are leveling to lock-in a torpedo drop, or a line of cruisers or destroyers is dueling, the immense force overwhelms mere men and contrasts with the delicacy of their existence. But even in the greatest tests of fire there is a sense of separation, a separate dignity, a separate identity. Sailors are delivered to war, riding, and even in the bloodiest engagements the sea cleans up quickly, quieting any chaos man can make and sealing the scene of battles with the inflow of innocent waves that whisper and relax.

In ocean racing you leave no track that lasts for more than minutes. Though each moment is fresh and dangerous, the rules never change: the only variations are in the way you play them. In racing, one moves not much faster than a man can run, tense and intent upon seconds, watching for maximum swell in the spinnaker, sensing the changing angle of the wind so that its collision with the mainsail leaves as little as possible of slip and escape. In this patient and continual sensing of that which cannot be seen, a sailor deepens in thought. Going around the world courting the invisible at every moment teaches not only that mystery has force, but that it can deliver.

That which cannot be seen, in this case something as simple and explicable as the wind, had propelled him around the world and called forth his unceasing attention lest an ungraceful move dismast or capsize his craft. That which cannot be seen had warned him of the storm far in advance of its coming. For ten days, subsumed by the rhythms of nature and necessity, he had been preparing for his final engagement, which now was rolling at him from across the Atlantic.

Though he was afraid, he was not afraid, and though his heart was broken he was happy. All the practical things had been taken care of. The money had long before flowed into trusts. Paintings and memorabilia were with Anna. The letters had been written, the plans laid out. In the last week, he had sold or sent the last of his valuable possessions. A few cartons of books were on their way through the mail. All he had left were his glasses, a watch, and clothing. In the bathroom, a toiletry kit. In the kitchen, a plate, bowl, wineglass, two pots, knife, fork, and spoon, can opener, and cutting board were the only hard items remaining.

In the days before the storm he had slept deeply and well, on the floor, with two blankets – one folded for a mat, the other, of the lightest weave, for the late hours when the wind made a cover necessary even on the Gulf Coast in September. Shorn of most things, feeling more and more agile as the storm approached, he found less and less desire to replay the scenes of his life. Now it was as if, in facing what was to come, he was able to pull from the past everything of value and make his peace with it so he could leave it behind. In truth, in leaving it behind as he had never been able to previously, a seal was set upon it. And when finally it left his hands and escaped his possession it took on a life of its own.

At the marina on the mainland most of the boats had been taken out of the water, a useless act, for the ocean would rise to lift them from their cradles and throw them inland to end their days smashed, demasted, and on their sides. The rain was already driving, though not yet in sheets and whirlwinds, and with everything battened down and wet, and the sky dark gray, it looked not like Florida but like Maine in a gale.

He was on the last barge, with the police, who had made their sweep. He guessed that within the hour not a single one of the fifty or sixty people on the barge or moving anxiously about on shore would remain. And there was not much more than an hour or two before one would not be able to navigate the passage out, even under power – and his boat had no engine. But it was an ocean racer, a Halifax 40, as stiff and strong as a lance, empty and light, with a keel that would enable it to hew to the windward side of the channel, closer than usual because the depth of the water had increased with the rise in the sea. The barge had slid right over the dock that it had spent years butting with its prow, the swimming pool at the marina was inches and minutes away from the jail-break of its waters, and the last-minute evacuees were rushing along flooded paths that were up to their knees.

He went to the shed where the luggage was stored when on holidays a crush of people went over to the island and the things they carried choked up behind them. Now it was empty, warm, and dark except for thin stalks of light pressing in through cracks in the siding. It was as good a place as any to listen to the sound of one's own heart and breathing, to know that even this close to the end, with answers not yet apparent, they seemed, nonetheless, beautifully close.

In the shed the water rose, flowing wavelessly through seams that had conquered its resonance. In the darkness, with his eyes closed, he was battered by the images of those who were gone and those he would never see again; of his father walking with him on an Atlantic beach in sunshine and wind; of his mother, tranquil and beautiful, in a white wicker chair in the second summer of the First World War, listening to a little boy who could hardly talk, but as rapt with attention as if he had been Ralph Waldo Emerson; of his angelic daughter, sleeping, secure in his arms; and of his wife, when she was young, in the bow of the *Inverness II* as it dipped and rose in the sea off Lahaina, when, for a moment, the world was perfect. These insistent memories, of his wife as she threw back her head to clear the hair from her face, of his infant daughter, her eyes squinting into the newly discovered cold wind, her little hands held up before her face to protect it, these insistent memories, soon lost but to God, he would take with him into the sea.

He had thought that time would pass very slowly in the confines of the shed, but it had raced, and when he looked at the tritium-laced hands of his watch he saw that he had overstayed. He unlatched the door, which the wind then threw open. Though they were yet to be stripped of their branches, the palm trees were getting ragged. He did not even have to look, but could sense that everyone else was gone. It was not quite like being alone on the sea, but he felt a sense of freedom. No man would be watching him, no one to confine, judge, or proscribe except nature itself. You could not be lonely when you were completely alone, but only when you were close enough to others to fail them or to have been failed by them.

As if eager to run into the heart of the storm, his boat was bobbing urgently near the top of the pilings to which it was moored. It had not been constructed to sit at a dock or cruise idly in middling seas. It had been made for the lower fifties and the highest sea state, and when he stepped aboard from the dock covered by two feet of water, he imagined that the boat knew it.

In a quick and final release, he cut away from the moorings. Never again would he tie up. Never again would he maneuver into a slip. There would be no alteration of action and rest, but only action building without cease until it became eternal stillness.

The boat moved from its slip into the channel, cutting to windward, picking up speed. With just a yard of mainsail he was making fifteen knots and leaving foam. This running of the slot was complicated, for if he had blown to the lee of the channel he could never get back, and would die in the muddy bureaucracy of the mangrove roots.

But all was going well and fast. The keel, a great underwater sail and balance for the power of the wind, held him on course like a straightedge. The difficult part was yet to come, the race to the sea. It was a short stretch, but if the wind blew straight down this untackable slot he would never get out to open water. He had counted on the fact that the storm had a north by northeast bias and the channel veered slightly northwest. He would know at the turn, where the wind came freely off the ocean, undisturbed by the now rapidly disappearing island.

He wished that at the turn, eighty-five degrees to port in two hundred feet, he could lift the keel and skate into position, but the keels of ocean racers are not centerboards and do not lift in shallow water, and the boats they steady were never intended to skid.

When the time came he spun the wheel and tightened the mainsheet. The stern swung around in a graceful movement and the boat reoriented even before it reached center channel. All it had to do was break through the waves sweeping down the slot.

At the turn, these waves had been five feet from trough to crest, and at the end of what once had been the jetty, fifteen. Even before he left the last qualified embrace of land he was in the storm and the boat was flying across the crests and thudding against the troughs. Before he sailed beyond what had been the beach, waves washed over the deck and tried to take him with them, but his safety lines held.

Then he cleared the land and sailed into the violence of the storm, his boat battered near to death not even two miles from his house. This would not do: his desire was to reach the heart of the storm, where he would match its rage with equanimity. At the heart of the storm, he believed, he would find love. Why he thought this he did not exactly know, but he thought that if in difficulty the heart rose, then what could be more promising than the heart of a storm? He swung the prow west-northwest and ran close in, lifting the mainsail another few feet. In wind that screamed in the halyards he could have made good headway just sailing with the mast, but he wanted strain, and he flew forward at more than thirty knots. No one alive would have been strong enough to hold a tiller in these moments, and for him, because he was old, holding the wheel was almost unbearable, but he held it, locking it when he could, and unlocking it to trim when he had to, hoping that it would not be pulled from his hands and spun so that the spokes blurred and he would have to run with the wind until the boat detonated against a beach made invisible by colossal surf.

Although he had never seen a sea like this, he had been schooled in long-lasting storms that had not been so different, and he managed to hold and persevere. As he moved forward and the hours passed in cold and exciting agony, he found regions of waves so high that sliding down them was like falling from a cliff. As it got darker, the tritium hands glowed more brightly, he breathed hard, and the noise of wind and water was so great that it hurt.

And when he had been out for so long that it was night and great hills of foam appeared in a malevolent glow and almost broke over him without warning, he felt very tired and ready to sleep, and that, at last, he was closing upon the heart of the storm, a terrible darkness tinged with light.

ACKNOWLEDGMENTS

J. G. BALLARD: 'Now Wakes the Sea' by J. G. Ballard, copyright © J. G. Ballard 1967, is reproduced by permission of the Estate of J. G. Ballard c/o The Hanbury Agency, 28 Moreton Street, London SW1V 2PE. All rights reserved.
'Now Wakes the Sea' from *The Complete Short Stories of J. G. Ballard* by J. G. Ballard. Copyright © 1963, 2001 by J. G. Ballard. Copyright © 2009 by the Estate of J. G. Ballard. Used by permission of W. W. Norton & Company, Inc.
RAY BRADBURY: 'The Fog Horn' by Ray Bradbury, first published as 'The Beast from 20,000 Fathoms' in the *Saturday Evening Post.* Reprinted by permission of Don Congdon Associates, Inc. © 1951 by the Curtis Publishing Company, renewed 1979 by Ray Bradbury.
ROBERT OLEN BUTLER: 'Titanic Victim Speaks Through Waterbed' from *Tabloid Dreams* by Robert Olen Butler. Copyright © 1996 by Robert Olen Butler. Reprinted by arrangement with Henry Holt and Company, LLC.
ISAK DINESEN: 'The Young Man with the Carnation' from *Winter's Tales* by Isak Dinesen, copyright 1942 by Random House, Inc. and renewed 1970 by Johan Philip Thomas Ingerslev c/o The Rungstedlund Foundation. Used by permission of Random House, Inc. and The Rungstedlund Foundation.
MARK HELPRIN: 'Sail Shining in White' from *The Pacific and Other Stories* by Mark Helprin, copyright © 1982, 1986, 1988, 1995, 2000, 2001, 2004 by Mark Helprin. Used by

permission of The Penguin Press, a division of Penguin Group (USA) Inc.
'Sail Shining in White' from *The Pacific and Other Stories* by Mark Helprin. Reprinted by permission of The Wendy Weil Agency, Inc. First published by The Penguin Press. © 2004 by Mark Helprin.
ERNEST HEMINGWAY: 'After the Storm': Reprinted with the permission of Scribner, a division of Simon & Schuster, Inc., from *The Short Stories of Ernest Hemingway* by Ernest Hemingway. Copyright © 1932 by Ernest Hemingway. Copyright renewed © 1960 by John Hemingway, Patrick Hemingway and Gregory Hemingway.
'After the Storm' from *Complete Short Stories* by Ernest Hemingway, published by Jonathan Cape. Reprinted by permission of The Random House Group Ltd.
PATRICIA HIGHSMITH: 'One for the Islands' from *Slowly, Slowly in the Wind* by Patricia Highsmith. Copyright © 1972, 1973, 1974, 1976, 1977, and 1979 by Patricia Highsmith. Copyright © 1993 by Diogenes Verlag AG, Zurich. Used by permission of W. W. Norton & Company, Inc.
'One for the Islands' from *Slowly, Slowly in the Wind* by Patricia Highsmith. Used by permission of Bloomsbury Publishing plc.
DORIS LESSING: 'Through the Tunnel' from *The Habit of Loving* by Doris Lessing. Copyright © 1955 by Doris Lessing. Originally appeared in *The New Yorker*. Reprinted by permission of HarperCollins Publishers.
JOHN UPDIKE: 'Cruise' from *The Afterlife and Other Stories* by John Updike, copyright © 1994 by John Updike. Used by permission of Alfred A. Knopf, a division of Random House, Inc.
KURT VONNEGUT: 'The Cruise of *The Jolly Roger*' from *Bagombo Snuff Box* by Kurt Vonnegut, copyright © 1999 by

Everyman's Pocket Classics are
typeset in the classic typeface Garamond and
printed on acid-free, cream-wove paper
with a sewn, full-cloth binding.